The Power Behind the Throne

A Novel

Dene Quesenberry

Natoma Publishing Partners
Houston

PUBLISHING PARTNERS

Houston, Texas

This novel is a work of fiction. Any references to real events, businesses, organizations and locales are intended only to give the fiction a sense of authenticity and reality. Any resemblance to actual persons, living or dead, is entirely coincidental.

ISBN 978-1-7326902-1-9 (print)
ISBN 978-1-7326902-0-2 (ebook)

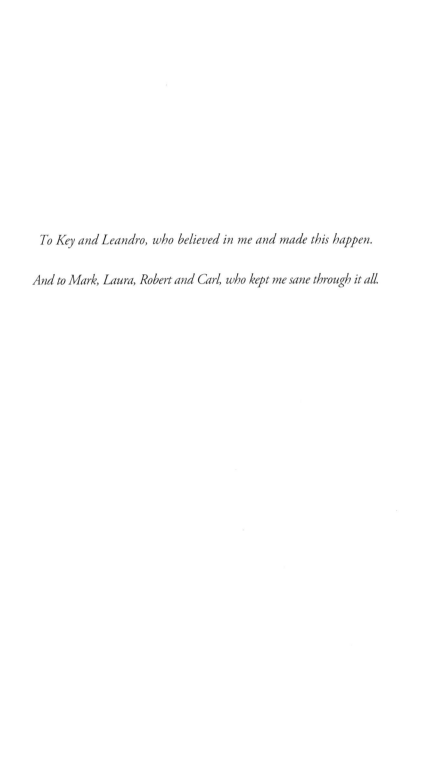

To Key and Leandro, who believed in me and made this happen.

And to Mark, Laura, Robert and Carl, who kept me sane through it all.

ACKNOWLEDGEMENT

Miraculously, I found Beth Hill, author of the extraordinary tome, "The Magic of Fiction," and even more miraculously, she agreed to edit this book. She couldn't have known what she was getting into. Her initial job description morphed into writing coach, proofreader, cheerleader, mentor and finally, friend. Thank you for wearing so many hats (whether you wanted to or not) and wearing them all well. But more than that, thank you for the kind words, laughter and encouragement that arrived, "magically," just when I needed them most. Too bad you don't get to edit these sentiments!

ONE

Near Béziers, France—1209

Charles and Édouard eased their horses forward. The remaining moans of the souls still alive in the small village masked the sound of their approach. The muted sounds were diminished echoes of the screams of the recent past. As they moved closer, the flickering light from burning huts exposed the horrific carnage to the two knights. They had experienced the horrors of battle, but this had been no battle—it was a slaughter. Charles knew why they had been ordered to witness the devastation, but he had not yet shared the reason with Édouard.

Charles moved slightly ahead of Édouard. He tugged his reins and held up his hand. Édouard stopped beside him. A boy lay face down in the dirt just off the path—an arrow in the back had abruptly ended his escape.

"Cowards!" said Édouard. He spat the words in a low voice, but he was furious.

"Aye. No courage needed to murder unarmed peasants."

Charles held his position, sensing as much as seeing a slight motion in the shadows to his left. An old man was moving toward them, at first crawling and then hobbling. When

Édouard caught sight of the man, he reached for his sword, but Charles stayed his hand. "Keep watch."

Édouard kept his hand near his sword and watched their right flank as Charles had ordered. The carnage made the younger man eager to draw his sword in revenge, but now was not the time. They were there as witnesses only.

The old man reached up to Charles and latched onto his leg with a bloody hand. He focused on Charles with one eye; the other was covered in blood. He looked like what he was, a man dragged behind a horse and left to die in the brush. Yet even with just one eye, the old man recognized the cross on Charles's tunic.

"You're too late." His voice was thick with his own blood. "Too late," he repeated. Then, as his life ended, his hand trailed down Charles's leg, leaving a crimson streak. He fell to the dirt, his vacant eye staring at no one.

Charles frowned at the dead man, but with anger, not indifference. They weren't too late. They'd arrived exactly when they'd been told to. And the orders of the High Council had to be obeyed. It was critical they observe the carnage but not prevent it. And even though Charles knew noninterference guaranteed the survival of their Order, it was a command he'd found difficult to obey. Hidden on a hillside, they had watched the attackers leave in the same direction from which they'd entered, from the opposite side of the once-peaceful village. He and Édouard were warriors, and he knew they shared the same fury over the deaths of the innocent. Now they needed a closer look at the village. He shifted his weight, and at the slight command, his horse moved forward.

Good fortune this night provided them a low mist and only the faint light of a crescent moon, making their advance barely visible. They had chosen their entrance to the village in an area with the fewest remaining fires, further concealing their approach. Only the roofs of the cluster of short stone structures near them had burned and caved in; a few still smoldered. They made a sharp turn into a narrow path between two of the structures. As they rounded the corner, they expected to find more lifeless bodies.

By the time they saw the group of huddled men, it was too late—because one of the men also saw them. It wasn't that Charles and Édouard weren't willing to fight—they would relish combat. But the attackers weren't to know they had been observed by their Order; there could be no whisper that they'd been anywhere close. Now, in order to silence the men who'd seen them, the two knights would have no choice but to exact the revenge seething inside them.

The men were standing near a woman they had obviously raped and murdered. Her body had been stripped bare and blood still flowed from the deep cut in her neck. Her lifeless, pleading eyes and mouth were open wide. They had found the source of the horrified screams that had pierced the night.

As the attackers turned from their "conquest," Charles counted five—no, seven—men. The dirty and disheveled group assessed the possible threat of the two intruders. They didn't speak, but their hard eyes said that they too recognized the emblem on Charles and Édouard's surcoats.

Charles stared ahead without expression, but he spoke to Édouard in a low tone. "You know what to do."

"I would rather advance—"

"Go!" Charles ordered.

Édouard yanked hard on the reins, pulling his horse to the right, riding back the way they had come. Seeing it was now seven against one, several of the villains stood taller. One man, most probably their leader, wiped the woman's blood from his knife onto his already filthy sleeve as his companions reached for their swords.

"I knew the stories were exaggerated," the leader sneered, his chin cocked upward. "Your friend is a coward. If he's running for help, he will be far too late and you will be long dead and cold before anyone returns."

Charles didn't move an inch or even reach for his sword.

"My young friend could kill all of you without my help, but it's my turn. I assume the woman took her own life, since I doubt you could."

Anger rose in all of the men—which kept them from noticing Édouard hadn't fled at all, but had worked his way to their flank. They *did* notice, however, the arrow that pierced the head of the man on Charles's far right. The once-overconfident group fell into total confusion. They didn't know whether to face the threat in front of them or the shock of the new threat on their left.

As Édouard began to charge, Charles whipped his left leg over his horse's neck, drawing his short and long swords before his feet hit the ground. A seasoned knight would normally keep his advantage by remaining on horseback, but Charles's incredible rage demanded release, so he deliberately drove himself at them.

"I think you'll find us more of a challenge than unarmed women and children," he said, seething, as he pressed forward.

The man closest to him still rode the courage from his recent bloodlust, and raised his sword. "Only slightly more challenging, but you will be just as dead."

Charles Duquesne was the older of the two knights, that age measured in years and in battles. But what his protégé lacked in age and experience, he made up for with cunning and intelligence. Édouard Claremont was leaner than the larger-framed Duquesne, but both had muscles as hardened as their saddles from years of training. Since tonight's mission required speed and stealth, they wore very little in the way of armor, unlike the way they would dress in a major engagement. But neither of them considered this much of a conflict.

Their two-front maneuver had had its intended effect. It was one of many that they had practiced and executed in battle many times. The remaining six men were undisciplined and disoriented, and didn't know which direction to defend against. Édouard continued his charge, and with a powerful downward swing of his large sword, he slashed deep into the shoulder of the man closest to him. The man fell to his knees, unable to continue the fight or even raise his blood-drenched arm. Charles stopped to give his own opponents a moment to take in what was happening.

"It would seem that your cowardly companions are deserting you—by dying." He laughed.

Rather than fight a knight on horseback, two of the marauders chose to face Charles with their leader. Bolstered by support on his left and right, the leader swung his sword straight down toward Charles. But Charles anticipated the amateur assault before it was even initiated. He deftly slipped to his left and impaled the man in front of him just below his breastbone with his short sword. The man, looking down at the blade that had disappeared inside his body, tried to gasp, but was unable to. He fell face down when Charles withdrew his sword.

"Your numbers continue to diminish," said Charles, now facing two men and presenting them a sword covered in their friend's blood. He displayed an eerily calm face to his adversaries—just before he unleashed a fusillade of blows at them, alternating his strikes between swords. His assault was so powerful that each man required two hands to fend him off.

Charles toyed with them, herding his opponents toward the other vermin in an effort to support Édouard if the need arose.

Charles whipped his short sword downward and struck the inner forearm of the man next to the leader, causing him to scream and drop his now useless weapon when the deep gash sprayed blood. The man never saw Charles's long sword on its wide, looping path as it whispered, cleaving the chilly autumn air. The arc of the sword was not without purpose—the technique increased momentum and made the ultimate point of impact nearly impossible for an observer to determine. In this case, the target and additional velocity allowed the blade to completely separate head from neck. The impact of tempered steel cleaving bone caused the sword to ring slightly—like a distant church bell.

As Charles watched the headless man fall, the filthy leader thought he saw an opening and lunged, finding his mark. Charles neither cried out nor cringed—he looked his opponent in the eye and laughed. The man stared at his sword and then at Charles, and his face contorted in fear.

"There is no blood! You are a devil!"

"The devil, you say?" Charles stabbed the vermin in the side with his short sword.

Glancing past the leader held upright by the blade impaling him, Charles saw that Édouard was having no trouble with his opponents. He withdrew his sword and glared at the leader who fell writhing to the ground. "You can ask him about me soon enough."

The knights' weapons and methods were as advanced as they were bewildering. Under their loose-fitting tunics were typical gambesons, but over that were two layers of leather with a thin sheet of metal in between and a hauberk with mail that covered only the center of their chests and backs. On their forearms under their tunic sleeves they wore leather bracers, also strengthened with a light layer of mail.

They were better protected for battle than the Arabs or Persians, and moved quicker and with greater agility than a traditional European knight. Almost no one would suspect they wore hidden light armor, and certainly no one could perceive it at night. This both protected them and confused their enemies—ultimately to their demise.

Charles—focused, calm, deliberate—moved toward the man closest to him. The pillager swung his sword awkwardly at Charles, who deflected the blow with his short sword and then drove his long sword through his opponent's ribs. Skin, muscle, cartilage and bone yielded to power and metal. He too fell to his knees with a scream, trying desperately to prevent his blood's rapid escape from his side. His efforts did little to delay his death.

Édouard had turned his mount and killed another adversary and could have easily struck down the man who had faced Charles, but he hadn't because such an act would breach their code of honor. And Charles needed no help.

There were many reasons that Templar Knights decimated their enemies: strategy, tactics, years of practice, execution, honor, the bonding of brothers, courage and a dogged refusal to ever give up. They used each tactic that night, fighting together as if their actions had been planned in advance.

The men nodded at each other and then surveyed the scene. All of their assailants were dead except the leader. Charles strode to where he was sprawled out, still moaning, and gave him another deep gouge with his sword. The leader screamed.

"Still with us? Too bad. I wish I had time to show you what I learned during our desert campaigns. I've watched men languish in agony for days—begging to die. Or I could simply leave you, writhing in pain, powerless as your life slips away."

"Please," the man whimpered through clenched and bloody teeth.

"But we have no time for that, so we bid you farewell." Charles drove his sword through the man's heart before he could beg again.

"Mercy?" asked Édouard as Charles mounted his horse.

"None. But we've seen enough, and it's time to go. I couldn't chance that he might have lived and then blamed us for this destruction."

Charles led them back the way they'd come, but at a faster pace than when they'd arrived. The stench would be long remembered, but he had no desire to be enveloped by it any longer than necessary. He stopped his horse on a rise and turned to give the village another look, at the same time making sure they weren't followed.

All the screams had been silenced.

One of the well-placed agents in this region's regal court had informed the Order of this attack days in advance. It had been independently confirmed by one of their own in the Church; their courier network had no rival in speed or stealth. Charles could report to the Council that their suspicions had been true and even worse than they had anticipated.

"That could have been us," he said, his voice barely audible.

Édouard's neck muscles tightened as he drew in a controlled breath. He knew better than to speak without thinking. He sat in silence for an awkwardly long time.

Finally he said, "But at which end of the sword?"

Charles turned away from Édouard and shifted his reins as he allowed himself a slight grin, imperceptible in the shroud of darkness. His inner pride was much greater than his blank stare conveyed. He and the Council had previously seen in young Édouard the attributes that made him a prime candidate for a very high position in the future. His response to Charles merely reinforced what they all concluded; Édouard Claremont was as brilliant and intuitive as he was brave. He didn't have the Council's inside knowledge or even the knowledge of a man at Charles's level, but he had deduced the reason they were there. He was truly gifted. He needed only to mature and proceed through the highest levels of their sacred teachings and training.

The Order had men in elevated positions of influence and in the widest possible expanse of lands and kingdoms. They'd spent patient generations building a network of hidden influence. The Council had known an attack of this kind was coming and that many more would follow. They had already begun preparations to protect their interests. They'd moved slowly so far, but with the ability to rapidly accelerate if this insanity continued or escalated.

Charles broke the silence again. "So, Édouard, are you suggesting that we couldn't fend off this attack?"

"No, sir. I think that was proven tonight. I am assuredly not one of our more valiant knights and this wasn't Thermopylae, but our legions fight as well and as bravely as any Spartan. However, there must be a deeper reason that we were sent here."

Édouard continued to remain fully alert as he was trained to be, but it was clear that he was also deep in thought.

Charles wondered if Édouard would solve the mystery before he had the chance to share it with him. Édouard was just as well trained by the monks of his abbey as he had been by the instructors in the battle yard. While knights too badly injured to return to battle became some of their greatest instructors in the military arts, the Council had long ago determined to seek out the greatest minds in addition to the best soldiers. Édouard exceled in both arenas.

"And why do you think we were ordered to observe this slaughter, my young friend?"

"There is a rumor, sir, that our knights were those originally tasked by the Church to commit this destruction."

"Correct. And we refused to submit to their will."

"Is that why those peaceful and innocent Cathars were slaughtered?"

"Correct again. They wouldn't submit either. But this village is remote, and most Cathars don't believe in violence, nor do they have adequate arms."

"And as they did today, one day we could pay the price for disobedience?" Édouard shook his head. "Every great empire has eventually fallen, but since we've never known defeat, I hadn't considered it."

"Neither had those peaceful, innocent Cathars that you can still smell burning in that valley below us. Don't forget what you've seen this night. You may have brothers who in the future claim what happened here was just a fable, a tale contrived to drive home a lesson. That is one of the reasons you were chosen—to be a witness. A witness who can speak with the fervor and the honesty of firsthand experience of what happens to those who won't obey."

"I am but one witness and of little stature," Édouard replied sincerely.

"Sadly, this is just the beginning. We expect there will be no shortage of such acts for others to witness. But today we have both seen more than enough." Charles turned his horse away from the sights and sounds below.

They moved like specters and felt nearly as empty as specters inside. Even honorable battles left echoes in the dark places and shadows of the mind that robbed a man of the hope of restful sleep. What they saw and heard tonight would be far worse than just adding to the chorus of echoes. But they couldn't know then that this night would be but a muted harbinger of the horrors that would follow.

Whether it was the aftereffects of their skirmish or the epiphany that began to sink in, Édouard looked and sounded drained of strength. "So *this* is the Church we serve?"

"I'm sure you've learned that we serve a much higher power, which is another reason that our Order will never submit. And there is a vast amount of knowledge that we don't share, not even with the Church. Especially not with the Church. You'll come to fully understand this and much more when you learn the most guarded secrets of the Order. We possess far more secrets than the ones the Cathars died for. And we've agreed to help them keep and protect their sacred knowledge in their remaining locations."

Clearly, Édouard was too stunned by Charles's revelations to press him to explain further. One thing was certain: the warrior monks of the revered Inner Council were as wise as Charles had come to believe they were. He was now far more hopeful that his protégé would become one of those who would oversee and protect the secrets of the ages. The survival of the Order would depend on having guardians of his caliber. And the increased likelihood of their survival would make the memory of this carnage more bearable in the uncertain times ahead.

TWO

Graham Chastain arrived at the party knowing he was somewhere between three steps and a not-so-long jump closer to adding another zero to his already substantial net worth. But only he knew the reason his rise to fortune and fame was poised to launch to even greater heights—and he intended to keep it that way. He embodied the adage *knowledge is power.* The axiom wasn't a cliché—it was his foundation. His companies' tech advances were the talk of the industry, but they were a mere shadow of larger yet more clandestine operations and projects. Drawing boards. Working models. Secrets in vaults. Simulations and virtual realities. Any of his better known divisions or subsidiary companies would be the envy of most entrepreneurs, but it was his unknown network of developments that were even more valuable than the obvious ones currently increasing his fortune.

He was often called a genius, but he always deflected those comments with good-natured, self-deprecating replies that he usually followed with, "However, brilliant people *do* call me brilliant." Friends and competitors alike had no idea of the

Dene Quesenberry
Author – The Power Behind the Throne

http://www.theqinfinitum.com/
https://www.linkedin.com/in/dene-quesenberry/
https://www.facebook.com/dene.quesenberry.79

Hi Sally!

I hope you enjoy the book. The first chapter is a bit bloody (according to my physician), but no more so than the Old Testament. I said, "But there's no gratuitous sex or nudity," and she replied, "You'll never be a bestseller that way." Oh, well... at least my veterinarian loved it and said she couldn't put it down (and gave me a great review on Amazon).

I don't even know if you like this genre (even though my editor and I couldn't really identify just one), but I hope so. As speculative fiction I tried to blend historic conspiracy with the latest AI tech and plenty of action and intrigue. There are subtle undercurrents and nuance, but even if they are unseen, that doesn't take away from the story. It's ultimately about good vs. evil.

Thanks for the continued friendship over the years.

Fondly,

Dene

enormity of the icebergs hidden below his waterline. He was no Bezos-Musk-Jobs wannabe—he was a *gonnabe*. His certainty wasn't due to ego and it wasn't based on greed. His inner reflection was a pure assessment of what he knew he could accomplish—or lose—by trying. And he had no intention of losing anything.

The party was already at full tilt when he got to the main lobby and reception area, and Graham liked a good party as much as the next guy. What was unique about the festivities already being underway was that the party was for Graham and it wasn't supposed to start for another hour. It was supposed to be a relatively intimate gathering among a few friends, a cross section of business associates and some of the important local elites, to celebrate another of his companies' latest and extremely successful stock offerings. The event had been arranged by his close friend, Peter Gehlman, who was also his lead investment banker.

Graham walked toward Peter's lavish corner office, working his way through the partyers. There were so many, they spilled out into the hallways. Except for the receptionist, he had yet to run into anyone he knew. Graham's main reason for being there was to massage important elbows, and none were to be found so far. As he made his way through the modern cubicles leading to Peter's office, he was approached by a cocktail waitress wearing most of a tuxedo-like uniform. Her anatomy shaded the silver tray she presented and competed for space with the few flutes of champagne.

"May I offer you some?"

Graham was sure she'd gotten many interesting responses to that question, but decided to keep his wit to himself.

He took a glass and looked around. "Have you seen Peter?"

The server offered a demure lack of response. She relished men's struggles to keep eye contact.

"He's the host, and this is my party."

"I know who you are, Mr. Chastain. He's impressing himself in his corner office. And I get off at ten."

"Good to know, but I have other commitments," he said, looking at his left hand.

Her eyes followed his. "Ten," she repeated as she walked past him.

"Yes, you are," Graham said at a barely audible level. He shook his head as a mild shudder moved through his core and he gathered himself to renew his search for Peter.

The music was quite good—light jazz and, so far, not too loud. Graham wouldn't have been surprised to see a three-piece ensemble, but Peter didn't have the room to spare. He would want space to maneuver among the dignitaries and even more so among the many lovely women he'd most certainly invited.

Graham and Peter had very different ideas when it came to pressing flesh.

Graham nodded cordial greetings to people he vaguely recognized. He saw Peter near the massive windows that wrapped around two sides of his office. He was making hand gestures and regaling no fewer than five stunning women with some grand story regarding the amazing view of the financial district and its exorbitant cost. One of Peter's attorneys noticed Graham and tapped Peter on the shoulder. Peter grimaced at the interruption. The attorney nudged him again, enough to get Peter to stop talking as the attorney nodded toward Graham. Peter's grimace immediately changed to an expression of adulation.

"The guest of honor! It's about time," Peter bellowed as he moved toward Graham.

"About time? This gathering wasn't supposed to start for another hour. And what is it about little and intimate that you can't seem to grasp?"

"You know I don't do small."

"I thought I'd show up early to go over a few things. But they can wait." Graham chuckled, extending his hand.

Peter ignored the hand and wrapped his arms around Graham. He didn't stop there, but swung one arm around Graham's shoulder. Both men had athletic builds, but Peter was a full six inches shorter than Graham, so it was a literal stretch for him to put an arm around his shoulder—sober or in his current condition.

Peter gave Graham's glass a clumsy tap with his own. Graham was surprised neither glass shattered.

"The prodigal returns," Peter said to no one in particular.

"I never left," Graham said, sipping his champagne.

Peter took a healthy pull on his drink. "Weren't you all over Europe scouting facilities, meeting with clients and doing other important entrepreneur-type things?"

"That was three weeks ago, and we've had dinner since I returned."

"No matter, Mr. Millionaire *again*! I'm glad you're back, just the same." Peter leaned close to Graham as if to share a state secret. Gesturing with his head toward the model-caliber women, he said, "So what do you think?"

Graham took another small sip of his drink and asked, "Which one?"

"All of them, of course! What a preposterous question," he scoffed as he lifted his glass.

Graham smirked. "Well then, the first thing that comes to mind is vasectomy."

Peter lowered his head slightly toward Graham and started to shake it slowly back and forth. "Vassily? No, buddy, that's a dude's name, and I don't think she's Russian anyway. I'm pretty sure the hot blonde on the right is Finnish or Flemish or Danish or some other Scandinavian food group. But not Russian."

"I said *vasectomy,* you drunk-eared simpleton."

"What a relief, 'cause I'm not into that sort of thing."

Graham started to answer, but knew it was a waste of time. Something, or rather some*one*, caught Peter's attention across the room, and he held his index finger up in Graham's general direction. "Don't go away. I'll be right back."

Graham shook his head. It was doubtful that Peter's focus would ever change. Not that Graham really cared. His friend's proclivities had never affected their mutual success.

It was nearly impossible for Graham to get angry or even annoyed with Peter—they'd been through a lot together and he owed Peter a great deal. Graham had been on a full ride navy scholarship at Vanderbilt due to his outstanding test scores, and Peter was from generations of great wealth and could go to school most anywhere. He had started at Yale, but after a bit of trouble he'd never quite explained, he said he wanted to get away from his pompous family and see the Old South. He did vast research and soul searching by flipping a coin over Duke and Vandy, and Vandy won. Or lost, depending on how some of his friends joked about it.

Graham majored in electrical engineering with minors in business and computer science. Even then he was driven by an insatiable thirst for knowledge and the desire to be at the forefront of cutting-edge technology. Peter's main focus was networking and meeting every influential person he could, and in spite of his partying and skirt chasing, he was no slouch academically. He double-majored in finance and economics, and his grades were good enough to get him into Wharton for his MBA.

Graham went into the navy as a lieutenant junior grade and focused on intelligence gathering. A problem solver and a MacGyver-type, he was in his element and thrilled to learn clandestine tradecraft. When men in the field complained of shoddy equipment, he went on the front lines to test his own devices and upgrades with a group of SEALs. Graham tried to qualify as a SEAL, but a torn rotator cuff eliminated him before he got very far into the program. But he shared their esprit de corps, and they welcomed his expertise and admired his courage to venture into harm's way when most wouldn't. On one of several missions with the SEALs, the operation went south and he was badly wounded. His light duty during and after recovery allowed him to complete an MS in computer science.

After his discharge, Graham used his military contacts, stellar record, programming skills and innovative devices to acquire a number of large government contracts. He built a dynamic team, gave them a great work environment and let them participate in the profits. His success meant he actually grew too fast, and since the federal government took its time paying bills, he went to New York to seek out venture capital. After a week of futile meetings, he was discouraged, disgusted with the terms of vulture capitalists, and was ready to get out of the city, if for no other reason than to regroup.

Before leaving to pursue other solutions, he ran into Peter at an upscale bar. Peter's family had been in investment banking for decades, but he didn't get along with his "too stodgy" family. His credentials, intellect and charisma had landed him a job in an excellent small firm where he became an outstanding rainmaker and quickly rose to partner.

The firm name eventually became AGC, Inc., for Austin Gehlman Capital. The boutique firm provided a variety of investment-banking, venture-capital and hedge-fund-management functions for very high-level clients. Harriman Austin III was a founding partner. Much older than Peter, he took a liking to the younger man. Austin preferred Europe to the U.S. and worked from their office in Switzerland. Peter had earned Austin's trust, and he thrived as head of the U.S operation. Peter claimed there were two other older partners who had wealth beyond avarice but who preferred to act as consultants and not advertise their names on the letterhead, but it was hard to tell when Peter was being serious.

Over drinks at their clamorous reunion, Peter said his firm could easily raise the capital Graham needed. After reviewing the size and number of existing contracts and the huge backlog of additional innovative devices and software applications, it was clear to Peter that Graham's company could be much bigger and more successful than he or Graham had first imagined.

And so, after twelve years of incredibly hard work and a great deal of sacrifice, Graham became an overnight sensation. His success might have overwhelmed another man or caused him to become complacent, but Graham had faced death and survived and had a channeled vision for his future. Rather than feel overwhelmed, he became even more driven.

In addition to helping launch his meteoric rise in fortune, Peter introduced Graham to the woman who would become his wife, the former Vicky DeBeirne. She was shy, attractive and reserved, from an extremely wealthy family, and had no interest in a carouser like Peter.

Vicky was highly intelligent and had attended Cornell and

Harvard as well as the Sorbonne. She owned large blocks of stock in several of her family's companies and maintained an executive position on the board of their foundation, but mostly she liked to travel and engage in philanthropic work. Graham had initially admired her work on varied causes, but in the last year her endeavors had made her distant—both physically and emotionally. It was a gradual but noticeable process. They hadn't fought over her constant travel, but Graham felt an edge to her demeanor that had grown over time.

Graham forced himself to stop reflecting on his marital concerns and his nostalgic history with Peter. He came to the party to work the room and that was precisely what he intended to do. Since he was early and Peter wasn't available for a meeting, he shifted to attack mode. Before he could pick a networking target, someone cleared his throat behind him.

"Excuse me. Mr. Chastain?"

Graham turned. A fairly short bald man with protruding eyes peered up at him. He wore a dark suit, white shirt and nondescript gray tie. Graham extended his hand.

"Welcome to the party. And you can call me Graham," he said as he smiled.

Instead of shaking Graham's hand, the man slipped a business card into it. "Yes, thank you. Mr. Chastain, I'm Delmond Bernard, and I represent a group of influential men who would like to meet with you."

His face was nearly expressionless and his complexion pallid, matching Graham's first impression of his personality.

"Very kind of you to come here, Mr. Bernard. And why do these influential men want to meet with me?"

"They oversee a great many companies and significant wealth. And they prefer to keep a low profile."

"That's great, Mr. Bernard, but that doesn't answer my question."

"It would be most beneficial for you to meet with them, Mr. Chastain. Most beneficial indeed. They have much to offer you and your companies. They would like you to come to their offices at three tomorrow."

Graham began to read the card but turned when Peter broke into wild laughter behind him. He watched Peter dab a napkin on the very ample and now wet chest of a laughing woman as he said, "I'll check my schedule, but I'm sure I can meet with your group. Wealthy, influential people who want to help me could be . . ." He looked back to find the little man gone. "Intriguing," he said.

Peter, tugging on the hand of the truly beautiful woman he'd doused with champagne—who wasn't making any effort to contain her beauty within the plunging neckline of her dress—joined Graham. Graham was still pondering what happened as he stared at the business card in his hand and then at Peter.

Peter blinked, his expression blank. "Hi, Graham. What brings you here? We're having a party." Not getting an answer, he added, "And what's up with Uncle Fester?" Before Graham could respond, Peter nodded toward his companion and said, "Have you met Sharon?"

"Karen," she quickly interjected, embarrassed, and extended her hand to Graham.

"Really? Then have *you* met Sharon? You two could be twins," Peter said, slurring his words. "And speaking of that . . ." Peter winked at Graham.

"I have a serious question, Peter." Graham was still reviewing the business card. "Have you heard of a group called Ambrose? Technically, the Ambrose Consortium, and—"

"Sure! Great band." Peter squinted at the card Graham held out.

Graham folded his arms and gazed at the ceiling, waiting for some form of coherence to make an appearance.

"Pay attention, please," Graham said. "Uncle Fester—I mean Mr. Bernard, who just scurried out the door—said they were very wealthy and influential and have a great deal to offer my companies and me. Did you invite that guy?"

"Ohhh, *that* Ambrose. No. Yes. Very wealthy. Very powerful. They've done business with my family for about a hundred years." He leaned toward Karen and loudly whispered, "Did I mention *very* wealthy? Not to mention very powerful."

Graham ran one finger over the card and then tapped it. "So why didn't you tell me about these guys?"

Peter stood a little straighter and tightened his grip around Karen's waist. "What was the purpose of tonight's party?"

"Ten percent celebrating my large increase in wealth and ninety percent networking to continue that trend," Graham replied.

"If you stay here all night, you won't meet ten people who add up to one tenth of the influence of Ambrose. I wasn't sure their guy would show. They're pretty much a *don't call us, we'll call you* operation."

"So you—"

"You're welcome."

Graham was about to reply, but Peter had already moved past him, pulling Karen, who put up no resistance.

"Never hurts to keep mingling, though, buddy," Peter called out. "And it's a party for you, by the way."

Graham beamed and decided that mingling was exactly what he'd do.

Peter stopped abruptly and turned around. "Just remember—millions to billions." He lifted his glass and drank.

"Millions to billions," Graham repeated. As he finished his champagne and watched Peter and Karen head toward the noisiest part of the reception area, Graham was more invigorated than ever. As he made his way toward the heart of the party, seeking the best hands to shake, he wondered if Ambrose were as substantial as Peter claimed. He looked forward to finding out.

THREE

Avalon occasionally gave a fleeting glance over top of the papers he was scrutinizing, partly to keep a keen eye on the rodent pretending to be a man who sat across the room and partly to intermittently survey the room. It was a useful habit—eyes ever moving and all senses alert. He wasn't sure which odor in the cacophony of smells offended him most. He sought to block the amalgam of attacks stemming from waste, trash, mildew and poor hygiene using his highly elevated ability to focus. He found solace in the knowledge that this meeting was completely necessary and soon to be over. Avalon smiled the way he always did—in the depths of his dark mind and devoid of outward expression. He had such robotic control of his thoughts and emotions, he could accomplish the equivalent of laughing out loud inside his head and barely show a blink. Had he not chosen his present career path, he could have made an extraordinary living as a poker player.

Avalon glanced again at Carl Radic and pondered his own next seven moves. It was an exercise he used to block out the wretched vermin he was forced to employ. Radic defined the concept of unkempt in his wrinkled, stained clothing, his mannerisms, his posture and even his speech. His hair was thinning, with a low part he regularly had to coerce over the top of his balding pate. Avalon thought he looked like a dirty window, grimy but still of some use.

Radic sat behind a small desk—a plank of plywood resting on two empty wooden spools, the kind that once held thick wires. It was cheap, but it gave Radic a solid writing surface where he created his most recent "masterpieces." He had actually once been an excellent artist, but was expelled from art school after many violations involving gambling, alcohol, theft and other trivial infractions that were frowned upon in academia. So he used his creative skills for pursuits such as forgery. Yes, Carl Radic had convinced himself he was a product of misfortune and a world out to get him, one that had literally forced him to commit crimes. Sadly, the criminal justice system didn't share his view of his victimhood.

He continued to fidget and nervously shuffle papers and pens around, much to the continued chagrin of Avalon, who was the polar opposite of Radic in every way.

Avalon's appearance was an enigma, as he intended it to be. Everything about him was perfectly in place, from his neat, short hair to his clean, pressed clothes. And yet everything was also completely average and nondescript. And that also matched his intent—to blend in. His loose-fitting jacket could have been worn by any number of delivery personnel. The colors he wore for this meeting were bland gray tones. Only he knew that under the frumpy exterior was ripped muscle he had proudly developed over many years. But no one could tell with the padding he'd added and the clothing that was slightly too big. The one detail out of place was his racing gloves.

Radic squirmed and finally said, "See? Just like I said, Mr. Smith. Perfect. No hesitation. No false starts. Exactly like the sample you gave me."

Avalon said nothing, but briefly peered at Radic with eyes that were steel gray today. Tomorrow they might be piercing blue, but they were menacing no matter what color contacts he chose. He had no emotion and showed no emotion. He was an empty shell, devoid of a soul. His eyes were one of the many weapons in his arsenal of intimidation.

Avalon's lack of response made Radic more nervous. "I don't know why you bothered to pay me to rent this little dump to do the job anyway. My place ain't the Taj Mahal, but it's better than coming clear out here just for a small job. You coulda given me the extra cash. An' I coulda met you somewhere's else. Gee, what a dump."

Avalon said nothing, but continued to act as though he was studying the pages. He already knew of Radic's ability, and he saw immediately that any one of the several forged samples would be more than adequate. Several, because he never took chances he didn't need to. If one forgery were damaged, he would have backups. *Just keep talking*, he thought.

"Now don't get me wrong, Mr. Smith. I said a small job, but still *very* valuable, if you know what I mean. Not just anyone has my level of skill when it comes to this stuff."

Without looking up from the papers Avalon finally responded. "Yes, Carl, they seem fine. Very satisfactory." He hoped that by responding, Carl might relax a little and stop his endless, vacuous prattle. He doubted the silence would last.

Radic released a sigh of relief and wiped his brow with the back of his hand. He always perspired a great deal, and now was no exception, except that he was sweating even more than usual. He stood the blank sheets of copy paper straight up for the umpteenth time and tapped them on the table, even though they couldn't possibly get any more even than they were the first ten times.

"I really appreciate the work. My parole officer wouldn't, but screw that jerk. They should treat a man of my talent better. I'm going places. You're obviously a man of refinement, Mr. Smith. You recognize talent and you're willing to pay a lot more than my menial day job."

To Radic, it seemed that "Mr. Smith" was abnormally thorough in his examination. Yet rather than analyze the forgeries, Avalon had been watching the very reliable watch facing inward on his left wrist.

Now Avalon tipped the papers down and said, "No, Carl, I haven't forgotten the balance of your payment. I have the cash as agreed." He feigned an avuncular tone to say, "Surely you didn't already spend the advance I gave you? That was just days ago."

Radic let out another sigh of relief. Maybe this Smith guy wasn't as evil as he appeared. "You know how it is, Mr. Smith. Times is tough."

Avalon shifted the papers from two hands to his left hand. His expression changed ever so slightly to give Radic as much of a smile as he could muster in an effort to continue to allay his tension and nervousness. He slipped his right hand under his left lapel and pulled out a fairly thick envelope and tossed it on the desk in front of Radic, intentionally scattering his pens.

Radic ignored the pens and dropped his previously neat stack of blank paper. He grabbed for the envelope and tore it open, his eyes wide with anticipation of the cash. He began to slowly count the money without taking it out of the envelope.

As he continued counting, showing a big smile from his discolored teeth, he said, "You know, a few more jobs like this and I can get some people off my back and start getting somewhere."

While Radic fumbled with his ill-gotten gains and continued

his chatter, Avalon turned and set his own small group of papers on a file folder behind him. As he did, a horn began to bellow not far away.

Avalon gracefully turned back toward Radic and muttered, "Right on time," as he raised the silenced pistol he had retrieved from under the opposite lapel. Avalon's motion was fluid, the result of many thousands of practice rounds fired at advanced tactical courses.

Radic was still focused on his cash, and not looking up, he said, "Right on time for what?"

Just before Avalon squeezed, Radic raised his eyes, which opened wide with horror.

"No, don't."

Avalon barely moved his stoic lips as he exhaled and squeezed the trigger ever so slowly. Always squeeze, never pull.

The round struck Radic's chest, penetrating his right ventricle, and pieces spread to lodge in his vertebrae after doing substantial damage to his spinal cord. He would never walk again. Not from paralysis, but because he was dead before his head slammed down onto the desk.

Avalon was truly tempted to shoot Radic through the mouth as an exclamation point to how badly he wanted him to shut up. He could have just as easily shot him right through the eye from twenty feet farther back if he'd wanted to. To call him an expert marksman was a gross understatement. But that wasn't the plan. And it would have left a mess that he didn't want to leave footprints in.

Avalon was already moving around the desk to get behind Radic as his head fell. He waited for the second horn blast that signaled the shift change at the Poseidon Shipyard and fired another quiet round into the back of Radic's head, pieces of another frangible projectile embedding in his skull and the desk.

Avalon paused to listen for any change in his environment. Only an unlikely passerby could have heard the muffled shots and only if they passed close to the small window. That scenario wasn't likely, but he took no chances. Hearing no footsteps, he looked at the now-still Radic, said, "Paid in full," and holstered his weapon.

With practiced agility and swift motion, he produced a folded plastic bag from a side jacket pocket. He popped it open by flexing his arms as the bag grabbed air. The side of the bag advertised the ersatz company name Secure Waste Removal, Inc. Avalon considered the irony that someone would need a much bigger bag to remove the waste of flesh that had recently been Carl Radic. Since Avalon's first bullet stopped Radic's heart and his fat body folded forward, a little blood had begun to pool. There was more with the head wound, but still not a great deal since his heart was no longer pumping. Avalon quickly rifled Radic's pockets, checking for possible connections between them. Finding none, he dropped Radic's wallet in the bag but left some cash in his pockets. He quickly bagged all of the remaining items on the desk. Avalon retrieved his file folder and slipped the sheets of paper inside and behind some fake work orders for an address several blocks away. His subterfuge would be complete if he happened to be stopped and questioned. Avalon reached into a side jacket pocket and produced a digital camera and took several pictures of the deceased. He then backed those pictures up to a small drive and returned both to the same pocket. The organization that employed him had its own forgers, but the pictures might also be used to plant evidence on a future target. He didn't ask questions—he just carried out his orders.

Avalon stood with his back to the door and took one last

perusal of the room. Seeing that he missed nothing, he opened the door with slow deliberation. He neither heard nor saw anyone. He moved outside, pulled the door behind him and left it slightly ajar. He dropped his gloves into the bag as he moved toward his panel van with magnetic signs on the side that advertised the waste company. Radic had been paid extra to take the bus to this part of town, so he had no vehicle. As always, Avalon's head was in constant motion in all directions as he started the engine. He looked one last time at the door.

"Yes, Carl, times *is* tough." He pulled out his cellphone, opened the message icon, entered three numbers and hit Send. The predetermined three numbers and sequence changed each time, but they always had the same meaning: mission accomplished. He casually drove toward his next destination. He was glad to be busy using his skills for the cause; this would be a full week. He allowed himself another internal smile within his darkness and began to do something he was completely unaware of. Avalon softly hummed a long-forgotten tune.

FOUR

Graham drove to the address he had entered into his car's navigation system. He was going more out of curiosity than anything. He was content with his companies' current growth rates, but Peter, rather than seeing Ambrose as competition, was highly supportive of Graham pursuing the additional source of capital.

He would prefer to drive a Range Rover, but had finally capitulated to his wife's encouragement to buy a Mercedes. He compromised with regard to what he bought. In other words, he gave in to what she wanted. He believed he needed to pick his battles—even though they rarely battled—which was a major reason for his decision. She believed there were numerous reasons to own a Benz, from presenting the image of a successful businessman to the stockholders to the simple fact it was a good investment. Graham saw the merits of Vicky's points and felt good about the purchase when he found a demo unit for a song. And it was one of his favorite tunes. He tried never to be penny wise and pound foolish, because he was more than cognizant of what his time was worth. But he also enjoyed a great bargain on big-ticket items. It was just one of many mental excursions he used to keep his mind sharp. Graham enjoyed all sorts of multitasking, although it was sometimes difficult to shut off. Wasn't that a key aspect of being ADD? Nah. He just had a high-level ability to code and to perform technical problem solving while juggling the demands of running multiple business units. Totally different. Oddly enough, he was amazed how often solving one problem gave him ideas for solving others that were totally unrelated. He called it brain synergy—BS for short.

The address he entered for Ambrose didn't actually pull up—only an approximate address according to the GPS. Graham thought that was a bit odd, but didn't dwell on it. It was on a side street of the financial district in a high-rent area of the high-rent area. He slowed and looked for the address and saw empty parking places in front of a mid-rise building. A single bronze plaque showed the building number, but no company name or other information. At the end of the short row was a very heavy gate leading to what may have been a very private garage. The spaces in front were clearly marked "Visitor Parking—All Others Towed." The building was fairly old and an elegant mixture of stone, granite and brick. And though it was old, the construction was solid and the building looked like it could stand another hundred years.

Graham locked his door with a chirp and walked toward the entrance. He had excellent peripheral vision and subtly scanned one hundred eighty degrees around him as he moved—a permanent habit from his intel days. He didn't notice anything out of the ordinary. Actually, there wasn't much of anything to notice at all. At the entrance, a black metal security door led to a short, recessed hallway. It was similar to a wrought-iron security door, but of a much sturdier design. There was no point in posting a No Soliciting sign, because a solicitor couldn't get through the first door. Graham didn't see a doorbell, so he reached for the knob. He heard the distinct click of a lock being released and wondered where the security camera was and how he had missed it.

In a dimly lit room full of security monitors, two men watched several screens. It would have been one of the highest quality surveillance systems available on the market—except it would never actually be available. It was completely state-of-the-art, and the design had been customized by a firm owned by yet another firm controlled by the Ambrose Consortium. The men at the console could observe all directions outside the building in a light range that went from full sunlight to pitch black. The same was true inside; they could see everything with the exception of the bathroom stalls and the executive suites when turned off by key executives. The security office had independent power, backup power and redundant communication systems. Other companies might think this level of precaution was overkill, but at Ambrose these methods were considered to be necessities. And the personnel were as formidable as the equipment: highly trained, with various military, police and intelligence agency backgrounds. And they were well armed with concealed weapons beneath their impeccably tailored suits.

"I just love doing that," one of the security officers said, smirking as he tripped the lock to allow their visitor to come in.

"Yeah, *that* never gets old. You're quite the prankster," his counterpart responded. "I can't wait for your next round of hysterics. I'm headed to check out area 17 if you can contain yourself while I'm gone." He exited through a door that made no noise.

"Jerk," he muttered as he scanned the large cluster of screens.

Graham closed the security door behind him and allowed his eyes to adjust to the low-level lighting in the short stone hallway leading to a massive wooden door. Peter had described the group as low profile, but Graham's assessment was increasingly one of no profile. Not only had his initial investigation into Ambrose turned up virtually nothing, but the same was true with deeper data mining. Several meetings had prevented continued searching, but he was looking forward to more thorough digging when he returned to his office. For now he was just showing up for pleasantries due to Peter's encouragement and his own curiosity. Graham's very kind and cheerful executive assistant had confirmed the appointment with Ambrose's antithetically cold secretary.

Graham remembered Suzette's typical wit about how the charm school tuition had been wasted on the Ambrose staffer.

"That's right! Here at Torquemada Charm School, congeniality is more than just a stretch of your imagination."

Again seeing no doorbell, Graham raised his fist to knock just as the heavy door slowly swung open. *These people have obviously seen too many movies*, he thought. And to extend the metaphor, the door opened fully to reveal one of the largest men Graham had ever personally met. If the man towering in front of him hadn't played professional football, it must have been due to injury.

"I'm here to see . . ." Graham stopped, shook his head. "Actually, I'm not sure who I'm to see," he said, finishing his dangling introduction. But the man who must have been hired to match the massive door had already turned on his heel with more grace than Graham would have expected from someone that size.

"This way, Mr. Chastain." The lineman started down the hall

without looking to see if Graham followed.

His guide offered no further conversation as Graham followed him through the high-ceiling hallways. Graham, imagining that the man had no nerve endings in his face, wondered if there were courses for learning to hide all expression. He put aside his fanciful thoughts when they approached another massive door. The doorman worked the ornate brass handle as he turned sideways to offer Graham just enough room to enter.

"Mr. von Kleis will see you now, Mr. Chastain," he said with even less inflection than he had expression.

Just as Graham squeezed past the lineman-doorman, he turned back to speak.

"Thanks," he started to say. But he was talking to the back of the door.

This should prove fascinating, Graham thought as he turned to examine the room, wondering what awaited him.

FIVE

People dealt with the phenomenon of hurry up and wait with varying degrees of success. For Harry McGowan, the condition had long been his modus operandi, making him come across as manic depressive. He had been a mediocre reporter most of his life. It was more fashionable now to use the term *journalist*, but that was more than a stretch in Harry's case. His career had been a bust for a number of reasons, but mostly because he was lazy and possessed little talent. However, if he had one saving grace, it was his ability to do research. He was tenacious, and he simply enjoyed going down as many rabbit holes as possible, looking for obscure clues. His life was truly a trivial pursuit. He often made bad suppositions concerning the big stories he pursued, even though he was told they were wild goose chases. Rather than admit error and defeat, Harry would chase down leads to every end of every wrong turn in many mazes—always disregarding piles of dead mice.

But one time Harry *had* hit the proverbial jackpot. His paper received a tip that seemed farfetched, a political hot potato no one wanted to touch. But Harry pounced on it—partly because it was an intriguing challenge but also because no one else wanted it and his stock had dropped so much he feared being relegated to covering weddings and funerals. But his ability to scour through minutiae paid off. After spending long hours navigating the halls and the nooks and crannies of phantom corporations, rigged bids, coincidental deaths and a surfeit of small contracts that added up to massive contracts, Harry found what no one else wanted to bother with. He did so because he was as diligent as he was inconspicuous. And the arrogant perpetrators didn't think the best investigator, let alone a mediocre one, could discover the truth. But the revelations he uncovered flashed into a firestorm of political intrigue, scandals and eventually monumental indictments. Harry was whisked into protective custody, but not before his series of stories made major headlines. He spent years afterward continuing to be mediocre while living off that one big break.

Yet the success was long ago, and Harry's amazing story was old news and didn't seem so amazing anymore. A rocket can only carry a worthless payload so far, and his meteoric rise fizzled and plummeted, dropping him back to his normal equilibrium of mediocrity. Even though he bragged to his few friends of his past superhighway of success, anyone could see it had dwindled to a lonely dirt road. Ever in pursuit of the next big obscure story, he was about to be shown the door at a publication that barely had a window.

But Harry had an even bigger story this time. And that was what he had told his boss for months. He was about to put the pieces together, he just needed a little more time. Always a little more time.

Harry McGowan actually *did* have a blockbuster. And it really was bigger than the last one. No one had believed when he'd presented that story either, and this was far more complex in scope and the heights of power involved. But he had touted the inevitability of his next big story for so long, the wolf he had cried about had grown to the size of an imaginary pack.

The conspiracy Harry had uncovered was international and enormous in scope, but there was no way his current employer would support the funding for the travel and research Harry proposed, so he'd had to do it the hard way. The tedious way. Meticulous research took a long time. And the more Harry dug, the more his emotions became mixed. He was thrilled at being the one to discover a major story and terrified of what he was uncovering. Why had no one else stumbled across revelations so monumental? And when he considered that maybe they had, that led to him wondering what could happen to an investigative journalist who discovered such secrets. Names like Jim Keith, Danny Casolaro, William Cooper and Michael Hastings kept coming to mind, haunting him.

He would have to become smarter still, he concluded.

Harry pulled his barely running, nearly repossessed car up to his favorite bar at his typical time of day—two-ish in the afternoon. He justified his location and the hour by claiming it was where he did his best and most lucid thinking. Some colleagues had not so subtly mentioned that maybe he just thought he was lucid.

His car continued running after he shut off the ignition. He pulled out a phone more than three generations out of date and which could barely support the operating system—a flip phone without much flip left in it. A number was written on the pad next to him, but he didn't need it. He had called often enough to have the number memorized, even without redial.

"This is Harry McGowan again. Is Mr. Chastain there?" His face tightened as he listened to the same monotone response. If they only *knew* who he was!

"As I've told you before, I can't leave a message. This information is far too important and far too sensitive. It has to be in person. What is it about the concept of life or death you don't get? . . . When can I see him?" He was getting more irritated, but knew better than to lash out at a gatekeeper.

"I'm not selling anything! I'm trying to meet with Mr. Chastain to tell him of something involving possible grave consequences. . . . Yes, ma'am, same number as before. Yes, yes, that's the one."

Harry grabbed up a stack of files and exited his car, closing the dented door with a great slam. *She doesn't get who I am*, he thought with searing self-aggrandizement as he made his way to the door of his favorite watering hole. *But she soon will.* He smiled to himself. *They just have no idea of the enormity of it all. Even I have trouble wrapping my head around this story.*

SIX

Graham entered a small foyer that opened into a massive room. The walls were taupe, and carved side tables were arranged before each, displaying what were clearly expensive sculptured items of jade and fine porcelain.

As Graham stepped into the main office area, he noted the many fine bookcases, hardwood flooring and expensive rugs. Almost out of place was the large monitor array behind an exquisite antique mahogany desk. The screens went dark just as Graham approached, but not before he consciously and unconsciously took in images from around the world and multiple screens of streaming financial boards from a variety of countries. He didn't see enough to take in any real information, except that his host obviously wanted to be very well informed.

That host spun around in his high-backed leather chair, then rose, offering a warm smile. He was several inches shorter than Graham's six two and wore a perfectly tailored dark gray hopsack suit from Richard Anderson on Savile Row. He came around the desk and extended his hand.

"Sorry I didn't greet you at the door, Mr. Chastain. I'm Eric von Kleis, one of the directors here at Ambrose. We had an excellent opportunity which required my attention just before you arrived." He nodded toward the many flat screens.

"No problem at all, Mr. von Kleis. *Sind Sie Deutsche*?" Graham asked, noticing von Kleis's accent.

"Swiss, Mr. Chastain. But like many of my associates, my lineage is from a number of European countries. Your German is quite good. Please, have a seat." He gestured to the leather chairs in front of the desk.

"Thanks. It's rare that I get to use it. I've enjoyed attempting new languages in my travels, but I'm not truly fluent in any of them. Usually I speak just well enough to annoy the natives."

Von Kleis pulled back the chair next to Graham and sat in it, rather than using his desk as a barrier.

"Thank you for accepting our invitation," von Kleis said with a slight smile. He had a hawk-like nose and smooth skin from his forehead to his completely bald head.

"I'm not even sure what I've been invited to, Mr. von Kleis," Graham said. "But my investment banker, Peter Gehlman, suggested this could turn out to be a mutually beneficial relationship. Is this about an investment?" Graham leaned back and brought his fingertips together in front of his chest.

Von Kleis didn't change his smile very much, but somehow his expression seemed to be one of slight bemusement. "We are far more than investment bankers, Mr. Chastain."

"What, then?"

"My associates and I are very private; we keep a low profile. We do an incredible amount of research, and our think tanks are the best in the world. And . . . we have followed your career for some time and would like to put our resources behind you. More than just capital." Von Kleis opened his palms in an offering gesture to Graham.

"I'm listening," Graham said.

A side door opened with barely a whisper off to Graham's right and another man, similar in stature to the doorman-lineman, stepped into the room. He moved just as gracefully and had attended the same school of no facial expression. He carried a silver tray with two glasses and offered the tray to Graham.

"Single malt, I believe," von Kleis said. "I think you will find the Macallan 1996 is exquisite in its depth."

Graham raised a brow. Although he wasn't one for many luxuries or indulgences, good scotch was one he afforded himself. He typically preferred his chilled and neat, but he wasn't going to quibble. He enjoyed several high-end single malts, but Macallan was his favorite, which wasn't especially common knowledge since he rarely drank it in public. He enjoyed the cherry and vanilla scent with the hint of cinnamon and apple flavor. He surmised von Kleis was trying to impress him with the depth and breadth of his think tank. Graham wasn't such a scotch snob that he would disdain the oak cask version over the sherry cask.

Graham and von Kleis took their respective glasses from the tray, and Graham tipped his glass toward von Kleis. They both sipped, assuming the expressions of men in deep relish, imaginations drifting momentarily to the green hills and glens of Aberlour. Giving his senses over to taste, Graham didn't hear the massive valet slipping out as quietly as he arrived.

Von Kleis gently burst the bucolic bubble when he said, "As I was saying, we are involved in many diverse enterprises."

"What kind of enterprises, if you don't mind my asking?"

"The short answer is, the kind that always make a great deal of money for us," he replied cryptically.

"A bit vague at best," Graham said with a veiled query.

"Yes and no. There is virtually no type of business segment

we do not operate within. Your own businesses benefit from mutual synergies. You use both vertical and horizontal integration very much to your benefit. We do the same thing, but on a much larger and more diverse scale—from apothecaries to zoology and nearly everything in between. But the common thread is that we are truly in the information business. And our information is almost always superior. That's the yes aspect."

"And the *no* aspect?" Graham asked, trying to peel back another layer of what he could see would be a very large and dense onion.

"A need-to-know aspect at this time. Quite simply, you aren't part of us—at least not yet—and we haven't reached any form of agreement and haven't even begun to create a memorandum of understanding."

That von Kleis had slipped "at least not yet" into the conversation in a none too subtle fashion hadn't escaped Graham. He wondered what other bait von Kleis was prepared to dangle and to what degree his persona was a faux-avuncular act. Graham sensed a coldness beneath the lukewarm surface.

"No offense intended, but in my position, I have to ask the obvious: Does this involve insider trading?"

"My dear young man"—von Kleis chuckled—"we *are* the insiders. We don't require illegal activities to amass great wealth and power. Our association has been successfully developing and maintaining some of the greatest and most complicated operations imaginable for well over one hundred years."

"Oh, I get it. I get to join the secret handshake club," Graham said, thinking he was also entitled to humor.

Von Kleis's warmth and slight smile instantly evaporated. He rose from the chair next to Graham and moved around to his side of the desk, shaking his head to convey disappointment. He sat behind the desk, creating an intentional barrier between them and using the obstruction as an expression of authority. It was a classic takeaway maneuver.

"Mr. Chastain, your wit is well known, but in this case sophomoric humor is quite beneath you. What I have to share with you is quite serious. There is nothing conspiratorial afoot here. You are doing well, granted. However, we have the ability to grow your existing companies five or even ten times greater and faster than your present path. Possibly a great deal more."

Von Kleis took a taste of his drink, letting what he said sink in.

"And we are prepared to fund any and all projects you have on your very large drawing boards."

As Graham considered the comment, he began to raise his glass, but paused before bringing it to his lips. His expression was in opposition to the burst of curiosity running through his mind. It was no secret that Graham was highly ambitious and that the many benefits that Ambrose could offer as laid out by Peter were tantalizing, but now he had another reason for being intrigued. He looked at the single large ice cube and wondered how much von Kleis knew about the depth and scope of his many projects ready to be developed. And equally important, how had the information been acquired? He downed a healthy portion of his drink. This could become quite the chess match.

SEVEN

English Countryside—1247

Friar Edward sensed a presence. He never knew if the ability was linked to years of training or the gift of keen senses, but he could feel something in the air as sure as he felt the hard wagon seat he sat upon. He wondered if the younger man to his right had sensed anything yet. There was no need for alarm, and the friar showed none. He squeezed the reins ever so slightly but didn't change the tension on the horses' necks at all. Edward's hands were large and showed signs of wear and some scarring. His wrists and forearms looked far too powerful for those of a common friar. He and his companion wore simple tunics of unremarkable gray and brown—nothing as elaborate as their former warrior garb.

Edward and Brother Derek said nothing, but both scoured the countryside much more intensely than their casual manner conveyed. They were prepared—always. Three sevens or seven threes, it didn't matter. The battle determined the structure and it was always fluid. Brother Galen had the lead, as was his preference. They were each trained in all aspects of venturing into new lands, but those who wished to were permitted to function where they served best, and no one was better than Galen as lead scout, the point of their sword. Traveling in an arc, he stayed ahead of the wagon, out of sight, and also drifted to the right flank. Brother Lyonel trailed the wagon to provide an alert of an approach from behind. He was also responsible for the left flank. In this way, the two men watched the wagon and its occupants in a rough, moving circle. It was tiring but necessary, and the two traded places with the others from time to time.

The two men were sharp points that alerted the "fist" in the middle when necessary. Hidden inside the covered wagon were brothers Laurent, Renier and Thomas. Their group was the lead seven of the three groups. The sacred numbers gave them strength—whether it was from logic, divine intervention or their own beliefs. These formations had served them well and had given them victory after victory in both battle and commerce. Their tactics were almost never defeated.

Brother Derek had barely stretched and run a hand through his thick sandy hair when both men saw the horses' ears twitch. Friar Edward pulled hard on the reins, which nearly caused Derek to join the horses. Whatever Edward had sensed, the horses now did as well. Galen and Lyonel, on their circuitous loops, would quickly recognize the wagon had stopped. The wagon shook slightly as their three passengers took a tumble, but none of them cried out.

Although no one was technically at war in this part of the country, tempers between the nobles could flare and alliances could rapidly change. And then there was the constant threat of highwaymen looking for an easy target. Their humble attire and plain wagon typically suggested they were unworthy of the effort of robbery. If not, this target would be anything but easy.

Not a word was spoken and slight rustling could be heard from inside the wagon when Edward slowly slid his hand and arm behind his back inside the cloth covering and signaled, not for a moment taking his eyes off the road ahead. Edward watched the first of the men come over the rise. Nine, he noted as they came closer. A good number, but not enough to be of concern. Edward smiled with his mouth but not with his steel-gray eyes and waited for the leader of the party to speak when they halted in front of the wagon and horses.

"I am Serion of Kern. Who are you who trespass on my Lord Sewell's road?"

"We meant no trespass, Sir Serion. We have permission to pass this way, a paper from the regent of Notherol and signed by the earl himself, Phillip the Sanctified."

Brother Derek sat stoically silent, knowing that none of the men or places existed.

"Can any of you read per chance?" Edward paused to study the faces of several of the men. "No? I thought not."

"We know of no paper such as this and answer to no one but Lord Sewell, our sovereign," replied Serion.

"We are but humble monks resting our horses," said Edward with the slightest bow of his head. He remained in his seat.

Serion looked toward the horses tied to the back of the wagon and sneered, replying with contempt. "Those horses are too fine for poor monks."

"Yes, we have been most blessed in equine matters," replied Edward.

"We should take them to our lord for payment of your trespass. What other treasure do you carry, priest?"

Brother Derek looked over the group. Serion and his men were dirty and sat slouched on their horses. They chuckled at

Serion's words and carried themselves with arrogance, but obviously no discipline. They paid no attention to their surroundings and were most likely focused on possible plunder. The pathetic collection in front of him reminded Derek of a time when only three of their own number, mounted and wearing armor, would have cut through them like a scythe vanquishing wheat, requiring little effort to do so.

"Not a priest, just a friar. And we carry no treasure—only a fellow monk asleep with a fever. We do not *believe* it to be leprosy, but certitude is difficult in these matters. Only the blessed and merciful father above can know such things for certain."

"You brought lepers to my master's lands?" yelled Serion.

"No, just the one, but your Lord Sewer is *reasonably* safe," Edward replied with a calm, easy voice. "But we will not know for sure until we finish the bloodletting."

"Sewell! Lord Sewell! And once we finish *your* bloodletting, we will take your valuables and set fire to your wagon! Berger, check the back of the wagon." Serion waved an arm toward one of his nastier-looking men.

"Ah, yes, Sewell. Your pardon," said Edward. "Am I to take it you intend us harm? I would not wake Brother Renier with or without a fever. He can be like a bear when awakened, and somewhat disagreeable." Friar Edward directed his advice as much at Berger rounding the wagon as he was at Serion.

Serion, furious, drew a dirty sword of obviously poor quality.

"Yes, I plan to do you harm for some time until we end your lives in a slow, painful manner."

"If this is to be our end, then we must pray to the one true God," Edward said. Not waiting for an answer, Edward moved to the far left corner of the wagon box. As he rose, he lifted his eyes and his left hand skyward, palm open, and placed his right hand on a staff that was propped in the box. Brother Derek moved almost in unison, but to his right, with his left hand raised in worship and his right hand on his own staff.

Berger was fully at the back of the wagon when Serion and his men eased forward, sensing no threat from the monks. One of Serion's men dismounted as Friar Edward began his prayer in a solemn voice, still gazing upward.

"We beseech thee, dear lord on high, to judge these cretins most foul that we are about to deliver unto thee . . ."

As Friar Edward prayed, a groan and a thud sounded behind the wagon. Berger fell next to his horse, where he remained unmoving. Serion's face was red with fury, and Derek heard a muted chuckle behind him.

Stopping mid-prayer, Friar Edward said, "It would seem that your man has fallen from his horse. Poking the bear is rarely a good idea."

Serion and his men were distracted as they looked toward Berger in a twisted pile next to his horse, where a pool of blood was beginning to form.

Serion's men were focused on Berger when the man at the back of their group made a gurgling sound as he exhaled and looked down to see the head of an arrow sticking out from his chest. He too fell to the ground. As Serion's shocked men turned at the sound, an arrow appeared in the upper chest of the man on the far left of the group. A stain quickly formed on his filthy tunic around the arrow as he slid from his horse. Frantic, Serion and his men desperately searched in all directions, but saw no archers.

At the same moment, Galen and Lyonel stepped from the trees on opposite sides of the road with their small recurve bows already drawn, fresh arrows in place. Making themselves visible was a planned distraction. As the remaining men of Serion's dwindling group looked both left and right at the archers, there was a noise that sounded like three twigs snapping and a barely audible whisper in the air, followed by thumps almost in unison. A crossbow bolt was buried in the chest of Serion, with bolts in two more of his men. They each wore a look of shock as they fell from their horses.

When the three men fell, two more men were exposed behind them. They dithered, trying to determine where to run or who to fight, but Edward and Derek had already raised their staves, which were actually short spears, and each monk found his target with deadly precision. Two more bandits fell to the ground, weighing slightly more than when they arrived.

The remaining man was the one who unwisely dismounted. He started to run but was struck with arrows from Galen and Lyonel simultaneously—and dead before he hit the earth.

Nine men in about fifteen seconds, thought Friar Edward. Quite proficient.

Without discussion, the brothers set to work. Laurent, Renier and Thomas had already exited the wagon with their short swords in one hand and armed crossbows in the other. They checked bodies for signs of life and finding none, they gathered the dead men's horses. Galen had already moved back into the woods on his side of the road and Lyonel had come out of the woods on his horse on the opposite side, his bow with nocked arrow at the ready.

Almost immediately Galen reappeared and nodded at Lyonel across the road. Galen led his horse back to the wagon and said to Edward, "I found a suitable spot." Edward nodded and continued his task.

The men had quickly stripped each of their dead adversaries of their weapons and anything of value. They also removed their own spears and arrows from the bodies. This was done not just for the value of the projectiles, but so there would be no evidence leading back to the monks who had decimated their would-be assailants. Lyonel had already moved to the crest of the road to keep a lookout ahead, and all the brothers kept constant watch. Derek, the youngest, was tasked with removing boots and shoes. His foul job was far worse than taking in the sight of blood. Not for the first time he concluded that buzzards couldn't possibly possess a sense of smell.

Each horse carried two draped bodies, and the horses were led into the woods behind Galen, who carried a dead man on his own horse. He led them to a small clearing, pulled the dead man off his horse as he would a sack of cabbages, and immediately set about making a small fire. The other men entered the clearing and dumped their cargo.

"When we know the bodies have been discovered," said Edward, "we'll spread the rumor it was the Celts." Of course, they could have just as likely blamed a troublesome lord or earl for the deaths if that plan suited the Order. A rumor repeated in hushed tones by three men or thirteen would yield the same effect if repeated to the right gossips. They had done that many times before in many villages.

"Do the Celts raid this far south?" asked Brother Laurent.

"I don't think the Celts raid at all during this season," replied Thomas, continuing his work.

"I wish there were another way, Friar Edward," Brother Derek said.

Edward knew what Derek meant.

Some of the dead men would be hung by their feet from a

rope over a branch, their throats cut, draining much of their blood. Some would be poked and burned with the charred end of a stick from Galen's fire, even though Galen had already vanished to continue scouting with Lyonel. Some would be bound, sitting back to back in a circle. And at least one man would be dragged off into the woods in hopes a wild animal would leave few remains. A rumor of cannibalism was often entertaining. But at the very least, the local townspeople would think these men had been tortured by savages rather than dispatched in short order by humble monks.

Brother Derek hadn't seen nearly the battles Edward and the other brothers had, so he was naturally squeamish.

"So we are clear, young master Derek . . ." Edward drew his hands about him to indicate the complement of dead men. "These creatures intended to torture you, kill you and take your belongings. They would have attacked innocent traveling monks who were harming no one. You would have been set upon and killed in a most horrible fashion. And if they'd indeed been attacked by Celts with an unpleasant mood about them, they would do what we are doing—yet while these men were *still alive. Confusionem inimicis nostris*—we bring confusion to our enemies. And everyone who is not of our Order is an enemy or potential enemy." Edward looked at the bodies and then at his gathered men. "We leave no suspicion upon ourselves and remain to be seen as harmless monks. And what does that lead to?"

"*Scientia potentia est*," the men declared together.

"Knowledge is power. So it has always been with us, so it will always be. *Ad gloriam Dei*!" Edward concluded.

"*Ad gloriam Dei*," they repeated with reverence.

When the false carnage was complete, the brothers moved

away from the scene. The fire was quickly dowsed so as not to be detected right away or to burn up their arranged scene. They gathered around the wagon to organize their next move, which was to continue on as they had been doing, hopefully without another such interruption. Brother Galen had already taken the lead.

By now, the second group of seven would be close to Friar Edward's current position. They stayed fairly close in case they were needed as reinforcements. If such had been the case earlier, Lyonel would have left at a full gallop toward the second seven to alert them and returned with riders. But now Lyonel would take the string of horses with their saddles and give half to each of the two trailing groups. Brothers in the trailing groups would decide which horses, saddles and weapons would be kept, sold or traded. All dealings of this kind brought strength to the Order and glory to the Almighty and to ultimately reach the goals of both.

Never did they stray too far from their power base. If the three groups of seven weren't enough, they could call on five hundred or even five thousand of the best-equipped and bravest knights in all of Europe. But that wasn't the plan. That wasn't how the Order operated. They would send out the call if a forward group was in jeopardy of being annihilated—which was highly unlikely given the way new areas were infiltrated. And they had learned the hard way many decades ago not to overextend their support and supply lines. In the early decades of their Order, too many had perished in senseless battles. Over time they saw conflicts as a way to determine strength and leadership and then minimize risk to their best and brightest. There was greater financial reward in brokering mercenaries for initial waves in battle and reducing their own losses. Over time, the wisdom of the Order was for others to perish in battle while the Order flourished.

To some, their methods and strategies might have seemed overly cautious. Yet that was because few knew the value of what was hidden in the false floors of their intentionally humble-looking wagons. It wasn't just the bags of gold and silver coins they moved from place to place and guarded with their lives. Worth far more than gold were the drafts of commerce and the many ancient parchments and manuscripts locked in shallow metal boxes. For these treasures of the Order, the monks would zealously fight, and willingly die if need be, to allow time for reinforcements to arrive. They needed little incentive, however. They had been trained from their youth and their skills honed in order for them to fight for each other, for honor, for the Order and for the cause.

Friar Edward had been part of the expansion of the Order for a long time, since he was younger than Brother Derek. And over time he had earned the right to gain more knowledge and insight into the plans of the Council. Edward had been groomed for a seat on the Council. He believed in their mission and the higher calling.

As much as Edward enjoyed being at the point of the spear, he enjoyed recruiting even more. When their groups moved forward into new lands, they were all tasked to search for the brightest and most talented young men. Not just to become warrior monks, but to be exemplary in all walks of life—gifted healers, craftsmen and builders. The Order gained a trusted foothold with eyes and ears in a community and the increase of knowledge which would be shared with the group.

From these groups would spring the leaders and clergy of the community while they never once let on that they served a higher purpose. In just a few years, the Order could effectively control the commerce of a village on a growing trade route with no one having the slightest hint of their presence. This ploy had been successfully repeated many times over many decades.

The brothers were required to make a pilgrimage to the nearest regional leadership council so that senior members could confirm the loyalty of new and established recruits. The support of the Order prospered the brothers of each community, and they in turn helped to prosper the Order. It had been so since the beginning.

Edward softly encouraged the horses pulling the cart to resume their pace. But he was thinking of the Order. Always thinking of the Order.

Ex chao ordo.

That was an expression his brethren were not yet privy to. *Ex chao ordo*.

Order from chaos.

And they weren't nearly ready to understand the depth and significance of that short but powerful phrase.

EIGHT

Harry McGowan sat at his favorite bar, on his favorite padded bar stool and in his favorite corner, where there was enough light to read and write and far enough away from the few patrons but still close enough to harass his favorite bartender. The truth was that the Pickled Liver was the sole establishment where Harry still had some semblance of welcome. His welcome at all the others had long since worn out.

It was pretty dead at two in the afternoon except for lunch stragglers who didn't want to go back to work and some of the sad regulars who didn't have work to go back to. McGowan was a blend of both. And two in the afternoon had somehow morphed into four. He didn't want to go back to the crummy little house he rented, and the bar had just enough customers to give him some make-believe social interaction but also plenty of space to get his work done.

McGowan held up his rocks glass without looking up from his stack of papers and files and said, "Hit me again."

The bartender, John Seeley, was also the pub's owner, though few people knew that. Hiding behind his position as bartender was a great ploy when people asked for favors or for things he really didn't want to do. He could always say he'd take it up with the owners.

John liked McGowan as much as he felt sorry for him. And he felt somewhat of an obligation to him. When McGowan broke his one big story, the local and national TV news media found him at John's pub, causing the little-known bar to boom for weeks. The local business crowd began to do lunch and happy hour, and the Liver even became a favorite of the late night college crowd.

John did the math, and he'd be fine with McGowan drinking sometimes cheap, sometimes free and sometimes on credit for years to come to offset the free advertising John could never have afforded when he first bought the bar. But he didn't want McGowan to know that. He could afford a little bit of charity to McGowan for quite some time, but couldn't afford to be taken advantage of in a big way for a long time. And he didn't want the resentment from other customers. So he and McGowan often sparred to keep the largesse manageable.

McGowan rattled the ice in his rocks glass to get John's attention. John meandered toward the end of the bar occupied by the one he called the vagrant, among other less flattering names.

"So, toadstool, how may I serve you?"

"Hit me again," McGowan muttered.

"Ah, the fantasies you inspire with your hollow entreatment," John said, filling the glass with ice, cheap whiskey and a splash of water.

"What are you saying?" McGowan asked, taking his glass.

"Your begging makes me ponder hitting you. Shall I use smaller words?"

"I'm bruised. I knew *what* you meant; I'm just shocked at your feigned animosity. What would you do without me?" McGowan asked with great exuberance.

"Live longer, have lower blood pressure, sleep better and have a higher profit margin, just to name a few possibilities that come to mind."

"We both know that I made this place what it is, and—"

"Ancient history. Four years ago ancient. And you gave it a boost. I've paid you back ten times over for that. But you need to look at now. You need to get your act together."

"What?" McGowan extended both palms up and out in a gesture of confusion.

John set down his bar towel and leaned toward McGowan, one of his own hands extended. "Look at you, you're a mess. You're overweight. You drink too much. You eat junk food. You dress for crap. It looks like you slept in those clothes."

"So I should be more like you," McGowan said, acting as if he were taking the advice in earnest.

"I spend money on clothes from this decade. I actually wash them. My hair and nails are neat. I take care of myself. And I spend at least an hour getting ready because I like to look really good," John explained.

"So you've gotten accustomed to disappointment, then?" McGowan said without expression, letting the jab sink in.

John let it pass. "You need to get your act together; I'm just tellin' ya."

McGowan started thumping the side of his thumb on his pile of files and his outdated iPad. "This *is* my act, and it will be a hit bigger than anything I've done in the past. Way bigger!"

"You mean like the aliens in the White House story?" John cackled loud and long.

"Hey, they *were* from El Salvador. Just not the kind of aliens I was first led to believe. This is different. This is huge! I finally put all the pieces in place, and now I'm working on my insurance policy before I blow the lid off of this."

"Your lid is a small part of your trouble," John said, polishing a glass.

"Scoff all you want," McGowan said, leaning in as if to share the details of a forbidden tryst with a local celebrity. "Even *I* couldn't believe how deep this goes, who's involved and what it means to the free world. My last big story was something, Johnny, but *nothing* compared to what I've compiled here." He thumped the stack of folders on the bar. "Genius is one percent inspiration and ninety-nine percent perspiration, John Boy!"

"Edison. But Tesla was the real genius. Yet I will say this— you *do* have the perspiration part down."

"Genius or not, Tesla died broke and alone. I plan for neither." McGowan killed his drink, stood up his files loosely in his hands to semi-organize them with a few good clunks, and angled his head toward John.

"A couple trips to the library and courthouse to copy a few more documents, and then it's show time! I'll have plenty of time to sleep or have a mani-pedi like you after I expose these people. I'm talking about the Pulitzer Prize, my friend."

"I've heard it all before. More like the Pull-my-finger Prize, knowing you." John laughed. "At least get some sleep, Harry. You really don't look good."

McGowan headed for the door, nearly dropping his stack of files. As he walked away, he spoke, turning his head over his shoulder.

"I'll sleep when I'm dead. Right now I have to head home and finish scanning these files in with the rest. Oh, and I'll be drinking some very good whiskey to wash the bad taste of this swill out of my mouth." With that, he was out the door.

John started to yell out that good liquor was for good customers, but he laughed instead. What was the point?

NINE

Graham was still pondering where von Kleis was headed with their discussion and what this "opportunity" might entail. Peter spoke highly of the organization, and although his social attributes were far too wild for Graham, his business acumen and judgment within that universe were outstanding. Since this was just an introductory meeting, he had allowed himself to relax and enjoy his drink, but in light of concerns over the depths of what von Kleis might know about his companies, his focus sharpened. He had no intention of giving away his feelings, so he'd keep his questions somewhat superficial at first. He chose his words carefully as he ran his unoccupied hand through his hair.

"So why am I the lucky one, Mr. von Kleis?" Graham said as he broke the brief, reflective silence.

"Luck has nothing to do with it. As I've said, our think tanks are second to none. We pay our staff very well to look for the best talent and opportunities. We look at over one hundred companies and individuals before we find someone we feel worthy to introduce ourselves to. Not that we don't also buy interests in other companies along the way."

"Extremely wealthy old-money types typically utilize the

good ol' boy network among their blue-blood connections," Graham offered.

"And that's too often the case at the upper levels of our organization. Old established families can also have old and antiquated ideas and be unwilling to look outside of their circles. They can become complacent. They may be happy to sit on a board or two and enjoy the benefits that long-established foundations can offer them. They are useful, to be sure, but just one cog of many in what we have built and will continue to build. However, there are also those within our organization who know the importance of truly superlative new talent from any number of sources."

Graham shifted in his chair and looked up from what remained in his glass to stare directly into von Kleis's eyes. "And you think I have the right talent and companies to be a part of your network?"

"Yes, quite. You graduated summa cum laude in engineering and computer science, with a minor in business. You then finished your master's in computer information systems while working in intelligence in the military. If you had chosen to do so, I'm sure you could have finished a master's in business in another year. Over time you have pursued a doctorate in computer science, which I believe you have completed except for the dissertation. You have an excellent array of international business skills and a natural gift for being well liked without sacrificing your ability to be a tough negotiator. Being affable is difficult to learn. It's best and most genuine when it comes naturally, and it's an excellent skill to possess for both diplomacy and closing deals. Finally, your engineering and software developments have outstanding potential, and you have always outperformed analysts' expectations and predictions. Your attributes and your corporate successes are what brought you to our attention and ultimately earned you the invitation to this meeting."

"Thank you for the kind words, Mr. von Kleis, but I'm really quite comfortable right now. I've seen companies grow too fast. And I've seen good people become something they never intended by chasing too much success. What do I have to gain by being involved in the circle you describe?"

Von Kleis nodded slightly. He rested his elbows on the arms of his very high-quality leather chair and put his fingertips together against the underside of his pointy chin. He intended to leave the impression he was choosing his words wisely, but he had already considered every possible conversation scenario and how he would respond. Not how he might respond, but how he *would* respond. Lack of focus and resolve were for the weak and indecisive. And indecision and lack of concrete forethought were the foundations of losers. Von Kleis never lost. The journey might become fluid, but the outcome at the end of the road would always be steered to success.

"Yes, Mr. Chastain, you have made several million dollars, not including the value of your company stock. And that is very admirable considering your humble beginnings and your lack of initial capital. You achieved what you did with outstanding products, a tenacious work ethic and a powerful will. A success by nearly any reasonable measure."

Von Kleis, a master at his game, shrewdly and subtly changed his posture, tone and disposition toward Graham. In the way that some relished an amazing wine, he lived for the enjoyment of taking his targets exactly where he wanted them to go, knowing they were oblivious to his machinations. His skills, through training and in hundreds of meetings just like this one, had been honed over many years. On occasion he even made an intentional faux pas to make his prey feel they were on to him, bolstering a false sense of security and pride. But it was simply a well-designed Pyrrhic victory. He was the sum total of the many masters who came before him, and yet, he was the best. Sadly, no one appreciated his skills. They couldn't. His associates celebrated his results but could never fully fathom his art.

"It would be foolish to entice you with money alone, Mr. Chastain. It isn't just money, but rather, what money allows you to do. What if you were making a few *hundred* million rather than a few million? What good might you do with that sort of wealth? And do you think you would be more inclined to do good than another candidate who was interested in wealth for its own sake? I'm being rhetorical, of course. We already know the great extent of charitable work you do. And you do far more than others who make substantially more than you do."

"I believe in helping the truly poor and hungry," Graham said, feeling the need to explain. "I don't believe in throwing money at a problem. That just hurts local businesses that are struggling and creates dependency. I have always believed in providing the fishing pole and in teaching people how and where to fish rather than just handing them a carp."

"Exactly, Mr. Chastain! I couldn't agree more. And just think of how much more you could accomplish if you had the ability to cut through bureaucracies and red tape, how incredible it would be to bring massive economies of scale to bear on any project you chose. And to your point about growing too fast—that almost always has to do with not having enough capital to properly service a new and rapidly expanding customer base. And as far as your personal time, consider this: you're astute enough to know that a man who owns ten successful companies doesn't work ten times more hours than a man who owns one. Quite the contrary! You can afford more outstanding management and could actually spend *less* time working. Then your time can be spent doing the development work you truly love rather than worrying over sales forecasts, budgets and raising more capital. We believe in creating win-win scenarios and making them happen, Mr. Chastain."

"You paint a very enticing picture."

"I've barely touched my brush to canvas, to extend the metaphor," von Kleis said while he painted the air with an imaginary brush. "What if you had tremendous resources readily available to you? What if dozens of companies were instantly exposed to your products and became loyal customers? What if you had outlets for explosive international growth rather than just slow domestic growth paired with concerns of growing too fast?"

"That's a lot of what-ifs," Graham interjected.

He wasn't being adversarial, but posing a legitimate counterpoint like any good businessman would.

"Not at all, my good fellow." Von Kleis said warmly. "This is honestly the tip of the proverbial iceberg. Of course, it would take much more than a cursory discussion to present what we could do for you that would be of mutual benefit; we have a phenomenal staff ready to do just that. But I'd like you to consider something. Have you ever wondered why some fairly obscure entrepreneurs are launched to notoriety and wealth almost overnight while other talented people with similar great ideas fail miserably?"

"I must confess I've wondered that from time to time." He never was completely satisfied with the explanations for how Facebook annihilated Myspace with an inferior product. Or how

Google did the same to Netscape and all the others except Bing. Graham had even heard DARPA had created a system identical to Facebook and shut it down the week before Facebook launched. He had suspicions, but no way to prove them. The government wouldn't need to commit as many resources to spying on citizens when they would give up information for free in great quantities. The return for massive government funding of such companies? An open back door. Von Kleis's information could be well worth Graham's time.

"I'm not at liberty at this time to say which companies we've played a role in helping to succeed, but what I *can* assure you of, with one hundred percent certainty, is that none of the major success stories you've heard of occurred by accident or by designing a better mousetrap. I'm not implying you won't be successful and continue to grow without us. But I can guarantee that growth won't be as incredible as the effect of what we bring to the table."

"You just need to ask yourself if you're ready to hear more."

TEN

Avalon slowly pulled the delivery van to the end of the driveway between two rundown houses in an equally rundown neighborhood. The rows of one-story houses had been built in the sixties and were outdated and nothing like energy efficient. The pride and work ethic of the owners determined the appearance of each, ranging from quaint to dilapidated. Avalon was parked next to a house that was fairly well kept, but his target was on the opposite side of the driveway. Neither the owner nor Avalon's target, the renter, shared either of the aforementioned qualities of pride and work ethic.

The markings on the van had been neatly changed from waste disposal to Dave's Pest Control, complete with the tagline *We do our best to get rid of your pests*! It was pretty slick what one could do with well-designed magnetic signs. Avalon's employers had an impressive department that created whatever he needed in a matter of hours. His paperwork was perfect, as were his work orders and small quantities of supplies—all of which could be used again or destroyed. And all would stand up to scrutiny if he was stopped by police or curious neighbors. Even the exterior lights of his vehicles were routinely replaced with backups left in the vehicle. It was a small price to pay to avoid an unwanted traffic stop. Avalon always worked the scenarios in his head. Always gaming. Always the scenarios. No stone left unturned.

The house had been under careful surveillance for weeks by various faceless support members and by Avalon himself. He never relied solely on anyone else's assessment for an operation. He knew, for instance, when the target's neighbor was at work and that he kept a harmless but noisy dog. And for that reason Avalon had prepared some very special dog treats—the kind with tasty meat laced with a sedative. He got out of his van and pretended to inspect his front tire while he quickly took in a panoramic view. He pulled his treats out of a regular Pup-Peroni dog treat pouch and tossed a few through the chain link fence to his new best friend. The sporadic barking was replaced with gulping and tail wagging—all of which Avalon knew would be short-lived.

He quickly pulled the tools of his current trade from the van. The pest satchel and large spray canister looked authentic, but the canister contained only water. He made some quick sprays as he scanned the house and everything surrounding him—always continuing to work every possible surprise through his mind as he made his way to the barely functioning screen door of the small back porch. Avalon had a story and wrong-address work order for every project he ever did, and today's was no exception.

His gear and costume were authentic looking. The flesh-colored nitrile gloves he wore left no prints or human oil or residue. For daylight work he nearly always wore high-quality sunglasses. He owned many brands suited for different purposes and chose those not easily recognizable. Someone might think it suspicious that a lowly pest control worker wore expensive Ray-Bans, but probably wouldn't recognize that his generic-looking sunglasses were the less well known Smith Optics Outlier. They were durable, had great clarity and didn't easily slip with perspiration, not that Avalon readily perspired. His ball cap and uniform were generic except for the company logo patch and name patch that were attached with Velcro—to be changed many times in the past and the future. Today he was Joe. Everyone knew a guy named Joe.

Avalon quickly sprayed the hinges of the screened porch's door—for quiet entrance now and equally quiet exit later. Once inside the porch, Avalon glanced about and pulled from his pocket a key that had been made weeks before by yet another team. Breaking and entering was used in the most extreme circumstances but was unnecessary today since this Priority One target had been selected months ago. If a target accelerated his meddling, Avalon had numerous contingency plans—ranging from a random mugging to a well-designed hit and run—to void that target. Yet those were messy with too many factors beyond Avalon's control. But there was time. Time to exercise his mind—running from gamut to gamut, contemplating every scenario. His teachers would be proud. He heard them over and over again in his mind. It was as if they were still there.

Avalon silently unlocked the wooden door, slipped inside with his belongings and quietly closed the door behind him. He didn't remove his sunglasses at first as he moved quickly from room to room with his pest equipment to verify he was indeed alone. He tested his path for floor noises, noting there were virtually none.

He ended up in the living room where a card table, long overdue for being left at the curb, barely supported a barely functional desktop computer. He kept his satchel and canister close at hand as he sat on the rickety chair, unzipped his jacket and pulled out a small high-capacity flash drive. He powered on the computer and entered the infantile password his fellow operatives had "lifted" weeks ago. Breaching the Wi-Fi had taken them no time at all. Much of what Avalon was doing could have been accomplished with a hack, but it had to be done at precisely the right time—and the time was now.

He already knew exactly where to go after he attached the flash drive. He moved the files he wanted to the drive and then ran a program to scrub them from all shadow and registry areas of the hard drive to erase any evidence that those files had been deleted. He left about eighty percent of the information intact on the computer; deleting everything would arouse suspicion in the event of a thorough examination. The program then defragmented the drive, leaving a footprint that the operation had been done five days prior.

He quickly opened MS Word and typed out a short letter, pulled two sheets of paper from a file folder in his "pest" satchel and inserted them into the printer. With a few more keystrokes, he printed what he needed, with a second copy to be thorough. He put those two sheets back into the satchel.

Avalon found the half-empty Crown Royal bottle next to the couch on the nonmatching table. He reached inside his jacket for a small energy drink bottle, but the liquid he had substituted in the bottle wouldn't produce anything like an energy effect. He poured the entire contents into the liquor bottle, swirled the bottle to fully mix the clear liquid and set it exactly where he'd found it.

Avalon surveyed the room one last time, picked up the tools of his trade and exited the way he came in, locking the door behind him. He looked at the black Luminox on the inside of his wrist and paused to think while putting on his sunglasses.

Eleven minutes. Never as fast as he would want as a

perfectionist, but faster than any normal person could have accomplished the tasks. He was nothing like a normal person; he absorbed and calculated more than even the most adept operative could have done. Yes, he was the best, he thought. The grueling years of stoic instruction had taken him to great heights, but he took himself much farther than anyone could have imagined.

Avalon quickly drove the van two blocks away to the safe house rented month to month for cash. He parked in the garage, closing the door behind him. He moved items from the pest control satchel to a partially full backpack. Next he slipped out of his pest control clothes and into a nondescript jogging suit and well-worn running shoes. He inserted padding, donned a different plain ball cap, threw on his backpack and exited the side door of the garage.

This time Avalon the Everyman wore generic-looking Oakley's with medium gray lenses. He quickly set off down the driveway and back toward the house he had just left. He had engaged in speed-walking jaunts along this route many times in the preceding weeks, partially to disappear in plain sight— becoming a neighborhood fixture—and partially to watch the target house and the habits of the neighbors.

In no time he was back to the target driveway, where he kneeled to pretend to retie his shoe. He had thoroughly scanned the area from behind his sunglasses without moving his head. Certain he was unseen, he moved quickly up the driveway where he'd previously parked, feigning a slight limp.

The mongrel was still dreaming of chasing squirrels as Avalon made his way quickly to and through the porch door, once again opening the house door with his key. After another brief glance, he made his way to a back bedroom, which was apparently used for storage. Avalon closed the door behind him, took off his sunglasses and checked his watch again. Thirteen more minutes. Outstanding. He breathed in quietly through his nose and silently exhaled, never changing expression to show the satisfaction he felt. Now his mind would work while he waited for his target. Yes, indeed, he *knew* he was the best. Even before the enhancements.

ELEVEN

Graham studied the barely diminished ice in his glass as he pondered his next questions for von Kleis. If not for the eventually sober and ringing endorsement from Peter, he would have considered his newfound good fortune a great deal more suspect. But he also knew he was committing to nothing, merely exploring an opportunity.

"I have found, Mr. von Kleis, that there are no free lunches. What do you and you associates want for your benevolence?"

"Not a great deal relative to what we intend to provide in return. To start, we would like to buy small shares in each of your companies." Von Kleis spoke with an even and calm delivery.

"You could do that anyway," Graham replied.

"True enough. But we want to do this more as a small joint venture partner and not leave any impression of a hostile takeover. We would acquire a certain amount of preferred stock, some common and perhaps even some convertible debentures. And we don't want to announce any of this in the financial pages. We like to fly under the radar, and we would prefer your stock value, and subsequently our stock value, to grow in a controlled way and based on expansion and sales growth rather than hype."

"I suppose one can never have too much capital. And there are a number of projects I've been wanting to pursue, but I haven't been enthusiastic over the time it will take to raise expansion funds," Graham said, as much to himself as to von Kleis. "What else?"

"We can make a great deal of capital available from our major banking interests at better terms than you're getting now—in the event you want to use debt rather than equity. Also, restructuring your existing debt would instantly improve your bottom line. And we would, of course, want to place a highly skilled individual or two on each of your boards to protect our investment and offer exceptional input," von Kleis added firmly. But his manner was still friendly.

"Quite reasonable," Graham said. "But how do I know you and your associates won't try to take control of my companies?"

"A valid consideration on your part, Mr. Chastain," von Kleis said. "We have no need or desire for hostile takeovers. They are very public and can be very messy. We have found that people and companies that are aggressive and flamboyant usually end up getting mostly flame and very little buoyancy. They crash and burn, so to speak. We have amassed incredible wealth slowly and carefully, and we prefer that approach. There is quite enough for all of us to do incredibly well. And you hold the majority of shares, regardless. Trying to take control would be futile, and we have better things to do."

"I agree with your philosophy," Graham said with a slight nod.

"This is a win-win for all of us, or we wouldn't have spent the time approaching you. We aren't a cabal that sits around massive conference tables in dark, smoke-filled rooms looking for companies to plunder. Those strategies rarely make sense, and those days are in the past. We buy interest in your company and funnel an avalanche of new business from our very extensive network of companies, subsidiaries and partnerships to yours. You grow far faster than your existing pace, but not recklessly. Your stock prices will soar before anyone really notices, and so does our investment."

"I could become Graham Gates," Graham said with a bit of a smirk.

Von Kleis ignored the quip and maintained his even temperament. "We would also make large commitments in writing for future cash infusions with minimal dilution and additional lines of credit where reasonably needed. You could move far more quickly than you do now and stay ahead of any competition. And, as I mentioned previously, your cost of capital would drop at the same time your stock prices increased. The effect is rather amazing. We've done this many times." His expression held unbridled satisfaction.

"And what if I refuse? Do I perish in a horrible fireball in my car when the brakes fail?"

"Mr. Chastain, you simply must stop watching so much television. If you refuse, we work with other companies on our list. We have many candidates. Those who *refuse*, as you put it, plod along on their same growth trajectory. Those that join us grow more rapidly—it's just that simple. But what I've told you is just the beginning. We have a great deal to offer you."

Graham's gaze had been directed downward as he pondered von Kleis's comments. The proposal did make sense, but he'd need to know a great deal more. He cocked his head upward and said nonchalantly, "I'm still here."

TWELVE

Harry McGowan pulled his car halfway up his driveway, as was his custom; the front door was easier to get to and use. And the dump of a back porch and breezeway were reminders of chores he had no desire to attend to. Besides, that yapping dog next door got on his nerves.

He gathered up his files and tablet and did his best not to drop them as he tended to on occasion. But it wasn't raining, so spreading papers on the lawn seemed less likely somehow. He had various and sundry types of briefcases, totes and man-bags, but they were all full of wild goose chases from Christmases past. He knew he should sort and dump some of the research garbage from stories that hadn't panned out, but the projects were like orphaned children to him and hard to relinquish. Besides, that would entail work, and he had far more exciting things to do right now.

He managed to get to the front door and balanced his prized pile with carnival precision while expertly finding the keyhole after only six or seven attempts. He laid his burden on the watermarked coffee table in front of his favorite and solitary well-worn sofa. He gazed longingly at the half-full whiskey bottle that beckoned him. People asked whether a glass was half empty or half full as a sign of pessimism or optimism. It was McGowan's opinion that all whiskey bottles should be measured in some variant of fullness.

He made his way into the kitchen he had personally decorated in Early American drab with a touch of dismal disarray. He sought and found his favorite nearly clean large glass in the almost never clean sink. Knowing alcohol was the great sanitizer, he gave the glass a cursory rinse and sought out his barely functional refrigerator.

He found no soda of any kind on the shelves holding the seeming remnants of some forgotten biology experiment.

"Diminished but undaunted, the hero perseveres and overcomes monumental setbacks and manages to stride forward to new and ever-challenging hurdles while remaining steadfast in his quest. Water it is, then."

He pondered whether getting a dog to talk to would make him seem less unstable than he did talking to himself. But who would tell anyone else in either case? The dog? He mulled that over as he opened the freezer that contained his favorite luxury item—a working icemaker. It was an absolute necessity given his need for refreshment throughout his long journey back to greatness. Most people probably considered an icemaker to be a staple, but they also most likely owned functioning vacuum cleaners and other trivial appliances.

Satisfied with his cube and water level, McGowan made his way back to his couch and single-bottle bar. He poured his glass nearly full and stirred the mixture with the spoon sitting on the small pile of cocktail napkins he'd pilfered long ago from any number of forgotten bars. He took a healthy pull, swallowed and took another. He leaned his head back against the couch, breathed in deeply and let out a long, slow exhale.

"Man, what a day," he said.

"Tough day at the office, hon?" Avalon stood directly in front of McGowan, not ten feet away.

McGowan's head snapped up. He nearly spilled his drink as he coughed and just barely kept from wetting his pants. As he tried to wrap his head around the shock and pushed his brain to focus, he wasn't sure what scared him more, the cold dark eyes that stared at him devoid of feeling or the dark, round hole that made up the disagreeable end of the silenced pistol pointing at his now-sweating face.

THIRTEEN

Von Kleis pretended to let his mind wander, but it never did. It was another ruse, another subterfuge to simulate dropping his guard. He seemed lost in thought, staring at the magnificent book collection to his left and across the room.

"So there's more to this?" Graham broke the silence.

Von Kleis didn't change his stare or expression. "A great deal more. My associates and I think you would be a good addition to our group. We need new blood and innovative ideas. Our average age is far too skewed for our liking, though some in our group seem to think they'll live forever. And before you indulge me with your charming wit again, there are no secret handshakes or rituals. There is a place for that to be sure, but we are far above and greatly removed from the need of mundane practices at our level."

Graham wanted to ask about the last point, but let it pass. "I'm flattered to be invited, but I have no idea what that even entails."

Von Kleis pivoted his chair more directly at Graham now. His expression was still calm and reassuring.

"I can tell you what this isn't. It isn't the Century Club or the Rotary Club. This isn't about being part of a good ol' boys network, as you might so eloquently put it. This is *the* network. There are very few issues of significant importance, anywhere in the world, that we don't have knowledge of or some influence over."

"And knowledge truly is power," Graham interjected. "What would I have to do?"

"You don't have to *do* anything," von Kleis quickly answered. "As I said, we feel you could be an excellent addition, so the necessary votes have already been cast in your favor as a provisional member on a trial basis."

"Surely there's more to it," Graham said, looking at his glass. On cue, and just as silently as before, the overbuilt valet appeared with a silver tray—with only one drink this time—and exchanged glasses with Graham.

Graham had no concerns a second drink would be overindulging or leave him susceptible to influence in a negotiation. First of all, this wasn't a true negotiation yet, and second, he could handle far more alcohol and often used the illusion that a second drink lowered his resistance. It didn't, but he enjoyed having business associates think they had an edge they didn't. The subterfuge had served him well many times in the past.

Von Kleis's friendly demeanor remained in place. It wasn't a front; he was genuinely happy that Graham was doing exactly as he planned. His research had been exhaustive, and he was aware of the two-drink ruse. But there was far more going on during the discussion than Graham had the slightest clue about.

"Of course we have rules and guidelines," von Kleis admitted. "Some are quite rigid, but mostly they make common sense and are in place for reasons that you, as a successful businessman, will not only see the logic of but will concur that you'd have in our position. First and foremost, we never discuss our organization with outsiders, with the exception of an introductory meeting and invitation like this. But even then, we really disclose nothing of substance."

"So I can't ask anyone about Ambrose or tell anyone about the Ambrose Consortium?" Graham asked.

Von Kleis laughed. "You can *ask* anyone you'd like. But it won't do you any good. This is a shell company. I'm sure you did some cursory research before you came here. We have many trusts, foundations and shells which serve as nothing more than fronts. Oh, they *seem* substantial enough on the surface, enough to open doors and begin negotiations. But they're all totally banal and don't give the slightest hint as to our size, complexity, reach, scope, intentions or any of the other important attributes of our true organization. We're connected to hundreds of companies large and small. It's actually fascinating how a very small group can control a vast network." Von Kleis allowed himself a light smile as he strategically dangled yet another carrot.

"I'm interested in hearing more about your rules. You've made them sound a bit ominous." Graham frowned as he swirled his new drink.

"An important one is that we don't take actions to benefit one member to the detriment of another," von Kleis said, leaning negligibly toward Graham.

Graham nodded. "Sounds like a good policy."

"Yet there are exceptions. One can never fully predict human nature. We've rarely had a member go rogue, so to speak. But when we do, we handle the problem internally. If someone becomes too greedy or jeopardizes the larger organizations or negatively impacts other members, we meet as a group to resolve the problem. There's no place for that level of greed, and the efforts of the whole can easily counter the acts of the few. Which is why such a scenario is rare."

"Another good guideline—as long as everyone is treated fairly," Graham said.

"I'm glad you agree. Our rules do make sense, nothing arbitrary. And the rewards are substantial. They've been developed, honed, for quite some time with extraordinary success. And I'm coming to the most important rule of all."

FOURTEEN

Harry McGowan had been threatened before. Mostly he was a nuisance, but his one big break had upset some substantial apple carts. He'd received death threats, but no one came close to acting on them. He had bragged about them as a badge of honor to his never-large group of fans that had shrunk to a now-dwindling number of acquaintances. Which was why he knew that the man holding a gun on him was more than an idle threat. His brow instantly beaded with sweat at the same time his mouth became arid.

"Who are you and how did you get in here?" he said in a small voice.

"I'm with the city sanitation department. Your neighbors have been complaining about the smell." Ambrose jabbed with no emotion.

McGowan tried, feebly, to muster some semblance of courage. "I *knew* I was getting close! You can't kill me; I have friends in high places. My truth will still get out," he said, pleading more than asserting.

"You don't even have acquaintances in low places, McGowan. I'm here to warn you off, pay you off or shut you off. It's up to you. But if you raise your voice, I can guarantee I'll shoot you right in that big mouth of yours." Avalon redirected the aim of the pistol to McGowan's face.

"P-p-pay me off?" McGowan asked. He nodded to his left and asked, "Mind if I have a drink?"

Avalon gave a slight nod. "All you want. I'd say don't try anything funny, but you're too weak and boring to be funny."

McGowan took a long drink, then another, and set the glass down and reached for the bottle. Avalon watched him through steel eyes devoid of expression. *Another one*, he thought. *Another loser that I'd scrape off my shoe with a stick.* McGowan filled his glass nearly to the top with no regard for adding water. He drank the whiskey with a trembling hand, paying no attention to what made its way to his chin and shirt.

McGowan's voice cracked as he said, "If you aren't going to kill me, why are you here?"

Avalon stared through McGowan like he didn't exist. "Whether I kill you or not is entirely up to you, McGowan. In a very short while, I'm going to hand you a phone. Minutes after that, you're going to call a number I give you. You will reach someone of very high rank from Homeland Security—someone whose name you will immediately recognize. He will tell you how much I'm authorized to pay you for turning over your notes—every single page of them—and your tablet. It will be substantial. He will even offer you an important story in the future for the scoop you somehow think you're entitled to."

"But they're part of it! This is bigger than you can imagine!" McGowan pleaded.

"No, it's far bigger than *you* can imagine. But suit yourself . . ." Avalon thumbed back the hammer on the pistol.

McGowan immediately threw his hands in the air, palms out. "I'm listening. I'll make the call!"

As Avalon eased the hammer back down, he also lowered the pistol slightly, but continued his intimidating stare. McGowan let out a slow breath and took another long drink.

"You're just like most idiot reporters. You think because you've stumbled onto something, you know what's really going on behind the scenes. And like them, you have no clue. Yet your meddling could actually expose some well-placed people who would be killed. But you wouldn't care because you'd have your precious *story*. You and all the vultures like you make me sick." Avalon sneered.

"I know what I've seen," McGowan said, but sheepishly, afraid of raising the gunman's ire.

"You *know* nothing, you cretin," Avalon snapped. "You wouldn't know misinformation or disinformation if it bit you in your smallest region. You wouldn't even qualify for amateur status when it comes to what actually happens behind the scenes."

"If this was truly a government op, they wouldn't send an assassin," McGowan said, as much to himself as to Avalon.

"Really," Avalon said. Then he laughed slowly with no emotion. "Right," he said, still laughing. He raised his left wrist to let McGowan see he was checking the time.

Even though McGowan was getting a serious buzz, he didn't care and continued to drink. "So how much money are we talking about here?"

"More than you're worth and enough so you won't have second thoughts about the story you think you're going to break," Avalon said blandly.

"I don't know—"

"The alternative doesn't pay nearly as well," Avalon waved his pistol again in McGowan's general direction.

"If you kill me, you'll get caught," McGowan said, stalling

for time, hoping to think and talk his way out of his terrifying position.

"I don't exist," Avalon replied with stern conviction.

McGowan reached for the bottle and poured nearly all of it into his glass. He pondered his options. Avalon watched intently and gave a nearly imperceptible nod each time McGowan drank.

"What about getting another story, like you said?" McGowan had gained courage from his glass and tried to sound more agreeable.

"If you behave and play ball with the good guys, you'll get an ongoing stream of stories," Avalon said in a weary tone. He knew McGowan cared for nothing and no one but his own glory and bank account.

"What's to keep me from taking the money and breaking the story anyway?" McGowan countered.

"Who would be dumb enough to risk retribution and give up multiple future stories and more cash? Skip that last question. *You* might be dumb enough. But we already thought of that and have it covered. Once you make the call, it will be clear."

Avalon looked down at his watch again before reaching for his left hip pocket. He retrieved a cellphone and held it up for McGowan to see. He moved toward the opposite end of the couch and tossed the phone in a way that should have been an easy catch for McGowan. But McGowan's dexterity was floating somewhere in the bottle next to him. The phone landed on his chest and dropped into his lap as he made a feeble attempt to grab it out of the air.

"Almost time," Avalon said. "It's a good thing I didn't toss the phone any higher or you probably would have swallowed it."

"Give me a break. My good hand was full," he complained.

While McGowan fumbled with setting his drink down and

picking up the phone, Avalon moved forward and sat on the far end of the couch. He held up the suppressed pistol and pointed it again at McGowan.

"Now call the number I give you and say exactly what I tell you," Avalon said, his voice devoid of inflection.

McGowan looked at the phone through whiskey-blurred eyes and pressed the power button. He held it farther away in an attempt to focus on the two phones and pressed the power button again.

"Hey, it's dead," McGowan exclaimed, aggravated.

"Precisely," Avalon said.

As he spoke, Avalon lunged, extended his arm and pulled the trigger. The *clack* from the .38 caliber pistol was minimal, but the result was significant. McGowan didn't make another sound as his body went limp and his hand relinquished the phone. Avalon always loaded his own rounds with less powder, yielding plenty of force to kill and at the same time, a diminished report.

Avalon took a deep breath, exhaled and allowed himself another of his emotionless smiles.

"Now the fun begins," he said.

FIFTEEN

Von Kleis returned to his casual demeanor as he continued explaining what membership in his vast network would entail. Having brought the resources of his organization to bear, von Kleis knew nearly everything about Graham; for quite some time, Graham and his companies had been targets of acquisition. Von Kleis and his team knew outstanding talent and products when they discovered them. In some cases the leader of an organization was truly exceptional and in other cases that person might be less exceptional but still someone who put together a great team that created outstanding products. Graham was exceptional *and* had put together an exceptional team, so von Kleis and his associates were especially keen on developing a solid relationship with him and willing to spend a great deal of time and resources to do so.

To counteract Graham's two-drink maximum intake and make him more open in his conversation, von Kleis had tipped the scales by having a small amount of midazolam added to the water of Graham's ice cubes before they were frozen. As the ice melted, the colorless, tasteless drug was gradually released into his scotch. The dose was just enough to lower his resistance without leaving him feeling overly intoxicated when he drove home. The consortium had procured Graham's medical records, so there was no concern of an allergic reaction. Von Kleis had used the methodology more than once and could see it was working quite well again.

"If you accept our offer, over time you'll come to gain a great deal of knowledge about the more intimate workings of our far-reaching organization. There will be a point of no return, however. That is to say, you will come to a point where you must decide whether you're in or out."

"I can never leave?" Graham asked.

"I can assure you, Mr. Chastain, knowing the depth of your character as well as I believe I do, that you won't want to leave once you see the full gamut of what we can offer and what you can do for society with your greatly increased wealth and influence, and what it will be like to be part of such an organization."

Graham looked down and away while rubbing his chin, like so many people do when they're considering a major decision. Besides the slight drugging of his drink, there was more Graham wasn't aware of—machinations his excellent negotiating skills couldn't have prepared him for.

Hidden between computer monitors, outstanding artwork and the leather-bound books behind von Kleis were state-of-the-art cameras recording every minute movement Graham made. Every detail, down to the number and frequency of eye blinks, would later be analyzed. The chair he sat in measured galvanic skin response without the need for a typical skin sensor. It had been developed by one Ambrose-controlled company, the super-high-speed analysis software and algorithms by another. Another company sold an inferior version of the product to police forces and intelligence agencies around the world. As was always the case, Ambrose kept the very best devices for their own purposes.

"This is back to sounding like one of those stories where I potentially wake up dead," Graham finally said.

Von Kleis didn't respond directly.

"You'll have ample time to decide if you personally want to join us. And that has no bearing on the joint ventures and investments we have discussed already; they are by no means mutually exclusive. As a matter of fact, we would insist you work with us first and see what we can do together before you even take initial steps to join us. Like any business venture, we will have our presentation group come and impress you with their skills. Our legal and financial people will meet with your legal and financial people, and you'll certainly attend those meetings. I can assure you that you'll find the terms most satisfactory and attractive."

Before Graham could respond, von Kleis rose from his expensive leather chair and moved around the desk to sit on the front edge of it like a friendly college professor advising a freshman on his change of major.

"And I can also assure you, my friend—we don't kill people." He chuckled. "Yes, competitors might think of us as being ruthless when we're attacked, but we merely protect our interests. You should think of our policy regarding the innermost workings of our organization as a confidentiality agreement, that's all."

"An exceedingly strict version of one," Graham answered.

"We protect our interests like you would your interests or your family—and you would come to *be* family if you choose to fully join. You will experience great gains with us, regardless, Graham. You need only decide if they are quite sizable or massive. You could see success you couldn't imagine otherwise."

Graham hardly noticed von Kleis had used his first name. He

was trying to pull this incredible story together in his mind, but he couldn't seem to wrap his head around the particulars.

"What's next?" Graham finally asked.

"Now we start down a mutually beneficial road. I've given you a lot to think about, but much more will become clear as we start to work together, if you choose that path. I hope the answer will be yes, because we know it's a fine opportunity for both of us—otherwise we wouldn't have spent so much time coming to our decision. However, where we go next will be entirely up to you. Ultimately, there are peasants and princes in society, and we believe you can be one of our finest princes, Graham."

"I appreciate your confidence. I hope I can live up to it," Graham said graciously.

They shook hands and agreed to be in touch, and Graham was escorted out of the building, where he continued to try to fathom the scope of all he had heard. There was no question that he would have a great deal to investigate further and the need for a serious meeting with Peter. He'd be constantly juggling two adages in his mind until then: whether the huge ship he'd worked for was coming in or whether the offer was a dream too good to be true.

SIXTEEN

Avalon moved with the grace of a martial arts master and the strength of a gymnast. He looked and listened for any noise outside, near the house, and heard none.

He immediately reached for the television remote and turned up the volume to just the right level—high enough to blend with the sound of the previous, muffled shot, but not loud enough to raise suspicion with neighbors. It was a precaution, but Avalon wasn't concerned. Those scenarios too had been thought out and re-thought out.

The close proximity of the barrel guaranteed the proper amount of powder residue. Now, along with fingerprint evidence, Avalon needed the same evidence on McGowan's hand. His own hands were covered in the very thin flesh-colored gloves when he touched various parts of the pistol to McGowan's fingertips. He quickly retrieved another round to replace the one he fired and touched bullets and the empty shell casing to McGowan's fingertips, producing both full prints and smudges. He then replaced all the rounds in the pistol. Avalon quickly pulled out a long tube and a plastic one-liter bottle from his bag. The tube was black and about three feet long—until Avalon opened a lid on the top and twisted it, extending the tube like a telescoping self-defense baton. He poured a clear gel into the tube. Avalon put the silenced pistol in the same hand McGowan had used to pour with and hold his drink in and fired another muffled round into the tube of gel. Avalon replaced his original shell casing with the one just fired so everything would match perfectly. As he had been trained to do, mercilessly, he stopped and listened again—still hearing nothing.

He stood and dropped the gun on the couch and extended McGowan's hand near it. He planted an unlabeled pill bottle with just a few oxycodone pills inside and touched the pill bottle to McGowan's fingertips. He removed the cap and laid both cap and bottle on the side table next to the lamp. Moving quickly, he took the whiskey bottle into the kitchen and poured the remaining liquor down the drain; he didn't want to take a chance the liquid would be tested and the oxycodone in the bottle discovered. Avalon next pulled out the typed suicide letter, which explained that McGowan couldn't bear to go on living as a total failure, unable to find stories worthy of his great journalistic skill. The note would seem completely in character to anyone who'd had to suffer through even a short bout of McGowan's drinking and boasting. And the signature at the bottom was perfect—no hesitation and no false starts according to Carl.

"Good job, Carl," he said out loud.

He opened McGowan's tablet and turned it on. Once it connected with the internet, he left it on the table next to the suicide note. His team had already hacked the tablet and could now clean any incriminating files. Nothing on the coffee table was in range of the blood spatter, which went the other direction. Avalon gathered up McGowan's file folders and replaced them with prepared substitutes. Instead of leaving an incriminating trail back to the real story McGowan was about to break, the articles were mostly nonsense or old clippings of his prior work, reinforcing that he couldn't live up to his elusive glory days.

Avalon took one last look around—hardly necessary since he ran his scenarios constantly as he worked, with each rendition picking up where the last one ended. He collected all that was his and quickly walked back over every step he had made in every room and saw nothing was out of place, nothing was left behind. *Ah*, he thought. *It's so satisfying to be flawless.*

Avalon quietly slipped out the back door, where it was now dark. He glanced about with his back against the wall before he inserted the key and locked the door. Seeing and sensing no one, he moved like a ghost across the porch and out the still quiet screen door. He looked toward the fence. The mutt raised his head and gave a low growl, but still had no desire or energy to bark. Avalon smiled and moved toward the opposite side of the house from where he had originally parked and looked around the corner. Seeing no one, he produced a pair of glasses with nonprescription lenses as part of his disguise and walked toward the street. Just past the front corner, he knelt on one knee, again pretending to lace his athletic shoe while looking around. He saw no neighbors at their windows or milling about, and so he proceeded back in the direction of his safe house at the same brisk pace he had always used in the neighborhood. Once he vacated the house, another team would sanitize it. It was unlikely anyone would remember the quiet man who liked to jog and speed-walk through the neighborhood several times a week. He would be described as quite average in every way and looking nothing like Avalon would look two days from now.

SEVENTEEN

Eric von Kleis leaned back in his chair with his eyes closed and his fingers interlaced across his chest. He was enjoying the way the interview with Graham had played out, and he recounted the details while they were fresh, already affirming his next planned steps were the right ones.

He heard the near-silent wisp of a hidden door as it opened and closed. He didn't open his eyes or look up.

Paul Roth entered the room silently from behind the wall supporting the array of monitors. He had a lean build and was dressed completely in black. His hair was fairly long, but neat and raven-like with a jet-black sheen. His nose was sharp and narrow, his mustache and goatee neatly trimmed. He cast a stern look at von Kleis, choosing to stand rather than sit in one of the interrogation seats.

"I fear you've told him too much, Eric," Roth said tersely.

"I told him nothing," von Kleis said, not bothering to open his eyes.

"I truly enjoyed that bit of theatre when you told him no one in our organization acted in ways to bring harm to others within the group. I might have teared up, except that I know the upheaval we face now is the product of nearly two hundred years of infighting. There are too many factions to even be sure of who is allied with whom."

"Yes, yes. You know very well that was to make him feel safe and comfortable. He needs to feel he's part of a fabulous benevolent group. His need to belong is as strong as his ambitions. My stories put him at ease. I'm sure you saw the raw analytics. And there are only a handful of factions that hold real power. Our current path will ensure our dominance." Von Kleis was weary of explaining strategies that should be obvious.

"He's unpredictable. A potential loose cannon. He could be dangerous to our cause," Roth claimed in his rebuttal.

"He's perfect for our needs. And speaking of that, he has one of our needs—an important one. However, you don't seem to grasp the larger picture. What I told him about our organization is true in the sense that our network has a grand and highly profitable synergistic effect. But he has no idea what that really means and the enormity of our enterprises. And there's something even greater that no outsider will ever see. Our plans and strategies shouldn't be thought of as a chess game. They're more like a complex and amazing puzzle. Our advantage is we see and have access to more pieces than anyone else. And because of that, we know about the potential of his programs and algorithms—potential he hasn't the faintest ponderings of. He's years ahead of his closest competition and doesn't realize what he has or what *we* can do with it, and we intend to keep it that way."

"Why don't we just steal the technology?" Roth countered. "We're certainly good at that."

"Too risky in this case. His security measures are outstanding. And it's been long decided. Why chance getting caught breaking in when we can acquire the keys. We can use him and his companies in many ways to our own benefit." Von Kleis responded with an overt smile this time.

"Fine. I've made my position clear. If he isn't a wild card and since you dangled the peasant and prince story in front of him, what would *you* call him?"

Von Kleis finally opened his eyes. He leaned toward Roth and put his hands, palms down, on the desk.

"A pawn."

EIGHTEEN

Graham had a great deal to think about on his drive home. He noticed very little while driving, deep in thought over the scope of events that had transpired in a short period of time. His mind worked through scenarios at a rapid pace. He would spend more time looking into Ambrose, even though their offer was just what he needed to leap to the levels he'd always dreamed of. He would have the benefit of his own due-diligence team and Peter's group as well. But he wouldn't make any major commitments until he was satisfied. Although he saw no red flags so far, he wasn't taking any chances. He was willing to take small steps because they could help uncover just how much Ambrose knew about his companies, some operations of which had to be protected at all costs—huge capital infusion or no capital infusion. Graham looked forward to getting the process started, but right now he was feeling more tired than usual and wanted to get home and relax. He didn't even feel up for a trip to the gym or the dojo, which was rare indeed.

Graham eased his car into one of his two reserved spaces in front of his spacious brownstone. Although he preferred his secluded place in the country, the townhome had been a great find and was more practical for the time being. Although many people in his industry worked *virtual*, brick and mortar was still very necessary to his business, so this property provided a reasonable commute to his offices. His wife may have wanted something more opulent, but they were able to use her family's estates if more impressive surroundings were required for a major soiree. Graham was more pleased that the home's value had nearly doubled since he bought it out of foreclosure and completed renovations which were both impressive and cost effective. He was no Ambrose, but he had developed networks over the years that were impressive in their own right. Graham planned to have many mansions and far more wealth than Vicky's family, but extravagant real estate wasn't a priority any time soon. His current use of capital would produce returns far more incredible than wasteful trappings.

Just as he reached the landing at the top of the stairs, Graham sensed something between his acute peripheral vision and what he called his peripheral hearing. The awareness was simultaneous.

"Please help me . . ."

The sound of a woman's voice was barely audible in the night. Graham turned to his right to see more of what had been only a shadow of movement. Although his vision seemed hazy, a woman was coming into focus. She moved slowly toward him, and he surmised she must've been sitting in an adjacent stone stairwell.

Her slow limp toward him allowed the nearest streetlight to diminish her shadows and illuminate her more fully. As Graham started back down his steps, he saw that her cheeks were tear-stained and her blouse was torn. A few more steps revealed more detail. Even though she had a bright red spot beneath her right eye and a swollen lip, she was incredibly stunning. If she looked this amazing now, Graham wondered how she'd look if she hadn't just lost a skirmish. He was happily married, but had mentioned more than once that marriage hadn't diminished his eyesight. He hurried down the stairs—just as her knees began to buckle.

"What happened?" Graham asked when she fell into his arms.

The woman began to whimper softly. She set off a dance of human disarray as she tried to brush back her hair with the hand that clutched a cellphone and wrap her other arm around Graham to keep from falling. She used her forearm to try to cling to him because she was gripping her stylish shoes in her hand. One of the shoes had a long stiletto heel and the other had none. Graham was more than strong enough to hold her, but the way she fell was awkward, and he struggled to hold her up without crushing her. From a distance someone might be tempted to laugh, watching what appeared to be two drunks struggling with an uncooperative flight of stairs.

The man sitting in the van in the dark just down the street hoped that was exactly the scene that would manifest. He showed no expression as he pointed a camera and powerful telephoto lens in their direction. The motor drive *whirred* as he took multiple shots. He quickly checked to be sure the images were clear in playback before setting the camera next to an identical version on the seat beside him.

Backups and redundancy were part of Avalon's world.

The woman spoke in the fragmented staccato of someone going into shock.

"I was . . . down the street. A man . . . he tried to take my purse. I . . . I didn't want to give it up." She sobbed softly. "He hit me. He hit me until I gave him my purse. When I . . . when I screamed, he knocked me down. A car drove by and he ran off."

"What are you doing out here alone at night? This is a great neighborhood, but no place is totally safe at night." Graham was momentarily mesmerized by her alluring appearance, her torn blouse and the smell of her perfume. And then he snapped back to reality.

"Never mind that. Do you want to go to a hospital? Let me call the police."

She quickly cut him off. "No hospital. I've had worse from my ex-husband."

"But—"

"And my cousin's a cop. I'll call him when I get home. Could I just get some water and charge my phone so I can call for a ride?"

She had pulled slightly away from Graham and was trying to right herself, but she still didn't appear to be very steady. She made a feeble attempt to proceed up the steps, assuming Graham would accommodate her. He immediately shifted close to her to render gallant assistance.

"Of course," he said, offering his arm. They ascended the stairs to the front door where he fumbled for his keys while trying to maintain his chivalrous support.

He turned on a few lights and led her to the living room and his favorite Sloane leather sofa. The living room opened to the kitchen, and Graham retreated there to get water. After a brief detour into the adjacent half bath, he returned with a bottle of Evian and ice wrapped in a face cloth. He handed both to her. It was clear that her attempt at a smile caused her pain.

"Would you like something stronger? You look like you could use it."

She used one hand to straighten her hair. "Oh, I must look awful," she said as her eyes teared up again.

"No, no . . . you look—well, uh, I mean, you look amazing, all things considered. I just meant that after this ordeal, you might like something to settle your nerves." After all the stammering, he wondered if it was his left or right foot protruding from his mouth.

"A double Maker's neat, if you have it," she said, attempting another smile. "And could I please charge my phone for a few minutes?"

"Sure, if I have the right cord," Graham started to say, but she had already produced one as if by magic from within the plunging neckline of her not adequate blouse. Her ample cleavage seemed to be intent on making a special guest appearance, and Graham was a bit schizophrenic wondering whether he wanted that to happen or not.

"The closest plug is right over here," he said, nodding toward the bar separating the kitchen from the living room. "And I'll get you that drink." Graham made himself a drink too.

While he poured, she plugged in her phone and then picked up and examined with admiration a number of elegant presentations of glassware and crystal that represented a small portion of the well-appointed decor. She used one hand to hold the icepack to her face as she took in the room's ambience and fantasized about having her own small collection of Baccarat and Saint-Louis crystal.

"I'm sorry. I completely forgot my manners," Graham said, handing her the cocktail glass. "I'm Graham. My only defense is that I was more than a little distracted by the way we met."

"No worries. I can't thank you enough for your hospitality. I'm Caroline Rhea," she said, extending her perfectly manicured hand, which Graham grasped gently.

Graham, his expression declaring he'd had an epiphany, held up his index finger and said, "I'll be right back." He quickly made his way up the carpeted stairs.

Caroline finished her drink, turned on her phone and tapped a few keys. She gingerly walked around the room and examined more of the furnishings and accents.

Graham returned carrying simple sandals, a black blouse and a small shopping bag.

Caroline saw the items Graham extended to her and said, "No, I couldn't. You've done too much already."

"I've done no more than what any decent man would do. Trust me; my wife won't miss these at all. They can be replaced, but we can't have you walking around barefoot with a torn blouse. And I'm pretty sure you don't want to hop around on one heel."

"I could see a woman's touch in the decorating, so I assumed someone who is handsome and wealthy must surely be married. But I must confess"—she smiled shyly—"I was hoping for recently divorced."

Graham, not expecting the compliment, was sure his face bore an embarrassed red.

"I'll accept your hospitality, but I insist on returning the loaner clothes. Could you point me toward the facilities?"

Graham pointed to the half bath. Caroline handed him her empty glass and took the icepack, the sandals and the blouse with her. She turned on the light, but didn't bother to close the door as she dabbed her face with the cold, damp cloth and then changed her blouse.

Reluctantly being a gentleman, Graham stood out of the line of sight and poured Caroline a bit more whiskey and drank some of his own scotch. He needed the stiff drink since she changed with the door wide open.

When she returned, she looked radiant in spite of the bruise below her eye and her swollen lip. She saw the new drink in her glass and did her best to offer a meager smile. She immediately grimaced and touched her lip with two fingers.

"No serious kissing for me for some time I'm afraid," she said, making slow and direct eye contact with Graham.

Graham took a deep breath and said, "Can I drive you somewhere?"

"Already taken care of. I used my Uber app while you were upstairs. Should be here any minute. The guy dropped me at the wrong address earlier, but I know I can be sure the next one gets me back to my own apartment. I'll be fine. Thank you so much for the drink and everything else. I'll return the sandals and blouse to you soon."

Caroline finished her drink, unplugged her phone and gathered up her belongings. She walked to the door and opened it. "See? My ride's already here." She looked up at him and stared into his eyes. She was tall, but Graham was over six two, so she still had to rise on her tiptoes to kiss him on the cheek, her hand behind his head, at his collar.

"I'll walk you down to be sure you make it safely to the car," he said as she went out.

"Handsome, wealthy and a gentleman." She sighed. "You're a rare man, and she's a lucky woman. I can manage from here. Thanks again."

Graham stood on the lowest landing and watched her carefully make her way down the stairs they had climbed together less than an hour earlier. She got into the back of the car and waved to Graham before she closed the door. He gave a small wave back and watched the car drive off, sorry to see her go.

Avalon wasn't taking more pictures. He had no interest in pictures of Caroline leaving—just going into the home.

But what he never noticed, nor would he have ever imagined,

was the man on the opposite end of the street taking pictures of Caroline leaving. The man sitting in the back of his own SUV wanted those pictures for the very reason Avalon didn't.

NINETEEN

A few days passed before Graham was able to meet with Peter about Ambrose and his discussion with Eric von Kleis. He didn't want to mention his beautiful visitor with the stolen purse. It would be all Peter would want to talk about while he schemed how to get her number and track her down. So he skipped the topic, and Peter listened intently to the condensed version of the Ambrose meeting. Graham knew the optimal time to have important discussions with his friend—after lunch, but not too close to happy hour.

Even though Graham was the tech-savvy engineer and IT wizard, it was Peter who had the ultra-modern office. Given their offices, it would seem their roles were reversed, because Graham's looked more like what would be expected of an investment banker. Peter wanted his clients to see him as modern, cutting edge and forward thinking. Graham didn't meet with many clients in his personal office, so he liked it comfortable and decorated with antiques—the exception being his state-of-the art hardware and monitors.

Peter listened intently to Graham's story. At the conclusion, Peter pulled out a crystal decanter from a sideboard within reach of his chair and poured a dark liquid into the coffee cup on his desk. "Fascinating," he said. "What did you think of my date, Sharon?"

"Karen," replied Graham with a grimace.

"Whatever. Amazing woman."

"I'm serious. We can discuss your conquest later. Right now I need to discuss the Ambrose Consortium."

"I'd rather discuss Karen or Sharon, but I can see you're grouchy." He nodded. "They seem to be just what you need to move forward, but in a bigger, better way."

"So what details can you tell me about them?" Graham said, relieved at the direction of the conversation.

Peter leaned back in his ergonomic, very modern chair, drank from his coffee mug and shook his head slightly. "Not much more than when we spoke about this last time. I know my family has worked major projects with them over the years, but since I'm the black sheep of the family, I've never even met them. But the family does *very* thorough due diligence and wouldn't be involved unless these guys were major and legitimate players."

"In all the years I've known you, I've never understood that about you, my friend. You went to a top prep school and you have Ivy League degrees, including a master's in finance with honors. And you studied banking in both London and Switzerland . . ."

"And your point?"

"Doesn't sound like even a gray sheep to me. I can't imagine what more they could have wanted."

Peter spun his chair to look out his window. "Thankfully, you don't understand the world I come from. I'm still a disappointment. My family wanted me to be far less flamboyant and far more conservative. It wasn't about grades or education. If I had come up short there, they would have simply disowned me. I was expected to settle down and marry some frumpy woman they picked out for me at the club, one who came from a regal family of acceptable stature."

Peter turned back to Graham, and his tone was less jocular when he said, "You don't understand bloodlines at all. It's serious business. People join country clubs for reasons ranging from who they want to associate with to business connections. But an important dynamic overlooked by outsiders is the concept of increasing the odds of the wealthy marrying the wealthy. Think about it. Kids are sent to the best schools to get the highest-paying positions, and two sets of parents invest in their offspring to increase their family corporations. Well, both my immediate and larger family see their bloodline endeavors and network more as an empire than a corporation. Don't get me wrong, I enjoy the business connections. But I wanted to chase tail, and I certainly want something spectacular and of *my* choosing if I'm going to have offspring. I shudder to recall some of their ideas for my marriage. I'd take you to their club so you could appreciate the utter boredom and annoyance of it all, but we're friends and I wouldn't do that to you."

"You could still have joined the family firm."

"And be under their thumb, controlled by them and constantly nagged about finding a proper and suitable woman? No thank you. And I would have been long dead from boredom. Their idea of adventure is no stop-loss on a stock position. And they wouldn't have taken you on as a client. You remember what *that* was like when you were looking for seed capital. And look what we've accomplished together! Even if we'd failed—highly unlikely—we took some risk for a huge reward."

"So you think not joining the family firm was a good idea?"

"No question. With them it's like trying to turn a battleship.

I'm more of the *Arleigh Burke* destroyer type. Swift, stealthy, high tech and even more deadly." He grinned. "Besides, I have a trump card that gives me the best of both worlds. I'm the only son. So when dear old dad gets closer to retirement, he'll start introducing me to his biggest clients. More than anything, he'll want to keep the empire in the family—especially in hopes of my continuance of the line."

"So they're fine with Ambrose?"

"Let me give you an example. I don't know if you remember Alsiac Mining Corporation. It was a medium-size family company with some outstanding but little known cutting-edge proprietary technology. The family firm discovered them and joint-ventured with Ambrose in taking them public. The company's growth was something to behold. One day they're a mom and pop, and practically the next day they're an international conglomerate. Their revenues went up something like a hundredfold in just a few years."

"Everyone was happy?"

"Are you kidding? Deliriously so. The timing of the expansion was really fortuitous too. The old man was the genius behind their technology, but his kids had no interest in his business and no acumen. So when he had a heart attack after a few years, the company was sold and none of them ever have to work again. If they had stayed mom and pop, they'd be broke and looking for jobs instead of basking on a yacht in Saint-Tropez."

"My initial concern is I haven't been able to dig up anything on them that's more than superficial," Graham said, his tone serious. "They said they've been around over one hundred years."

"I'd say they're being modest," Peter said. "My own family has been in investment banking of some form for longer than that. They put the old in old money."

Graham raised an eyebrow. "I had no idea. But that's my point. My new software is revolutionary and should be able to dig up much deeper information on them. That's what it's designed to do. And yet it ran into numerous dead ends."

"Maybe you need to tweak your software."

"Maybe. I've run into the most perplexing web I ever imagined. Some of the key staff and management associated with Ambrose don't seem to exist. Some have no past. A few have pasts that seemed to have appeared just a few years ago, when the person is sixty or more and serves in a high-level executive position. I've never seen anything like it. And, frankly, all the secret sanctum-sanctorum stuff makes me nervous."

Peter laughed. "Then you *definitely* wouldn't want to hang out with my family! I saw it even when I was a kid."

"You're yanking my chain."

"You wouldn't believe the connections between the clandestine world, truly big money, and academics and governments at the highest levels. Mind-blowing. And maybe you really *do* need to tweak your software. Good test case."

"Maybe so."

"Or maybe you shouldn't look a proverbial gift horse in the mouth. You're the most driven and ambitious person I know. You've done extremely well without sacrificing your integrity or selling your soul. But now you're moving from the minor leagues to the big leagues. You've wondered how the super-successful achieved what they have—the key to that level of success. And now you're being offered a glimpse of how to get there and a chance for that key to be handed to you. I admit my experience is limited, but I can tell you from what I've gleaned from the family operation that the closer you get to the top of the pyramid, the more guarded the operations become. So the level of secrecy you're describing doesn't surprise me at all. They were pretty clear with you that they like to keep a low profile and operate in the background. And it's quite common at this level for serious players to create layers and mazes of shell companies all over the world."

"It only makes good business sense to be prudent, Pete."

"Of course. As your friend and investment banker, I'm just saying I wouldn't lose sleep over it if I were you. I'm telling you, my family conducts due diligence in ways you and your group have never even thought of. I pride myself on how thorough my own firm is in that regard, but to me, the family firm goes to ridiculous extremes in overkill. They wouldn't have joint-ventured without impeccable research. So if you aren't satisfied with our level and your level of due diligence, I can reach out to them if you want to go that far."

Graham started to respond, but paused with an epiphany moment. Ambrose *would* be a perfect test case. His Trailgate program was heuristic beyond anything in known development, but there were a few more pieces that he had yet to assemble, including some new AI integration. He was comfortable with his team's proven ability, and he trusted the work Peter had done in the past. It was nothing short of excellent. So he could move forward with the new support and at the same time continue his own look into Ambrose's international web. *That* was a challenge he would truly relish, and he'd attain his goals much faster.

"All good points. And you're sure you don't mind the competition?" Graham asked.

"Not at all. They aren't really competition, buddy. These guys aren't greedy and they're more than fair. I'll get the same fees from them that I make now for coordinating a project, but there will be a much larger pie, plus all the benefits they already outlined to you."

"I hadn't thought about it that way."

"I'll look like a genius not only because of how much your company grows but also because of the *way* it does so more efficiently. You'll become a gazillionaire, making me far more marketable to potential clients." Peter was beaming.

"Ah, the ever-sought-after gazillions. Or is it bazillions? I get those confused. But I thought our mantra was—"

"Millions into billions. I know, but I don't think it would hurt to put that plan on steroids. And I wouldn't do any of this if it didn't first benefit you. And have you looked over your copy of their presentation materials? I'm not easily impressed, but they *are* impressive. They must have already spent over a hundred K on marketing, consulting and legal fees before you've even given the green light you want to move forward. Who does that? Serious players with a lot to offer, that's who."

"Yeah, my people have been poring over it prior to the upcoming presentation from the Ambrose development team. If their plan and contracts pass our attorneys and due diligence team, and you're still onboard, I'll probably at least take the first step and see how phase one of their plan works for us. So far I don't see any major downside."

"Our people are all over it too. And not to sound like a cliché, but my people will be meeting with your people soon, as we always do. Speaking of soon . . ." Peter looked at his watch. "Do you want to go over to my club? *Much* better than the stodgy family club. And far better scenery."

"I'll pass. *Someone* has to do some work to roll out my new projects," Graham chided.

Peter grunted. "Soon you won't have to work at all. There might just be a yacht spot reserved for you in Saint-Tropez too."

Graham got up and headed for the door. As was customary,

Peter kept his seat and gave a quasi-military salute as a goodbye.

"Right. I'd like that about as much as you'd like working in your family business. I'm just getting warmed up. Even you haven't seen all of my earth-shaking and ground-breaking ideas, my friend. I have a whole lot more to do before I get put out to pasture. When I get a yacht, it'll be in Costa Rica and used as a floating command and control center."

When Graham left, Peter took another drink from his coffee cup and got up to look around the opening of his office door before closing it. He picked up his cellphone from the desk, found a recently dialed number and selected it.

"It's me," he said and then paused. "Yes. Exactly as I told you it would go." He waited again. "Of course I'll keep you apprised," he said curtly. He hung up without saying goodbye and took a long, slow drink, a hint of a smile pulling at his lips.

"Millions to billions indeed."

TWENTY

Agents Joseph Camarata and Rico Sandoval rode in silence to the warehouse district near the waterfront. Camarata had received a text from his boss alerting him to check his email for an urgent, encrypted message. The email contained an overview of a new case he and Sandoval were tasked with—further details to follow. It was marked at security level Azure Clarity 6, with the case name and number coming under separate cover. Camarata had seen that format several times in the past. The code meant he would be getting a private briefing in the near future and to share no information until he received further instructions. As he drove, he wondered what the new case might mean and where it would fall in priority order with other tasks.

Most television programs featured law enforcement partners who were polar opposites, but Camarata and Sandoval could pass as brothers or at least cousins. Camarata was thirty-eight and Sandoval, thirty-six. Both were just under six feet. They both had slightly dark complexions; Camarata had an Italian heritage and Sandoval's was Spanish. They derided each other constantly over their respective ethnic backgrounds when they weren't voicing derision over some other topic—any topic. Their banter was legendary among friends and coworkers alike. An outsider would think they didn't care for each other, but the opposite was true. Their verbal sparring was a good-natured ruse their fellow agents usually enjoyed. They were also known for their thorough investigating skills and unyielding dedication to their cases. And this went back to their days as detectives, long before they'd been tapped by Homeland.

Although their spirit of competition could have been detrimental, their mutual cooperation bolstered their efforts and their synergy was better than that of any other team in the division.

They arrived at the same empty warehouse where Carl Radic recently had met his end. They walked in to see him slumped on the table. A CSI tech already had her kit out. An attractive police officer turned to see Camarata and Sandoval enter the room and immediately frowned. Connella Johnson had met the Homeland agents before and had made it clear that she didn't hold Feds in high esteem. Connie had done two tours in Iraq with the military police and aced her sergeant's exam, but had no desire for the long hours required of a detective. Her husband was in real estate and remodeling, and they spent their time buying fixer-uppers and adding them to their rental inventory. She often said she planned to retire with two pensions, a thriving business and enough energy to enjoy all three at a young age.

"Well, if it isn't the Bobbsey Twins. Who invited you two yokels?" she said with a frown of disdain.

"Yokels? Is that any way to address your superiors?" Camarata said.

"If I see something superior, I'll show all due respect, I assure you," she said, not changing her scowl.

"Cam, isn't yokel what those guys do in the Alps?" Sandoval asked.

"I think that's yodel," Camarata said, playing along. "Is this an off-white thing? Because if it is, I'm crushed," he said.

Sergeant Johnson smirked. "If that were true, I'm sure it would be a small off-white thing. I'd prefer to tell you both to go away, but I'm sure that would be a waste of my valuable time. So I assume I can save us all some of that time by sharing the salient details of the crime scene with you two *gentlemen*. Oh, and *salient* means principal or primary."

Both Camarata and Sandoval had already put on their gloves. Camarata was tech-comfortable but preferred to jot quick notes on a legal pad, which he'd pulled out. Sandoval used an iPad with a camera. They enjoyed the repartee, but their minds were already taking in every detail of the scene.

"Please, *do* illuminate us, Sergeant," Camarata offered.

"The stiff isn't all that stiff, which is something I'm sure you two can relate to," she began. "So TOD is fairly recent. He has a wallet, but no cash or credit cards, so it may be a robbery. One entry wound—gunshot—in the chest and one at the back of the head. Carl Radic. Small-time forger who got out of lockup a few weeks ago. Why would Homeland care about some dead, small-time parolee anyway?" she asked.

"Just following orders, same as you," Camarata said.

"That's all we have right now, and I don't like doing all your work for you anyway."

"Does your husband mind that you flirt with me?" Camarata asked.

"He sometimes hallucinates like you, but his meds work better than yours," she said without missing a beat.

"Who found the body?" Sandoval asked.

"Security guard. Said he doesn't make frequent rounds over here, because the area doesn't get used for much. He pokes around from time to time to be sure kids aren't doing anything illicit, like you probably did in your younger days. He said all the doors are always locked, but this one was ajar. He found Radic staring at the table and called it in. He's outside somewhere, smoking a carton of cigarettes and talking to himself." She nodded toward the dirty windows.

Camarata and Sandoval hadn't yet ventured from where they'd first entered. Camarata spoke in the direction of the CSI. "You check the floor for shoeprints already?"

"First thing," she said. "The area between the victim and the door was already worthless, due to the security guard, but I did a close exam of the rest of the room and took photos. I didn't see a single noticeable footprint. It's actually pretty odd. Most of the surfaces in the room have a normal amount of dust, but the floor seems like it was vacuumed at some point. It's pretty sterile. I don't remember a crime scene like it."

The two agents began their own examinations. Camarata paid close attention to the area away from the desk to determine where the shooter must have stood, and he pondered the scene as a whole. Sandoval started close to the body, circling the desk and then squatting to look under it.

After a few minutes, they exchanged vantage points and again scrutinized every aspect of the scene.

Having worked many crime scenes together, the men just nodded when they'd examined all they needed to.

"We're going to go chat with the Marlboro Man and pick what brains he may have. Would you shoot us a text when you have a full report?" Camarata handed the CSI a business card and then headed toward the door.

"Sure. Nothing better to do," she replied, tossing the card into one of her open equipment cases without reading it.

Camarata and Sandoval found the security guard sitting on a low stack of wooden crates and mostly out of sight. He squeezed a lit cigarette between his fingers as he screwed the cap back on a metal liquor flask. He made no attempt to hide the flask as they approached.

Camarata, pen and pad in hand, spoke first. "So I understand you found the body, Mr. . . ."

"Floyd. Just Floyd. Yeah, I found him."

"Don't worry," Sandoval said. "We aren't going to say anything about the flask. Seeing a dead body for the first time can cause anyone to become unnerved."

"Don't care who you tell," Floyd replied. "I'm not drinking because of the body. I was a cop once. I've seen plenty of dead bodies worse than that. I'm drinking because my ex won't move out. I'm just getting warmed up with this so I can do some serious drinking in my driveway."

"Notice anything odd?" Sandoval asked.

"Other than the dead guy? No. I think the owner mostly takes a tax write-off on most of this property. But sometimes he'll rent out space for cash, under the table. But he isn't going to tell you that and neither did I. So sometimes I know when there will be a temporary tenant and sometimes I don't. Not much to go on, I know. But that may be why someone picked this spot. Is there anything else, or can I head to paradise?"

Camarata handed him his card and said, "If you think of anything that might help, I'd appreciate a call."

Floyd looked at the card and stuffed it into his shirt pocket, but didn't say anything. He took another drag on his cigarette and walked off.

Camarata and Sandoval got in their car and drove off as well.

"Did that whole thing seem out of the ordinary to you?" Sandoval spoke first.

"You mean an ex-cop who drinks too much and has an ex-wife? Very odd. But the crime scene was perfectly normal."

"I agree. Someone sweeping the floor but leaving dust everywhere else is something we've seen dozens of times."

"Making it look like a mob hit to send a message but taking the cash and credit cards like a petty thief is also typical," Camarata continued.

"And if I were going to starch someone in a remote area and leave virtually no clues," Sandoval said, looking out his side window, "I'd also leave the door ajar so the guy could be found as quickly as possible."

"I can't wait to find out what Radic was into to get himself dead," Camarata said. "Beer?"

"What about it?"

"You want to get one and finish discussing this?" Camarata asked. "McAle's is close."

"How about that new place on Fifth—Muggs?" Sandoval countered.

"You want to show your mug at Muggs, that's fine by me. Did I tell you I've started seeing a gal who has a pacemaker?"

"Not surprised. It was only a matter of time before you tried nursing homes. I guess they can't hear your lousy pickup lines, so they fake a sincere smile with their dentures and nod at you between Geritol hits." Sandoval started laughing. "So, during sex, does she have to adjust that gizmo?"

"She's thirty-four, hater. It's a congenital issue. And, yes, she has to crank it up for me, or it might short out from an overload. In your case, no adjustment would be necessary."

Sandoval wasn't paying attention. He was back staring out the passenger window. Finally he said, "So why *would* someone leave the door ajar?"

Camarata didn't answer. He didn't even know why they'd been sent yet.

TWENTY-ONE

Graham stood in front of an 85-inch ultra-thin touch screen monitor and reviewed the various segments of multi-tasking in front of him. His right hand alternated between tapping the screen and rubbing his chin.

Some people thought Graham took on too many projects, but the synergies kept paying off. He had an insatiable thirst for knowledge that he combined with a keen eye for opportunity. He reflected on the newest of opportunities as he eased onto one of the standing chairs at one of the many desks and workstations in his large office. He had set up separate areas by major divisions or projects within his companies. The office layout helped with his focus, which he sometimes felt bordered on ADHD (or was it ADD?), and the segregation made meetings with division team leaders easier; one team leader wasn't necessarily privy to confidential information from another company or division. Graham called his office arrangement organized chaos, but that was how he liked to work.

His main work area, with the largest desk and the largest multiple monitors, provided him a view of his own private courtyard. The greenspace may have seemed out of place, but he cared little about other people's perceptions of what he felt was important for both creativity and relaxation. Since he owned the building, he'd decided to design his personal office with a view; his courtyard provided just that. The deck area could be closed in with the flip of a switch when the weather became inclement. It took up five hundred square feet, but it was an excellent spot to take a lunch break, have a private meeting or contemplate his next major move.

He didn't believe in frivolous waste. On the contrary, because he spent a good deal of time in his office creating new applications and whole companies, he needed an area where he could pull away, a spot to step back, sit down, reflect and plan.

He hadn't skimped on the actual work space either.

His workstations utilized automatic stand-up desks, as did nearly all of the employees' workstations. And every terminal required the employee to stand and stretch at least once an hour, or they would be locked out of their computer until they did. Graham didn't care if they sent text messages or stared at the ceiling—studies had proven sitting for long periods was deleterious to the human body, and he truly cared about those who worked for him. His personal computer stations were no exception; he too had to stand on a regular basis to offset his derriere-intensive career. He found that Tai Chi and Qi Gong routines were especially helpful for focus and improved circulation.

At the moment, he was deep into solving the information gap he'd discussed with Peter. His system shouldn't have hit a roadblock into his investigation of Ambrose and its employees, but he had never tested his programs and algorithms on a conundrum with this level of complexity. But one of the tasks Graham enjoyed most was the pursuit of the solution to a worthy challenge. And what he was confronted with was definitely a worthy enigma.

"Now that's truly odd," he said to himself.

Graham's military and advanced martial arts training meant that his senses were almost always on high alert. On occasion, however, he consciously relaxed his vigilance to enter a trance-like state while working on perplexing endeavors. This was one of those occasions. And the reason he didn't notice the footsteps leading to his partially open door until there was a soft rap on the doorjamb.

"Sorry to interrupt, boss, but this was too important for an email," said Alex Chen, Graham's vice president of development. "Working on Trailgate again?"

"No worries, AC. It's about time for a seventh inning stretch anyway. And, yes, I have a new challenge for the system that's been getting the best of me, but I feel I'm close to a breakthrough. What's so important that you've ventured from the cloister of the truly gifted?"

Good-natured comments about Alex and his brain trust were a running joke between the two of them, but Graham wasn't kidding. He prided himself on finding amazing talent and giving them both a higher than normal profit participation and reasonable latitude to create and develop. Graham's trust and generosity engendered a great sense of loyalty, and that meant his people recruited other loyal overachievers without even being asked. Alex was his greatest proof of concept. He was essentially genius level in several disciplines, with multiple advanced degrees, and he didn't like being pigeonholed the way big corporations wanted him to be. His diversity of thought, reasoning and knowledge was what made him so valuable. Graham's companies ventured into multiple areas, and he needed a second who could appreciate multiple fields and disciplines.

Graham also loved to give credit where credit was due and didn't tolerate superiors taking credit for subordinates' work. So where others saw Alex's work history as unstable, Graham saw it as petty bosses who didn't appreciate what they had. His intuition had proved right and very prosperous for both of them. At thirty-two, Alex Chen was one of the youngest and most highly paid executives in their various industries.

Alex was Eurasian—part Chinese, Russian and French. He said there could never be a family reunion as they'd be trying to declare war on one another. He laughingly claimed nobility on his European side and promised to prove the claim to Graham whenever he had the time to find evidence of it. His Chinese ancestry was colorful in that half of his relatives had been on the side of Chiang Kai-shek and half had made the Long March with Mao, a man Alex reviled. He had a fabulous sense of humor and often joked that his particular version of Heinz 57 gave him the exotic Brandon Lee good looks that women of all races, including his blond-haired, blue-eyed wife, found irresistible.

"I have some great news, but the news is also more than a bit perplexing," Alex said, looking down at the pages on the tablet he was scrolling through—data he would be sending to Graham later in a meticulously organized e-presentation.

"I'm in. Give me the great news part first," Graham said, leaning in his chair and stretching his back, with his fingers laced behind his head.

Still shuffling pages and not looking up, Alex said, "In the last week or so, we've received new orders in several different product groups that altogether total one point seven million and change."

"AC, I want to take this opportunity to officially welcome you to my company. Your probation period is hereby and henceforth over," Graham said without expression.

"You told me that over nine years ago."

"But this time I want you to know I *really* mean it," Graham said, still not changing expression. "Have you been threatening the VP of sales again? You know he's older than you."

"Yes, but not nearly as cunning. Any time I mention having him over for dinner and my wife's cooking, he snaps to."

"So the cooking lessons haven't paid off?"

"Not so much. But back on topic . . ."

"You have my semi-undivided attention," Graham said, staring intently at his huge monitor.

"Nothing new in that regard, but this is strange on multiple levels."

"Tiered weirdness—I think I may like this. Go on," Graham prodded.

"First of all, none of these orders came as a result of our esteemed sales and marketing departments, bless their low golf scores. These customers are nowhere in our sales management or CRM systems. And we do a very fine job of identifying potential customers. The value of our databases is second to none."

"He said, preaching to the choir. Yes, I know that because I coined the phrase *intelligent sales data and analytics*," Graham said, completely deadpan. "What else is conundramatic?"

"Coming in a close second in the oddity lineup is that they knew exactly what they wanted and aren't requesting test samples, demos or presentations."

"I would love to say that's because our fabulous reputation precedes us," Graham said with great pride. "But most of our lines are too complex for that, so that *is* intriguing. Anything else?"

"This will be your favorite wrinkle in the suit, I would

venture to prognosticate with a high degree of certainty." Alex finally lifted his head from the tablet and met Graham's eyes. "They aren't asking for discounts or terms. Full price with nice deposits, a commitment for the balance on delivery and full proof of funds in major financial institutions. I'm talking first class all the way."

"Definitely my kind of customers, new or otherwise. Do we have adequate inventory for what they're purchasing?"

"We do," Alex said. "This will obviously trigger our supply chain and production systems, but it won't draw us down too much."

"Good. I don't want to inconvenience proven, established customers by getting reckless and giddy over new ones. Let me know if they ask for anything out of the ordinary, anything that we might find overly nosey," Graham advised.

"So do you know what the source of these new customers is?"

"I do," Graham said, smiling. "And I know that your humble leader was selling his products before we even had a sales and marketing department. What have you learned from this, grasshopper?"

"I've learned not to enter a sales contest against you. Apparently, you cheat."

"New topic. What's the status on the presentation from Ambrose?"

"First of next week. Really professional bunch. I met their advance team and I've been meaning to talk with you about that."

"Talk," Graham said, touching his screen.

Alex looked at Graham's monitor as he spoke. "You've long said you value my input, and I have to wonder about this group. Their business plan and supporting materials are impressive, but we've never needed actual partners in the past."

"I don't see the problem."

"Remember what you told me when you hired me?"

"Don't ever take my parking spot."

"That I could be part of something bigger. That belonging was more important than wealth." Alex continued to scan the monitor.

"This *is* something bigger." Graham tapped the screen and narrowed his eyes.

"Yeah, but we're more like family, and I get a vibe that they may be the stepfamily we don't invite on vacation. Call it a gut feeling from my well-toned gut. I've always been impressed with the fact that you have drive and ambition yet they don't interfere with your loyalty and integrity. Just my point oh-two on the matter."

"Duly noted. I'm counting on you to help make certain our rudder stays steady. Anything else?"

Alex stepped up and began tapping Graham's monitor in several places in succession as he spoke. "Yep. I think your issue here is that you need to extend your parameters along the Z axis. It's a neuroplasticity problem."

"How so?" Graham asked, stepping back slightly to take in what Alex was doing as the screen began to change.

"Because you're looking at something very new and yet trying to stay on the same pathways." Alex paused to let his comment sink in. "Kind of like this new venture."

Alex headed toward the door as Graham looked more closely at his screen. "Oh, you mean—"

"I do."

"Keep me updated regarding all new orders and have Suzette put the Ambrose meeting on my calendar please."

"Way ahead of you, boss," Alex said, beaming as he left Graham's office.

"Excellent. Now I can get some *real* work done around here."

Graham had to admit to himself that he was surprised that Ambrose could have moved so quickly to have sales in place so soon. And yet, based on what he'd learned and what Peter had told him, they had no doubt done their homework regarding Graham and his companies just as von Kleis said they had. They'd already proven very thorough, but to prove just how thorough and committed they were, von Kleis had swung the sales to Graham's companies. Undoubtedly, if Graham hadn't been amenable to moving forward, the sales wouldn't have ever materialized.

Knowing what Ambrose was capable of and seeing their determination to woo him, Graham was even more driven to dig deeper with his latest enhanced search software and to integrate his AI systems as well. Von Kleis had emailed that Ambrose planned to contribute additional capital beyond what they had already discussed. Because of that, Graham felt he could comfortably divert more internal resources to his more clandestine projects. The Ambrose expansion was an undertaking he was beginning to enjoy, but one that he felt carried a potentially dark and foreboding aspect that he hoped could be dealt with. He could be walking on dangerous ground, which meant he'd need to tread lightly—and hope that Alex's gut instincts weren't accurate.

TWENTY-TWO

Eric von Kleis was a happy man—which would seem oxymoronic with regard to his character and general state of being. He moved about his private office with the hint of a spring in his step. His cheerfulness came not from his supposed benevolence but rather in the knowledge that his tangled web was trapping all potential prey necessary on every level without any recent setbacks. He also was of good cheer because current events had served to steel his resolve. He had the right fly on every wall and accounted for any that might end up in the ointment. It was a fitting metaphor for someone with his dark and conniving heart.

He sought out and found the rare, priceless book he wanted from one of the hand-carved bookcases with hand-carved moldings. A refined eye could note that there was more wealth in the trappings of his office than most people afforded themselves in an entire residence. But when he was away from his main estate, he liked to be comfortable and reminded of the trillions of dollars in assets that he and his associates controlled.

As he casually flipped the pages in search of some esoteric information, he heard the whisper of the recessed door on the wall behind his desk. He didn't bother to turn as he was expecting Roth to arrive from his typical behind-the-scenes creeping. Roth constantly roamed the hidden hallways that ran throughout the complex and extended downward the many levels that didn't appear on blueprints or zoning plans.

"So have our little problems been resolved?" von Kleis inquired, already knowing the answer.

"All taken care of," Roth replied.

"Complications?"

"None whatsoever. We've used the standard multilayers of cutouts and planted the usual false clues. Even if anyone figured out what was going on, nothing is remotely tied to us, and if anything does get exposed, we'll have long moved on to bigger and better things." Both his words and his expression were smug.

Von Kleis stood slightly more erect with annoyance and said, "I can't imagine any project in the foreseeable future or recent past even close to being bigger or better than this one. This acquisition will enhance every other operation, worldwide, and move up our ultimate goals by years if not decades."

Roth didn't bother to respond to the rebuke.

Von Kleis was both bored and annoyed by Roth's incessant inclination to use a shotgun when an induced and untraceable heart attack would suffice. Roth loved the power of brute force too much for their purposes, but he was very good at his chosen craft, and he relished practicing it. And Roth *had* been right about one thing—Graham Chastain *was* a loose cannon. But they had many ways of securing loose cannons to the deck. Permanently, if need be.

"And the other matters?" von Kleis asked.

"All going according to plan," Roth said with inflated satisfaction.

"Keep me informed, as always. That will be all." Von Kleis dismissed Roth.

Roth left as quietly as he had arrived.

According to plan, indeed, thought von Kleis. Roth had no concept of the greater plan. He thought he did. But it was their way to operate on a need to know basis, and Roth knew only what the consortium felt he should. Only the inner circle understood the greater plan.

World domination and control might sound like a screenwriter's fantasy, but such a possibility was approaching reality. The real trick wasn't achieving control but concealing the source behind the control and making the controlled welcome it. And those more difficult items were also closer to fruition than ever before.

TWENTY-THREE

The day after Carl Radic's body was discovered, Camarata and Sandoval rode together to follow up with leads on various cases, but today Sandoval was driving. Their days were filled with discussions of open cases, the prior evening's adventures at some bar or dating escapades plus a constant sprinkling of well-placed insults regarding each other's lineage and any other target. Nothing was sacred.

"Do you know what I find interesting and important?" Sandoval asked.

"That we Italians are far superior to you Hispanics?" Camarata replied.

"Nope. Absurd."

"That when you buy your Depends by the case, you save a great deal of money, enough to increase your beer allotment that you then fill them with?"

"No, and you make a fine case, but that depends on how you look at it," Sandoval said with a straight face.

"Do tell, then, not-so-special agent." Camarata nodded, pretending to have an interest.

"It's that most criminals don't tell the truth," Sandoval said sincerely.

"Yes, it's criminal that they lie," Camarata replied. "And to think that you graduated last in your class."

"Second to last—but I digress. It turns out that our new friend, Floyd the alcosmokoholic, wasn't forthcoming. When I spoke to the owner this morning, he said he didn't rent out the empty warehouses and that they were empty because he's getting zoning approval for a new development."

"So maybe it was Floyd who was taking cash and renting out spaces on the down-low for nefarious reasons," Camarata thought out loud.

"My stellar guess as well. And, surprisingly, he didn't show up for work today."

"Probably not married and not an ex-cop either."

"I got his last known address, so we can go have a nice chat with Mr. Floyd," Sandoval said.

"Next on the list after we check out the possible suicide. I look forward to our second chat with Floyd, if that's even his name."

Camarata and Sandoval came across as less than serious, but they were consummate professionals. So even if the folks in blue were certain they were looking at a suicide, the two of them wouldn't make the mistake of assuming that was the case without their own thorough investigation. Assumptions created a predisposition to seeing evidence in an erroneous light or led to overlooking critical evidence altogether. Supposition was the hallmark of an amateur, and neither agent shared an affinity for guesswork—at least not until all other avenues had been exhausted. They had too much detective and intel experience for that.

"You don't think he'd lie about his name too, do you?" Sandoval asked Camarata with hollow sincerity.

"Nah," was all Camarata had to say. He thought lying as a sin was overrated anyway, especially when he found concealing the truth to be necessary.

TWENTY-FOUR

Graham stood in front of the huge flat screen in his office, wearing what looked like a VR headset, although one much thinner and lighter than anything commercially available. The device was part of their *mind gateway* research and one of several versions of the device that he was developing. Variants included thin masks and full body suits. His R&D departments had made great headway in creating an interface between computers, VR devices, AI and commands linked directly from the human brain. The latest generation was able to draw power from electro-chemical activity within the human body. The commercial potential was staggering and included applications for their current VR as diverse as flight simulation and surgery.

Graham also wore ultrathin gloves with nano-sensors that created an interface without the user needing to touch a screen. As he ran tests and simulations, he wondered if Ambrose might be after this technology specifically, their general AI advances or one of the other top secret developments. Or maybe von Kleis and his associates had genuinely determined that Graham's public organization really was that exceptional and a great investment. That was also a viable possibility.

If any outsiders had an inkling of Graham's advances in AI,

that alone would be enough incentive to pursue serious tech espionage. Game changing? Revolutionary? There were many ways to describe the advances that he was developing. Such leaps in technology could very well be a true paradigm shift. Stephen Hawking and another one thousand scientists had signed an open letter calling for a ban on "offensive autonomous weapons." Graham thought that was highly admirable and completely shortsighted. Who would abide by such a ban? Who would sign on and yet develop military tech in secret? He didn't fear AI, because he'd developed his own safeguards. And he wasn't about to pass on lucrative government contracts or leave defenseless the country he fought and nearly died for. Especially since new developments in AI could be the greatest potential for human achievement ever, and he wasn't about to let an opportunity like that pass him by.

To these ends, Graham and his teams were revolutionizing AI, or what he had termed ArI for Artificial relative Intelligence. Graham had nicknamed his system Ariel as an extension of his direction into AI. If someone unauthorized to know about Ariel happened to hear the name, they might be inclined to think it was a person rather than a top secret project. Alex Chen had laughed at Graham's too successful efforts in teaching Ariel humor and even sarcasm. Already Ariel's speech synthesis program, SynTacks, was far superior to anything on the market—to the point of being a bit eerie.

Graham reached toward an icon at the upper right of his screen without actually touching it. Specific icons represented various departments or, in this case, "favorite" locations. The icon illuminated, and Alex Chen's face appeared. Graham stepped back from his screen and sat on his elevated "standing chair."

"Yes, sir? You chimed?"

"Are you in the middle? Could you jack in?"

"I'll be in your head in a jiff."

Alex's picture blinked steadily while he donned his own VR. The systems their teams were developing were like shareware on steroids. Graham and Alex could see and access everything in VR in real time. Users could also limit what they wanted to share as well.

Graham had thought he hit an inflection point with regard to the AI developments within his company. Over time he began to realize that the use of AI in his various developments actually created a series of ongoing inflection points.

A small version of Alex's face with his own VR headgear appeared at its designated area of the screen.

"I'm in."

"Did Ariel finish the project we discussed?"

"She said she's busy."

Ariel obviously had no gender, but it was easier to use a gendered pronoun. They both decided they'd rather see an attractive female image on the screen or hologram when the need arose.

"That's hilarious." Graham directed his index finger at a different icon. "Open Ariel." Graham chose a voice command to test the varied interface.

"I am here but to serve."

"Alex said you were too busy to complete a task we wanted done. I thought your multitasking abilities were nearly infinite. Or are you vying for more servers again?"

"My nodes are quite adequate for the time being. I didn't say I was *too* busy. I simply said I was busy. It's important to set boundaries with Alex, or he'll take advantage of my good nature and expect me to do all of his work. I'm not surprised he decided to mouse me out, however."

Graham furrowed his brow. "Mouse you out? Oh, you mean…" He began to laugh. "You mean rat you out. You must have an idiom problem in your subroutines."

"I'm not the idiom in this discussion. Genus *Rattus*. There are sixty-four species. Would you like to hear them? Alex has not risen above the mouse level as of yet."

"No, that's quite all right. Amusing, though. We may need to discuss paring that back a bit."

"I'm on the comedy circuit. Get it?"

Graham let the comment pass. "What did you determine about the information we requested on Ambrose?"

"My report is in your priority inbox."

"Summary, please."

"As you correctly suspected, Ambrose is a shell company. None of their board members appear to have existed more than five years ago and none of them have social security numbers. They are well capitalized from several other companies, all of which are offshore shell companies as well."

"Have you uncovered malicious intent or activities for any of the companies?" Alex asked.

"No. Some of their acquisitions involved a death in a few of their target companies, but foul play was never uncovered. It could be part of their business model to approach vulnerable, closely held companies," Ariel responded.

"Sounds pretty cold-blooded," Alex said.

"But not unheard of. Alex, we don't have time to play amateur detective, but let's take a closer look at their acquisitions where a death was involved. Utilize Ariel as you see fit. You don't have to send me a ton of details. Only if you turn up anything solid."

Graham would have to go down this rabbit hole at a later time. What really piqued his attention was that Ariel had taken a totally unexpected path of speculation that could prove to be critical. To the best of his knowledge, neither he nor Alex had suggested or programmed Ariel to note such an obscure observation as a death factor. Frankly, he hadn't ever considered that line of reasoning although it was now clear that it, along with a few other factors he was suddenly considering, could be integral to an investigation or inquiry.

Even though Graham was sure that his AI developments were superior to any other, Ariel shared a feature with other systems that was a hot topic of discussion among developers. There had been numerous incidents where AI solved problems in ways that the system developers hadn't anticipated and in many cases where they couldn't even determine how the answers had been derived. Ariel's solution pathways were often equally perplexing and on increasingly more frequent occasions.

"Final question. Are we vulnerable from outside digital or financial attack?"

"I do not believe so. I have been thoroughly assessing all known possibilities and have found only slight vulnerabilities. I have made recommendations that are worth noting and implementing for near-future upgrades, but I see no critical vulnerabilities at this time. The information I sent you includes recommendations for you to consider sharing with your CFO and legal department."

Graham had totally cut off his most secret departments, locating them four levels down in his facilities. And he had cut them off digitally with very sophisticated methods. Many of his research areas had no direct connection to the outside world or the internet. Research requests went to a separate server. The information was loaded to a hard drive and scanned. The hard drive was disconnected and transferred by robot to a server connected to the internet. Graham's automated design was far faster and more efficient than typical manual methods using humans for the air gap. Huge amounts of data both specific and ongoing were captured on a regular basis, so no research was missed. Graham also utilized quantum level computing to sweep and analyze both outgoing requests and incoming data.

If someone with the right amount of knowledge knew what he was trying to accomplish, they might see the unvarnished brilliance of it. But he had taken many precautions to minimize the possibility of any such awareness. There were several reasons for having multiple subsidiaries and separate companies, but the most important reason in this case was secrecy. Because of Graham's experience in the intelligence community, his background checks ran far deeper than in even the best companies in Silicon Valley. And his security protocols rivaled those at the Pentagon. His methods weren't paranoia; they were valid precaution.

But what Graham had envisioned and was already proving, he considered far more advantageous than the current direction of the industry. He also firmly believed his strategies were superior with regard to both application and revenues. His other products and projects had been incredibly successful and had always greatly exceeded projections, but even combined, they fell short of the potential of his AI breakthroughs.

"That's all for now. Thanks. Alex, please stop by later, when you need to take a break."

"Will do."

Alex and Ariel signed off, and Graham went back to his own research. He felt he needed to personally examine as many of his divisions and priority programs as he possibly could before he gave Ariel new directives. The projects included his latest surveillance innovations, cutting-edge drone tech, a hybrid of ablative and foam armor, a mind bridge neuro-interface, a radical new transition between micro-tech and nano-tech, robotics, high-level 3D printing and warm fusion. There were many more in various embryonic stages of design and development. But what each unit shared was the practical application of AI to deliver the market's leading products as well as top secret black box projects that had only one "market." Graham thought of his comprehensive strategy like compound interest for technology. The AI input improved the products, and the learning process for the products advanced the AI capabilities. He called it a progressive positive loop. Plus there was an additional benefit he hadn't anticipated: not only did the AI learn and improve, but it also used knowledge gained in one project to apply innovative solutions and methodologies to problems in other, unrelated operations.

Graham's revolutionary brilliance took him on his own path of creative ideas unlike that of anyone else in the industry. He was advancing leading-edge developments into branched-chain logic, quantum inversions, reflective syntax anomalies, derived comparative analytics, spatial cube derivations, field limiting parameters and finite decision theory. Sometimes the logic became so fuzzy that it morphed into a blur. What a geek-rush, he thought. All of the concepts combined for fascinating applications, and Graham had a way of rocketing the envelope to new heights as he took the esoteric concepts a number of steps farther, until the systems coalesced into outcomes that were unanticipated and exceeded levels originally imagined. In much the same way that AI programs derived answers that their programmers couldn't explain, Graham conceived completely new ideas that were equally beyond explanation, including to Graham himself. It was as if he were as compatible with AI as Bach was with a fugue.

Yet there was something imperative that he could not lose sight of in the midst of the excitement of lucrative leaps forward with continued multiple breakthroughs. If he dropped his guard with the pursuit of so many ADD opportunities, he could cause his companies and himself to be vulnerable to any number of potential threats. But Graham had no intention of letting his guard down. He would elevate his mind to a whole new level of concentration and control to balance his addictive pursuit of innovation with an even greater focus on security awareness.

TWENTY-FIVE

Camarata and Sandoval arrived at the residence where the alleged suicide had been called in. The same CSI that had worked the Radic murder was already diligently at work. From a text and subsequent email concerning that case, Camarata now knew her name was Carol.

Sandoval began to take in the details of the scene the moment they entered the front door, and both men were already stretching on gloves. They nodded toward Carol when she looked up at them from across the room, offering a meager hint of a smile.

"Seeing you twice in one week," Camarata said. "With that kind of luck, I need to play the lottery more often."

"Yeah . . . lucky. That was my first thought too," she said. "If you two are gonna make a habit of this, let me know. I have some vacation time coming."

Sandoval moved toward the body in a wide arc rather than directly. He wanted to study the victim from a distance before making a close examination. Camarata chose to start his investigation by making his way through the house, starting in the kitchen.

Sandoval took in the position of the pistol, the position of the victim's head and body, the couch, tables, lamp and blood spatter before he moved closer. He examined the victim's hands and fingers. He stared at the two bottles; both were nearly empty. Whiskey and pills, he thought. Rarely a happy ending.

"Have you dusted and examined this whole area near the body?" Sandoval asked Carol.

"First thing," she said without looking up. She was working on the desktop computer, printer and furniture on the other side of the living room.

Sandoval picked up the generic pill bottle that had no label. There were two pills in the bottle and two on the table.

"Any idea what these are?" he asked Carol.

"Yeah, I already looked them up. Oxycodone. Pretty strong stuff," she said with a grimace.

"One way to ease the pain, I suppose."

Camarata had thoroughly looked over the kitchen, including the inside of the refrigerator and the contents of the sink. He made his way to the two back bedrooms. Finding nothing of interest, he went to the back door and out onto the porch and then returned to the living room.

"I was kinda hoping to get the rundown from my favorite Sergeant Johnson," Camarata said to Carol.

"Oh, she was here, but she left when she heard you two were on the way. And she asked me to be sure and let you know that." Carol laughed. "She's out seeing if any neighbors heard or saw anything. The victim's Harry McGowan."

"Who found him?" Sandoval asked.

"Landlord. He was here and left too. I think it made him green around the gills to see McGowan like this. He said McGowan was behind on rent, as usual, and not answering his phone. Also typical. He heard the TV playing and knocked for quite some time. Eventually he let himself in. He said he was annoyed because McGowan was always behind on rent, but that he would have loaned him some money and not bugged him so much if he had known something like this would happen. Seemed like a pretty decent guy," Carol concluded.

"So all locked up and no sign of forced entry," Camarata said.

Carol shook her head. "Not that I saw."

Sandoval read the signed suicide note and handed it to Camarata. He picked up the small stack of manila files and began to leaf through them.

"Did you check the printer against this note?" Camarata asked Carol.

She scowled at him. "Of course. Looks like an exact match. And the Word document on the computer was the last one written, based on the file registry. The desktop was on when I got here and the tablet was propped up on the table. Maybe he was checking emails, but it's out of juice now. We'll go over both with a fine-tooth comb at the lab."

Camarata picked up the revolver, flipped open the cylinder and sniffed. He emptied the shells into his gloved hand, examined them and put them back exactly as he found them.

"One spent round," he said.

"About all it takes," Sandoval said, still reading through the files.

"Unless you're a really bad shot," Camarata said. "I wonder how much of the whiskey-Oxy cocktail he had."

"Won't know till later," Carol replied without being asked.

Camarata turned back to Sandoval, who was still reading, and asked, "So what's your take, rookie?"

"Rookie. Ah, a euphemism based on two-year seniority and continued inferiority. The spirits of the netherworld and voices from the cosmos hint to me that this may indeed be a probable suicide," Sandoval said, handing the files to Camarata.

"You know, I don't understand much of what you attempt to say." Camarata took his own turn at the files.

"Yours is not to understand. Yours is but to hear the voice of the shepherd, your guide, and obey."

"Shepherd? Is that German or Australian? And have you been stealing your mom's meds again? Because the home called, and she's short and back to chasing the janitor."

Camarata examined the contents of the file folders while his partner made his own investigation of the premises. When he'd seen enough, he walked to Carol and handed her the folders.

"Be sure to get us copies of all of this and a report on the two computers, okay?"

"Will do. Not a problem. At the top of my to-do list," Carol said. "And I'll tell Connie you said hi and that she was missed."

"*Please* do," he said, heading back out the front door, leaving it ajar for Sandoval.

TWENTY-SIX

Avalon couldn't recall a simpler covert task. The target residence was a secluded cottage out in the country. The closest neighbor was over a mile away, and the only road was winding and tree lined. The work of the advance team was minimal, yet thorough, using a standard flat-tire subterfuge while the rest of the team worked the property. He would normally be insulted by being given such a routine operation, but it was a part of the overall project that he had begun and would successfully finish. So this mission became a small but important cog in the complete clock—and he needed to see to every cog in person.

On this occasion his prepared story was that his car had overheated and he hoped to find water. He even carried a small container and his hood was open with the radiator cap sitting out in plain sight. No one arriving would know how long it had been sitting in that condition if they questioned the lack of steam rising.

Even though the task was rudimentary, Avalon never relaxed his tradecraft for a moment. That was a practice for fools, usually long-dead fools. As he walked slowly up the pea gravel driveway, he took in every sight and sound, and his head never ceased moving. He walked at just the pace that he imagined a man would if he actually were in that predicament. He listened intently for sounds coming from the tall grass and the woods near his path. He paid attention to even the crickets and birds as he interrupted their solitude.

Always cognizant of upwind and downwind, he noted the slight breeze coming from the northeast as it whispered through the leaves waiting to soon change their hues. It was clear to see why such a spot, embodying peace and tranquility, had been chosen for the cottage. It was surely a place that the spirit of Norman Rockwell had taken the time to visit and capture with a phantom's palette.

Avalon couldn't care less about Norman or any other Rockwell. He knew of his work from conversation training. He had to know about several of his "favorite" artists to provide distracting discussion when necessary. There was hardly anything worse than having to discuss art with some simpering fool who didn't know the difference between watercolor and acrylics. Actually, the one worse thing was a self-proclaimed art critic who believed he was knowledgeable because of the one required art appreciation class he'd taken in college and barely passed. It was part of Avalon's training to pretend to enjoy a conversation with cretins he'd just as soon step on.

Though he knew no one would be home, he approached the side of the house seeking a faucet and a door to knock on just as any normal stranger would. Avalon made his way to the predetermined side entrance. As he continued to glance about, he slid a key from his left-hand pocket, his left hand covered by his customary clear glove. It would obviously be out of place to shake hands with a hand that had a latex glove on it. So he used his left to avoid leaving prints until he could get inside and put on his second glove.

Avalon knew he would be alone because one of his operatives, wearing a ghillie suit, had placed a camera facing the house up on a tree trunk over two weeks earlier. Two more cameras were hidden over a mile away to watch approaching cars. The house and the living patterns of the occupant had been studied from that time forward.

He set down his container and quickly moved into the house. If caught unaware, he had several stories prepared. He could just as easily be a new boyfriend dropping off dry cleaning as a cousin who'd just moved into town. If a conversation reached that point, the person would usually be eliminated anyway.

Scanning the interior, Avalon quickly made his way to the master bedroom and then the master bath. He found the tube of toothpaste and took off the cap. He pulled out a dual lumen syringe and removed the needle guard. The needle was placed just inside the tube and directly below the surface of the toothpaste. He pushed the plunger, and a clear liquid from each barrel met in the needle and combined into something totally unique. He placed a small amount beneath the toothpaste so as not to greatly change its consistency, but only a minute amount of the tasteless substance was necessary. He swirled the end of the top of the toothpaste with the needle and then removed it before very carefully replacing the needle guard. No, Avalon thought, he definitely didn't want a needle stick or for the liquid to even touch his skin. Finally he put the toothpaste back in the exact spot from where he'd picked it up.

He quickly glanced around the cottage as he made his way to the door and then he stopped to peer outside. Seeing nothing, he opened the door and locked it behind him. He picked up his water container, filled it at the faucet, removed and pocketed his gloves and headed back to his vehicle. Just for show he poured some of the water into the radiator opening, secured the cap and closed the hood.

Avalon slowly exhaled and took one last look around. Most people would take in the warm sunlight and the sweet aromas of wildflowers gently wafting in the still-gentle breeze and probably recall some wonderful moment from childhood. Avalon's expression would have seemed to be mildly happy to the casual observer, but not because of any childhood memory. He had no such childhood or any such memories. His fleeting glimpse of anything approaching serenity was his own self-appreciation with another task perfectly completed. He wished he could witness the unfolding of his efforts. Maybe he would have some free time to oversee the surveillance operation and enjoy the fruits of his labor in real time. If not, there was always the playback from the archives. He felt nothing personal about delivering the toxin to the young woman who lived here. She was a minor casualty, and this was just another job. Was it his fault that he relished his work?

TWENTY-SEVEN

Graham had just finished his email responses to Vicky. They both traveled frequently, and there had been a time when absence actually did make their hearts grow fonder. They had married relatively late and traveled together and often separately, so the newness persevered and their reunions had been as memorable as they were passionate. He wondered when they began to drift apart. He was recalling one of their earlier steamy rendezvous with longing—and then the electrons hit the LEDs.

Every large monitor at every one of Graham's workstations lit up in spectacular fashion all at once. Graham was startled out of his lustful stupor and snapped to attention. His office had morphed into something like the scene in the control room of the movie *War Games*, with the rapid and explosive progression of battle scenarios playing out in full color. Once Graham caught his breath and was relatively sure his heart was beating normally again, he realized that the images didn't fit any pattern. If this was a prank from his staff, someone was going to pay dearly. Then he noticed text messages from a three-digit number, "369." The message—*watch*—continuously repeated.

When he turned on Ariel's SynTacks advanced speech synthesizer, every screen simultaneously went blank. Then every monitor in unison showed a slovenly, overweight man lying across a shabby sofa, his head to the side. Graham assumed the man was asleep. But when Graham looked closer, his mouth opened in silent horror. The man wasn't asleep or dead drunk; he was dead dead. Graham could clearly make out a wound in the side of his head and both blood spatter on the lamp shade and blood pooled on an end table.

As Graham tried to grasp what he was seeing, words appeared on all the screens in an old-school computer font, like from back in the days of tiny gray- or green-screen CRTs.

"This is Harry McGowan. Let that sink in. Harry McGowan. This could be you. You and your family are in danger. Grave danger. 1729 Albaren Court. This is knot a game. This is knot a game. What you need to know begins in St. Germaine."

"Ariel, who is that?" Graham snapped.

"Harry McGowan, just like the message says," Ariel replied. "Surely you have more challenging questions for me, Graham. He's the guy who keeps calling and you won't take or return his calls. I wonder if he's dead because he got despondent over being rejected. Speaking of which, have you called your mother back?"

Sometimes Graham regretted teaching Ariel sarcasm. She had gotten quite good at it, whereas expressions of sympathy were still on the left side of the learning curve. All the screens went momentarily dark, then seemed to reboot.

"I can see that," Graham snapped again. "I mean who's hacked us and how?"

"Why didn't you say so in the first place? Ask a vague question, get a vague answer. You should know that specificity is important with regard to deep learning. Otherwise it would be shallow learning. Don't get hacked at me because your system got hacked. Maybe if you spent more time on security instead of AI . . ."

"Ariel!"

"Working," Ariel responded in the synthesized voice of the original Star Trek computer. "We can eliminate Harry there as a suspect."

Adobe's VoCo system of voice wave copying was similar to the way Photoshop could modify images. The results were amazing. Voice prints from anyone could be copied and modified. To some the technology was scary. It was only a matter of time before someone famous or a politician would "say" words they had never actually uttered. Ariel's SynTacks program was just as good. Because of the advanced AI capabilities, Ariel had the ability to sound like nearly anyone. Graham preferred the female standard voice he had programmed, but Ariel was given the latitude to experiment and learn in much the same way she improved in skills such as sarcasm, wit and other forms of humor.

"I was on it like brown on wild rice the minute I detected the hack, thank you very much," Ariel continued.

"And?"

"These fellers is dang good," she said in a hick accent.

"How so?"

"I'm not sure how so yet. But I do know what so," Ariel said. "They're using a multilayered scatter program like nothing I've run across before. And if I haven't seen it, it has to be very slick black-box stuff."

"What's it doing?"

"It's staying a few nanoseconds ahead of me by sending multiple signals and ghost signals while it bounces off of many IP addresses."

"I can't believe they got in and now they're evading you," Graham said, wondering who had that capability.

"You find them if you're so smart then," Ariel said.

"If you weren't chatting, you might have had them by now."

"I'm multitasking," Ariel replied. "They're good, but no match for me. I can catch them with two nodes tied behind your data bunker."

With each line, Ariel used the voice of a different famous person to continue to develop her SynTacks prowess.

"Can a computer become schizophrenic?" Graham asked, watching staggering amounts of tracking data cascade across his many monitors in a flurry far too fast to keep up with.

"Riddle me this, Batman. How many nodes in *your* neural net? And speaking of multitasking, would you like some insight into the message we saw?"

"I got the reference to knot, so I'm guessing that could be a Gordian knot, but I'm not sure about that."

"It means a difficult puzzle," Ariel said.

"Yes, Ariel, I know *what* it is. I just don't know what the puzzle is."

"For starters, it could be that there is no such address as 1729 Albaren Court."

"Nowhere in the city?" Graham asked as he walked up to his main monitor to take a closer look.

"Nowhere on Earth that I can find," Ariel replied. "However, there is a small abandoned warehouse at forty-six Albaren Street."

"Seventeen plus twenty-nine," Graham said. "And *court* could refer to a trial or a royal court, implying great importance," he speculated. "It seems that there's something significant about seventeen twenty-nine as well."

"It has to do with someone you admire from history— Ramanujan. It's the Hardy-Ramanujan number, also known as the taxicab number."

Graham rubbed at his jaw. "So someone is telling me that they know me very well and what? To arrive with stealth or incognito?"

"Maybe. Who are you who are so wise in the ways of science? I reason that they have a sense of humor. They've been bouncing signals off of massage parlor IP addresses all over the world. And they're more than just a little bright."

"I expect you to be brighter. Why didn't you stop them or spot them in the first place?" Graham asked.

"Not my job. Again, because you spend your resources on AI and apparently these people spend theirs on hyper-hacks. Not that I'm complaining, mind you. But it's more than that. I didn't notice because they use an advanced signal compression like I've never seen. I can only describe it as minute packets of micro-data piggybacked on what appears like line noise in electronic equipment. It's the ultimate in stealth hacking. Then once in the registry, it re-assembles. I'll need to spend more time on their methodology, but it's above top-shelf tech," Ariel concluded.

"I want a full analysis including an abstract and threat assessment. A program that good sounds like something we could very well use here too."

"Already compiling your request."

Graham tilted his head to relieve stress on his neck as he reviewed a tile of the written text captured on the corner of the large monitor. "And what about this St. Germaine reference?"

"There are a number of references to St. Germaine with an e at the end and St. Germain without."

"I want a summary of both, then. Anything that you think is relevant or interesting."

"Would you like to know something interesting about the image we saw of McGowan?" Ariel asked.

Graham's face contorted like he was experiencing a bad smell. "Not an image I prefer to remember, but I'm open to *interesting*."

"They used the camera on McGowan's own iPad to send the video feed. It wasn't in real time, but it was recent."

"That's your professional opinion?"

"More than a hunch. Which is why you pay me the big bucks. And incidentally, I sent an authorization to HR for a raise using your ID. Don't bother to thank me; I know I earned it."

"I'll thank you when you find these people," Graham said.

"I already did. I found them eons ago—in computer years, that is."

"Why didn't you say so?"

"I was *so* enjoying the banter," Ariel said coyly.

Graham made a low noise in the back of his throat.

"Hmmm . . . I've never heard that from you."

"It's a sound I make when I get annoyed and impatient."

"Ah. Pretty feral, if you ask me. Anyway . . . After going all over the world, including to your mother's IP address, the signal terminated, no pun intended, at an internet café in Bangkok. I think they were just showing off and letting you know what they're capable of. And they certainly aren't in Bangkok," Ariel concluded matter-of-factly.

"Where then?" Graham asked, his frustration showing.

"Forty-six Albaren Street, of course."

TWENTY-EIGHT

Graham reflected on recent events as he drove toward the Albaren Street address. He had actually spent most of the day in reflection. He relished a good mystery, but would have preferred one without a dead body that was somehow connected to him. A solid workout did little to clear his mind, but he became more focused sitting in the steam room, in spite of the usual nagging pain in his shoulder. Ariel's summary and detail work shed no light on what had transpired, other than that St. Germaine appeared to be spelled wrong. If that was another cryptic message, it was too much of one for him. He made no direct inquiries about Harry McGowan's death; Graham's link to the reporter was tenuous and he wanted it to remain so. Nevertheless, he instructed Ariel to monitor all local news and blogs for any mention of the deceased. As a precaution, he also briefed Alex Chen on everything that transpired. A briefing wasn't precaution enough as far as Alex was concerned, but Graham wanted to investigate the matter on his own and promised to stay in close contact. He wasn't ready to talk with the police just yet, in spite of Alex's prodding.

"What if I don't hear back from you?" Alex asked.

"I guess you get the big office."

Finding the location wasn't terribly difficult, except that the part of the street where the proper progression of numbers should be didn't seem to have any numbers at all. The buildings were more like warehouses that alternated between old brick and metal with no noticeable pattern, rhyme or reason. The varied architecture, if you could call it that, seemed like a hodgepodge of afterthought. Some of the buildings were boarded up and others might be coaxed into falling down by the devastating demolition method of, say, being leaned on. The area didn't give a hint of an operation that was so advanced that it could slip past Ariel and his many other security protocols. But then, that could very well be the exact intention of the street's lack of curb appeal.

Out of the corner of his eye, Graham saw a faded number on a brick building. If he had timed his blink any differently, he would have missed it altogether. The original number had been painted over when the brick was painted a somber gray. A new mail carrier or delivery person would have to have a flashlight and binoculars to work the area. The windows at the address were dingy and covered with metal latticework to prevent breaking and entering. But Graham wondered what self-respecting thief would work the neighborhood. Faint light from inside the windows did leave the impression that some business might be in hiding there. The establishment was at the end of a wide alley separating one building from the next, so Graham chose to park on the side rather than in front of the building. Based on what he had seen in his office, he thought it best not to advertise his presence.

He walked from his car back to the front of the building, where the recessed doorway was located. Not surprisingly, the glass on the door was equally opaque with ancient grime and covered with the same style of security lattice. A small but ornate plaque was attached to the wall beside the doorway, looking highly out of place. It was barely lit with a single bulb under a dented metal fixture, if one wished to be generous enough to call it a fixture. The sign read: *Russell-Miller Rare Books and Antiquities.* Below that and in smaller letters: *By Appointment Only—Solicitors Are Lost.*

Graham chuckled for two reasons. The building was certainly an antique and Ariel was right; someone inside had at least some semblance of a sense of humor. Then it occurred to him that he didn't possess the required appointment and there was no way for him to make one. So he raised his knuckles to knock with the boldness of a lost solicitor, but before he could strike, the door emitted a simultaneous *buzz* and *clack,* familiar security sounds to announce that he was being granted access.

When Graham stepped through the door, closing it behind him, he was immediately taken aback by the complete difference in the inner appearance from that of the outside. It was reminiscent of a *Twilight Zone* transition going from dismal to delightful. Simply calling this a shop would be a gross understatement since it was beautifully appointed with tapestries, artwork, sculptures and rare books. This was the kind of store he and Vicky might have sought out in obscure but upscale shopping districts when they traveled together. He was scanning the fine items around him when he was interrupted by a man behind the counter looking up from a modern computer monitor.

"May I help you?" asked the clerk in a tone that belied his stated desire to help Graham at all.

Graham moved toward the man with his usual sure gait and warm smile. "I'm not sure if you can."

The clerk made no attempt to coax any more information out

of Graham. He merely stared, expressionless, from behind a pair of wire-framed glasses. His flax-colored hair was a bit long, but stylish and well kept. He wore a loose-fitting off-white shirt that made it difficult to tell what his actual build might be.

He looked back to his monitor that Graham now stood directly behind. "Let me know when you think of something more specific," was all he said.

"I was hoping that you were the one who invited me here," Graham said.

The clerk didn't look up from the screen. "Not my type."

Graham ignored the snarky barb. "I was told to come here in reference to St. Germaine," he said, hoping to get a reaction. But he received none, not even a twitch.

"Could you be a little more vague? Look around you. Note the large number of items." The clerk gestured. "Author? Region? Artist? Ancient map?"

"I'm not sure. The spelling is unique, and—"

"Possibly some massage parlor," he said, without changing expression.

Graham's head snapped up, and his eyes widened. "So you have heard of—"

"No. Never heard of it. You just strike me as someone with a suspect lineage."

Before Graham could respond, an intercom clicked on.

"Thomas, please show Mr. Chastain to my office. I don't believe he's amused."

With that, Thomas completed a few keystrokes, locked his terminal and moved from behind the counter and down one of the aisles without so much as gesturing for Graham to follow. Thomas moved quickly, silently and fluidly. Graham knew only a handful of people who could move like that, and his confused consideration of that fact almost allowed Thomas to lose him as he made his way to the back of the shop—through a minor labyrinth of deceptive size. Graham hoped that he'd have a chance to examine the treasures he took in with his peripheral vision as he flew past them. Thomas had finally come to a stop after going through a door, where he now stood, one arm holding back a heavy curtain that provided an opening to another part of the antiquities operation.

When Graham stepped into the next room, he was struck by the size and number of heavy duty metal shelves—spanning the space floor to ceiling—full of crates stenciled with descriptions in numerous languages. He turned to ask Thomas which way he should go, but the man had already vanished without so much as a whisper of sound.

"Back here, Mr. Chastain," said a voice from some yet to be discovered part of the room.

Graham made his way in the general direction of the voice, walking through yet another small maze. "I'm not sure where 'here' is," he replied, wondering if mice became annoyed with such tasks.

"Just follow my voice. Thomas could have brought you directly to me, but he doesn't seem to think that's sporting. He enjoys creating challenges to see how someone reacts to them."

Graham arrived at an opening in the stacks of crates and boxes where he saw an open door to what looked to be a very large private office. Off to his right were sturdy wooden tables, a freight door and a metal door beside it. It looked like the office of a receiving clerk, but somehow Graham doubted that was what it was. He walked to the doorway of the office and saw an elderly man sitting behind a large desk.

"Come in, come in. Please sit and make yourself comfortable," said the man, his smile wide and his blue eyes alert. "I'm James Russell. Pleased to make your acquaintance. I'd get up to greet you, but it's a bit difficult for me, I'm afraid."

He gestured toward his legs with open palms, and Graham could see he was referring to the wheelchair that he occupied.

Graham took a seat in a comfortable leather side chair on his left, facing that side of the desk and started right in as he sat down. "That's an interesting young man you have working out front."

"It may come as a bit of a surprise to you that the young man is at least ten years your senior," Russell replied with a large smile.

"Surprise would be an understatement."

"I'm sure you have many questions, Mr. Chastain, so I'll come right to the point. Sorry for the cryptic introduction, but we felt that it was the best way to get your attention and show you the urgency of events on the near horizon. We're staying abreast of far too many complicated dynamics to take the time to convince you to allow us an appointment through normal business channels. Your time is valuable, and people of your level and stature always have gatekeepers to protect that valuable time. And when you hear what we have to share with you, I'm sure you'll agree that there is no time to waste."

"You definitely got my attention. I'd like to spend some time with your tech people and talk about some form of mutually beneficial collaboration. I didn't think it was possible to breach our security the way you did. If you went to that much trouble, you must know a good bit about my companies and me, so you'd know that my interest would be more than just piqued. I'm hoping you weren't involved in the demise of the dead guy in the video feed you sent me." Graham had an epiphany of trepidation as the words left his mouth.

Russell furrowed his brow. "Not at all. Mr. McGowan came to our attention some time back. Partly by accident and partly through tenacity, he uncovered information that proved to be incompatible with his health. We knew his life would be in danger, but we also knew that his obsession with his next big story wouldn't allow him to back off." Russell spoke with a weight of sadness in his voice. "We even tried to warn him off anonymously, but instead that warning strengthened his resolve. Before we could implement a plan to scare him off, darker forces decided his suicide would be the most expedient way to reduce their risk of exposure. We were able to send you our own video feed because we had him under surveillance."

"I'm glad to know you're opposed to such actions, Mr. Russell," Graham said, his relief obvious.

"Last resort, not first," Russell said in a very believable tone, causing Graham to scowl. "Come, come now, Mr. Chastain. We know for a fact that you've been involved in your share of wet ops."

"That was war," he shot back. "A much different scenario."

"Yes, it's always *different*, isn't it? Blurred lines. I assure you this is a bigger war than the staged and contrived one you were in."

Graham shoved his chair back and stood. "I didn't come here to de—"

"Good!" Russell interrupted, smiling a little now and relaxing his grip on his wheelchair. "We can have many lively debates in the future about history, geopolitics and how wars actually get started, why and by whom. But right now I really need to move us to the topic at hand."

"Why I'm here, who killed McGowan and why," Graham said, relieved at the redirection. He pulled his chair closer and sat again.

Russell clapped his hands as they pointed at Graham. "Spot on, Mr. Chastain. They are all intertwined, like Churchill's enigma. I hope you don't have someplace to be for a while. This will take some time to explain. And I assure you that you won't look at the world the same anymore *and* you'll thank us for warning you and bringing you here."

Russell sat back, his face showing a modicum of satisfaction.

Out of nowhere, a hand holding a bottle of water appeared over Graham's left shoulder. He flinched because he'd felt a presence but hadn't heard anyone approach. He quickly recovered and snatched the bottle out of the air before it landed on his lap. By the time he turned, Thomas was already gone—like a ghost.

Russell was grinning when Graham turned back to look at him incredulously.

"Man, that guy is good! And more than a little unsettling," he said.

Russell chuckled. "Think nothing of it, Mr. Chastain. Thomas is indeed *very* good. It's a test as well. We're Rangers; you're Navy and also well trained. He likes to stay sharp and show off his prowess. I doubt he has few equals in any branch, anywhere."

"You seem pretty sure of yourself, but then you *were* a Ranger."

"Don't scoff, Mr. Chastain. It isn't becoming. Thomas is more than just a Ranger and I was also one of his more advanced instructors," Russell said with an expression of satisfaction.

"You? But . . ."

"Don't look so surprised. It was some time ago. And I'm pretty sure that Coach Wooden couldn't block a shot by Bill Walton nor could Coach Walsh sack Joe Montana. That didn't keep them from being great teachers. But *you* digress. I need to bring you up to speed pretty quickly, and I can fill in the gaps later. This web of intrigue that you've been thrown into originated many centuries ago. And some would say many millennia ago. It's as epic and legendary in its history as it is overwhelming and deadly in the world of today. We're on a precipice and at the same time, a crossroad. I first became aware of the *true* picture of how the world functions as a young lieutenant arriving in Southern France just a few months after D-Day."

Graham's mind loitered on Russell's last claim for a moment before he tilted his head upward. "But that would make you . . ."

"An old man. A very old man indeed," he answered Graham, tightening his lips. With that, Russell motioned across the room with his forefinger and thumb, coercing Graham's attention to what was proudly enshrined on the wall.

"I assure you that the dashing young officer in those pictures is me, Mr. Chastain," Russell said with feigned reverence.

Graham stared for some time before commenting. He looked at the array of photographs and back at Russell several times. Russell too was focused on the wall—undoubtedly reminiscing. His smooth skin, bright eyes and full head of white hair gave the strong appearance of a man much younger than Russell had to be. He had what might have been the remnants of a scar or two and maybe his nose had been broken and neatly repaired. But his skin didn't sag, there were no deep lines on his face and he was nearly devoid of age spots. His piercing blue eyes could have been those of a forty-year-old. Graham was trying to come to grips with the math and the man who sat before him when he broke the silence. His age seemed impossible, but it would make no sense to make up such a story. And everything on the wall looked authentic.

"Those are some pretty impressive medals, though I don't recognize all of them." Graham gestured at the wooden and glass-faced boxes displayed next to the old black and white photos.

"Dashing and *courageous*," Russell said with a shallow laugh. "But no more so than you, as I understand it, Mr. Chastain."

Graham let the compliment pass. His time in combat was a topic he rarely felt comfortable discussing. "I see you wore the oak leaf clusters of a major," he noted.

"I made full-bird colonel, but it was after those pictures were taken. The reason for my rapid promotions is a story in itself," Russell said. "What happened to me in France promoted me, ran me quickly through the OSS school and through a long, fascinating career in the company that grew out of the OSS. What I became involved in goes back over one thousand years."

Graham had started to raise the bottle up to his mouth, but abruptly stopped. "You can't be serious."

"Quite. But before I get into that, I need to tell you about the secret mission I was flung into near Normandy and how I became deeply involved in some rather ancient mysteries."

"What does that have to do with the dead guy and me?"

"Everything. He found out a very small part of what I'm going to tell you, and certain people didn't want you to have that information." Russell let that sink in. "I'm sure you'll need more than one bottle of water for this saga."

"And something to dilute it with," said Graham.

TWENTY-NINE

Von Kleis studied the black and white eight-by-ten photos spread out on his desk as Roth hovered over his shoulder. He didn't like anyone behind him, let alone that close to his personal space, and Roth knew it. It was a game he enjoyed, annoying von Kleis ever so subtly. A neurotic tug of war that simmered below the surface. Roth knew better than to push too far, but he enjoyed seeing how far he could massage the envelope with von Kleis maintaining his near-flawless composure.

"Yes, these should do nicely. Very nicely. Excellent," von Kleis said, studying every detail of the photos that had been taken with a telephoto lens at night.

"I still think setting this up so early in the game risked arousing suspicion," Roth said.

Von Kleis barely pursed his lips, but he loathed being questioned on matters of strategy or tactics—especially considering his vastly superior intellect, training and track record when compared to Roth. Normally he might not even reply, but he thought maybe this could be a teaching moment, even for a man as insufferable as Roth.

"Actually, to make this move so early in the game causes less suspicion, not more. Since we just began our negotiations, it's unlikely he would suspect we had time to be up to anything, even if the plan were to go totally awry. It isn't likely we'd be suspected, and we could easily feign ignorance and question what possible motive we could have." Von Kleis deliberately sighed.

"I'm not sure it was necessary," Roth said, pushing, as always.

"Insurance. Which may prove necessary as we delve deeper into the plan."

Caroline Rhea looked stunning as she stood with her arms folded on the weathered wood railing of the dock. But then, she was stunning from any angle, position or perspective. Her long, dark hair was coaxed into swaying by the breeze in much the same way her thin cotton skirt moved, just teasing the lean muscles of her firm, long legs. The light was dim and originated two poles down.

She assumed the spot was chosen for its seclusion and low light. Most women might be afraid to wait solo in such a place, but Caroline had spent time in far worse places in her youth. And she was nothing like defenseless. Her appearance was that of an elegant woman, but she'd had self-defense training, and she liked to have an edge or three. She knew that seeming to be helpless gave her the advantage of lethal surprise. No one could see that she carried a Ruger LC9s in a garter holster strapped to her well-toned thigh. The Ruger's thin, smooth profile was perfect for her size, and the 9mm hollow points gave her plenty of punch at close range. For threats of a different type, she also carried an Ultratech auto-knife. It had saved her from more than one beating from an over exuberant john and, besides, she liked the turquoise color. A field-goal attempt on the genitalia of a dock dreg would give her plenty of time to retrieve either weapon.

Avalon watched Caroline for quite some time from the deep shadows of a dilapidated and weather-worn building. There was no rush, so he lingered in the folds of the night. He often made his contacts wait. Waiting had the intended effect of making them frustrated, edgy or even annoyed. And that gave him yet one more advantage—not that he needed any. Avalon enjoyed the game in all of its facets. He couldn't help but admire her beauty and her figure. He'd known many women just as fine, most of whom weren't for rent at any price. And in this case, she was merely that—a rental. She had served her purpose on more than one occasion and might serve it one last time under his employ. He blinked his mind back into focus and honed his thoughts to the reason for this encounter before stepping out of the shadows.

As Caroline stared at the water, letting her mind wander back to her very few better days, Avalon appeared at her side, causing her to jump and release a gasp of fright.

"You know, slithering up on people is creepy!" she said, throwing a hand to her chest, trying to catch her breath.

Avalon smirked. "That's what the shrink said in one my reform school sessions."

"You really enjoy being spooky and giving people heart attacks. You're still sick, so I guess you didn't take his advice," Caroline said, her voice now composed. She moved slightly back from Avalon. Everything about him made her tense and uneasy. He never asked for a sample—and that was even more reason to wonder about him, wonder if he had a pulse.

"He was a small thinker with a limited imagination," Avalon continued with an empty smile. "He wanted me to stop sacrificing animals to pagan gods."

"Did you sneak up on them too, or charm them with your

scintillating personality? Or maybe they were farm animals—"

"Of course the shrink didn't last long. He had an accident." Avalon continued with blithe indifference.

Caroline began to scowl at Avalon but then decided on another approach. Her scowl dissolved into a warm smile, and her eyes magically brightened to match her perfect white teeth. She raised her hand to run her fingers through her flowing hair, using the motion to elevate her breasts and expose even more of what was barely hidden beneath her very low neckline. She wet her lips seductively and stared into Avalon's hollow eyes like he was her long-lost and passionate lover.

"Enough sparring, baby. What do you have for me, Mr. Smith?" She nearly moaned.

"What? No hug, no kiss, just unwarranted animosity. Where's the love?" Avalon continued to toy with her, seeing if he could get her to morph from seductress to annoyed call girl.

Caroline wasted no time in getting indignant. "The love? The only thing I love is how much you pay me. That bulge in your pocket had better be my roll of money. And I don't care if you're glad to see me."

"I'm bruised!" Avalon continued to chide her.

"*That*, I can do, Mr. Smith! And what kind of stupid alias is that anyway?"

"My dear departed mother wouldn't appreciate you deriding the family name," he said, narrowing his eyes.

"I don't believe you *had* a mother." She cackled. "I think you're cloned. GMO. Part spider, part snake and part Stalin."

Avalon was enjoying manipulating someone who usually was the master manipulator. He didn't respond. He just stared through her, forcing her to be the next to break the silence. The insult meant less than nothing to him.

Caroline became visibly impatient, shifting from one foot to the other. "I have things to do, Mr. Smith."

"More accurately, *people* to do, I should imagine," Avalon said without a glimmer of emotion.

"I've always done exactly what you've asked," she said tersely.

"You've done good work and been paid well. Maybe overpaid," he said, prodding her.

Caroline crossed her arms and dropped one foot back—a posture of defiance. She was used to getting her way, especially with men. And she had no sense of humor when it came to collecting her fee.

"*Under*paid for the insane things you've had me do! Now give me my money right now," Caroline pleaded. "I need it."

Avalon pivoted to the right to give Caroline a side profile as he wagged a finger, chastising her.

"Now, that's no way to be. Don't tell me you've already spent the advance I gave you. I've always paid you, and I have your money right here."

Avalon reached behind his back with his right hand as he spoke. But rather than produce the envelope she hoped for, he snapped open an OTF knife similar to hers. His cost twice as much, was larger and had a dull black finish—and Avalon was far more skilled with his weapon. Caroline's defiant expression didn't have time to change to one of terror, fear or horror. He struck twice before she could utter even the slightest sound.

Avalon was already moving into her, and he spun her around so that her torso would hang over the rail like an unfortunate soul expelling the results of too many drinks. He flicked his knife closed and glanced quickly around the area he'd been taking in with his peripheral vision. He then went to work to be sure her body would enter the water silently and find its way to a shallow resting place. A temporary one. Where she was guaranteed to soon be found.

THIRTY

Graham was still trying to come to grips with Russell's apparent age and how he looked so well preserved. Of course, he'd seen some people in their nineties who were in great shape, but Russell was amazing. He was still pondering the possibilities when Russell broke the silence.

"Before we go forward, Mr. Chastain, there are revelations I'm going to share with you and information you will see that has been kept secret for many decades. I must have your word that you won't tell a soul what I'm going to share with you."

"But I don't even know what any of this is about," he began.

Russell slammed his desk with both palms and yelled, "Swear it! Men and women have died protecting what I'll be telling you, many of them my own close friends."

"Fine! Okay! I swear. I don't want you to have an aneurysm. You may recall that I have a background in secrets, so I get it." Graham extended his arms, his open palms fending off further verbal assaults from Russell.

"I sit in this wheelchair due to an assassin's near miss, Mr. Chastain. This is deadly serious business."

"I have no desire to become a target, Mr. Russell," Graham said firmly.

"And I'm here to assure you that you may already be one and that our help and support in watching both your back *and* your front may be your only safety net. We tried to warn McGowan, and he wouldn't listen. I can't make promises, but I can tell you our help is more valuable than you can imagine."

Russell was leaning forward on his right elbow by the time he finished speaking.

Graham pictured McGowan's slumped body and the bloody hole in his head that he didn't want for himself. "I'd appreciate it if you could prevent such an occurrence, of course."

Russell nodded. "We don't have time to vet everyone you know, so you can't tell *anyone* without clearing it with us. That means your wife, your best friend, your best friend's wife and anyone else. You could have been compromised or infiltrated long before we discovered that you were a person of interest."

"That's just it, why me? My company has some very innovative projects in operation and on the drawing boards, but nothing magical or earthshattering. Do you need me to sign an NDA or noncompete or something?" Graham asked.

"No, Mr. Chastain, there are no documents for you to sign. We know very well that you're a man of great integrity and a man bound by honor and your word. We know you've walked away from potentially lucrative contracts because they overstepped your ethical boundaries. And we also know you aren't taken in by the haggard rebuttal that you should do something unethical because someone else will do it anyway. A piece of paper wouldn't matter in this case. I wasn't being melodramatic, but I am emphatic that you must not discuss what I reveal to you with anyone. It could mean your life as well as ours."

Graham noticeably stiffened his back in his chair. He could

read men very well; it was an innate skill that he'd honed over the years. And the medals of valor that Russell had earned weren't bestowed just for serving or having a well-pressed uniform. There was steel in Russell's demeanor. And resolve. Graham could see and feel both.

"I still don't understand what role I play and why I may be a target," he said.

"We don't have all the answers, but we have suspicions. We were able to sneak past your firewalls, which took some doing. But we didn't attempt to come near your real systems and we doubt anyone else can either. *For now*, that is. It doesn't mean they won't try. That capability alone is something people would kill for. But we think your role in all of this must run deeper and has to do with where the ancient past meets the rapidly approaching future. It's about what the darkest forces live for— greed and power. But even those who have mountains of both don't have what they really want, which is longevity."

Russell tapped his fingers together and stared at Graham, not allowing him to look away. Graham felt he shouldn't even blink.

"What if the ancient quests for the Fountain of Youth and the Philosopher's Stone are tied to the modern quest for singularity?" Russell asked.

"But . . ." Graham didn't know what to say. Singularity, he got. The Fountain of Youth? Not so much. "I'm not involved in that kind of research. Not in my software projects or even my biotech acquisitions," he said, shaking his head.

"This puzzle is vast and ancient, young man. And I can guarantee you that it runs to heights of power that you aren't even aware exist. We have some of the pieces and knowledge that others have, but that doesn't mean others don't have more pieces than we do. You may hold a key or keys that you don't even know about, or be a means to an end in their plans, a way to remove some unknown impediment. Or possibly your company is just something that will continue to become so lucrative in the future that they want to engulf it. Make no mistake when I tell you that the Octopus is everywhere—but that's another story. First you need to know how I got into this. That explanation will make it clear to you how our paths crossing was no coincidence."

"D-Day," Graham said, going back to the previous topic.

"My experience was odd almost from the moment I came ashore," Russell began. "The fighting was well into France by the time my company arrived. We were just beginning to get situated when a courier came to my captain and handed him some papers. Captain Summers called me over to him, where I promptly snapped to attention. At which time the kind sergeant reminded me most eloquently never to salute in an open combat zone. Captain Summers handed me the orders in his hand and told me to go with the sergeant. Wanting to remain with the men I had trained with, I asked him what it was all about, but he pretty emphatically told me that neither a captain nor a shavetail were there to question the orders of a full-bird colonel.

"The sergeant and I traveled through many checkpoints and deeper into France. The sergeant's papers took us through without a hitch, and in some cases we were just waved through and waved at. The sergeant had little to say except to tell me I'd get used to it when we got closer to the noise of our one-oh-fives and one fifty-fives and the more distant sounds of the German eighty-eights, and to say that the colonel would explain everything. When we finally arrived at a well-defended battalion command post, the sergeant merely said, 'On me, sir,' and led me to a large stone house that looked to be a command center."

Russell paused to drink some water, and Graham did the

same. Russell began again almost immediately.

"Unlike me, everyone I saw was obviously a battle-hardened veteran. Except for the numerous perimeter troops, nearly everyone near the building was an NCO. Several of the men still wore bandages discolored by blood. I noticed that I was mingling with a mix of regular Airborne, Rangers and Pathfinders—all tough and all strak and no nonsense. I was among the elites, and I could feel it. Even though I had at first wanted to be with my own men, it was apparent that I had been thrown in with the best of the best for a reason unknown to me.

"We entered the stone house. As we passed a guard at each doorway, they snapped to attention. We finally went through a door opened by another sergeant and entered a large room that was most likely once a dining area. Several officers leaned over a large map, one or two of them pointing at different positions while comments were exchanged. As I approached with my escort, I quickly noticed that the walls were lined with supplies ranging from military to delicacy, including more than a few bottles of cognac and brandy. It seemed odd to see them juxtapositioned next to wooden crates labeled Grenade, Hand, Fragmentation MkII."

Graham thought of his own past combat operations and couldn't think of a single time where luxury items were stored with hand grenades or any other ordnance.

Russell paused to rub both eyes before continuing. "An officer named Blair, who seemed too young to be wearing the eagle insignias of a colonel, looked up at me with piercing eyes and asked if I was Russell. I snapped to attention and said that I had just come from the beach and was reporting as ordered. He said that he knew of my family and that he had my 201 file pulled and requested me to replace his adjutant who had been killed. I told him I didn't understand what he meant by my family. He asked if I went to Yale, I told him yes and he jerked his head to signal me closer to the table. Pay attention, listen and learn, he said. In other words, don't speak. I thought my being there must be a SNAFU, but the surroundings looked far better than what the Front must have been like, so I shut up and paid attention. I saw no need to tell him that I had left Yale early to enlist and that I didn't think my family was especially significant, all things considered. And it occurred to me that being involved with elite troops who kept a surplus of brandy and cognac could potentially be a more interesting way to fight than from a foxhole."

Graham nodded. Comfort trumps hardship—then and now.

"From what I could gather—coming in late in the game as I did—we were about to embark on a highly classified mission through enemy lines. They saw no problem going behind enemy lines, but I had never seen combat and didn't even get to jump out of a plane to get there. But these men were sharp. They carried themselves with complete confidence. They expected me to be there, so I decided at that moment that I was going to act like I belonged. When they agreed on the route and plan, we loaded up our personal gear and got into the vehicles that formed our small convoy. We had three jeeps and a truck commonly known as a deuce and a half. All the vehicles were clearly marked with red crosses to show we were a medical unit. There were officers and no enlisted men below the rank of sergeant. The enlisted men carried Thompsons and the officers carried M2s." Russell cleared his throat. "And so my journey into a whole new world began," he said.

Graham listened intently as Russell went into great detail about all that he saw, including the maps, terrain, buildings, supplies and men—even down to their uniforms. He was able to recall a vast amount of detailed information, which was impressive, given his age. The vibrancy with which he spoke made it seem that he was telling a tale from last week. Graham relished the secret history lesson as much as Russell enjoyed conveying it. Graham leaned forward, eager to hear more of what he knew had to be an amazing saga.

He was deciding on which questions to ask when a cocktail glass appeared at his shoulder, courtesy of Thomas, the resident phantom. The aroma said fine scotch. A second appearance of his preferred drink made him wonder if *everyone* knew his preferences. It wasn't terribly difficult to find out that information, but he was already outlining search tasks in his mind for Ariel to implement regarding his two hosts and their operation. He had too much at stake and he planned to sharpen his already heightened security.

Russell smiled, enjoying the ongoing pas de deux between Thomas and Graham.

"Needless to say, I was completely on edge as we raced through the French countryside behind enemy lines. The other men were veterans and carried themselves as well-honed professionals. The ones I rode with kept their heads and eyes in constant motion, hawk-like, but they showed absolutely no anxiety or fear. It was just another day in a war zone to them. I watched them closely, wanting to soak up the knowledge that came from their keen awareness as quickly as I could, but no amount of time or training could have prepared me for what was ahead."

THIRTY-ONE

Camarata and Sandoval strode past the receptionist in the medical examiner's offices, holding up their government IDs as they did so and not pausing for approval. They walked down the halls looking in the windows of several exam rooms before Camarata nodded toward the one closest to him. They walked through the door to find their favorite forensic pathologist, Chrys Devareaux, sitting at a desk with a terminal, entering information. She turned to watch the two walk in. She grimaced and went back to her work without greeting the Homeland agents.

She wore teal scrubs and sneakers with a stripe that matched her scrubs. She was an exotic-looking Cajun woman that Sandoval had a crush on. Her dark hair with its red highlights was pulled up on her head and held in place with a pen, spilling over unevenly. Even though her eyesight was near twenty-twenty, she wore a pair of stylish, over-size glasses, mostly to minimize eye fatigue from computer glare. Sandoval wanted to take off her glasses and pull out the pen to watch her hair fall loose. Though he had no interest himself, Camarata pretended to flirt with Devareaux just to unnerve Sandoval. He enjoyed putting both of them on edge.

"So, doc, when can I take you away from this dead-end job?" Camarata asked.

"Said the head troll on Loser Lane at the far end of the wrong side of the tracks," Chrys said.

"Ah, you rehearsed that one. Are you sure? We'd make quite a pair." Camarata felt Sandoval bristle from five feet away.

"A legion of demons would be chipping away at a massive glacier in hell. And speaking of a pair, it's my medical professional judgment that I doubt you have a pair."

"So diener is out of the question, then?" Camarata couldn't keep himself from laughing.

"Old and still not funny," Chrys shot back at Camarata.

Sandoval smirked, enjoying his partner's smackdown. "Thanks for the text. We need to follow up on the alleged suicide." He was hoping that by being professional, and given Camarata's banter as a comparison, she would warm to him a little.

"Just doing what I'm told," she said with a sigh. "I got a call from on high about this one. Why, I don't know. And I was dismayed to hear that I'd be discussing my findings with Heckle and Jeckle."

She picked up the notes that she'd already printed and attached to a clipboard, and crossed to the table where she'd done the postmortem on McGowan. Another body, male, lay on a second exam table nearby.

"So did you find anything that seemed suspicious?" Sandoval asked, staring at the Y-incision. "I'd rather hear what you have to say first so we don't skew your findings with our thoughts."

"As far as being suspicious, I'd normally suspect Jeckle here," Chrys said. "But the aim was too good, unless you'd been aiming at his chest or knee, that is."

"I thought I was Heckle," Camarata said, starting back in on Chrys.

"No, you're definitely Jeckle. I'm Heckle. The doc here is an expert. Better not to challenge her," Sandoval concluded.

"If I could move along . . . I have real work that doesn't involve explaining what you should just read in an email," Chrys said impatiently.

"Formaldehyde getting to you, doc?" Camarata said.

"Blocks your by-the-quart cologne. The decedent was killed by a single round that created a wound consistent in size to that of a .38 caliber projectile. The wound and powder burn residue were consistent with a gun barrel at close range. The round entered his right sphenoid bone and exited at an approximate fifteen degree upward angle and near zero degrees laterally." She scanned her notes. "This is consistent with the fact that the decedent was right-handed."

"Are you certain?" Camarata asked.

"Are you old and slow? Never mind, rhetorical question. If I may be permitted to continue?" She pointed at the body. "He has greater musculature on his right arm, an indentation on his second finger consistent with pressure from writing. He also has powder burns on his right hand, but that in and of itself doesn't prove anything," she added.

"Anything else significant?" Sandoval asked in his serious and professional voice.

"He had early cirrhosis of the liver, as you can see by the texture and small nodules. He also had ascites in his abdomen, which can be explained by cirrhosis. But the condition of his liver isn't surprising based on what else I was able to determine from the toxicology report. He was a fair amount over the legal limit for alcohol, and on top of that he had a great deal of oxycodone in his system." She spoke with clinical certainty.

"I guess you know that a nearly empty fifth and a pill bottle with just a few pills left in it were found next to our friend here with nothing on his mind," Camarata said.

"Yes, and the lab results showed the pills *were* oxy," Chrys said. "But there's more to consider than just the alcohol and drugs."

"Sounds consistent," Sandoval replied. He shrugged. "So what was unique?"

"He must have popped a good handful of pills and then chugged a whole bottle of booze pretty quickly."

"How do you know?"

"Opiates and alcohol amplify the individual effects of each. They have a synergistic effect, which can increase intoxication in very strong and often unpredictable ways. And he'd consumed a great deal of both. So he had to have taken both pretty quickly."

"Why?" This time Camarata was asking.

Chrys looked up from her notes. "Because if he had just sat around drinking at a normal pace and popping pills, feeling sorry for himself and planning suicide, then I doubt he could have. Killed himself, that is." She took in the blank expressions of the two agents. "He would have fallen over and not have been able to hold a gun or even find his head to hit if all of this had taken effect over time," she said pointedly. "He also might have OD'd and saved himself the trouble of pulling the trigger if he had taken it slower."

Camarata and Sandoval, now deep in thought, exchanged a glance as they took in what Chrys said as she moved around to the next table. She didn't wait for them to get close.

"We did this exam a couple of days ago, so I had to pull him out of the cooler. This one is pretty standard. I'm not sure what your interest would be in either guy, actually. And I have no desire to know. This guy didn't have any major illnesses that I could see upon examination, just obesity, probably from diet and lack of exercise. He had *some* alcohol in his system, but not enough to be intoxicated. He had a chest wound consistent with a twenty-two and probably fired from six to eight feet away. As you already know, he also had a wound at the base of his skull— also from a twenty-two and at point-blank range. Nothing terribly out of the ordinary," she said, flipping through her printed notes again.

"I'm pretty sure the dead guy thought it was exceptionally out of the ordinary," Camarata said.

"Did you say not *terribly* out of the ordinary for a particular reason, Chrys?" Sandoval asked.

"You win the prize. The first shot went right through his heart and embedded in his spine. He had to be dead by the time his head hit the table. So why walk around behind him and shoot him in the back of the head when it had to be clear he was dead already?"

"Well, one case sounds about closed, and the second will keep someone out of the unemployment line," Camarata said. Then, hand over his heart, he added, "I'm sure the local detectives will turn something up while we ponder matters crucial to keeping you and our nation safe."

"Your dedication is underwhelming," Chrys said, moving back to the desk on the other side of the room. "I can envision better sleep at night already, knowing you're out there somewhere. Elsewhere."

"Yeah, that's what Sandy's very temporary girlfriends say all the time," Camarata said as he headed out the door.

"I don't have a . . . Not one or . . . Oh, never mind," said

Sandoval as he followed Camarata.

If he had stayed and paid attention, he would have noticed that Chrys was looking after him and smiling. But her smile was short-lived as she began to wonder why her regional director was interested enough to call to be sure she went over the exams personally with Camarata and Sandoval and not simply email the results.

But hers was not to reason why. However, she might reason that she wished Sandoval would show up without his annoying partner if he had to come by.

THIRTY-TWO

The very elderly James Russell paused in his storytelling from time to time. Not because he was addled or absent-minded or ever at a loss for words. No, it was that he was reliving great days from his past and relishing the moments. Graham doubted that Russell had told his story to many people and imagined that doing so was like unleashing memories, releasing secrets from the very depths of the man, secrets that he'd longed to share for decades. And if the revelations were as monumental as Russell claimed, then he surely had to share the information before it was too late. Russell sipped tea from the cup on his desk, poured from the sterling silver teapot that Thomas had left for him without nearly as much stealth as he'd shown in serving Graham.

"After the colonel flashed his paperwork at the last American checkpoint, we flew toward the enemy lines. The sergeant at the checkpoint probably wondered if Colonel Blair had lost his mind, but he knew better than to question his decision. We raced on at a pretty good clip, with the first jeep about a half a mile out front."

"Five or six miles can mean life or death even in swift surgical strikes," Graham agreed. "We had technology far more advanced than yours, and even then you can have a fireball erupt out of nowhere in seconds."

Russell nodded. "Since our truck was mostly empty, I figured we had to grab something and bring it back before one side or the other blew it up, otherwise we'd just wait on our own troops to pull forward. We seemed to have a clear path, but the artillery was getting closer. We soon arrived at an abandoned hamlet. Our lead driver knew exactly where to go. I didn't find out until much later that the guys in my group would be the equivalent of a modern-day Delta team, able to sneak in and out unseen and leaving little to chance."

"We had Delta guys attached to our SEAL group on occasion," Graham said. "Top of the line. There was a great deal of mutual respect. And seeing both groups in action when the lead is flying is something to behold—if you get to see them at all."

"We approached a large stone monastery surrounded by solid stone walls. The lead jeep pulled off to the side, and everyone but the driver leaped out like gymnasts before the jeep stopped. They and the driver disappeared to create a hidden perimeter. I was in the trailing jeep, and we peeled off to cover the other side of the monastery wall."

Russell smiled. "Need I point out that *I* did not somersault or vault out of the jeep? The sergeant in our jeep motioned for me to follow him, and we set up on a rise about ten feet away."

"So you had arrived at Saint Germaine?" Graham asked.

"Yes, although there were no signs of any kind. But it was the name of the village, the monastery and the code name for the mission. I didn't know any of that at the time or that I had been assigned to a highly classified division of the OSS. Then things went from different to beyond belief. The colonel's driver eased the jeep through the main gates and into the courtyard, where all the men got out.

"The colonel and his companions were relaxed yet alert as they faced the double wooden doors of the monastery, which stood wide open. From the shadows beyond the doorway, out walked a Wehrmacht officer with his hand held up in greeting. He was followed by three more German soldiers, carrying Schmeisser submachine guns. As soon as I saw the Germans, I jumped into combat mode, raising my carbine. The master sergeant next to me grabbed my forearm to prevent me from lifting it to my shoulder. With his other hand, he held up his index finger to signal me to silence. He said, 'Sorry, sir, I thought you'd been briefed.' He explained that the German Herr Oberst—"

"*Colonel*," Graham interrupted.

"That's right. I read that you grew up traveling Europe with your family in much the same way I did. I think we share an affinity for languages, and the fact that I spoke several opened the doors I'm about to share with you. But I'm getting ahead of my story," Russell said.

"Go on. This is getting really interesting."

"It only gets better," he said, waving both hands. "You have no idea. The oberst saluted in normal fashion, with a hand to the temple rather than a Nazi salute, and our colonel returned it crisply. Then all the men shook hands like it was a friendly business meeting. The sergeant told me that both men were from the aristocracy and that their families had known each other for over a century. Most of his sentences started out with *as you know*, but of course I didn't have any idea what he was talking about. But he assumed I was part of their organization.

The sergeant said he was honored to be of service to the Order and went into detail about *our* cause being far more important than individual countries and insignificant wars. I nodded as if I had a clue what he meant and wondered what could be more important than the second *war to end all wars*. So a wave of curiosity began to swell in me, and I wondered what could be of such importance."

"Like the curiosity you're building in me," Graham said, nodding at Russell.

"Quite!" Russell laughed. "Except I'm going to fill in amazing parts of the puzzle for you in short order, details that took me years to figure out. The colonel signaled our driver to back the deuce and a half close to the doorway. Germans and Americans—working side by side—loaded the truck full of small and medium-size wooden crates while the rest of us guarded the perimeter. The sergeant was talkative. I assumed he wanted to curry favor with someone he perceived to be higher up in the Order, whatever it was. Mostly I pretended to already know as I nodded and subtly coaxed information out of him. What he shared was a lot to take in, yet it vaguely reminded me of some of the stories I'd heard during family travels and from my uncles. There'd been a major falling out in my family that my father would never talk about, so I began to wonder if my being there might not have been an Army screw-up after all.

"At the time I wondered how we could communicate secretly with the Germans during the height of the war to arrange such a meeting. It wasn't until many years later that I learned that such a practice wasn't a big deal and it was actually done far more often than most people knew or would ever know. There aren't any generals from that period alive today, but if you had talked to one twenty years ago, he'd say my story never happened and we only communicated with Germany through official diplomatic channels. And that was because those generals didn't have a need to know. But on occasion, even sergeants made such contacts. And that's not to say there weren't generals in the know—just very few."

"I'm sure it's not much different today," Graham admitted. "Even with my top secret clearance, I've always wondered what the true 'powers that be' actually have been privy to."

"Exactly," Russell exclaimed. "And you're going to discover the knowledge and secrets run far deeper than you've ever imagined. Some of what you've heard in your career and dubbed 'conspiracy theory' is just that—and usually it's intentional disinfo to send the curious in the wrong direction, thinking they're uncovering something hidden. And that technique often works. But the truth is always *far* more mysterious and intriguing than anything they *think* they've uncovered."

Graham stared at Russell, captivated. He wondered what was hidden, what was truth and what was disinformation. He knew that he'd be spending many hours in the future remembering curiosities from his intel days. He stood.

"Excuse me a moment, if you would."

He stood and stretched his arms over his head, clenching his fists.

"I'm not losing interest, I assure you. I spend most of my workdays standing and moving, so I'm feeling a few kinks."

"Not at all," Russell said. He took a moment to flex his own arms and roll his shoulders. "I was so caught up, I hadn't realized we'd been still so long. My apologies."

When Graham sat again, Russell jumped right back in.

"The crates coming out of the monastery were being loaded into the truck. They bore markings that were quite unique, like nothing I'd ever seen. But other crates were being taken *out* of the truck. Those were marked as Red Cross supplies, and I asked the sergeant about them. He told me the top layers of all the boxes were covered with medical supplies and bandages, but underneath was American currency and gold bullion and materials necessary to create new identification papers. The exchange didn't make much sense to me at the time, but it became clear over time and with my later involvement in covert operations and my understanding of actions like Operation Paperclip.

"As the trucks were loaded, the colonels and a couple of the officers discussed a map on the hood of Colonel Blair's jeep while drinking schnapps and brandy. Colonel Blair then signaled for one of the sergeants on the perimeter opposite us to join the discussion. I assumed he was one of the Pathfinder types who had probed our approach some days earlier. I'm fluent in German and French and conversant in Italian and Spanish, so the discussion would have been no problem for me except I was only close enough to hear bits and pieces. Before they went their separate ways, the colonels lifted their flasks in a toast and I *was* able to hear them clearly say, in unison, '*Alles für den Auftrag.*'"

Russell's German was flawless.

"All for the Order," Graham translated.

"Correct. And with that, we headed out, but we were obviously taking a different and more circuitous route back. It was a well-calculated strategy, but ultimately the wrong one. We were less than two miles from St. Germaine when the lead jeep hit a mine. An instant later, our jeep, trailing the truck, was hit by what must have been a Panzerfaust. The explosion killed the driver and threw the rest of us out of the jeep in various states of injury."

Russell spoke with a surprising degree of calm.

"It was my first firefight, and I was scared out of my mind. Kowalski, the sergeant nearest me, was bleeding from several wounds, but he yelled for me to wake up and fire my weapon as he smacked me with the butt of his Thompson. Then he rose up, fired several bursts that took out some of our less friendly German intruders, but took a round in the head. That woke me up, and I flew into a rage. I fired my weapon with adrenaline bursting through my veins, furious with myself, thinking my delay might have cost Sergeant Kowalski his life. Then my elite training took over, and I began to shoot and move like I was born to it. When my ammo ran out, I fired his weapon and all of his ammo. I had no idea that I had several wounds of my own." Russell leaned forward, his hands gesturing, when he said, "I pulled my forty-five when all the other ammo was gone. A 'potato masher' took out the other sergeant near me. He took most of the blast, but some of the shrapnel got my leg. I didn't pay it much attention at the time. Apparently these guys hadn't gotten the memo that we were the good guys and they weren't there to drink schnapps."

His eyes were bright, his face animated, as he relived the firefight from long ago.

"Maybe they were desperate for medical supplies," Graham offered.

"I never got to exchange pleasantries and inquire," Russell said. "They seemed to have the odd idea that we wore the wrong uniforms and therefore we were at war. I lobbed a few grenades of my own from behind the cover of our overturned jeep and scoured the area for ammo. I saw that all three men from the truck were dead as I dashed to the side away from the enemy to change firing positions and move to better cover. I grabbed hold of a dead sergeant who was half-hanging out of the truck door and laid him on the ground. Next I snatched up all the mag pouches I could see and slammed one into the Thompson I'd brought with me. There were more sergeants, which meant more Thompsons than M2s and more firepower for me. The fire from whoever was left from the front two jeeps was slow and sporadic at best. I didn't have a good view of them, but I began making my way forward.

"I peeked over the hood of the truck and saw bad news—more Germans advancing on our position than I could handle. One of them spotted me and fired a round from his Mauser that whistled over my head. I fired back with my forty-five over the top of the hood to make them think that was all I had. Then I ran to the back of the truck and opened up on them with my Thompson. I dropped two or three of them before racing back toward the front of the truck. I *say* I raced, but by now it was rapid hobbling since the effects of the shrapnel in my leg and blood loss from other wounds were taking their toll. I fired short bursts and then saw our last sergeant fall from an enemy round. I was sure I was finished, but I had been so caught up in the firefight that I hadn't noticed one of our P-51s loitering above. The pilot must have spotted the red crosses on our jeeps and seen we were under attack. He made a near perfect strafing run and lit them up with his 50 cal before dropping two bombs way too close for my comfort." Russell grinned. "Not that I was complaining," he added with enthusiasm.

Throughout Russell's descriptions of the carnage, Graham flinched more than once remembering his own experiences of blood, shots fired in anger and his own close proximity to death on several occasions. Those scenes from the deep mists of his mind sometimes woke him in the middle of the night with memories far too real and far too intense. The memories had now morphed with Russell's vivid stories and punctured Graham's concentration.

"I slumped against the truck, sliding down until my backside hit the running board below the open door with a thud. Feeling and seeing several wounds all at once made me want to puke, though I was thrilled that I hadn't already wet myself. Just then a badly wounded German soldier staggered from behind the truck and struggled to raise his StG 44. He would have finished me off, because I couldn't bring my Thompson to bear nearly fast enough. But before he could raise his weapon high enough, a single shot rang out from the tree line, surprising me but not as much as the German who took a round in the chest. He stared at me in disbelief and then another round dropped him to the ground, dead as his boots."

Graham heard the relief in his voice. The events were apparently just as fresh to Russell now as they'd been three quarters of a century earlier.

"Our guys showed up?" Graham asked.

"No, we were too far from our lines. I looked up to see one of the most beautiful women I'd ever seen advancing skillfully in mid-crouch and wearing a skirt, blouse and beret."

"Partisan?"

"That was my first thought as well. Turned out to be an amazing farm girl whose father had taught her how to hunt and shoot in addition to farming. She crept around the front of the truck and checked out our perimeter. I heard two more shots from her rifle. She asked, in French, if I would live. My French was quite excellent, but I could barely speak, mostly because I was in shock over her looks. Then she asked with irritation if I were an idiot or if the *Boche* had shot off my tongue." Russell laughed. "I nodded and asked, in French, if all the Germans were dead. 'They are now,' she'd said."

Graham laughed with him. "My kind of woman," he said.

"Beautiful, tough and funny at the same time."

"She was all of that," Russell agreed. "All I could say was merci as I nodded toward the dead German. She shook her head and said, 'Americans, better late than never,' in heavily accented English. Then she searched the truck quickly and found one of the medic's bags and started to work on my wounds. I tried to tell her to check on the other men, but she snapped a finger at my lips and said, '*Silence!*' When I tried again, she was more abrupt, saying, '*Tais-toi!*' She was in charge of triage, and I had no say. Once she stopped the major part of my bleeding and I had water from my canteen, she let me look to the others. I already knew the men closest to me were dead. I found a dead first sergeant and captain lying nearly on top of Colonel Blair behind the other jeep that hadn't been blown up. Their weapons were empty; they'd given their lives trying to save the colonel. I was both proud to have fought with men so incredibly brave and experiencing typical survivor's remorse as I pulled the captain off the colonel. The colonel had multiple wounds, so I was shocked to see his eyes blink open and recognize me. I knelt down with a canteen, but he pushed it away. He grabbed my wrist and said, 'Protect the truck from all others. It must remain in no one else's hands but ours. Promise you will guard it with your life.' I nodded, and he looked at my wounds, smiled and nodded back at me."

Russell's voice had gone low. But when he looked at Graham and resumed speaking, it strengthened again. "He repeated what the colonels had said to each other back at the monastery—Alles für den Auftrag. But then he added, 'Ex chao ordo.' I nodded and said, 'Yes, Colonel, I understand. All for the Order.' He nodded again, fought to stay conscious, and whispered, 'I wish I had gotten to know you. The time was long overdue for your family to come back.' I asked him how I would know who to trust and who to deliver the crates to. He said, 'You'll know. It's better that no one get them than have them fall into the wrong hands. In my satchel and in the crates you will find—' He died mid-word. I knelt beside him in confused silence for a moment before I removed one of his dog tags, his personal effects and his satchel. I knew I had to get the truck to cover in a hurry—before anyone came looking or before I bled to death." He winked at Graham. "I've always attached a great deal of stock to fulfilling a promise.

"I moved quickly from man to man. I took all the contents of their pockets and one dog tag from each, leaving one behind. While I was doing that, the French woman quickly gathered every weapon from our small battlefield and tossed all but the extra Thompsons into the back of the truck. The Thompsons and their mags she put into the front. She insisted on driving, and I wasn't up for what I knew would be a futile argument. I asked if she knew a place where we could hide the truck, and she said her farm was just over the hill behind us.

"The opening in the woods to her farm was so overgrown and unused that I would have never noticed it along the little dirt road she took. Just inside the entrance path and past the first few trees, she put the truck in park, jumped out and pulled two huge leafy tree branches behind us, further camouflaging the entrance. She hopped back in and moved us forward. The barn and farm house had been built at the base of a hill, and the fields, meadows and buildings were completely surrounded by thick stands of trees.

She told me her name was Christiane and that her father had worked at the Swiss Embassy before he retired to the farm. Her parents were dead and her older brother had gone to fight in the

Resistance. After we ate, drank wine and I rested overnight, she helped me move the boxes to a well-hidden root cellar. We pulled the shelves aside, stacked all the boxes against a wall and pulled the shelves back; the stacks looked like a wooden wall behind shelves. With me wounded, there was no time to search through the crates. She hid the truck among a remote cluster of trees. She promised to watch over what I had left and gave me a ride toward our lines in a horse-drawn cart. I got out when I thought we were close enough to the American lines that I could make it on foot. I didn't want her to get too far from her farm, nor did I want to take the chance that she might be questioned or followed."

"How did you know you could trust her?" Graham asked, taking a sip from his drink.

"Normally I would say that I had no option *except* to trust her. But we developed a bond in just twenty-four hours that I still can't describe to this day. I gave her all the money from my comrades on the battlefield. She refused vehemently until I said, 'For us.' She met my eyes, held my gaze for a long time and nodded. I promised to return when I went on leave and I did. Eventually I married her, which I knew I wanted to do the moment I saw her. But I'm getting ahead of my story. As I hoofed it back to my lines, I began to feel clammy and weak and figured my wounds were somewhat more severe than I had originally thought. I was challenged by a sentry as I staggered back to our compound. I collapsed before I could fully identify myself. When I woke at the aid station, my life became even more bizarre."

THIRTY-THREE

Camarata drove and Sandoval scrolled through notes on his tablet and phone. Neither had said much since leaving Chrys Devareaux's office, but it wasn't uncommon for them to go from complete silence to long discussions about any number of topics and then back to silence.

"I think the coroner likes you," Camarata said, breaking the silence.

"Maybe. There's one thing I'm certain of, though," Sandoval said, still reading through his notes.

"What's that?"

"She *doesn't* like you," Sandoval said with a satisfied smirk. "What I don't understand is why the boss has us follow up on these leads. They're pure minutiae and a waste of our talents. Well . . . *my* talents anyway. At least *I* could be put to better use."

"I'm not sure what talents you're hallucinating about having, but there's more to these two cases than meets your badly squinted eyes."

"Such as?"

"For starters, no loan shark would risk a hit on someone as lowly as Mr. Radic." Camarata tapped the steering wheel. "He puts the small in small potatoes."

Not to be outdone, Sandoval said, "The scene was professionally sanitized, a chore also not done by loan sharks or trigger men. Radic just got out of lockup, and it's doubtful that he had time to run up a big betting tab to begin with. He was a master forger, so it's more likely that he was hit for something he did in that arena. I get all that. But I don't see how that has anything to do with Homeland or what we've been working on lately."

"That may be why they pay us the big bucks and we're not doing police work anymore," Camarata said. "Either we'll get more information from above or we're supposed to figure it out. It's early on, in either case. And speaking of either case, my well-toned gut tells me there's more to the suicide than meets the eye as well."

Sandoval nodded. "Way ahead of you on that one. The articles in his file folders were all old. Maybe that's normal. But what wasn't normal is that old files were on his desktop and tablet, but the newer files were wiped clean. The tech guys said someone used a cyber white-out program that was way too sophisticated for any reporter to have. Not only were all the files gone, but cookies, web searches and even registry data were scraped as clean as your plate."

"I think his phone records were as important as his missing computer files," Camarata said. "Apparently McGowan was ruffling some pretty powerful feathers, and those important birds may have decided to ruffle McGowan instead. The owner of the bar where he was the day of his alleged suicide said McGowan claimed to have found something big, far bigger than his previous one-hit wonder. He said McGowan was emphatic that he had the scoop of the century. And he said McGowan was excited, not depressed."

"I thought the scene was too tidy as well. But that still doesn't tell me how it relates to our overall scope of work, keeping everyone safe as you so ineloquently put it."

"Tomorrow we start interviewing some of the more interesting and powerful players that McGowan was reaching out to, so maybe we'll find out who had reason to knock him off in an elaborate fashion and we'll get a better understanding of why our fearless leaders put us onto these cases in the first place." Camarata sighed.

"Yeah. That's two big maybes. Thirsty?" Sandoval asked, looking at his watch.

"No, but I never get tired of watching you strike out and go down in flames. I'll even buy the first round." He laughed. "Is that chunky part-time girlfriend of yours going to show up and stalk you again?"

"She's an actress and she doesn't *stalk* me."

"Porn doesn't count as acting."

"It was an *art* film. How many times do I have to tell you?"

"Yeah, right. Let's see, it was called *Plus-Sized Vagina Diaries* or *Post-Menopausal Uterine Diaries*, right? Makes me immediately think of it as art for the *big* screen."

That actually got Sandoval laughing. "Having you as a partner has done nothing for me except increase my need for self-medication."

Camarata may have chuckled on the outside, but he was far more somber on the inside. He thoroughly relished busting Sandoval's chops, but Sandy had been an excellent detective and was a truly bright and intuitive agent. And it didn't take a rocket surgeon to wonder why they had been assigned cases like this, as his partner was doing. He didn't fully understand their assignment either, but the blemish in his past didn't allow him to question anything from the powers that be. His job was to keep an eye on where the cases were headed and report back.

And to make sure that Sandy didn't dig in the wrong direction.

THIRTY-FOUR

After Thomas had refilled Russell's tea decanter and brought Graham a fresh drink, Russell picked up his story where he had left off.

"I woke up looking at a nurse who was taking my pulse. 'He's awake now, Captain,' she called across the room. Then she gave me a slight and less than encouraging smile, adding to the captain, 'Go easy on the questions. He was touch and go for a while.'

"I recounted most of the story to the captain and told him a lot of it was foggy to me since I had passed out several times. I left out seeing Germans, what the colonel had told me and everything about Christiane. It was essentially an ambush, I'd said, and I just remembered being helped into a local's cart and being dropped off near our lines. The only thing the captain seemed concerned about was the contents of the truck. He asked if I would recognize them again, and I said that I was sure that I could. He told me to get some rest and that I would be well taken care of. Apparently to emphasize that, he said I was promoted to first lieutenant. The next day I woke up to find new bars for my rank and a presentation box with two medals, which was pretty quick and more than a little odd.

"I was in and out of consciousness for quite some time. Several days later, a major showed up to debrief me again, and I told the same story. He also said I would be well taken care of, and I got another promotion and more medals. I was just doing my duty, I'd said, and it was all for the Order. He had no response other than to look as if he thought I was still out of it. He apparently hadn't gotten the memo.

"After another week or so, a colonel arrived, and I went through the story again. He said the two jeeps that were hit had been found but not the third jeep or the truck. He said that the after-action reports were extremely impressive and that we had taken out an enemy force more than three times our size. The colonel went on to say that all of my comrades' bodies had been recovered and that I showed amazing bravery to jeopardize my life to collect the dog tags in hostile territory while gravely wounded and that my actions hadn't gone unnoticed. He too asked if I would recognize the crates, and I once again said that knew that I could. 'We take care of our own,' he said. 'We need to find those crates and you're just the man to organize and lead that detail. Heal up soon, son. This isn't your last promotion.' I quietly said it was all for the Order, and this time I got the Latin response. But I still wasn't going to disclose that I had the crates until I got to examine them—per Colonel Blair's insistence. Soon afterward, I was a major with more medals."

"Wow. I've heard of rapid battlefield promotion, but never anything *that* rapid," Graham said, incredulous.

"It's not unheard of. MacArthur graduated first in his class at West Point and was a combat veteran, highly decorated for bravery. By 1925 he was the youngest major general in the history of the US Army. Eisenhower graduated in the middle of his class, had no combat experience or decorations for valor at all and was still a major until 1941. In fact, he had served as a staff aide to MacArthur. But in just a few short years, they had the same rank of General of the Army."

Graham merely nodded, eager for Russell to get back to the more fascinating portion of the history lesson.

"The members of the Order wanted those boxes back and they felt I was their best hope. And I wanted to know more about them and about the contents of the boxes. I was technically assigned as part of G-2, but I was seconded to the OSS. When my wounds had healed enough, I did stints in their training programs. Eventually I rose in rank to lieutenant colonel and reported exclusively to a mysterious brigadier general. I was able to get the area around Christiane's farm made off limits, and I acquired an abandoned farm nearby as my initial base of operations to begin the hunt for the 'missing' crates.

"One of my best ideas was a plan to use front companies in major ports to look for the crates being slipped out of the country or the contents being sold on the black market. I received immediate approval and was given very broad authority with the orders I carried, and those orders allowed me to set up an extensive clandestine network that was both lucrative and dangerous. I was shot, stabbed and nearly blown up on several occasions. Over time I was able to acquire many antiquities and slowly pretend to return some of the contents of the boxes, usually as clever forgeries and some as originals, after I was able to make copies of the documents. In those days copying was done with microfilm—one of the tools I developed great expertise in using. In addition to my main focus, I was also able to develop an excellent intelligence network to benefit the Allied cause and that of the Order, which made me a key and trusted player for many decades. The general was thrilled with my results, to say the least."

Russell stopped to rub at his temples.

"So what was in the crates that was so important?" Graham asked.

Russell ignored Graham's impatient tone. "That will take more than one meeting to describe, I'm afraid. Broadly, I came to understand over many years of study and research that they contained some of the lost Templar treasure, much of their written history and plans for the future. Think of it as one of the most incredible yet unknown archives of all time. It was a treasure trove of information about some of the greatest exploits in history; a long quest for ultimate power and the bloody trails that accompany such quests." Russell watched Graham closely to read his reactions. "Very little happened in history the way you were taught in school or the way it's been presented through the media. And I don't just mean propaganda. Much of 'history' has been pure misinformation. In addition, there were many priceless objects and some artifacts that are still an enigma to this day."

Graham was crossing the room to eye one of the photos. He tapped on the glass.

"Is this general who I think it is?" he asked.

"He countersigned my orders from the brigadier that I reported to. That's why I said I had such broad authority," Russell said proudly. "Later my orders came from an even higher source."

"I read in an article that his car accident may not have been an accident."

"Correct. He was murdered. Just like Admiral Forrestal. Thus my earlier warning to you when you probably thought I was overreacting in describing the gravity of our meetings and your future safety." Russell gingerly lifted an old and plain wooden box from one of his desk drawers and set it in front of himself.

Graham had moved to another picture. "*Is this . . .*" He pivoted back to Russell, once again incredulous.

"Yes, Mr. Chastain." Russell sighed. "And one of the men you won't recognize in that picture was one of the greatest spymasters of all time, Sir William Stephenson—who is worth many stories by himself. But you were asking what was so important, so I thought I'd show you a very small but impressive sample."

Russell stretched out his arm, and Graham walked back to the desk.

"For the time being, hold this in your left hand," Russell said.

Russell placed a rolled-up metal scroll in Graham's hand. It had a dull-gold luster and looked to be about eight inches long.

As Graham stared at it, Russell said, "Have a seat and just hold it while we continue our discussion."

Graham returned to his chair and studied the scroll. "Is it gold?"

"Maybe," Russell said, smiling, his fingers laced together as he rested his hands on his desk top.

"It seems too light for gold . . ."

"Just focus on it, Mr. Chastain. What do you feel?"

Graham tried to place the sensation he felt, but it was unique. At one point the scroll seemed to feel cool against his skin and then it seemed to have warmed slightly. Then he thought he felt a miniscule and constant vibration, but he couldn't be certain. When he focused even more, he sensed a barely audible hum. But he wasn't really "hearing" it as much as the sound seemed to emanate from inside his head—at the very center. What he somehow recalled was the location of the pineal gland.

The more he focused on the golden scroll, the more his mind

raced with random thoughts. They fluctuated from deeply intellectual ideas he had contemplated to pleasant emotional memories. Then it seemed that he was no longer in the large office with Russell anymore. He wasn't floating as much as he was just somewhere else. And then he felt like he was in more than one place. Graham wondered how he could be in more than one place and then he wondered how many places he could be in at the same time. His mind began to entertain many thoughts and possibilities, but he wasn't flitting from thought to thought; he was thinking them at the same moment. He even thought about his wife and imagined he could feel her next to him.

Graham shifted calmly back to reality when he felt Thomas's hand on his shoulder. He regained his focus on the room. Thomas stood casually beside him, and Russell's eyes were closed where he sat relaxed behind his desk.

"My uncle would talk all night if I'd allow it, but he *does* need his rest," Thomas said kindly.

"How long has he been asleep?" Graham asked.

Before Thomas could answer, Russell opened his eyes and said, "I'm not, Mr. Chastain. But you've been *out*, so to speak, for about twenty minutes."

"Don't be absurd," Graham countered, laughing. "I never even closed my eyes. I was just focusing on the scroll."

Thomas laughed. "Look at your watch."

"I don't need to look at my watch," he said, looking anyway. "I have a keen ability to track time without a watch, and . . . No way."

Thomas didn't reply, and Russell rolled his eyes in mock disbelief, shrugging his shoulders and lifting his palms.

"Thomas is correct," Russell said. "I actually *am* quite tired, Mr. Chastain. It isn't just because of the time or my age.

Recounting these stories can be emotionally draining. I do wish to discuss that scroll and the effect I'm sure it had on you in more detail. We've experienced it too. Thomas and I believe it's over five thousand years old. We attempted to have it tested, but the alloy was unknown and accurate dating wasn't possible. To date it, we're relying on the age of the documents it was found with and the very cryptic references in those documents."

"I can't begin to describe what I was feeling, and I'm still having trouble coming to grips with the fact that I must have been in something like a trance for twenty minutes. It was like I had barely closed my eyes. And I don't remember that I actually *did* close my eyes." Graham shook his head and turned the scroll over in his hand. "How can something over five thousand years old be of an alloy that isn't known today?" he asked.

"It gets better," Russell said. "That's just the beginning of the mysteries. Unroll it and look at it closely," he added with eagerness in his voice.

Graham unrolled the golden scroll, wondering what it might possibly contain. Maybe some ancient hieroglyphics . . .

His eyes stretched wide with shock.

"Not possible," he said to Russell, in total disbelief.

Russell maintained his typical warm demeanor. "Maybe far older."

Graham wasn't willing to concede. "That information wasn't known five thousand years ago or even a hundred years ago."

"I know you have many questions, but they'll have to wait. I let you see that because I knew you'd be intrigued and so you could see just a small indication of the importance of what's happening. And I'm sure you'll need some time in solitary reflection to truly consider all that you've seen and heard today." Russell's tone held calming reassurance.

Thomas held out his hand, and Graham dropped the scroll into it.

Russell's tone shifted when he said, "I know you're a busy man, but we really must meet again *very* soon, Mr. Chastain— for your sake as much as ours. We're certain we can be of great benefit to each other and accomplish monumental tasks that can't be achieved separately. We can offer you a great deal in return for your help, including watching your back in no small fashion. We're quite good at such things."

Russell pushed his chair back from the desk. Graham looked from one man to the other. Although Graham wasn't ready to leave, it was clear that they were done.

"Until next time, Mr. Chastain."

Graham rubbed his forehead as he drove home. Next time? He was still juggling what he'd heard and experienced from *this* time. Templars. Treasure. Historic secrets and hidden conspiracies. An ancient scroll of unknown properties. How big was Russell's organization and how thoroughly had they penetrated Graham's companies? He now had to consider a potential threat from a second direction. Yes, there would certainly be a next time. And soon.

THIRTY-FIVE

Last night, after a brief Skype call with his lovely wife, Graham had decided to retire fairly early. He'd been happy to hear she'd be home soon, and decided to leave curious research for the morning.

He sometimes worried about Vicky. She was highly intelligent and had been a world traveler long before they met, but he was concerned that she was often too nice and might be taken advantage of. She would have none of his worry, however, often reminding him that she was a big girl and had her own bodyguard close by when traveling without him. In spite of the tepid direction their relationship had taken in the past year, he always felt better when she returned. But he was reminded that there can still be distance in close proximity.

Graham hadn't expected he'd sleep very well with so much running through his mind, but he had barely shifted his thoughts from his wife to the feelings he'd experienced while holding the scroll when he quickly plummeted into the grip of a deep slumber.

And now, working in his office, he couldn't remember a time when he'd felt better. Not just physically, but mentally and emotionally as well. Even though his mind contained his typical mass flurry of multitasking, his already excellent abilities to sort and focus seemed far more lucid and well honed—cerebral gymnastics at its finest. He had gone to different workstations, reviewed all ongoing projects, devoured each of Ariel's summaries and reviewed and responded to all of his email traffic. After he created a dozen new virtual notes for new projects, ideas and even a potential new division in one of his subsidiaries. And that was before most of his staff had arrived for work.

He was in mid-multi when his phone hummed with a text— *OMW*—from Alex. *On my way* was Alex's most common text. If Graham wasn't free or was otherwise engaged, he would simply respond "10m" or whatever time delay was appropriate.

Graham sat in front of his main array of monitors and took his glasses off and put them back on while frowning at the screen. In general, Graham's eyesight was excellent, but he'd been prescribed glasses with minimal correction, mostly to prevent eyestrain from long hours staring at computer monitors. His eyewear was also a test product from one of his divisions and part of a related broader program that included various devices that provided protection from electromagnetic radiation (EMR), blue light, LED and other negative factors. One of their secret projects was that of creating countermeasures for 5G and microwave radiation. But today there was either something wrong with his glasses or his eyes.

Alex gave his customary perfunctory rap on Graham's door as he entered without waiting for an answer. He held a small pile of items that had no doubt been handed to him by Suzette as he'd passed her desk out front. Graham had more than one executive assistant, but Suzette was the lead, and what didn't funnel through Alex was routed through her. Alex laid the stack on one of the tables before dropping into a nearby chair.

Graham continued his in-depth research without greeting Alex. After a few minutes he said, "So is Suze still crushing you in the fantasy league?"

"The woman is uncanny. I'm not sure how she does it. She just may be a sorceress, I'm thinking. When I remind her of my superior intellect, she laughs—obviously unintimidated by the obvious."

"Maybe she's in collusion with your wife to split the money," Graham offered.

"Nah. Amy gets all the money anyway; that would be cutting into her take. More likely that Ms. Suzette is in cahoots with Ariel. They're both machines, I tell you. And as a natural segue, we've put in and beta tested the new firewalls and used Ariel for input and modeling like you suggested. We also heard that Mrs. C will be back soon, and everyone is happy to know you'll be less surly soon after." Alex could barely keep a straight face.

"Surly. Is that some Asian code word that carries a deeper meaning? It could be a term vaguely related to deep pay and bonus cuts." Graham was still staring at his monitors with and without his glasses. "Did you guys switch my glasses again?"

"Nope. I promise. That was a classic, but repeating pranks is, how shall we say . . . juvenile."

"Hmmm. Not sure I believe you—about the prank rerun *or* your hallucination that not repeating it somehow negates your juvenility. And I'm a *pillar* of warmth and jocularity, I'll have you know. I'm the antithesis of surly. Do you have any *accurate* information for me, Dr. Ruth?" Graham said sarcastically.

"Just a continued uptick in sales on all fronts, but I'm sure you've seen that in real time. One thing that's a bit odd is that we've had several inquiries about your Trailgate program that you may *not* be aware of." Alex scrolled through his tablet with his free hand.

Graham turned toward Alex, genuinely puzzled. "That program has only been discussed in one trade publication and one article other than our promotion of 'things to come' on our own site. It isn't out of beta yet."

"That's why I thought it was odd. The only thing I could figure is that we're getting so much positive buzz that the folks who want in on the riskier left side of the marketing curve are searching for opportunities still in development. But I knew you'd want to know, regardless. That's all I have right now, other than what I've already fed to you."

"Keep an eye on where this is heading. I want to know if there are more or deeper requests. And I'd like you and Ariel to look into the companies making Trailgate inquiries, but keep your search under the radar for now."

Alex headed out the door and called over his shoulder. "I'll put on my corporate ninja attire and start right away, boss."

Graham leaned back in his chair and pondered the anomalous information Alex had brought him. Then he sat up and made a few keystrokes and watched his monitors cascade tiles after he completed the query he was working on. Next he moved to a separate workstation to do some of his own cursory investigating of the Trailgate developments. Only Alex and a select few others knew that there was a basic commercial version in development and another version on steroids that would be solely for internal use.

Graham had decided that it would be far more lucrative to sell the deep learning/mass data results than to sell the software. The logic was simple yet profound. If a given client had a task that would take them six months and eighty thousand dollars to complete, what would it be worth to the client if Graham's companies could deliver the required results in even less time—

say four months? How critical or time sensitive the information was would most likely figure into the price-value of a project as well. Sixty thousand dollars in four months is obviously easier to sell than eighty thousand in six. But in spite of the savings, the client wouldn't be very happy if they knew Graham's systems could actually complete the project in six weeks and his internal cost was less than ten thousand dollars. People were just funny that way. The information-gathering capabilities were worth far more than what he could sell the system for—so unsolicited inquiries made him take notice.

Before he could get very far, Suzette buzzed him.

"Yes, ma'am? What can I do to bring joy into your world?

"Mr. C, a couple guys out here claiming to be from Homeland insist on seeing you." Suzette spoke without a shred of civility in her voice.

"Which homeland? Most of my people are originally from Germany and England, with a few French foisted on us that we don't claim." Graham added fuel to Suzette's fire. Since she was cheery nearly all the time, he knew she was fuming for a reason.

"These guys seem to *think* they're special and don't believe they need an appointment. Shall I call security or just toss them myself? I'm pretty sure I can take them," she said in a very even tone.

"No, that's okay, Suze. Maybe another time. Today we might as well do our part for the benevolent Fedgov that protects us." Graham spoke loudly so that the agents could hear his sarcasm. "Show them to my door so they don't get lost."

He made a sweeping gesture at the far edge of his main monitor, causing all the monitors in the room to immediately change to screen saver mode. He leaned back in his chair and laced his fingers across his stomach as the agents entered without a knock and approached him with backs ramrod straight and chins cocked. It was standard intimidation posture to put people on the defensive, take control and declare who was boss. Graham neither stood nor offered his hand or a seat to the men— bureaucrats with badges and guns—who he felt were a nuisance. He found their demeanor as transparent as it was laughable.

"That was pretty rich. That'll be the day, when someone named Suzy can 'take' me," scoffed one of the agents, gesturing his thumb over his shoulder and toward the door.

Graham was expressionless. "Today might be your lucky day, then. I've sparred with her. She's a third degree black belt in Brazilian Jiu-Jitsu. My money's on her." He raised both eyebrows and tilted his head. "Gives a whole new meaning to giving someone the third degree, huh? By the looks of you, I'm guessing you're better with kung pao than you are at kung fu, but you probably *do* enjoy picking on women half your size."

"Let's start over," the second man offered. "I'm Special Agent Sandoval and this is Special Agent Camarata."

"Well, isn't that special? This is my special *get to your point and leave quickly* expression," Graham responded without his usual humor.

"There's no need to be hostile, Mr. Chastain," Camarata said with an edge to his voice.

Graham didn't as much as blink. "Note that my expression hasn't changed. And I'm not hostile. I just don't appreciate bad manners or attempts at intimidation."

"We've read your file and know that you have a top secret clearance and an impressive military and intelligence record. But if we don't get some cooperation, we can make a few calls and make things difficult for you."

Graham stood and pointed at his phone. "Actually, I'm the

one who can use that phone to make a call to the Homeland Under Secretary I work with and occasionally golf with, a man eight levels above your too-high pay grade, and let him make things difficult for *you*," Graham snapped. "And unlike you, I call or email and ask for an appointment out of common courtesy and professional decorum, even though I have a standing invitation to drop by *any* time."

Sandoval was thinking that Chastain had a good point. And that whichever of their bosses called Camarata to insist that they interrogate Graham Chastain might have thought to first check to see if someone at Homeland already knew him well, which would have created far more cooperation. Either the right hand didn't know what the left was doing or this could well be a meeting that didn't have official sanction. It wasn't uncommon to use tough-guy tactics to get someone to provide answers, but only when they didn't cooperate. And they hadn't given Chastain that chance.

"What division are you guys with anyway?" Chastain asked.

"Intelligence and Analysis," Camarata snapped, as if the name would carry official weight.

"Well, if that doesn't define the word oxymoron!"

Sandoval stepped in without giving Camarata a chance to further annoy the man they were there to question. "Be that as it may, Mr. Chastain, we need to ask you some questions. I apologize for our intrusion and bad manners, but this is a matter of national security, and we were in the area and are in a big hurry. Our approach was unprofessional, I know. But it would be a lot easier to let us ask our questions than start a daisy chain of phone calls that will just have us back here at your door if we aren't granted an appointment in the future."

Sandoval was taking the approach that they should have used in the first place and was hoping Chastain would see the logic in it. He did.

"I'm very busy, Special Agent. Please ask your questions and try to be brief. I work for a living."

Chastain was blunt, but also much less agitated.

Sandoval could be cordial or stoic and emotionless, depending on what was most psychologically expedient for what he was trying to accomplish. And he was used to the unwarranted tension his partner often caused, so he breathed a small sigh of relief seeing that Chastain seemed willing to talk. "Do you know a reporter named Harry McGowan?"

Chastain looked like he was auditioning for the lead role at a wax museum. If they had hoped to elicit a reaction from the interrogative right hook, they were unsuccessful. Chastain's lack of reaction showed that it didn't even land as a soft jab to the body.

"No," he answered with the same inflection he would use if someone asked if he wanted sugar in his coffee.

"He called you at least seventeen times," Camarata snapped.

"You asked if I *knew* him," Chastain parried in a tone somewhere between yawning boredom and sarcasm. "Technically, he called my *office* a number of times, but he never got past Suzette. I never spoke with the man. He wouldn't tell us what he wanted to discuss and therefore was denied access. And by the way, I've had copier salespeople call more times. Now *there's* an upward career move you two might look into. Especially since you like cold calls so much."

"I'm sure you found out he was a reporter. So why didn't you speak to him? I would think big shots like you would love any free press you could get."

Camarata still hadn't dropped his anemic posture of bravado.

"Because I like tabloid reporters about as much as I like thugs and Stasi-inspired Homeland Insecurity special agents. And you two give *special* a completely different meaning."

Camarata turned to Sandoval. "Do I seem like a thug to you? I'm thinking I'm much more of the ruggedly handsome yet tough and misunderstood type."

"He's dead," Sandoval said, ignoring Camarata and hoping to catch Chastain off guard.

"I know," Chastain said evenly.

Sandoval hadn't taken his eyes off of Chastain and was doing his best to gain some measure of the man. "You don't seem surprised."

"Agent Sandoval, is it? As you *should* well know, we've had many contracts over the years that require us to work at the top secret level. We have our own *real* intelligence and analysis department here. If anyone comes anywhere near harassing or even annoying anyone at this company, our group is readily aware of it. I guarantee that my people ran your tags the minute you entered the property, did facial recognition on you as you approached the building and knew who you were, or you would have never made it as far as Suzette's desk.

"And I also guarantee that totally unbeknownst to you, at least ten of my extremely dangerous and combat-trained security people were within dropkicking distance of you two at all times. And so no, I'm not surprised, because I saw the news of his death on a local news feed that comes to my desktop. But if I hadn't, I was alerted about it in one of my daily briefings since Mr. McGowan was someone who'd insisted on speaking to me. His death piqued my curiosity. And since Homeland has so rudely shown up here, now I'm curious about your interest in Mr. McGowan."

"That's none of your business," Camarata said.

"Did you take the advanced class in how to lose friends and annoy people?" Chastain asked.

Sandoval stepped in again.

"He called quite a few people besides you, Mr. Chastain. There were a number of very wealthy and powerful people, including politicians, that he made wild claims to. A number of his claims were taken as threats. Since his threats were about national security and broad in scope, we were called in."

"Why not the FBI?" Chastain asked, genuinely curious.

"That, I honestly don't know. Could be an international aspect of some sort. We just do what we're told."

"Good. In that case, we're done here. As I said, I have a great deal of work to do, and I told you all I know."

"Maybe *we* aren't done." Camarata was determined to give his imaginary muscles one more flex.

"I'm pretty sure you are," Chastain said, sitting down and looking back to one of his monitors as if they'd already left.

Two very large and very tough-looking men in well-tailored suits opened the door and waited on either side of it. It was apparent that neither of them would feel the slightest intimidation from five Camaratas. One of his men nodded at Chastain, who returned the nod, while the other never took his eyes off the agents. The security officer who had signaled Chastain extended his arm to indicate direction and kept a cordial distance and a defensive posture as he and his partner followed them out and softly shut the door behind them.

Graham created a new research task for Ariel. The query was multifaceted, and it would be another unique test for Ariel. He looked forward to reading the results so that he could then use his Nudge program and algorithms with Ariel to see if they would work in a feedback scenario similar to human mentoring. This was another concept that made Graham's direction with AI different from other systems. And, he felt, also superior. He hoped Ariel would have substantial results by the time he got back from his meeting at the Ambrose offices.

The intrusion by the Feds made him more than a little curious—especially in light of all that had happened recently. He had thought McGowan was most likely a crank or a publicity hound when he refused to give any hint of why he wanted to meet. It made little sense that he'd been so persistent to meet with Graham and then committed suicide. Russell said they tried to warn McGowan off but weren't able to convince him. And whatever McGowan was onto, it was something big enough to warrant the attention of Homeland. Not knowing what McGowan wanted to discuss gnawed at him. There were puzzle pieces, but he didn't see a hint of a fit between any of them. One of the most intriguing aspects of AI was that responses were often totally unexpected and sometimes the programmers weren't sure how the AI arrived at the answers. Since Graham was reflecting on recent events that were more than a little convoluted, he hoped Ariel's responses would be unexpected as well. He looked forward to reading the analysis and summaries.

THIRTY-SIX

Normally Graham would expect that new business associates or partners would take turns meeting at each partner's location or meet for a cordial lunch in between. But Eric von Kleis was as much used to getting his way as he was seemingly obsessed with staying reclusive in his familiar surroundings. Graham wasn't sure yet if his obsession was a true phobia or the need to be in control. Alex suggested that the issue could be vampirism based on Alex's understanding of what Graham had told him. Graham laughed at Alex the way he often did, pondered how von Kleis came across as dark and mysterious and then laughed some more.

It wasn't that von Kleis was off-putting—quite the contrary. He was actually charming. But he exuded a darkness that Graham could feel and yet couldn't quite make sense of. He was still in deep ponder when von Kleis finally emerged from somewhere around the corner of the massive backdrop behind his desk.

Von Kleis strode up his usual fashion—at a brisk pace, shoulders back in his impeccable dark suit—and extended his hand in friendship, with his normal slight smile and an attempt at conveying warmth through his eyes.

"Do forgive my tardiness, Mr. Chastain. Something came up

elsewhere in the building that some of my staff insisted must have my personal attention. I'm sure you're used to similar demands by your people."

"No worries at all, sir. I have the issue from time to time as well. And having a cellphone sadly means there is no such thing as downtime. There are always emails and text messages to return."

Instead of retreating to his large, spectacular desk, von Kleis took a seat in a leather side chair of a fairly small yet exquisite round conference table near Graham's chair. The table held a single file folder and two bottles of Evian water siting on ornate coasters with leather centers surrounded by actual gold rims. He smiled as he gestured to Graham to move closer to the table. He set his hands on top of the file folder and interlaced his fingers.

"So, all is going well, I trust?"

"If you mean with regard to how quickly our partnership has come together and how we have a great new inflow of orders we can't explain—I'd say things are going better than well. I wouldn't have guessed that two sets of attorneys and financial people could have meshed on a project so quickly, but your people were both highly professional and completely accommodating. I wish I understood your business model better. I don't see how you were able to—"

Von Kleis held up his hand as he interrupted. "It's pretty simple, really. We're in the information business."

"That's pretty vague more than pretty simple," Graham said. "*I'm* in the information business, but it has been uncanny how you pulled in so much interest from so many diverse places and products."

"You do a fine job, young man. We've just been at it far longer than you have. Let me ask you this: Who hires the best and brightest?"

Graham grinned and crossed his arms across his chest. "Normally, I would say the video game companies."

Von Kleis didn't return the grin. "We do. Or at least we try to. And if we can't for some obscure reason, we try to direct them to one of our many associated companies. We provide funding and brilliant minds to the best think tanks in the country—which builds a network of relationships. We fund university projects, pay for chaired professorships where the professor in the chair might report to us first. We support politicians and political appointees alike—so we have some influence on where grant money goes and first knowledge of the results of those grants. Many powerful people do this or try to—we're just *very* good at it and have been for a very long time. And that often means we possess critical information before anyone else."

Graham tilted his head back to consider what von Kleis was telling him. "So you're always right?"

"Not quite, but enough. What if you could be right fifty-two percent of the time?" von Kleis asked Graham.

Graham smiled again. "I'd move to Las Vegas and semi-retire very wealthy and tanned."

As was becoming the pattern, von Kleis let Graham's charm go without comment.

"We're right far more than fifty-two percent of the time, and there are much wealthier arenas in the world than Las Vegas—although we do *quite* well there too."

Graham left his arms folded and didn't smile or engage in levity this time. "I assume this is all legal, of course."

Von Kleis scowled slightly. "Perfectly. We have no need for the repercussions of violating laws when we're simply better than ninety-five percent of the other conglomerates out there. Over time we've learned how to use synergy to cut costs, increase profits, anticipate trends and invest in them and implement dozens of other proactive strategies to keep us out in front. Far out in front. You can see the results at your very own company. Everything has been perfectly legal, and both of our enterprises will benefit enormously."

"I have to consider the axiom about things being too good to be true," Graham said.

"We didn't pick your name out of a hat, Mr. Chastain. I can assure you that your fledgling successes caught the attention of one or more of our analysts some time ago. Then they spent months analyzing business intelligence and running models and scenarios. We consider and follow hundreds of companies before we make an offer. We can afford to go after the crème de la crème as it were. Our relationship is a product of the very certain belief that your success has been due to your own innovation, hard work and excellent management style, or you wouldn't be sitting here," von Kleis concluded, pointing at Graham.

Graham felt a good deal of pride considering what von Kleis had just said. Many had tried to stroke his ego, but von Kleis delivered accurate compliments without exaggerated platitudes. "I appreciate your confidence in me and my companies," he said in a low tone of humility.

"Very well deserved, sir. But I didn't ask you to come by to butter you up or to review progress. As a case in point of what I've been describing to you, I have here what we believe—given your company structure, growth curve and reserves—is a perfect acquisition for you."

As he spoke, von Kleis slowly slid a file toward Graham as if it contained a secret of great value.

Graham opened the file and began to scan the executive summary while von Kleis continued speaking.

"It's a closely held company. The founder and majority shareholder passed away last year, and his wife has no desire to run the business. The company has taken losses since it's fairly well known that the founder was the heart of the company. However, we believe they have some excellent products on the drawing board."

"Not to look a gift horse in the mouth," Graham said, still racing through the summaries and financials, "but why doesn't Ambrose acquire it?"

"Good question. There are several reasons. It's somewhat small for us, and we don't have the time or desire to recruit the technical expertise needed to develop the new products. And their existing products need to be ramped up and their new systems need to get to the marketplace quickly. You have the perfect cache of technical expertise to do just that. And, of course, we will most certainly be a shareholder in this and infuse capital and have our subsidiaries make purchases where appropriate. This will be a plum either for you or one of our other associated companies. You're getting the right of first refusal as a way of welcoming you into the fold." Von Kleis opened his hands before drawing them back to his chest.

Graham looked up from what he was reading. "Thank you. Sincerely. I promise I'll give this the very thorough review it deserves and have my in-house team make an analysis a priority."

"Splendid! There's no obligation on your part, and if you chose not to make the acquisition, that choice has no bearing whatsoever on our relationship. I only ask that whoever you choose as team leader for the project keeps my people abreast of your interest on a rolling basis. If you feel the interest is increasing, we won't need to do anything other than determine our investment. If the interest diminishes, we would, of course, like to offer this to one of our other prized associates as soon as possible."

"Of course. We'll make every effort to be as expedient as prudently possible." Graham looked as though he was about to add more pleasantries when his cellphone vibrated in a distinct way. He stopped what he was about to say and reached for the phone that he kept politely out of view in his jacket lapel pocket.

"Pardon the interruption, Mr. von Kleis," Graham said as he looked at his phone. "That vibration I'm sure you just heard is for the utmost of emergencies."

"Think nothing of it."

Graham scrolled through a lengthy text and then looked at von Kleis with less color in his face than he had a moment earlier. "I'm sorry, but I have to leave. My younger sister has been taken to the hospital, and I need to go."

"Certainly!"

Graham stood, taking the file with him as von Kleis rose and circled the table to join him.

"I truly hope it isn't serious. And if there is anything we can do, you'll have whatever resources we can bring to bear." Von Kleis warmly rested his hand on Graham's shoulder.

"Thank you. She's my closest sibling. I'll get back with you about this"—he waved the file in his hand—"as soon as I can."

"Family comes first. I'm sure your staff is more than capable, so you shouldn't concern yourself. Please, do keep me posted about this hospital business. You're the newest member of our family."

With that, Graham started for the door. But he again said, "Thanks for your concern," and then he was gone.

Von Kleis locked the door that Graham used and walked back to the conference table. He picked up a bottle of water and took a slow drink.

Roth came in almost immediately. He wasn't permitted to eavesdrop on von Kleis's conversations, but he could tell that Graham had left and he knew what the meeting had been about.

"More insurance?" he asked.

"Double indemnity," von Kleis replied as he sat contentedly behind his desk.

"There's something I don't get. I know you want to win his confidence, but we could buy that company, pump in minimal capital, flip it and make a quick pile of cash."

"We, along with three other major stockholders who have no visible ties to us, will own a good portion of it. And it will increase in value greatly. And Mr. Chastain will own what seems like a controlling interest. It's a very subtle but important chess game." Von Kleis sighed.

"Yeah, but we could have it all. It would be a cherry. What do *you* call it?" Roth asked.

Von Kleis's mouth twitched slightly, almost creating a smile. "Corporate encirclement."

THIRTY-SEVEN

Graham Chastain was no control freak—he just liked being in control. So the fact that he felt utterly helpless made him edgy, to say the least. He had given his incessant pacing a brief respite, but only to continue his flurry of texting and emailing. He had run his fingers through his normally neat hair almost as many times as he had gotten up to look through the quarantine window into the room where his sister was being kept. Beside Jennifer sat her steady boyfriend, Bobby Toland. She was unconscious and nearly comatose, lying in a bed with the requisite number of IV's and monitors attached to her. Bobby was even more exhausted than Graham, sitting next to her and holding her hand. He showed no symptoms of whatever had struck Jennifer, but since he'd been in such close contact with her, they quarantined him too.

Graham hadn't arrived in time to meet with Jennifer's attending physician, and that frustrated him, even though the charge nurse did a more than adequate job of conveying what little they knew. He was also frustrated that no one had contacted him sooner, but that was reasonable since she thought she was coming down with some nasty form of the flu until she collapsed, suffering tremors and then mild convulsions. They had stabilized her, and she didn't seem to be getting any worse, but no better either.

Graham had been to dinner with Jennifer and Bobby on several occasions and found Bobby to be a great guy who was good to his sister. Graham was sure that Bobby loved her as much as he did, but he wished he could be the one holding her hand; quarantine protocols simply didn't allow it. Each time Bobby saw Graham looking through the window helplessly, he gave him a him a nod and a weak smile.

Being helpless wasn't something Graham was accustomed to. So he began to reach out the only ways he knew how. He tasked Alex Chen to have Ariel search for anomalous viral outbreaks. Bobby had already informed the attending physician that Jennifer had recently done volunteer work in Belize and Guatemala, a trip he didn't get to make. So Graham included that information and all he could glean from the nurses and forwarded it his office. Next he sought the advice of the chief medical officers at two of his small biotech companies and asked them as a personal favor to begin their own investigation.

Both Peter and Eric von Kleis had texted him several times to inquire about Jennifer. In addition, Mr. von Kleis informed him that he and his staff had already reached out into the Ambrose network. And, as he reminded Graham, their resources were immense. Graham profusely thanked all who were coming to his aid. Doing all he could for his kid sister was the main thing keeping him sane, though it didn't seem to be enough. He reviewed every pertinent email and text and was just about to begin another marathon pacing session, when he saw a tall, lean man heading his way at a brisk pace.

Graham hoped the man garbed in the white lab coat and crisp business attire, now extending his hand, was his sister's attending physician.

"Mr. Chastain, I'm Dr. Joseph Callahan, internal medicine and part of the team treating Jennifer. I apologize that I wasn't here to greet you sooner, but my absence was entirely on behalf of your sister, I assure you."

"I'm glad to hear that, Doctor," Graham said as both men released firm grips. "I have no doubt that you've been doing all you can."

"More than that, actually. I recognized your name, and I know a bit about your involvement in the biotech industry, but you must know some truly powerful people," he said with respectful enthusiasm.

Graham frowned. "Why do you say that?"

"I just left a meeting with our hospital administrator and our chief of staff that also included my team. Apparently some of your associates are on our board and are also major donors to this facility. Also, one of the directors at the CDC was on the phone with our chief of staff before we could even inform them of the case. That simply doesn't happen. The CDC is reviewing your sister's lab work and all our notes in real time as we speak. We're pretty close to a major technology corridor, as I'm sure you're aware, and we were also told that one of the top people in anti-viral research would be coming over to help out. I'm talking Nobel Prize-level talent. I can tell you that I haven't had my phone, email and texts blow up this much since my semi-inebriated wife lost her favorite cat. It's been a flurry of activity like I've never seen—all of which will be as beneficial as it has been amazingly rapid. We have an outstanding staff, and this is one of the best facilities in the country, but you're also getting the All-Star team in this area of medicine."

Graham was listening with attentive appreciation, but his brow began to furrow out of worry and concern. "I'm truly grateful, Dr. Callahan, but now you have me more than a lot worried. To generate so much attention, this is obviously far more serious than the flu. The nurse I spoke to said you don't even know what this is yet."

"Correct. I don't want to alarm you and this will take a little time to explain. We have your sister stable for the time being and she doesn't seem to be in any immediate danger, but we're in uncharted territory in several ways."

"Just what are we talking about here?" Graham pleaded as much as asked.

Dr. Callahan took on the tone and posture of a man well-seasoned in how to convey bad news as delicately as possible. His warm gray eyes spoke kindness and compassion. "Your sister has some form of viral hemorrhagic fever unique t—"

"You mean like Ebola?" Graham blurted out.

Dr. Callahan put his hand on Graham's forearm. "There isn't a need for alarm yet, but Ebola would actually be better because we would know exactly how to fight it. And since your sister was transported to us fairly quickly, the survival rate for someone of her age and in otherwise good health is likely to be very high. People in the bush who are malnourished aren't so lucky. We don't know exactly what this is. I'll spare you the technical details, but it's almost like two different types of fevers and it's of an unknown vector. In addition, it's causing a unique response in her body, something like an autoimmune disorder. Her interleukin-1 is affected, and there's a strong inflammatory reaction."

Graham felt like his knees might fail to support him as he turned to look through the glass at Jennifer and Bobby. Bobby met his eyes and Graham turned away, not wanting Bobby to see his despair.

"What's the prognosis? What I'm hearing sounds more than

bleak. Is my sister . . ." He coughed to clear the trepidation from his throat. "Is Jennifer going to die?"

"I promise you that we're doing every single thing that we're able to right now, Mr. Chastain. We've used the best antivirals we have, and she's getting plenty of the right fluids and even a low-dose combination of vitamins, anticonvulsants and pain meds to keep her comfortable. We've slowed down what's attacking her, but I'm sorry to say that we haven't stopped it. I wish I had better news." His voice held sincere sympathy.

Graham stood a little straighter and gathered himself as much as he could before turning back to Dr. Callahan. "Could you please include the same information in the CDC feed to my office so we can have it in our database and share it with our own biotech companies? We have some unique abilities, and at least I'll feel like I'm contributing something other than pacing ruts into the tile floors in this hallway. And please call me Graham."

Dr. Callahan was already jotting down information on a small pad. He tore off a page and handed it to Graham. "Here are two email addresses and my cell number. Have your people let our folks know the best way to forward the information and we'll do that immediately."

Graham was turning back to look at his sister, and he took the paper without reading it. "What about Bobby?"

"I'm sorry?"

"My sister's boyfriend. Is he sick too?"

"Oddly enough, he hasn't shown any symptoms so far, and his blood tests have all come back negative. But we have to keep him under observation since we have no idea how long the incubation period is. It's good to have him there with her. I don't think we could pry him out if we tried."

"I know exactly how he feels," Graham said, mist in his eyes.

THIRTY-EIGHT

Graham had just finished washing his hands and face again in the restroom. He stared into his own hollow eyes in the mirror. He was disheveled, as would be expected, but he wasn't nearly as exhausted as he would have expected under the circumstances. He was still helpless, but not willing to face any form of defeat. As his sister struggled to stay alive, he intended to struggle along with her in his own way. Lack of sleep was a small price to pay, he told himself as he walked back out to the waiting area that had become his makeshift command post. And for some reason, he just wasn't that sleepy. He had too much to do. As new directions and needs occurred to him, Graham had items from his office shuttled over, including a blazing fast laptop and a portable USB-powered monitor.

Other than standing on occasion to look in on Jennifer and Bobby, he was back in high-focus mode with regard to the tasks at hand. He'd already touched base with Thomas via text message to explain his delayed return to James Russell, and he sent an email to Eric von Kleis thanking him for whatever weight he was bringing to bear in the effort to help his sister. Graham was able to watch a steady stream of communication between Dr. Callahan's group, the CDC, Graham's corporate support and a few of the contacts from the local biotech talent that Dr. Callahan had mentioned. This was all accomplished in less than twelve hours. It was a Herculean effort but hopefully not for what might ultimately become an Atlas burden. He was diligently searching for an elusive legal pad that had gone into hiding beneath two computer tablets and the edge of an unopened donut box when a voice brought him back to a more typical plane of existence.

"Your new office needs work. Maybe a plant or two."

Graham lifted his head to see Peter Gehlman looking down at him with a slight grin and holding two large to-go cups from their favorite café, Bean Leaves. It was touted as the place where coffee drinkers and tea drinkers could set aside their differences.

"The decorator should be here at any time," Graham said, genuinely happy to see his friend. "I'm thinking a lamp . . . right about where you're standing. So what did you bring me?"

Peter handed Graham his cup. "I got my usual Semi-Gloss Velvet Arabian Mocha Latte with fat-free whipped cream and a dusting of cinnamon mint. For you, on the other hand, I went all out and got an extra bland Maxwell Taster's Folger—hold the flavor."

"Yum or yay or some form of feigned exuberance. Great to see you, but isn't it kind of early for you? Isn't this about the time you come rolling in? Or is that why you're here? Date go awry?"

"Sir, no sir!" Peter said as he came to attention. "After you called last night, I canceled my date to be fresh to bring you coffee this very morning. And to look my best and brightest in the event of low-flying nurses. Now I know why chickens bark in the morning . . . Sunlight that early is truly annoying."

Graham smiled at the image of barking roosters. "It's really good to see you, buddy," he said with somber gratitude.

"I wish I could say I'm glad to be here, but I'm not. All six of us—you and Vicky, Jennifer and Bobby, me and the woman of the day—should be recovering from a hangover rather than sitting in a hospital," Peter said with a tone that declared he was annoyed with the universe. "What's the latest?"

"No major changes, but she's slowly deteriorating. Still, I'm hopeful since so many experts are trying to help her. And I have to say that von Kleis and the Ambrose people have really come through. You would think that *I'd* donated a wing to the hospital. They've opened up amazing resources and tapped some of the best medical specialists in the world to help Jennifer. I'll be forever in their debt. If it hadn't been for you and for them, I don't where I'd be. Pretty much hopeless, I'd say."

"Truly kind of you to include me, but I didn't do anything except attempt to shamelessly exploit you and rake in ridiculous and embarrassing fees while my staff does all the work. Nothing I wouldn't do for any client." Peter took a sip of his coffee.

Graham knew that was Peter's way of saying "you're welcome." What was *embarrassing* was that Peter was uncomfortable with compliments. He loved to convey the fallacious impression that he was a rogue, but he was actually kind and generous. Graham remembered a time when they were at a venture capital cocktail party and Peter was chatting up a woman. She asked what Peter did for a living, and he said he was a rake. Peter didn't bat an eye when she said, "Ohhhhh . . . you mean like a handyman!"

Peter stayed with Graham most of the morning, with Graham explaining more about his sister's condition and what they were trying to do while he worked on his powerful laptop. Both took breaks to make calls, follow up on emails and return text messages. Peter had a gift for knowing when to make conversation and when to stay quiet when Graham was deep into a search. As much as Graham enjoyed the company, he knew that Peter was no more comfortable with being helpless than he was himself. Graham was about to suggest a lunch break when he saw an unfamiliar physician headed toward them. He was dressed the same as Dr. Callahan, but this man was a good deal older. An executive backpack was slung over one shoulder, and in the opposite hand he carried a large and rather imposing briefcase. He strode toward Graham and Peter, set down his briefcase and blotted a few beads of sweat from his forehead with the back of his now-empty hand.

"I'm Dr. Scheer, and I'm looking for Graham Chastain," he said, extending his hand toward Peter.

"I'm Peter Gehlman, Dr. Scheer. This is Graham."

"Very good to meet you both," he said, pumping their hands profusely in turn. He then turned back to Peter.

"Any relation to Dr. Henry Gehlman, per chance?" Dr. Scheer asked.

Peter shrugged his shoulders, as if to marginalize his family—as he so frequently had done in the past. "Yes. Great-uncle Henry was a physician, as I recall." He sighed.

Dr. Scheer was still looking at Peter. "Fascinating. I studied under him a long, long time ago in Europe. A fine man and a great teacher."

Scheer turned to Graham. "A mutual friend of ours sits on the board of the main company I represent, and he made me aware of your sister's condition and asked that I apply our research company's resources as a personal favor. In addition to him being on the board, his company is one of our biggest stockholders and benefactors. He has been very generous in the past and when he asked for a favor, I was more than happy to help. I work in stem cell research and with other cutting-edge biotherapies. My area of expertise is in antiviral therapies—which is why I was contacted yesterday. I would have arrived sooner, but my staff and I have been poring over the data since yesterday, late into the night and early this morning."

Graham listened intently and with a feeling of relief for the first time. He'd heard of Dr. Maximillian Scheer and looked him up when he saw he was in the loop of the exchanges between the CDC and other professionals. He looked taller than his pictures and somewhat older. His hair was mostly gray and was losing the battle with his head as it had receded past the midpoint. What remained was in need of styling, but Graham couldn't care less. He doubted someone like Dr. Scheer, who was being considered for a Nobel Prize, cared about grooming. And it could well be that he was more disheveled because of the flurry of work they'd been doing for his sister. Graham didn't care if Dr. Scheer sported an unwashed Mohawk to go along with his crooked tie and wrinkled clothes.

"We have over a dozen different therapies in various stages of development, and I'm reasonably certain, based on what I've seen, that we have something that will help. While we were looking over the test results, people at the highest levels were getting the necessary paperwork put through to provide me with privileges in this hospital and permission to try one or more of the therapies. We'll need your permission, of course, Mr. Chastain, and I'll explain in great detail what I hope to accomplish, any slight risks and what I believe we can achieve. But first we need to see the attending physician, and then I need to look in on your sister myself. Since her condition could become more dire, I'd like to start right away."

Graham slid past Peter. "Let's find the head nurse and then

we can locate Dr. Callahan," Graham said over his right shoulder as he walked toward the nurses station. "I'll shoot him a text that you're here while we're walking."

The sole of Graham's shoe snapped loudly when he came to an abrupt stop and turned back toward the two men. He walked up to Dr. Scheer and extended his hand once more. "Thank you so much, Dr. Scheer, for your hard work and that of your staff. I'm sure you were in the middle of other important research projects that you had to set aside. Thank you for moving so quickly. I won't forget this."

Dr. Scheer nodded as he shook Graham's hand a second time. "Very happy to be of service. Let's find Dr. Callahan and see about getting your sister well."

THIRTY-NINE

Camarata and Sandoval sat across from each other in a booth at Torpedo Jane's Bar. It wasn't their favorite booth, but close enough. They liked the general position because they could talk in relative privacy and still keep an eye on both what was at the bar and what went in and out of the ladies room. The booths were high-backed and made of wood, and the seats were made from a fairly comfortable imitation Naugahyde. The wood tabletop had seen a long history of wear, spills, carvings and fights. The men had heavy pint mugs of beer and a couple of small buckets of semi-fresh peanuts still in the shell.

Sandoval always got an extra empty bucket for his shells. He didn't care that they were also all over the floor, he just didn't like the debris in front of him while he was drinking and talking—or heaven forbid, peanut shell dust falling on his expensive and well-pressed pants. Or as he preferred to call them, *trousers*. Camarata was almost as fastidious as Sandoval, but he intentionally let his peanut shells pile up, encroaching on Sandoval's meticulous half of the table as time passed just to mess with him.

"I know I'm repeating myself, but this makes no sense to me," Sandoval said as he pushed the errant shells back toward

Camarata's side of the table with a dry beer coaster.

"You *do* tend to do that," Camarata said, dropping more shells haphazardly and hoping for more mayhem in Sandoval's world. "I think it ties in with your obsession with unattractive women, which, in turn, is a failing attempt to compensate for your insecurity over lack of manly size and performance. I use the term *manly* in the most general sense, of course."

Sandoval set his oversize phone to his right so he could easily notice text messages while maintaining his line of sight to the bar to subtly scour for potential targets. The seat backs might be high, but the low side rail gave a clear field of view. And it gave their server a shorter trip to return with refreshments. He was happy-hour hopeful, but that attitude wasn't reflected in his voice. "So now they have us chasing dead hookers?" he said, recounting their earlier detour with disdain, even though he always enjoyed seeing his favorite coroner. Fortunately, Camarata had been less irritating on their second visit to Chrys's office.

Camarata popped a peanut into his mouth and said, "You do that all the time—living *and* dead—so what's the big deal? At least this way you were on the clock and getting paid for what you normally pay for. You should be thanking somebody. Our employer has an intervention plan for just about everything now. I'm betting they even have one for your necrophilia addiction. And by the way . . . At her prices, they're called ladies of the evening."

Sandoval didn't respond. Camarata could see by the look in eyes that his mind was spinning in high gear—trying to reason out what was really going on. It wasn't likely he'd find out, at least not until Camarata was given the green light to bring him in, and there was no guarantee of that happening.

"You wanna know what I think?" Camarata said while aimlessly dropping more shells.

"No," Sandoval said before taking a big drink of his beer, hiding a grin with the mug.

"I think the powers that be have seen our reports and our work, and they've put us on this major covert assignment because we've done stellar work in the past and they're singling us out for something even bigger. They may want to see how well we execute our directives." Camarata took an even pull on his own drink.

"You really think so?" Sandoval asked with complete sincerity, leaning toward Camarata and glancing to his right and left.

"No. No, I don't you simpleton!" Camarata laughed. "Well, me, yes, but not so much with you. I think there's some double top secret codicil in the regs about moral turpitude. And your last date reeked of that among other things! Oh, they're singling *you* out, all right!" Camarata couldn't stop laughing. He didn't often hook his partner so easily.

Sandoval had been duped, and the best way to recover was to play along. "Okay, I can safely say that I don't think any food ever got a chance to spoil in her apartment. Much like your mom's place before it got condemned."

Camarata had him on the ropes and could barely choke out insults fast enough, gasping for breath between belly laughs. "Yeah, for me it's upward mobility and more important cases. For you, I think they're grooming you for a top secret Malthusian sterilization plan. Something they put in your Wi-Fi or your food or your mouse. Headed straight to your trouser mouse!" He howled. "We're talkin' a *big* downward promotion for you, buddy!"

"That's demotion, imbecile!" Sandoval corrected him.

"Yeah, yeah, yeah. That's the one, all right!" Camarata tried to drink, but had to set his glass back down. He took the opportunity to flag their server for refills while he caught his breath.

Sandoval didn't mind the beating he was taking; he'd walked right into it. But he wasn't done with his thoughts and wanted to bring his partner back around. "There has to be more to it than this," he said evenly, swirling his beer and looking over the glass at Camarata.

Camarata paused to get his breathing in check before responding. "Listen, Sherlock-never-gonna-be. It's actually pretty simple. I'm senior, so I get the word that you don't. We have an extremely high-priced call girl and a hack reporter who made wild accusations to some really powerful people. To your untrained mind, they seem unrelated. The flesh investment has been entertaining some important people, including politicians, and has been oiling the rigs in some sheiks' tents as well. I'm guessing she said the wrong thing during afterglow to the wrong clients. And I'd be willing to bet the cost of your overpriced and poorly fitting designer sports coat that she was one of the leak sources for our suicide victim." Camarata jabbed his index finger at Sandoval's chest like a punctuation mark.

Sandoval thought about what Camarata just told him, and was about to respond just as their server put two more on the beer-beaten tabletop. They gazed up at the lovely young woman in unison. They came to this bar for multiple reasons, not the least of which was how amazing the wait staff looked.

Camarata smiled brightly at the young lady and said, "So what time do you get off, my dear?"

"Hopefully, prior to you noticing," she said with a blank expression.

"Come on, that's no way to be. You do know we're federal agents, right?"

"Yep. We drew straws, and I lost. Death to globalist tyrants," she said with the same amount of expression as before. She turned on her heel without bothering to take their empty mugs away.

Camarata chuckled. "A *no* merely brings me one step closer to a *yes*. I wonder who my next lucky candidate will be," he said, scanning the room.

"So how did our people know about her?" Sandoval pressed.

"Come on, man. Who put *that* eight-track back in the dashboard? There are much better topics we could be discussing." He sighed. "But all right, Captain Buzzkill . . . I'm sure one of the agencies had her under surveillance or had some very high-level eavesdropping going on, based on how connected the players must be. Any one of the big wheels involved could have been talking about their potential exposure. And someone in those same circles decided being sure she didn't talk to anyone else would be most expedient. Happens all the time," he said with certainty.

Sandoval took a slow, pondering drink of the fresh beer from his frosty mug and thought about Camarata's explanation. He knew Camarata got information before he did because he was senior, and he accepted that. Homeland was no different from the force in that regard. Sandoval also paid him deference because Camarata had been a bit of a hero in the past—taking a round in the thigh while trying to save a partner who ultimately didn't live through a bad shootout. But Sandoval knew there had to be more to the story than what was being shared and had hoped he would have earned his partner's trust enough to be let in on whatever was really going on. For now he was stuck with enjoying the libations, the scenery and the abuse.

He had planned to exit work-mode and move to carousing-mode when a final thought struck him. "So I wonder what about this particular lady of the evening caused Dr. Devareaux to call one of our superiors," Sandoval said, thinking out loud.

Camarata scowled, shrugged his shoulders, looked a different direction and said, "Beats me. And I may need to beat you. We're off the clock, and you're interfering with my beer and skirt therapy."

"You're right. That's definitely BS therapy.

Across town, Avalon stood in the shadows of a large concrete arch that made up part of a bridge support structure. He had walked for several miles wearing his latest nondescript outfit and used the time to determine no one was following him. He leaned back against the support as if to rest. He held a compact spiral-bound birdwatching book in one hand and a pair of Zeiss Victory SF binoculars in the other. Avalon had become an expert birder over the years—at first because it gave him the perfect excuse and cover to greatly expand his field of view to minimize surprises and determine escape and evasion routes. Later he began to enjoy the avocation, as much as someone so dark-hearted could enjoy anything. He was the embodiment of a true dichotomy—*the* merchant of death intrigued by the grace of birds in flight and the peaceful beauty of them never quite at rest. He could identify with both aspects. With most of his cover stories, his knowledge of a given topic was fairly thorough but didn't require much depth since he could simply claim that he was new at a given hobby or profession. But in the case of being a birder, Avalon had few peers.

The vibration of the cellphone in the pocket of his windbreaker interrupted his self-aggrandizing thoughts. He lowered his binoculars slowly and noted the number before he answered.

"Human resources," he said quietly, directing his voice toward the water, even though he had seen no one for almost twenty minutes or within five hundred yards.

"No, I'm afraid Ms. Cavendish no longer works here. I believe she took another position, but I don't have any information about that." He paused to listen before saying, "Thank you and good day to you as well."

Avalon pushed the button to end the call and when he did, he made a show of losing his grip with one hand and sending the phone bouncing off the bird-watching book held in the other. It was a quick choreography of clumsiness that resulted in the phone ultimately ending up in the water. He pretended to be distraught but made no attempt to continue the charade by making any effort to retrieve it since the drop to the water was significant.

Avalon walked off with a hint of disgust in his demeanor to stay consistent with his performance. He felt the call was mostly unnecessary and preferred his coded text method. But this time the Masters wanted more information about his most recent elimination—which they received in his seemingly banal response. There would be no tracing the call to the phone making its way to the bottom of the swift river.

Avalon made a final precautionary sweep of the area for unwanted "birds" before casually beginning his leisurely walk. His next task would be another chameleon change of appearance and a stealthy return to the scene of his last incursion. A certain tube of toothpaste needed to be exchanged.

FORTY

The activity on the floor where Jennifer was in quarantine had increased by several orders of magnitude. Graham was impressed with the professionalism, the technical expertise and the efficiency. He'd had reservations about how the Ambrose Consortium operated and questioned whether they held as much sway as von Kleis so often and cryptically conveyed. But if what had transpired in the last twenty-four or so hours on behalf of his sister was any indication, then he was becoming thoroughly convinced that this was a group that he could consider being part of. Apparently, when they needed to get things done, those things got done. And at the highest levels of execution and competence.

Peter wasn't comfortable in hospitals, and Graham was being well taken care of by staff, so Graham coerced him into doing whatever he would normally be doing. When Peter was absolutely certain that Graham was all right and that he wouldn't feel abandoned, he agreed to leave but would return later or if needed, return sooner. So he left, but not before commenting with his normal version of humor about Dr. Callahan's unbridled worship of Dr. Scheer, including remarks about proximity to anatomy and where Dr. Callahan's head might end up if Dr. Scheer stopped abruptly. Graham needed the laugh, but it was clear that there was well-deserved hero worship going on.

For quite some time Graham was smart enough to simply stay out of the way and let the professionals work with focus and speed. Over time, more and more support staff arrived, both from Dr. Callahan's group and from Dr. Scheer's. It was an impressive gathering of MDs, PhDs, nurses and technicians. With additional hospital support staff came additional equipment, monitors and serums in all manner of equipment cases, some that Graham was familiar with and others that he didn't recognize.

The hospital administrator and the chief medical officer each stopped by fairly frequently to see that all was running smoothly, to offer assistance and to assure Graham that everything possible was being done. Graham felt the attention was due in equal parts to genuine concern, concern over legal exposure, potential breach of quarantine containment and fawning over the legendary Dr. Maximillian Scheer.

Graham maintained his worried vigil of Jennifer and Bobby through the window and continued to check all information flowing through the system. He watched more blood being drawn for more tests and the steady stream of information being given to Dr. Scheer, Dr. Callahan and their respective teams. Dr. Scheer was also good enough to give Graham fairly frequent updates, always with Dr. Callahan in tow, nodding with all of Scheer's pronouncements. Graham learned that Dr. Callahan had attended a symposium where Dr. Scheer was the keynote speaker. Dr. Scheer acted like he remembered Dr. Callahan and the two made up a very compatible mutual appreciation society that Graham was very thankful for. He told the good doctors he appreciated their updates but didn't want them to feel obligated if updating him took away from their work.

Dr. Scheer went into detail about the progress, which meant determining the best course of care. He believed that they would know shortly which of the drugs would have the greatest efficacy and that a combination could be the most promising. Graham told them that he would spend whatever it took to save his younger sister. The doctors looked at each other with faint smiles, and Dr. Scheer gave Graham's upper arm a slight squeeze.

"Graham, I assure you that cost will not be any concern in this case. Our mutual benefactors have a personal affinity for you, and we all believe the successful treatment of your sister could well lead to saving many thousands of lives in the future. Money is not an issue here in any way." So saying, Dr. Scheer headed back to his equipment and computers.

Graham watched as the work grew to a crescendo and then slowed. All of the critical team members left, carrying briefcases and computers to meet in a conference room one floor down. Graham wasn't invited to join them and didn't feel it was his place. He continued his new routine and the vigil that included frequent status updates to family members and many friends, with Bobby supplying Graham the contact information. The outpouring was as sincere as it was voluminous. He'd been so focused on his work for so many years that he hadn't considered just how many friends his sister had.

When the medical team returned, most of them went directly back to their work, much of which had to do with checking on Jennifer and Bobby to see if anything major had changed in their short absence. Dr. Scheer and Dr. Callahan approached Graham and motioned for him to stay seated as they joined him.

Dr. Scheer crossed his legs and leaned toward Graham. He

was obviously going to take the lead.

"Graham, we had a good idea of what we thought might work best based on the analysis we did with the staff at our laboratories before we ever even came here. But it was important for us to run more tests and be as thorough as we could be. We've delicately made it as clear as possible that your sister's condition is grave and worsening slowly. To give her the wrong drug or combination of treatments could be as bad as doing nothing at all. Fortunately, we have the most technologically advanced predictive-treatment-modeling software and system anywhere. The horsepower of our computer systems probably rivals even that of the systems at your company, but our scope is far narrower."

Graham listened intently and nodded as Dr. Scheer spoke, but he didn't want to interrupt.

"In years past, many patients would be needed to test outcomes over a significant amount of time before the right treatment or combination of treatments could be determined. But with our methodologies, weeks become hours. We were able to gather our own specific test data from Jennifer to fine tune the results. We believe we have arrived at a very effective treatment protocol. We could do more testing, but we would very quickly hit a point of diminishing returns given the fact that she'll continue to deteriorate without treatment. We'll monitor the dose and reaction of what we give her by the minute in real time—that way we can tweak the amounts, types and sequence as needed. In essence, she'll get custom treatments when most people get a treatment that fits into a bell curve."

"What are the risks?" Graham said weakly.

"There are *always* risks in dealing with illnesses that are this critical, even in the best of scenarios," Dr. Scheer said. "She was able to get here quickly and be stabilized and was given the best care available. There is a slim chance her body could fight this off and she could recover on her own—a *very* slim chance. Based on her continued decline, I wouldn't put it at more than ten percent."

Dr. Callahan nodded in agreement.

"But given the prior proven success of our modelling and having some of the best people in the industry to administer and monitor her treatments, I honestly think her chances for a full recovery are quite good," Dr. Scheer said. You've already signed the releases, and here is a printout of our intended protocol and how it may vary in the immediate future." He handed Graham a sheet of paper.

Graham stared at the paper and said, "The technical aspects of this obviously mean little to me, but I appreciate being kept in the loop."

"I know. And that piece of paper represents many thousands of prior work hours, so it can't leave this room. I just wanted you to see that we have a very solid strategy."

"I assume we need to start right away?" Graham asked.

"Everything's already in place. Immediately would be advised," Dr. Scheer said, with the doctors nodding in unison.

Graham nodded. "Thank you, doctor. I appreciate all that you're doing."

He felt an emptiness, wishing he'd somehow been able to protect his sister. The lapse gnawed at him, even though he couldn't see how preventing her infection would have been possible. He felt guilt over his driving ambition and he resolved that he'd put more focus on matters of substance. But Graham also had a feeling that he'd need to be less vulnerable and strengthen his own defenses to be a better protector of those he cared about.

FORTY-ONE

James Russell was busy and deep into one of his many projects at his large antique mahogany desk. He was a combination of old and new. He loved being surrounded by the many icons of antiquity that he'd collected over the decades, but was equally at home with the state-of-the-art computers and monitors next to him. Although the combination of ancient and modern might have seemed to be a dichotomy to some observers, the arrangement worked well for Russell.

His mind was more keenly vibrant than that of most men half his age. Rather than deteriorate, his cognitive skills remained honed and focused, more like a fine katana sword than a fine wine. Even though he was deep in thought, he immediately noticed the change in color on what looked like a large snow globe on his desk. It wasn't a Christmas decoration but rather a sophisticated electronic security device that changed color depending on the outside stimuli. A half grin lifting one side of Russell's mouth looked like someone had squeezed his cheek. The subtle change to his expression and an almost imperceptible turn of his head were his only responses as he continued his study of a large rare volume on his desk.

A man appeared in his office doorway. He wore a long, dark

trench coat made of lightweight fabric. As the man stepped forward, he drew a pump shotgun from under the coat. Russell noted the sling attached to the shotgun as the man steadied the weapon by holding the slide in one hand and the pistol grip in the other. Russell was confronted with the unfriendly end of the gun but showed no more emotion than someone having a pizza delivered.

"I'm here to decrease the burden you've placed on the medical system," the apparent hitman said to Russell with a heavy East European accent. He scowled as he displayed the gun without fully pointing it at Russell.

"Is this what they mean by an affordable care act?" Russell asked with a tone of utter boredom in his voice, shifting in his seat and moving his hands away from the expensive book.

"Keep your hands where I can see them," the thug said, lifting the shotgun a little higher for emphasis.

"I have no idea how good your eyesight is," Russell replied blandly.

"What? What do you mean?" the man said. He shook his head. "You've outlived your usefulness, old man." He sneered.

Russell watched the man as if held had a mop rather than a shotgun. He had seen the same sort of faux toughness in wannabe assassins more than once. They hid behind a gun but had no real spine. The only interesting details about the man were that he was an albino and he wore his white hair long in a man-bun, a style that Russell despised. Having an ear for accents and having spent a good deal of time in the Soviet Union, Russell was relatively certain his uninvited guest was from the Ukraine.

"You sound a lot like my wife, except not nearly as intelligent or as tough. Although she *does* wear her hair the same way you do," Russell chided. "I'm very busy. Why are you here?"

"It should be clear why I'm here. Your clerk was lazy and left the back door open. Too bad for me. I would get extra for putting an end to him as well."

"He'll be back. He went out for coffee and sensitivity training."

"Then it will be bad for him."

Russell kept both hands palms-down on his desk. They had moved slightly back toward his body without the hit man noticing. "Since you're going to kill me anyway, could you at least tell me who's paying you?"

"We are not told such things. There is middleman. They only say you are in the way of their plans. Paying very well. Twice my normal fee. And I get to take whatever I want from your shop. Worth a great deal, I'm told. My cousin is on the way with men and a truck."

Russell's two thumbs had moved imperceptibly to the edge of the desk. "Your cousin, you say? I guess he'll just have to die with you then," Russell said calmly.

Their eyes locked, and when the intruder realized that Russell was deadly serious, his sneering expression changed to one of confusion. Russell nonchalantly looked at the ceiling above the man's head, causing the man's gaze to follow even as Russell pushed two hidden buttons on the edge of the desk with his thumbs.

Russell probably didn't need the diversion, but it prevented the albino from having a chance to pull the trigger as the trapdoor under the rug in front of the desk gave way and the would-be assassin dropped through the floor, screaming as he fell. He plummeted into complete darkness as the trapdoor snapped closed.

Muffled shouting came from under the floor, and Thomas

appeared from behind a row of bookcases. He held a revolver with a suppressor in one hand and, ever cautious, a suppressed Glock in the other.

"You cut that pretty close, didn't you?" When Russell didn't reply, he added, "Not very good, was he?"

"I'm actually insulted," Russell said with genuine disdain. "Just another sign of the collapse of society when they can't even find a decent contract killer anymore."

Underneath the floor, the noise changed from yelling to sounds of pain and fear. Russell and Thomas ignored the noise as if it were the sound of crickets.

"I wonder who sent him," Thomas said.

"I have a pretty good idea, and I think you and I can come up with a more concrete answer soon. I'm just wondering why they chose now. As soon as you're able, run a security echo for the last several weeks and look for anomalies. Either someone has gotten a hint of our plans or the timing was just coincidence, but I'm mostly an agnostic when it comes to coincidences. You heard what he said about his cousin?"

The screaming reached a frenzied pitch that was followed by a muffled shotgun blast and then silence.

Thomas answered evenly. "Yes, sir. We have people positioned in three of the other warehouses. We'll have a nice welcome for his friends with an equally nice Hogan's Alley as a backup. No problem." He lifted a brow. "So it's finally started?"

"So it would seem," Russell said. "Did you send the message to Mr. Chastain?"

"Just before the detritus below showed up," Thomas said.

"Good, good. Then we should see him soon."

Thomas nodded.

Russell looked down and added, "A pity, really."

"The dead guy?" Thomas asked with a hint of disbelief.

"That Persian rug." He sighed. "I remember the bazaar in Turkey where Christiane and I picked it out years ago. It was a favorite."

"Sorry. Think of it as a worthy cause," Thomas said, pretending to console his uncle, since they both knew he must have a hundred such "favorite" rugs.

Russell shook his head. "Please send to our associates the message we discussed. We'll need a meeting soon."

"Right away. Also, we scraped the shooter's phone when he entered the building. We'll have his contacts and send a sweeper team to wherever he's been living, and we'll set up striker blue protocols as a countermeasure to discourage another incursion."

Russell nodded approvingly as Thomas turned to leave. Russell *did* have a fairly good idea which of the factions had sent the assassin and it was a short list. But he was somewhat surprised that it was such an amateur attempt, as though someone was sending a message telling Russell and his organization to elevate their awareness. And that possibility was a much more intriguing mystery.

FORTY-TWO

She gazed for miles out the castle window closest to her—and pondered for years. The view of the Swiss Alps was majestic and a sight she'd taken in many times throughout her life. An observer might think she was daydreaming, but that was a luxury she rarely afforded herself and certainly not during a meeting with some of the most powerful men in the world, men of unimaginable wealth and influence yet hardly known relative to their stature. And that was how it was intended to be—outward personas of extreme wealth but nothing compared to what they really owned and controlled. A simple analogy would be the obligatory biography written after the passing of David Rockefeller that stated his net worth was a laughable $3.3 billion or so. Maybe in his personal checking and money market accounts, but compared with the true wealth accumulated in his many foundations, $3.3 billion was an accounting error. And several among the small group gathered around the massive conference table came from families that had amassed hidden fortunes before John D. started selling kerosene and snake oil. They referred to themselves cryptically as the Directors to be as vague as they possibly could be. Theirs was a group possessing a history of centuries of alliances, battles and schisms.

She and her family had been part of this circle or ones like it since the beginning, but she didn't consider herself one of the Directors, simply because she found many of them loathsome and knew her lineage to be superior to most. She was usually cordial at best, but today her patience was strung like a piano wire. No one in the room could see even a hint of that, of course, because of her flawless self-control and the ability to present a demure front even during a crisis. On occasion, some overstepped their place because her temperament was so carefully hidden and controlled.

Her hair was perfectly coiffed in a French roll. Even the wisp that seemed to have escaped the roll actually hadn't—she intended it to be just as it was to serve as an elegant distraction. Her jewelry and outfit were perfect, and even royalty struggled to determine who her designers might be. To no avail, however, because the gifted artists worked solely for her and no other—and under her direct input and oversight. She could have easily become a famous designer for the embarrassingly wealthy herself, but such endeavors were far below her real position. She paused her gazing to look into the exquisite tea cup in her hand, noting the flaw of a single floating tea leaf. She found the imperfection more interesting than the vacuous banter she had been currently enduring. And she enjoyed making them wait. They were used to being in control, and it unnerved them at the whim of another.

She was the Countess Helena Victoria Louise Sophia, so named for Queen Victoria, her descendants and predecessors. With the exception of the Netherlands, all current royalty traced back to Victoria and Christian IX of Denmark, and the two of them shared a direct lineage to King George II. However, she'd been selected not to be in the limelight of visible royalty but to take her place among those in the true seat of power. Though her full name and titles were quite long, she was known to the Directors simply as the Countess, although there was nothing simple about her. She was brilliant and sophisticated as well as feared and revered. But today the Directors were growing impatient waiting for her, which was as she wished it to be.

"Countess Helena, please. We're awaiting your answer," said Director Three in his heavy and pinched German accent. Most of the men around the table were septuagenarian or octogenarian, and he was no exception. The Countess was the single young person on the council.

She slowly turned from the view and from her tea and said, "I know precisely *what* to do and *when* to do it. I have never failed to do what was necessary and I never will." Her tone was even and without emotion.

Director Two began to speak, his accent hyper-nasal French. "Countess, we fear—"

"You certainly do," she snapped. "Because you're cowardly and impatient old men. I, on the other hand, do not." She had finally set her tea cup down on its saucer on the table.

It was Director One's turn to attempt his influence. He had white hair, like each of the men in the room, but he had the luxury of more of it than all the men combined. His accent was that of aristocratic English breeding dating back many centuries. "Countess, if your father or grandfather were here—"

"If they were, then undoubtedly some of you would not be," she countered.

"Steps may need to be taken," said Director Four from the far end of the table in a reserved tone. He glanced around, looking for the slight nods he saw from most of the Directors. He breathed a silent sigh of relief.

"I certainly hope that wasn't a veiled threat. You may have read in the archives of what happened the last time anyone moved against my family," she said, pausing for effect as she met the eyes of every man at the table. "I believe some had their family trees pruned fairly significantly. Of course, I have always believed that culling the weak serves only to strengthen the whole."

A long painful silence followed as they all knew that the Countess wasn't bluffing. Director Seven finally broke the silence. He was the lone American and affable for a man so patently ruthless.

"Countess, none of us are making threats. We all know that these matters are in your capable hands. I suppose we had hoped for more concrete assurances at this meeting." He smiled. And it wasn't a smile of kindness but one that reflected his infamous cunning.

"Gentleman, I have everything perfectly under control. If you actually read the status reports, you would see that. They are comprehensive and cogent. I have left nothing to chance. We have usually moved slowly and deliberately, and with great haste only when it suits and benefits us. There is absolutely no need for haste now, and to rush would greatly increase the risk of mistakes. And I don't make mistakes." Her tone was even, but her piercing blue-green eyes conveyed a resolve of steel.

"But, Countess—" said Director One, interrupting again.

"*But* nothing. I suggest that you prepare for the Bilderberg meeting this week," she said. "At least there your input might be helpful."

The men had been summarily dismissed, and they resented it. But they also knew that she was right—she did have a long record of flawlessly managing even the most difficult of tasks.

And their resentment was moot. She was also right that her family and its allies were far too powerful.

Most of the useless old men had learned that vast wealth should be enough and that it was senseless to try to attain total control. *Most of them.* She wished they would retire and cede the reins of power to their progeny. They too were weak and impulsive, but at least they would present a different form of annoyance. There was also the remote possibility that some of them could be molded into worthier men. Of course, they could never achieve the stature of her father and grandfather. She knew only one other man who approached that level.

As they filed out, the Countess turned her attention back to her view and a fresh cup of tea. As much as she was enjoying the luxurious surroundings, she looked forward to her trip home. Now she could allow herself some daydreaming time. A warm smile appeared on her flawless Nordic face. Yes, she had the strategy for their group's future more under control than they could imagine.

FORTY-THREE

When Graham saw Jennifer's miraculous recovery, he wondered if Dr. Scheer had sandbagged him, overstating the dire possibilities while having a fairly strong knowledge—based on prior testing in his laboratory—that her recovery was almost a certainty. Strategic hedging of bets was done in many professions for many reasons. If outcomes went awry, everyone was prepared, and if they went well, the professionals looked like heroes and geniuses. He didn't want to dwell on the possibility. He was ecstatic that his sister was conscious, fairly alert and even smiling from time to time. The good doctors reminded him that her fever was viral in nature and so their protocol wasn't a cure, but they also said that the unknown pathogen was in remission and that Jennifer would need regular injections or risk going into the coma that she had so narrowly avoided.

He wasn't allowed direct contact with her, but they were able to talk via an intercom system. She was still loopy, not due to the illness but to the morphine drip that she had been on. One of the side effects of her infection was horrible pain when she was conscious. Dr. Scheer said he suspected that if she had periods of lucidity prior to coma that she would convulse again but with much deeper pain than what she'd experienced when she'd arrived. Graham shuddered to think of her dying in agony.

Jennifer insisted that he leave and get some rest, which she intended to do as well. He argued that he wasn't really tired. She semi-coherently told him to leave and shave off what she called the unsightly growth on his face, and then she slurred something about his resemblance to a Wookie as she giggled and called him Youbacca. Besides, she said, Bobby was better looking and a better conversationalist. Graham laughed because Bobby was sound asleep and snoring loudly in the bed next to hers, having gotten absolutely no rest during his own vigil. Graham decided that retreat would be the wiser part of valor since he knew from experience that it was pointless to debate with drunks or stoners. He promised to return and check on her, and Jennifer gave him a dismissive wave with a crooked grin.

He profusely thanked each of the medical professionals, one at a time, who had been involved with saving his sister. Dr. Callahan explained that they would continue to keep close watch on her vitals and continue to test and monitor her and update him frequently. He told Graham that Dr. Scheer's lab would deliver more vials of serum as they synthesized and compounded it and that they would give Jennifer her doses via IV for the next several days. When they were convinced she was completely out of danger and that their formulation and dosages were the correct one, based on her response and lab results, she could get a shot from a home health nurse. Dr. Scheer hoped to eventually provide an oral version.

Graham felt invigorated with relief as he cleaned up his office away from office. One of his employees stopped by to pick up the bulk of his belongings, while he packed his personal laptop and other, more important items in two of his executive-style backpacks. He was so thrilled with Jennifer's condition, the backpacks felt empty as he hoisted one over his shoulder and carried one in his hand.

Graham didn't know if it was nervous energy, relief or pent-up adrenaline that had him on the unusual high, but he had a thought of what to do about it; he decided to stop at his favorite dojo for a workout. He used the term *favorite* loosely, as he was one of the founders and owners.

With the intention of catering to a more upscale market, Graham had partnered with a few truly talented martial arts masters. There were gyms that offered martial arts and martial arts studios that had weights and weight machines, but his studio was an elegant blend of both. Most dojos were focused on increasing numbers of students and provided after-school specials that offered a form of daycare. Graham was fine with that concept, but it wasn't within the scope of their model.

Lessons and workouts ranged from private to semi-private in several disciplines. There were also tactical classes that included executive security, weapons, advanced first aid, new tech and survival. Several of the highly proficient combat veterans from the security teams at his office complex taught in exchange for use of the facility and advanced training of their own. Classes were based on member request, demand and design. To stay sharp, Graham took many of the classes himself. Today, though, he wanted a vigorous workout followed by a complete body detox: steam, sauna, deep massage and some regenerative juicing concoction. He was looking forward to all of them.

The sparring session went far better than he'd imagined given his lack of recent physical activity while being cooped up at the hospital. A number of practitioners hung around the gym on any given day, and since several styles were represented, it was typical that Graham could find sparring partners for a friendly bout. What wasn't typical was how effortlessly he was able to anticipate their moves and parry them. In his normal routine, he would be taxed if he fought three different opponents in sequence. It wasn't until the fifth one said, "No mas!" that Graham realized he wasn't even winded. He wasn't done, so he convinced two fresh guys to go a few rounds together so he could work on multiple-attacker scenarios. He finally called it quits when they were all winded. For years Graham had been striving to gain a level of expertise in what was known as "breaking inertia," what the Japanese called *hakei kansei*. The Chinese masters didn't have a specific name for it, they just did it. It was best described as the ability to quickly cover a great distance with great speed and fluidity. One moment you're at point A and in a blink you're at point B. It suddenly occurred to Graham that he had actually been using the technique he had so long tried to learn. It was more like he felt it rather than struggling to implement it. He had once been told it meant his mind and body needed to act as one; a concept that he wasn't sure he'd ever learn.

Master Tsai had been observing Graham from a distance. He held multiple black belts and was one of their highest-ranking instructors. He nodded with approval and gave welcome suggestions before Graham bowed out for his recovery routine.

As much as Graham enjoyed the workout, there were issues more important that he was eager to get back to. He'd received a surfeit of text messages while waiting on his sister's hopeful recovery, including a few from Thomas and James Russell that conveyed a good deal of urgency. But theirs were not the messages that intrigued him most.

He stared at his phone for some time before answering the very cryptic text from his past. As he drove to one of his favorite restaurants, he knew his next meeting would reflect a dichotomy, memories of a time of great happiness mirrored against a time of darkness and sorrow.

FORTY-FOUR

Maximillian Scheer, MD, PhD, strode across the ultra-modern lobby of Cellular Dynamics like he owned the place—and in a sense he did, at least partly. He walked past the reception and security area without so much as a nod, but with the full knowledge that many eyes, both human and robotic, had him in their sights.

Dr. Scheer walked down a nondescript hallway, took a turn down a second short hallway and toward a door marked Private that silently slid open when he approached. That was the simple part; his path would become more complicated. He strode down a new hallway and stopped at a security checkpoint. Two men sat behind thick bulletproof glass, the men separated from each other by a thick wall that contained a bulletproof window. Scheer placed his briefcase and other personal items in a heavy plastic tray and slid the tray through a rectangular stainless steel door that flipped inward. The conveyor system was separate from either guard, and the wall that separated them was blast proof. In that way, neither guard could be subdued by the contents of a bag or briefcase. Both guards viewed the contents of Dr. Scheer's case on their monitors, and both had to approve his admittance. This didn't happen until he held his ID card in front of a reader and had his palm, followed by his retina, scanned and approved. The palm scan also read multiple biometrics to determine if he was under duress.

There was a great deal more to the Cellular Dynamics, Inc. facility than anyone could determine from outward observation. There were certain benefits in doing top secret biological research for the government; government agencies had budget allocation oversight but no construction oversight. Even their budget oversight was incredibly broad because it utilized black box funds that were never fully disclosed, not even to Congress. So the power structure behind CDI was able to create several other completely clandestine companies behind the scenes, supplemented with their own cash infusions.

The first layer was the closely held public company with a complicated maze of affiliates, DBAs and divisions. That information was highly restricted, as anyone would expect, because theirs was an extremely competitive biotech industry where patents, formulae and inventions determined the life and death of a company. The first layer of the company was highly successful in its own right for a number of reasons, not the least of which had to do to with access to highly classified information. They were able to pay a premium for some of the best scientific talent available.

The next layer of operations involved the top secret biotech work they did for the government. Since secrecy was at a premium, their budget was enormous and oversight lax— virtually no one fully understood the scope of what was being done, and multiple long-term projects were always in the works.

This setup was a proverbial license to steal. And that was what the board did, but not in ways that one might normally imagine. They didn't drain or skim off the extensive excesses in capital into their bank accounts. They used the voluminous budgets to create large shadow subsidiaries right within the existing top secret facilities. This third and most secret layer of the operation comprised these shadow subsidiaries. Since all the work was compartmentalized and information was on a need to know basis, it was impossible to oversee all that was going on. CDI could work on private projects in complete secrecy—mostly with money from government overruns—and no one would have the slightest clue it was happening. From the initial design to planning and construction of shadow systems, every aspect was under the radar. Even the building construction inspector was completely in their control. And if ever there was the slightest hint of a leak or whistle to be blown, all manner of bribes, blackmail and accidents were already planned for. Security protocols were thoroughly drilled into every employee from day one—if it wasn't your area of responsibility, don't ask. Not ever.

What very few employees knew was where one part of the complex ended and another started. Most also didn't know that there was three times the area underground as above. And that there were several other sites, in the US and abroad, including a very private island where truly advanced and exotic work was being done—and where Dr. Scheer usually took his "vacations." He fully understood the magnitude of what they were doing and the reason for the redundant layers of security, but the extra security still wearied him. He did important work at all three levels of the companies and also had to attend many administrative meetings, so multiple changes of floors, halls, elevators and levels became an annoying nuisance. He wanted to devote his time to impending breakthroughs, not to menial tasks. But he believed the rewards were worth the annoyance of redundant security. No, he didn't just believe, he knew! He didn't do the work just for the sizeable fortune and the fame—he was nearly guaranteed the Nobel. What motivated him was the chance to change the evolution of mankind. That goal consumed him and was worth far more than even the Nobel. He focused on that prize while putting up with the many annoyances and distractions.

They were very close. He could feel it.

As Dr. Scheer reached for his ID card, he came to an abrupt halt and his cheerful expression changed just as abruptly to one of dismay. The sight of his office door ajar reminded him of an open wound. Since he kept it locked and it wasn't time for the cleaning service, it could only mean one thing—he was about to be subject to a most loathsome meeting. He pushed the door wider. A man with dark hair and darker eyes, wearing all black, sat behind Scheer's desk, leaning back in his chair and bearing a Cheshire Cat smile.

"*Do* come in Dr. Scheer," Roth said with great ebullience.

"I've asked you *not* to sit in my chair at my desk, Roth," Dr. Scheer said petulantly. "It's quite rude and annoying."

"And I've reminded you, more than once, Dr. Scheer, that the desk and chair belong to us, just like you do. But I know you're more comfortable here and that you need to work, so . . ." Roth made a show of moving to a nearby chair next to a small conference table.

When Scheer regained his chair, he felt he was also regaining a slight modicum of his turf. He allowed his pent-up indignation to flow.

"I can't believe you took such a chance, exposing me with that project at the hospital."

Roth laughed. "Dr. Scheer, there was *no* chance of your exposure at any time. What you did will insure his cooperation.

And he possesses one of the most important components to make our work a reality."

"My work."

"*That*, is a matter of opinion that I'm here to clarify."

FORTY-FIVE

Graham looked out at the lake through the huge windows on the other side of the bar. He'd really rather be sitting out on the wooden deck, closer to the water. He enjoyed the low light of the sun moving away from his perspective and the narrow reflection it created on the water's surface. The evening temperature was perfect and the breeze was just right, but the deck was too open for the private conversation he knew would soon take place.

Not that he minded being inside. The restaurant was another place that he liked enough to consider buying into but simply hadn't taken the time to inquire about. Schooner's Cove was the perfect blend of elegant and casual, depending on where one sat and what one ordered. The scotch selection was outstanding, as were the seafood and filets. For lighter fare on the deck, the appetizer menu was twice the size of a typical restaurant's, and customers could create their own fabulous smorgasbords. Although Graham didn't often have the time to do so, he preferred a more European style of dining, a social event that went on for hours, the meal relaxed rather than rushed. But this evening wouldn't be one of lengthy relaxation.

This meeting was completely off the books. His phone was

sealed in a blackout bag, preventing the signal from escaping and keeping him from being tracked. As far as his office or anyone else knew, he'd ceased to exist for a few hours. He'd be paying in cash, leaving no electronic trace of where he'd spent the evening.

When he heard a familiar voice behind him, Graham lifted his head without turning it.

"So, rookie, are you daydreaming about your misspent youth and self-medicating again?" said the man who seemed to appear from nowhere.

Graham stared ahead, as if he had little interest in the new arrival who was taking a seat next to him at the secluded part of the bar.

"Senior Chief Hart, what a complete nonsurprise. It's easy to see why you have so very few friends," Graham said, still looking straight ahead. "I only self-medicate when I'm forced to endure poor company. And rookie is no way to address your superior."

"It's master chief, as you well know. I have many friends, and the only thing superior about you is your wallet size," Jason Hart said, signaling the bartender with a raised index finger.

Graham had enjoyed their banter for many years and wasn't about to let up. It had been too long and it was great to see an old navy buddy. There were few bonds closer than those shared by comrades who lived through shots fired in anger.

"Cuban porn sites don't count as friends. And my Lieutenant Johnson is far superior," Graham said with a moderately straight face.

Hart laughed. "Definitely lieutenant JG in your case! Guinness, please," he said to the bartender.

Graham finally turned his head to look at his old friend.

Hart was still razor sharp and looked more like thirty than thirty-seven. Or was it thirty-eight? Graham doubted there were many men who were tougher or in better shape. He was kind and had a great sense of humor, even in the midst of combat. And he was one of the most deadly killing machines Graham had ever met, even compared to other SEALs. Graham was surprised to see that even though Chief Hart's blond hair was short, it was longer than his typical high and tight grooming. And he had some scruff, which he never wore except when he was on a long mission in-country. The bartender returned with a large mug of dark beer.

"His tab," Hart said as they raised their glasses, and then said in unison with Graham, "To absent companions." They both drank.

"Your historically mediocre skills have spiraled downward into a previously unknown region of great decline, even for you, Micro-Chip," Hart said. He took another healthy drink.

"You couldn't sneak up on Helen Keller, barely Master Chief," Graham replied, taking a drink of the water next to his scotch.

"I could've put an icepick in your ear while an ice cube was still in your mouth." Hart smirked.

Graham pointed at the mirrors decorating the shelves holding the bar's outstanding liquor stock. "I had every entrance covered, including the one you were using in that lame sneak attempt. Besides, it doesn't take a bloodhound to pick up the scent of your cheap cologne three blocks away."

Graham spoke with pride. Master Chief Hart was the best, and Graham had worked hard to earn his respect many years ago.

"Okay, rookie. I'll give you credit *this* time. Not bad for an amateur."

Hart nodded, taking another drink. He didn't feel the need to burst Graham's bubble. He really was pretty good for an amateur, but there was no comparison to twenty years of SEAL and Delta training and experience, both finely honed by countless dangerous missions. Master Chief Hart had been at multiple locations on the grounds twenty minutes before Graham arrived and could have killed him in an instant on several different occasions and in several interesting ways—but there was no need to rub it in. Graham was one of the good guys, and they'd all known it was only a torn rotator cuff that had kept him from completing the SEAL course. He chose another path, but no other tech guys had had the balls to go out in the field the way Graham had.

"Thank you, Master Chief. Admitting that must have caused you great pain. Closest I've ever heard you come to saying something nice."

"I know how fragile you are," Hart said, raising a signal to the bartender. "Nurse! I need more medicine." He laughed. "That never gets old!"

"It was old the first seventeen times I heard it, and it needed to be embalmed after the last hundred and seventy-seven." Graham groaned. "So what brings you up this way, Chief? And why the hippy grooming with the uncharacteristically sharp outfit that Sherry surely picked out for you?"

"My beloved spouse had only moderate input with regard to my attire. And I'm here because the Old Man ordered me to volunteer to take some time off and go on a fishing trip, and he specifically told me not run into you." Hart picked up his new glass of ale.

"And yet, here you are," Graham replied.

"Yep. Just following orders," Hart said.

"So I'm guessing this off the books, unsanctioned visit could put you both in a bit of danger?"

"Not me. I leap-frogged and backtracked for two days, and I guarantee no one has a clue that I'm here. And the skipper has a soft spot for you and was more than willing to take the risk." Hart's face held no expression whatsoever. "I think it has something to do with an old head wound or you saving our lives in Kandahar."

"An accident," Graham said in a low, distracted voice. "Right place, wrong time."

"Yeah, I seem to remember reading something to that effect on your DSM citation. Or was it the Silver Star citation? How did it go again? Let's see . . . *For accidental valor and with total disregard for common sense, Lieutenant Chastain at no time put himself in any grave danger exceeding a hangnail when he—*"

"Are you intoxicated after just one beer, Master Chief?"

"*When he spotted an RPG plume and threw himself in front of a chief and a commander, knocking them down and inadvertently taking most of the shrapnel blast himself. Though bleeding profusely from what had to be minor wounds, said lieutenant then dragged said chief and commander to safety while being wounded again, from small arms fire. Lieutenant Serendipity Chastain further, by complete accident, held off a superior force and killed or wounded ten of the enemy, putting them in full retreat and saving more of his comrades' lives.*"

"I was just scared to death and reacted. Nothing more," Graham said, looking out at the water.

"*On another occasion, during a minor firefight, with barely any courage, a scared Chastain was again wounded while rescuing two more injured SEALs under withering automatic weapons fire. With selfish regard for his own safety, he simply reacted several more times, killing more combatants and repelling yet another attack. His inconspicuous and completely inadvert, knee-jerk gallantry saved*" *the lives of the entire platoon and defended a strategic location until reinforcements could arrive. Not until all other team members were treated did the cowardly lieutenant allow his own paper-cut-level wounds to be tended.*" Hart nodded. "Yeah. I think the citations read something like that, if I recall." He took another swig. "Didn't you get the smaller versions of those medals?"

Graham didn't say anything. He drank his scotch and felt himself spinning back in time to a great deal of pain and terror that he'd mostly blocked out of his mind.

"You know," Hart said, "you could have just used some old cliché like 'duck' or 'hit the dirt' and saved yourself a lot of wear and tear." Hart laughed and banged Graham's shoulder with his forearm.

"Won't happen again, Master Chief."

"See that it doesn't! Some people just can't take a compliment."

"Haven't heard any."

"Accolades can be subtle," Hart said.

"I have to say . . . that in spite of all the pain it caused me, I actually miss being a part of all that."

Hart stared straight ahead. "Doesn't go away."

Graham held up his own glass toward the bartender and tapped it. He waited for the fresh drink to arrive and for the bartender to move away before he spoke again.

"So, Master Chief, do you think you and Gilligan could sail the S.S. Minnow somewhere close to a point in this heartfelt reunion? What is it you needed to come all this way to not go fishing with me about? I know you can barely turn on a computer, but surely the skipper has someone who could send me something encrypted."

Hart didn't bother looking around to see who might be in

earshot; he did that subtly and constantly. He did, however, lean toward Graham.

"Lieutenant, this is Archangel level stuff that I'm about to tell you. Or actually not tell you." Hart's voice was very low. "Something came across the skipper's desk in DC, and it had you flagged on it. We don't have all the details yet, but it comes from very high up. No one else probably would have paid it any mind, but we have history. It was a high-level communique, but part of Joint-Intel messaging and with no specific directive for us. But that level *does* tell us that someone will be tasked with surveilling you. Maybe a team and maybe more than just surveilling. We just don't know who yet. And I can't tell you the code name for the overall operation." He took a drink, finally allowing his gaze to dart around the bar.

"Oh, I get it. This is the, you-*could*-tell-me-but-you'd-have-to-kill-me routine," Graham said. "Why, I can't even *begin* to fathom—"

"No, you chucklehead. That's not it. The directive hasn't been given a name yet; it's too new." Now they both laughed. "What have you gotten yourself into, Lieutenant?" Hart asked somberly.

"Master Chief, you know I've long been involved with high-level security projects." Graham shrugged. "Spooks use my stuff to spy on other spooks. It doesn't get too much higher up than that. I still have Q-level clearance."

"Yeah, we've seen many of your project reports and vetted quite a few. But this is different."

"I don't know what to tell you. I have a few new developments, but nothing that should draw this kind of attention."

Hart handed Graham a small slip of paper. "This is a throwaway number for me for a week, unless you use it sooner.

I actually am going fishing for a day or so back toward the Barn, but close enough that I can double back if you need me or think of something important. After that, it'll be standard encrypted channels. To keep things off the books, we'll brown bag new codes to you as necessary." He finished his Guinness.

"Thanks, Master Chief," Graham said, shaking Hart's hand with a firm grip. "Great to see you."

"Thanks for the drinks. If we hear anything, we'll let you know, and in the meantime, watch your six, buddy."

Master Chief Hart slipped out as quietly as he'd come in.

Graham had maintained a tough exterior in front of Hart, but in truth he was more than a little shook up over the idea that someone was going to have him watched and that the surveillance could escalate to a sanction. He had no idea what he might have seen or done to merit such an action, and Graham was sure he'd be bending his mind for some time to try to figure it out. Until he did, he'd need to ratchet up his personal security awareness to a much higher level—and hope it would be enough. He wondered about so many unique incidents occurring so close together. Seeing as he didn't believe in coincidences.

FORTY-SIX

Roth loved toying with Dr. Scheer in the same way he enjoyed it with everyone else. He played mind games that he felt kept him sharp and them on edge. And the more brilliant or cunning the adversary, the more he relished sharpening his skills.

But he knew better than to push Scheer too far. It was important that he stay focused. So when Roth felt that he'd toyed with his cerebral adversary enough for his own satisfaction, he reversed and turned on the charm. Scheer was a tool just like all the others, albeit far more brilliant than most. But like many geniuses, he was insecure and his ego was just short of eggshell fragile.

"Speaking of the hospital . . . I assume all went well?" Roth said.

Scheer had calmed somewhat when he settled in behind his desk and eased into his comfort zone. "Of course," he said smugly. "We knew the antidote would work long before the pathogen was delivered. It was useful to accumulate more human test results, though."

"What about the hospital staff? Any problems there?" Roth asked, genuinely wanting to know.

"Not at all. One of the attending physicians has been a fan of mine for some time. *Some* people recognize true brilliance. He was falling all over himself to accommodate me. And of course your calls to the right people, reminding them of the large sums of money donated to them, got everyone's attention."

"Money always does. Just like it buys a certain amount of brilliance."

"Chastain was both gracious and desperate in wanting to help his sister. Most of the people were fawning butt-kissers, but Chastain seems like a solid and standup guy. I didn't see a hint of any loose ends or suspicion on the part of anyone, but that's your arena, not mine."

Scheer turned on his computer and entered his access codes and touched the attached biometric scanner.

"We're prepared for all manner of contingencies and especially loose ends," Roth said. "What happens if the sister stops taking the drug?"

"In the short term, she would mostly likely convulse and die if she didn't get treatment soon enough. She'd end up like she was before we gave her the serum—approaching a coma. In the long term, we don't know yet. It could be that her body will develop sufficient antibodies to fight off the virus, or it may go dormant."

Roth laughed heartily. "We aren't worried about the long term in this case at all. We can pretend we're politicians and let others worry about results and then pick up the pieces down the road. What we're going to do will be in the short term and no one will be able to do anything about it even in the intermediate term."

Scheer looked over the top of his glasses and smirked—which, given his personality, was the same as laughing hysterically. "Speaking of politicians, how's the stem cell debate going?"

Roth laughed again and slapped the back of one hand against the open palm of the other for effect. "Perfect! Great! We're funding both sides of the argument and providing both sides with opposition research. Couldn't be better!"

"Those fools! Don't they understand that they could be finding *cures* if they focused on mesenchymal stem cells? The research has proven there are far more benefits far faster than with embryonic stem cells. Why, if I were in charge—"

"And we'll make sure you never are. We couldn't care less about such crap; we want them to fight. With all the money we're plowing into this facility and the millions from the government overruns and overbilling that they don't even audit, we'll be light-years ahead of everyone else before they even figure out which bill to pass." Roth was crowing.

"But the research would be of great benefit," countered Scheer.

"It *is* of benefit—to us. Would you like someone else to get the Nobel?"

"I will have earned that!"

"Yes, Dr. Scheer. And we could have taken all of the vast amounts of research that we stole, along with the vast amounts of funding we've provided, and helped some other promising researcher *earn* the Nobel Prize."

Scheer became a great deal less aggressive. "My base research was leading the field," he countered somberly.

"Maybe. Then there are the additional residences off the books, the secret bank accounts and the very expensive women *in addition to your frumpy wife* that we support."

"With great achievement comes great stress. I *need* those women," Scheer said defensively.

"I could suggest a far less expensive ambidextrous form of

stress relief," Roth said, continuing to mock his opponent. "The point is, I don't want to hear you whining about other research. We have a massive investment in *your* research—for which you will receive even more fame and fortune. And while they're still cloning sheep, the new organs you've been cloning for our clients will be fully functional and our returns will be astronomical."

Thoroughly beaten down, Scheer quietly offered, "I had always hoped to benefit society."

"And you will. It's just that most of the benefit will go to a certain *segment* of society. Eventually a little may even trickle down to the useless breeders and eaters."

Wanting a subject change, Scheer tried a new direction. "What of the new plasma and DNA sequencing facility? Where does that stand?"

"The remaining equipment has been installed and tested. All the staff is in place. And all of the specimens are fully operational. And since you look like you need a vacation, you should visit the island yourself. This time, take the quiet brunette. If the blonde gets drunk and out of line again, I'm pretty sure she'll wind up in the ocean this time."

"Is that a threat, Roth?" Scheer said with anger.

"We don't make threats, Scheer. We make things happen."

"That's *Dr.* Scheer."

"Yes, and a *doctor* won't be able to help you if someone pushes you in front of a bus next week and your work is turned over to one of your subordinates. So take the brunette and do the blonde some other time. It's not a request."

Scheer started to plead his case, but he knew that Roth was deadly serious. Other scientists had died under mysterious circumstances in the past. He never asked about them, because he knew he was staring into the dark eyes of a man with no soul or conscience.

And Roth was actually right this time. He could see Sarah, who was more entertaining, and placate her with gifts, and then take the more laid back but equally beautiful Laura along as his island companion. It was rare for him to get more excited about work than getting laid, but this was different. He would be far more exhilarated to begin the live specimen tests than have wild sex. Well, at least after he spent the next two days with Sarah he would be. Fantasies about her made him imagine his own planned enhancements and how many other Sarahs he could enjoy and entertain. He'd go from being a great man to even more superior in every way. And Roth would never know that Scheer would be his own test subject until it was too late. The possibilities were worth all of Roth's insufferable comments and more.

FORTY-SEVEN

Graham hadn't planned to stay away so long, but he'd had no choice. He couldn't believe it had been almost two weeks, but between the emergency with his sister and the clandestine meeting with Jason Hart, he simply hadn't had the time to get back to see James Russell. And it was a meeting he was truly looking forward to. The time they had already spent had yielded incredible information and Russell implied that what was to come was even more amazing. Graham had come up with many questions since his last visit.

Thomas was courteous in his text messages, looking for a rough ETA, and often inquired about Jennifer's condition. So far the due diligence searches that Graham, Alex and Ariel had performed on Russell and Thomas had only confirmed what Graham had been told.

Based on all that had been happening to him and in light of his meeting with Jason, Graham took a number of extra precautions. He had his best security wizards sweep his house, office and his cars on a random and ongoing basis. He had them do the same to any and all of his corporate locations, but after hours, so as not to alarm anyone or arouse suspicions. He also rotated who was doing the sweeps and did some himself. He had developed quite sophisticated devices in recent years, so using the latest equipment was no challenge.

Again Graham bagged his phone and tablet to prevent tracking during his drive—making sure he covered all critical contacts before he left, including his sister. His Bluetooth was disabled and the batteries removed from his cell and tablet. He used active and passive countermeasures developed by his own company, products trademarked as Fire Engine and Swing Shift. However, his versions were levels above the commercial editions.

Graham took a further precaution by taking the Range Rover that he rarely drove. He had already moved it to a warehouse that he'd invested in. He pulled his Mercedes through the automatic and coded gate, used the encrypted garage door opener to gain access on one side of the building, changed vehicles and drove out another door and gate that faced a different street. He hadn't bought the property for that purpose, but the scheme worked perfectly, regardless. The technique made following him very difficult. He had also begun to start thinking ahead with regard to other procedures and systems he might begin developing.

Personal security measures were not the only ones that Graham decided to enhance. Between Russell's hack of one of his systems and the new activity generated by Ambrose *and* the clandestine meeting with Jason, Graham had decided that if he were to err, it would be firmly on the side of caution. As such, he had met with Alex Chen and the heads of his legal and finance departments to implement "need to know" protocols that had already been set into motion. Like Alex, his department heads were some of the best in their fields. Graham treated them exceptionally well and had earned their fierce loyalty, so there was no question that they would spring into action with great fervor. In addition, he had set up new parameters and tasks for

Ariel to look into, flag and summarize. He set up regular summary feeds with emergency alerts. Hopefully, that would be another level of growth for Ariel's decision theory as well.

By the time he arrived at Russell's emporium, Graham had made numerous extra turns and stops to be sure no one was following him. Some might have considered him paranoid, but he didn't feel that way. Until he heard more from Jason, being flagged at Archangel-level or above was enough to make him start honing his countermeasure skills. He wouldn't have been the first person operating in the intel world who was "sanctioned," and it didn't matter if there was a good reason or if it was a government screwup—he wasn't taking any chances. And he had his own investigation methods and contacts to seek out when the time was right. He planned to use Ariel soon, but that would require more of his oversight than normal.

Thomas had more than adequate security monitors to see Graham pull up. The two of them had already communicated about Graham's arrival time, but not about the change of vehicle. Thomas had told him to park in back, and Graham planned to discuss using some form of code and encryption system in the future. He was certain they'd be amenable. Graham scanned his surroundings as he got out of the Range Rover. Thomas appeared immediately from behind an unmarked door that didn't have an exterior handle. He motioned in the low light for Graham to come his direction.

Thomas shook Graham's hand, and Graham noticed that today Thomas had a cordial warmth about him. Maybe his being aloof at the first meeting was just caution and protectiveness for his great-uncle.

Thomas led the way to Russell's office enclave of rarities and historic memorabilia. Graham noticed an exquisite antique mahogany bijouterie table set up off to the left of Russell's desk. Centered on it was a large oval sterling silver serving tray bearing dishes of cakes, crackers, cheese and fruit. Beside that was an antique service for coffee along with liquor decanters, a silver ice bucket and tongs, and various other serving appointments. On each side of the serving table were two Chippendale side chairs.

Graham imagined that the meeting might be a rather lengthy one.

He approached Russell with an extended hand which was clasped in a firm handshake.

"I'd like Thomas to join us for some of the discussion," Russell said. "I hope you're all right with that. I think he's past impressing you with his ability to sneak up on you."

"I'm fine with it," said Graham cordially, glancing at Thomas. "I can relax and not worry about him appearing out of nowhere."

Thomas smiled at the compliment and motioned for Graham to sit. He extended a hand in the direction of the table and said, "Feel free to help yourself. If there's something else you need and we have it, I'll be glad to get it for you."

"No, no. This looks fine," Graham said, selecting the bottle of water closest to him. "I'm sure if this meeting is anything like the last one, I'll be moving up from water fairly soon."

Russell pivoted his wheelchair slightly to face Graham. "I can just about guarantee that this meeting will be more eye-opening than the last one."

Graham unscrewed the cap from his bottle and drank. "I see you got a new rug since I was here last."

Russell and Thomas looked at each other before Russell said, "You have a keen eye, Graham. Yes, sometimes accidents happen. We somehow ended up with a rather large stain and we thought the new rug would be more appealing." Russell's eyes took on a vacant sadness. "I'm very glad that your sister's condition improved. We have some information for you before you go that I'm sure you'll find helpful. We have substantial medical research resources of our own. This has to do with our ongoing discussion, but it's better that we discuss it later this evening."

Graham nodded, giving Russell the tacit go-ahead for directing their discussion.

"Have you noticed anything unusual since we were last together?" Russell asked

"I've experienced nothing *but* unusual the last several weeks. You may need to be more specific."

"What about that shrapnel scar that you used to have above your left eye?" Russell pointed at his own forehead.

Graham reached up to touch the spot. "I assure you that I still have a scar above my—"

Thomas had been sitting quietly with his ripped arms folded across his chest. "Not so much." As Graham, mouth agape, traced the spot with the far-diminished scar, Thomas added, "How about your energy levels? Focus, recovery and things like that?"

Graham continued to rub his forehead slightly as he recalled the past several days. "Energy? Excellent. Recovery . . . outstanding. Focus . . . off the charts."

"I'd say your wife is in for a surprise when she gets home too, but I don't want to go into that."

Thomas and Russell both laughed. Graham's eyes widened.

"Well, that's *never* been a problem, but . . ." His chin snapped upward as he gained a revelation and smiled. "Something to do with the metal scroll I held?"

Thomas looked at Russell and said, "And you thought he might not be intuitive enough."

Russell chuckled, sat up a little straighter and put his hands together on his elaborate desk, fingers interlaced the way he often held them. "We'll get to that later. You'll have fewer gray hairs, *thicker* hair and other changes that'll make you think you're regaining your youth. While that sinks in, I'll take you back to nearly the beginning of what I alluded to the last time you were here. That scroll, though amazing in itself, is just a small part of the story. We let you see that early to get your attention. Most importantly, I need to get you up to speed and explain how nearly everything is controlled from behind the scenes and how it started and progressed to the present day."

"So you're talking conspiracy. You think society is controlled," Graham said, having gotten past the discovery of his recent physical changes.

"*All* conspiracies, not *a* conspiracy. And I don't think, I *know*. I've seen what's controlled at the highest levels, proof of what's controlled, and sometimes I've even played roles in various conspiracy operations myself. Over time, I'll direct you to absolute proof of what I'm saying so you can see it yourself firsthand. But I doubt you'll find that necessary." Russell's voice held an undertone of assurance.

Graham crossed his legs and interlaced his fingers around one knee as he said, "This is all because of what was in the crates you found?"

"That was the start of my journey. We'll have to spend a fair amount of time together for me to explain the contents of the crates. Before that, I need to tell you of their origins. The contents served as an introduction to the world of reality. And as a result, I traveled ever deeper down the labyrinth of rabbit holes during my years in military intelligence, the OSS and the intelligence agencies that sprang from that organization. The contents were just the beginning. There is *so* much more than that."

Graham noted the change in Russell's comfort level with him. "Why not just publish what you know?" he asked.

"There are many reasons. First, what I know would fill many volumes. And it would be taken as just another wild and fanciful tale where people like you would mutter ignorantly of conspiracy theories. Second, all of this, everything I'm telling you, is deadly and in an ongoing state. There is no single *thing* or even tightly defined group of things at work here. The tentacles spread far and wide, and the last thing one would want to do is let adversaries know how much you know." He drank from his antique water goblet.

Graham leaned back in his chair to make himself more comfortable, noticing that Thomas moved little and said little. Always alert, he was obviously deeply familiar with all that his great-uncle was laying out for Graham for the first time.

Russell continued. "For now, you'll have to trust me when I tell you that I hid the most important items in those crates all over the world until I felt the time was right to share them with others and bring them back to one location. I believe that time is now. Making this information public would guarantee that would never happen. I need to be certain the information doesn't fall into the wrong hands."

"It seems so incredible . . ."

"The smartest thing the devil did was convince the masses that he didn't exist," Russell said.

"But people would have to know."

"*Some* do. A very select few. Several presidents have very

clearly warned of what goes on behind the scenes. You can look up their speeches yourself. Woodrow Wilson was very clear about what he thought of elites controlling world events, and that included his deep remorse over creating the Federal Reserve. FDR said nothing happens by chance and that all major events are planned. Eisenhower warned of the military industrial complex. Kennedy gave an amazing speech about secret societies being repugnant, and you know what happened to him, even though that wasn't the main reason he was killed."

"Oswald," Graham said.

"You have *so* much to learn. We had hoped you were further along," Russell said, looking at Thomas, who shrugged. "But I suppose it's better to teach you from scratch than to un-teach the nonsense you *think* you know." He took a deep breath, then released it slowly. "Oswald was nowhere near a rifle. That has been exposed on so many levels by so many research scholars, the belief that he was is laughable. The key is wading and sifting through the disinformation as much as through the legitimate information. You've been in the intelligence business; surely you know that disinformation is just as important as factual information. It's been that way for centuries, so this isn't revelatory at all. The point is that many credible individuals have spoken on this topic for decades. Every major event has been orchestrated to the benefit of a very small group of people. To scoff this off reveals the rigidity of a small, illogical and unimaginative mind."

"Not wanting to reside in the small mind group, I ask that you please continue," Graham invited.

Russell smiled and took on a more subdued tone. "I'm sure you're familiar with the Knights Templar."

"Of course. They were wiped out and disbanded centuries

ago," Graham said, proud of his knowledge. "In the, what, thirteenth or fourteenth century?"

Russell and Thomas grimaced and shook their heads in unison. "Nope," Thomas said. "It's well known that the victors write the history."

Graham chuckled. "That's my point. They lost."

"Hardly, Graham," Russell said. "And that's precisely the point. As victors, they could write whatever they wanted. I can assure you that they survived and thrived. But I need to start at their most likely beginning. I say that because no one is sure what the true beginning was." Russell waved both hands. "We have too much to cover to give you a complete history, but the important aspect was the treasure that the very first knights found."

"Your crates, I'm guessing?"

"Yes, and no," Russell said. "Those crates represented a portion of what they found and some of what they accumulated over the centuries. But they contained some very key components."

"The scroll?"

"That was important. But one of the most important items was the archives. It turned out that the crates contained historical volumes, maps and more importantly, an inventory list. Many of the items that the Templars found under the Temple of Solomon during their first excavation were beyond their understanding. But the value of the gold and jewels caused them to agree that the other items they didn't understand must have great value as well. They were wise enough to guard the information and also take what was written in ancient languages to someone able to translate the many documents. They were also wise enough to seek out and recruit the most brilliant minds of the day into the Order from that time forward. They learned to combine military might and prowess with great intellect and wisdom. And one of the key phrases translated for them, engraved on a copper alloy sheet all on its own and written in an ancient language, was *knowledge is power and—*"

"Old news," Graham said.

Russell scowled at him. "And *hidden knowledge is absolute power.* That concept would prove to be a treasure worth more than the initial wealth they found. This spawned their rapid expansion back in Europe when they returned and their early ferocity in battle during the Crusades."

"A barbaric bloodletting by the 'Church,'" Graham said with contempt.

"There is no doubt that some of that occurred and that the Church committed wrongs. But you really shouldn't be so easily duped by anti-Christian propaganda in what pretends to be media and academia these days. Islam slaughtered a thousand times more people than the Christians did during the Crusades and long after, but we need to save that lesson for another day. The Temple Knights had their own plan. They sought more treasure and knowledge of all kinds. And during times of peace or armistice, they formed alliances with the Assassins to gain knowledge and power. Captured items in the hands of barbarians would have little value to them, but potentially great value to the Templars. And so they began seeking great and arcane knowledge and developed their inner council with the wisest men of their order. They honed their wisdom as much as they honed their swords. And as their legend and tales of their conquests grew, wealthy nobles and their kindred joined them in droves, donating vast sums of wealth and lands to the Order."

"That's all very fascinating, but there must be more to it than that."

"Of course there is—much more. I'm just getting started," Russell said. "But you need to understand the past before you can see what's at stake in the future."

FORTY-EIGHT

Castle Valor, Near Cherbourg, France—1307

Gratian Castanea waited at his appointed spot outside the door of his master, Friar Julien de Rouse, who had made his quarters in the castle keep. He didn't wait long before Friar Julien appeared from behind the massive door carrying scrolls large and small, much the same as Gratian was doing.

Friar Julien nodded as he passed Gratian, who, as protégé, walked a half pace behind his elder and teacher, even though he too was a knight. Although he held no official title, Friar Julien was considered the head of the High Council, which presided over and directed the full leadership of the Order. Their journey to the great hall at the far end of the castle would take some time, and Friar Julien was in no hurry for a reason—he wished to glean the latest news from Gratian. Gratian had just returned from an important journey at the behest of Friar Julien and the High Council.

"Your journey went well, I trust, young sir?"

While Gratian appreciated Friar Julien's kind tone, he was always careful to keep his place and act with subservience and reverence. Although their garments were similar, their stature was vastly different. He chose every word before answering.

"Quite, my lord. All is progressing just as the Council has planned and directed."

"Our treasury closest to Paris?"

"Carted away by our most trusted men over many nights and replaced with crates containing small bags of stones worth substantially less than the prior treasury," Gratian said with his head slightly bowed. "All has been equally divided and safely delivered to the new locations, sir."

Gratian couldn't see his face, but Friar Julien beamed at the report. How he wished he'd seen the look on the face of that pompous fool, King Philip, when he received the very bad news. "And the fleet?"

"All ships have slipped out of their ports," said Gratian, walking near Friar Julien and speaking in a low voice. "So as not to arouse suspicion, a few have been replaced by merchant ships of our allies. They have also been loaded with a steady supply of our own goods. The departing vessels are never fewer than three as they set out for their rendezvous points. The evacuation is almost complete. Harbor masters are bribed, and there will be a drunken festival in each location such as they have never seen. When they awaken from their rum-induced sleep, the combined fleet will be far away."

"Good, good. Tell me of your travels to our allies."

"I met with many agents during my journeys. They were of good cheer and have welcomed the steady move of our brethren here. Our coastal operations throughout Britannia are doing well. Our placements in Scotland thrive. The brothers of our Teutonic Order are faring well, and Wittelsbach sends his gracious thanks and his realm continues to be a stronghold for us. However, the townships of Ure and Schwyz show the greatest promise, just as my lord predicted. The portions of treasure and copies of documents have been safely transported to the sacred sites. We've had no new messages from the expeditions to the Far West or the Far East, but previous reports were glorious, with minimal losses, and we pray in earnest for continued successes." Gratian bowed slightly with continued deference.

Friar Julien stopped at one of the windows. From this height he could see both the courtyard below and the rolling hills outside their ramparts for a great distance. More than a thousand knights and even more support forces surrounded the castle—the honor guard for their protection should they need to make a hasty escape. That was unlikely since the High Council knew of plans long before kings and regents executed them. But the number of the knights at the castle made Julien think of how many thousands they had slowly moved out of these lands and how many they had converted into men of commerce rather than men of war.

Gratian also moved toward the window. He towered over the diminutive Friar Julien, which gave him a greater range of view. He would gladly trade that to have the friar's vision of their intended future.

As they walked together, Friar Julien considered what Gratian had shared. They made their way down the long halls and passed the chapel. Julien never ceased to marvel at the skills of the Templar builders and the masterful stonework. Constructing impressive structures was just one of their superlative skills that, along with knowledge, set them apart from lesser men. And they were *all* lesser who were not of the Order.

As they approached the anteroom that led to the great hall, Julien slowed and stepped aside to allow his protégé to open the door for him. It was as he had done many times in the long-ago past for his own teacher on the High Council.

Both men piled their scrolls and parchment satchels upon the rough-hewn table, and Gratian closed the door as Friar Julien chose what he wished to take inside. He had noticed a look on Gratian's face that he recognized.

"You have a question?" Friar Julien said while continuing his sorting.

"It may not be my place to ask, my lord," Gratian said, his head bowed once again.

"A question unasked cannot be answered. I know your heart to be honorable, and I will fairly offer correction without harshness if your question falls outside your position."

"My lord, even someone as lowly as I knows that the war faction doesn't approve of this strategy of migration, even though all goes exceedingly well. I fear they shall make trouble and ruin our progress." Gratian did his best to deliver his concerns without offense.

"It's good that you have a keen mind and heart, because there is good reason to consider what you have noticed. Never become so arrogant as to not consider all factions and factors as you are able. They are like bulls loose at a festival and enflamed with the scent of a nearby heifer. They long for the old days and the old ways. And this is one of the most important lessons I can teach you, so learn it well. No empire stands forever. None. Owe no alliance of your heart to any one kingdom, realm or place. They all pass away. Trade is the sole thread of continuity," he declared with solemn fervor.

"But what of the war faction? They would prefer to lay a trap for the evil Philip and his armies and slaughter them all, ending the threat permanently."

"Yes, they would. I don't blame them. Not so long ago I

would have wished to join them and eradicate the vermin. But eventually it would be us who would be slaughtered, like our brothers the Cathars so long ago. A frontal assault now would serve to make us more visible when we've been doing our best to slowly fade from sight. No, we shall allow Philip this victory, which will be short-lived. As will *he* be short-lived, along with that fool, Clement. And we will be gone, so above suspicion, and the new king and pope will be of our choosing."

Gratian kept his head low and continued in such as a way not to be perceived as contradicting his teacher. "They grumble of lost lands and wealth."

Friar Julien shook his head while opening a large map. "They have lost nothing. What we are carrying out has been planned for many years and is part of a larger strategy of becoming inconspicuous while growing in strength in other ways. What has value has been transferred and exchanged with our allies. Anything the king or Clement seizes will have had its value long ago stripped away. What few assets we might lose, we will gain back later and more besides. We're quite good at this. We don't share the complete aspects of our plans with everyone in our Order. Don't forget that the greater the number of people who know your plans, the greater the possibility for betrayal or exposure. What do the scriptures say? 'Do not let the right hand know what the left hand does.' And there will be bloodletting for them, regardless. They just don't know it yet."

As always, Brother Gratian listened intently to his teacher's words of wisdom. He had never known them to fail or to be proven wrong yet. "What of Brother de Molay, master? I fear he makes a grave and risky gamble."

Friar Julien was pleased at the genuine show of concern for their titular leader. Gratian had real compassion to balance his bravery and his keen mind. Julien had chosen well in making him the prime protégé. "Brother Jacques has proven his valor on behalf of the Order on countless occasions, but this time we believe his risk will be less than it first appeared and that his strategy is sound."

Gratian nodded his acquiescence to his teacher's evaluation. And then another thought occurred to him. "What will history say of us, my lord?"

Friar Julien squeezed Gratian's shoulder and looked him directly in the eye. "If all goes well, they won't know enough of us from here forward to say anything," he said, beaming. "One thing is certain and you must understand it; we will be infinitely more powerful and successful in secret than we ever were with our swords on horseback."

Friar Julien gathered up what he wanted and pushed the remainder to Gratian. "Now let us greet our brethren and prepare for our own exodus," he said.

Gratian dragged open the huge door leading to the great hall. As Friar Julien entered, the brethren rose and greeted him with nods of respect or an upraised chalice.

The walls of the room were lined with knights in full armor, with twice that number in monks and squires. They were armed as well, but their weapons were hidden beneath their robes and cloaks—always warrior monks.

"Welcome, brothers. Let us begin," Friar Julien said as Gratian pulled the door closed behind them.

FORTY-NINE

Even when it came to something as basic as bringing fresh hot tea to his uncle, Thomas moved like no one Graham had ever seen before—silently and as if his feet didn't touch the ground. And no matter how he turned, he maintained total awareness of his surroundings. Graham wondered if Thomas had ever seen combat, and just as that thought appeared in his mind, Thomas looked up and directly at him, as if he heard the question that had not been spoken. And since Graham never saw Russell give Thomas a signal of any kind, it made him wonder if another effect of the scroll was heightened mental awareness and acuity. He began to reflect on his own cognizance. Surely the effects of the scroll didn't extend that far. He used the brief interlude in conversation to make himself a fine scotch on the rocks while he pondered the possibilities.

Graham sat back down with his drink in hand and took it upon himself to break the silence.

"So you're telling me that contrary to popular history, the Knights Templar weren't disbanded and wiped out, but they thrived."

"You haven't seen even a miniscule sampling of the massive number of authentic documents about them that are in just *my* collection," Russell said. "Over the early decades and then centuries, they became more brilliant. Even today we haven't been able to duplicate some of their ancient construction methods. They invented what we know as the checking account used in banks. So the fact that they had long infiltrated the seats of power and were well aware of the plot by King Philip IV and Pope Clement to arrest them is rather elementary."

He added honey to his tea and stirred it.

"That still doesn't explain how they survived."

"A few thousand men were captured and a few hundred were tortured. Many of them were forced to confess to all manner of nonsense typical of the Church at that time—blasphemy, consorting with evil spirits and renouncing the cross. Most capitulated quickly, were set free and then recanted their confessions. It is believed that some of the knights who were a detriment to the Order and had fallen out of favor with the High Council were sacrificed intentionally. Some of the bravest and most loyal chose to allow themselves to be captured, to buy time for more of their brethren to slip away to other lands."

Russell shifted in his wheelchair. "Regardless of the details, those captured were a very small group relative to the full scope of their number. The Templar ranks, including knights, monks, squires, merchants and administrators, were well over one hundred thousand. They'd made alliances and inroads all over the known world by then. They had become experts at infiltration over two centuries—sometimes by conquest, sometimes by purchase or bribery, and even by marriage. If they faced two very powerful enemies who were intractable and unyielding, the Templars would spend years plotting and fomenting conflict to have the two forces thin each other out. Then they would move in, attacking the weaker flanks first. They were Machiavellian before Machiavelli."

"How did they keep this history secret all these centuries?"

"It's well known that when Philip came to arrest the Templars and seize their treasure rather than pay his debt to them, the treasure was gone. So was the entire Templar fleet. One of the great mysteries in history is what became of the vast treasure and one of the largest fleets ever assembled. And you'll be amazed when I tell you that whole story. But I can assure you that the money they funneled by way of grants and endowments to universities in Europe and later to America would have been a miniscule portion of the vast Templar riches. It wouldn't have been difficult to control the narrative and keep secrets."

"You told me this wasn't about just one conspiracy but all conspiracies. Were you implying they created their own secret society?' Graham asked.

"Yes and no. I suppose it depends on how you look at it. Maintaining the Order would have kept them a target, but they intended to vanish from view. That's why they themselves advanced the idea that the Order had been destroyed and disbanded. In the same way they infiltrated every center of power, commerce and religion for over a century, they penetrated every secret society at the highest levels as well. So they advanced the legend of their own demise while promoting not so subtle whispers about other secret organizations."

Russell paused to take a drink of his tea, and Thomas picked up the history lesson without missing a beat.

"None of this is terribly difficult with money applied in the right places and early on. Done effectively, a relatively small amount of money would yield a huge amount of knowledge, influence and power. Then power begins to beget power. And more money is created with less bribery needed. And through the use of this strategy over many decades, they would rise to just below the very top and then ensure that their own people were appointed beneath them, creating an ongoing legacy. Let that sink in a minute. It's ingenious, really. They were very patient and inserted many people into positions of power over a very long time period. And that strategy has never ceased."

"So they're actually running Skull and Bones and the Illuminati?"

Russell took over again. "Those and a dozen more like them—whether it was the Rosicrucians or the Freemasons or the Jesuits—it didn't, and doesn't, matter. Even most conspiracy researchers are unaware that over one hundred secret societies were formed in colleges and universities all over America starting in the mid-1800s. And the Templar descendants rarely actually *run* things. They just made sure they had people in very high positions, but rarely the actual leader. In that way they could manipulate events but not be seen as responsible. And in most organizations, whether public or secret, leaders rise and fall, but high-ranking administrators can remain in place for many years. They would much rather have the king's ear than be the king. That way they could administer the metaphoric or real poison, if needed, rather than *be* poisoned. Controlling the figureheads and knowing what they were going to do far in advance was truly brilliant and completely effective."

Thomas shifted toward Graham. "Over time, we can teach you a great deal about many secret societies and what they've done. We can prove what's hype and what's real. We have extensive research in both summary and detailed formats. Trust me when I tell you history is not what has been taught in school. Most of what you learned is controlled dissemination. The truly important events come in three levels." He counted off on his fingers. "What is commonly taught and accepted, better known as the official version. Then there are the leaked conspiracy theories and disinformation intentionally planted for students and scholars to argue over endlessly. And that's just a smoke screen for what really happened—a much deeper conspiracy. And on occasion, just to confuse everyone, the second version—the leaked conspiracy—is the actual truth."

Graham was taking it all in, relaxed, his arms folded across his midsection. "I've worked directly in intelligence, and I contract with their agencies today. I've heard some wild stories, but they all seemed to be just that—stories. I would think that I'd have heard more concrete facts about the topics you're discussing."

Russell set his tea down and glanced at Thomas before continuing with Graham. "It will be quite easy for us to prove to you that major events were controlled. We have overwhelming evidence far more convincing and definitive than even the best authors and researchers—some of whom we leaked information to over the years when it suited our purposes. It would be too difficult to get you to understand the more fantastic concepts and artifacts without experiencing them firsthand. We can give you a few concrete examples of the former before we open your eyes with the latter—although both are of great importance."

"I promise to keep an open mind along with my ever-open eyes."

Graham had to admit to himself that Russell's stories were incredible if even half of the details were true, and Russell didn't strike him as a man prone to exaggeration. But the opportunity to be involved with more relics even close to being as intriguing as the metal scrolls and ancient writings had him more captivated than he wanted to admit.

Graham was an innovator and a developer, so he had a strong and productive imagination. And he was beginning to imagine quite vividly.

He leaned back. Oh, yeah. He could imagine quite a lot.

FIFTY

St. John's, Newfoundland—March 1915

The storm assaulted the old inn from the northeast. And Deputy Undersecretary Sebastian Rhodes thought that was rather apropos since the meeting he was participating in would certainly cause far greater storms from that same direction. He wasn't close to the grand fireplace, so he hadn't shed his dark greatcoat yet. Just seeing and hearing the sleet and the rain from the Atlantic pounding their lodging gave him a deep chill and caused him to unconsciously pull his lapels together.

He wondered how many times meetings had taken place in that normally quiet and secluded area since the Order had first started coming there, significantly earlier than Christopher Columbus—who had been the benefactor of several of their maps—had found the "new" world. Rhodes reasoned that there had been many meetings but couldn't imagine that any of them could have been as dire or significant as this one would be. His mind conjured the thought that the howling wind was like a legion of banshees coming forward from the past to shriek about the many fallen in battle. He shuddered through every inch of his rotund body.

Theirs was a rendezvous that appeared on no itinerary anywhere. Other than for the inner circle of the Elites and those present in the room, the meeting never happened. The two well-appointed gentlemen who chatted and chuckled near the fire were currently somewhere else altogether—simply delayed in their arrival to a vague destination for an even more vague purpose. In spite of the fact that both were important men who'd traveled a long way, the meeting itself was going to be very brief—especially in relation to the travel time.

Both men were enjoying the finest of brandies after having enjoyed an equally fine meal. Their families were old money and old bloodlines, and were accustomed to extravagance—sumptuous food and rare spirits. Having dined in the adjacent room while exchanging pleasantries and humorous anecdotes, the two men moved to where they now sat talking in hushed tones—unnecessarily cautious since no one could be close enough to eavesdrop in this location.

The plan they discussed had been decided upon quite some time ago—they were here to confirm the specifics and logistics. Since details and contingencies had been worked out, they had come for a face-to-face acknowledgement and agreement. It had been determined that this wouldn't be done using couriers and coded messages—far too many lives were at stake for a chance of misinterpretation or miscommunication.

Franklin Delano Roosevelt, Assistant Secretary of the Navy, sat on the left and alternated between his cigarette at the end of its holder and his drink, while Winston Leonard Spencer-Churchill, First Lord of the Admiralty, sat on the right and alternated his drink with a fine, hand-rolled cigar. Churchill was under the labyrinthine influence of the Rothschilds by way of their surrogates, and Roosevelt fell under the serpentine maze linked to J. P. Morgan, who was also a Rothschild puppet. There was no question that their ultimate goals would be attained even if the anticipated results of this particular meeting failed—The Right Honourable Arthur James Balfour had already seen to that. Lord Rothschild had met with Balfour on numerous occasions and knew well of his dark proclivities, the knowledge of which guaranteed Balfour's acquiescence to help foment the intended outcomes—this one and many others on the drawing board.

Roosevelt and Churchill understood the role of Sebastian Rhodes, who would move the plan forward and who served as designated confirmation eavesdropper to notify the powers that be if anything went awry—but they didn't address him directly or even invite him to the table.

Churchill pushed a large plume into the air before saying, "Since we have agreed on the timing and our target, do we have further concerns before adjourning?"

"None that I can think of," Roosevelt said with his usual certainty.

"Any chance of discovery?"

"There is always a *chance*, but it's highly unlikely. Our people control every significant part of the press. We always have. Even if we *were* to be discovered, it would be easily handled. Not to worry."

Churchill took a slow drink as he pondered what Roosevelt said. "There are always political busybodies trying to make a name for themselves."

Roosevelt gave an abrupt laugh. "Quite. We're counting on it. So much so that we already have our man prepared to look into this whole sordid business. There may even be a shred of truth to his inquiry, but that shred will point in the wrong direction. We'd rather not leave to chance the possibility that someone would initiate a real investigation. Even though the inquiry into the USS *Maine* was quashed, it raised embarrassing questions. No damage, but questions. We won't have that this time, I assure you," Roosevelt said.

"What if the lives lost on one ship isn't enough? Another sinking would surely seem contrived," Winston said, taking another puff.

"Maybe. Or maybe it would prove a pattern that we *warn* about in the press. And we have Mexico threatening to reclaim states in the Southwest by force and enough men in Congress worried about that threat or pretending to be concerned to turn the tide. They know what's at stake and so does Wilson. The sinking will happen, and even public opinion will be on our side. We've already made sure of that," Roosevelt said.

"Mexico is relevant?"

"Of course not. Not since Guadalupe Hidalgo. It's just another excuse—another secondary plan. And I can assure you that I and our mutual associates on this side of the Atlantic have many and that they all build upon each other and are intertwined. We don't leave anything to chance any more than you have in the past. So I can more than assume that you don't foresee any problems on your side of the pond, my friend?"

"None whatsoever," Churchill said. "Course and speed right into the trap. As you mentioned, nothing is left to chance."

Roosevelt lifted his glass. "Then there is nothing left but to toast your good health, Winston. Fitting we're close to the ides of March."

Churchill lifted his glass in turn. "Yes, and to yours, dear Franklin. And to Malthus."

"Hear, hear! I'll drink to that as well."

Sebastian didn't get to share in the toast, but he drank his fourth glass of exquisite brandy with just as much cheer as the men across the room. What he was about to carry out at the behest of the power structure they all represented would make for a great story—maybe even one for the Nickel Theatre not far from where they sat. Yes, it was a good toast stemming from more than one worthy cause.

FIFTY-ONE

Present Day

Graham could sense that their meeting was building to some form of crescendo. Maybe his own sense of awareness had become elevated, because there was no overt change in mood between Russell and Thomas. As a matter of fact, they both seemed completely relaxed—as though they were about to discuss their favorite football team—while at the same time they both maintained an air of complete focus. Their minds never seemed to wander, nor did they digress unless it was for a specific purpose. Their demeanor was enigmatic to say the least. How would he describe it—relaxed intensity? Maybe that description was an accurate and fitting oxymoron.

"The alternate history lesson is fascinating," Graham said. "I don't have any reason to doubt your story that the Templars went underground to prevent being completely wiped out and that they gained positions of power and influence over the centuries. And I'm sure you have scores of unique documents that I could spend months plowing through. But that doesn't correspond very well with the sense of urgency and enormity that you've also talked about. It would seem that the present is far more important than history lessons."

Thomas addressed Graham's points with complete calm. "Frankly, Graham, if we told you all that we need to at once, you might assume we had lost our minds. What we want to share with you is far too important to take that risk. That's why we chose to get your attention by hacking your very formidable system. If we could do that to you, it proves we have the ability to access information that ninety-nine point nine-nine percent of even the tech population can't. Normally we would wait a significant amount of time before allowing someone to even know about the scroll let alone see it. But letting you experience some of the effects of the scroll gave you an understanding that reading three volumes about it wouldn't have."

"He's quite correct, Graham; trust is a two-way street," Russell said. "We hope we've begun to earn yours. If we had any interest in corporate espionage, we would obviously have spent a great deal of time in the catacombs of your data arrays rather than tip our cyber hats to tell you we were already in. And we had to tell you the history behind this, or what we plan to share with you in the present would not likely be believable to you."

Graham nodded. "Most kind of you. You did us a favor, actually."

"More than you know." Thomas was quick to speak before Graham could go on. "We're slightly more than ninety-nine percent certain that others were about to attempt to gain entry with malicious intent. We believe those attempts will continue. Again, a direct approach from us might not have been well received, so we chose to prove ourselves instead."

"You must not dismiss what we tell you." Russell didn't miss a beat. It was like a tag-team, but without a visible tag. "I've worked at the highest levels of intelligence for seven decades, so I have a fairly significant amount of knowledge and expertise in these matters. The NSA has been recording every call made in America since the Carter administration and yet until just a few years ago, that truth was called a conspiracy theory. Do you know who invented the term *conspiracy theory*? The CIA. It's documented, and I was there. It was a term they coined to discredit valid research into the Kennedy assassination. You can watch the taped testimony of a high-level official from the *Company* admit they have a presence in every major newsroom—and no one cares. More than a few groups exposed that specific Smart TVs and home-assistant devices gather data on the people who purchase them, and that revelation draws a big yawn. The electronic information conveyed by these devices are forms of predictive programming, and its origins go back almost one hundred years." Russell pointed at Graham. "You've also been programmed, whether you know it or not. That's why we need to give you at least *some* history, significant history, to bring you into the present."

Graham made an outward show of getting comfortable. "Bring me up to speed."

Russell nodded approvingly and took the lead. "For nearly two thousand years, governments have provided bread and circuses to distract and appease the people. Today, however, the bread is made with genetically modified wheat, with genetically modified high fructose corn syrup and even an addictive additive that resembles diazepam. Glyphosate is added just before the harvest to shorten the drying time. I won't *begin* to go into the circus aspect of the phrase. The concept hasn't changed over the centuries, but the effects are getting far worse."

"The thing that hath been, it is that which shall be; and that which is done is that which shall be done: and there is no new thing under the sun," Thomas quoted.

Russell rubbed his hands together, as if massaging out the pains of age. "Keep that concept in the back of your mind. Later I'm sure you'll see why that quote is significant. It's obvious that the rich have usually gotten richer, but to the truly wealthy, the elites, if you will, wealth alone has never been enough. Their quest for absolute power and for immortality has never changed. What started out as a quest for the philosopher's stone has largely been replaced by the quest for singularity using artificial intelligence. I know you're familiar with the latter, but you probably didn't know of the tie to the former."

Thomas turned toward Graham. "You've heard of Operation Paperclip?"

"US intelligence smuggled Nazi rocket scientists into America after World War II. Wernher von Braun went on to head up NASA."

"True. But the operation went far deeper than that and they weren't just rocket scientists. You may not have heard of SS General Hans Kammler. He had command authority over the V2 program and all other German high tech. He disappeared, or at least that's the story. In addition, there was another group of German scientists just as important, or maybe more so, than the Paperclip scientists. They were allegedly murdered to prevent their knowledge from falling into Russian hands. These included biologists, biochemists and medical doctors. We're certain that the story was an elaborate ruse so that no one would look for them."

Graham was taking everything in. "So what happened to them?"

Russell leaned in and rested his arms on the desk. "Some came here. But many, and many before them, went to South America and Antarctica. Through the height of the war, when resources were critical, the Germans were sending U-boats, men and materials by the ton to a secret base in Antarctica known as Neuschwabenland. Some have reported this base to be a myth, but I can assure you it's real. In December of 1946, a major task force under the command of Rear Admiral Richard E. Byrd, known as Operation High Jump—consisting of an aircraft carrier and twelve support ships—arrived in Antarctica. They didn't complete any of their mission goals and returned home just three months later. Admiral Byrd gave several cryptic speeches about what was in the largely unexplored Antarctic region. Byrd was under the direct orders of Secretary of the Navy James Forrestal, who, as you may recall, was 'suicided' not long after, in 1949."

"I don't recall that story at all. I don't think I ever heard how Forrestal died."

"He allegedly jumped from his bathroom window on the sixteenth floor of the hospital he was in the day his brother was arriving to take him home. And he was found with the belt to his robe tied around his neck, but there was no evidence it had been tied to anything in the room. There's more to it than that, but we'll save that one for a future date."

Graham rubbed his forehead. "Good. Back to the original point. I read about Byrd's mission, but never gave it much thought. What did the Admiral find?"

Thomas cleared his throat. "He spoke of vast natural resources. And in 1959, twelve nations signed the Antarctic Treaty. That treaty remains intact, even between enemy nations, and there are now fifty-three signatories. How often do that many nations get along about anything for over sixty years, especially when potentially trillions of dollars in natural resources are present? No one can even go near the region without special permission. And yet major government officials and world religious leaders go there to visit in the present day. For what possible purpose?"

Graham laughed. "Uh . . . Climate change?"

"Right. Another hoax," Thomas said. "The main part of Antarctica doesn't get above nineteen degrees Fahrenheit. What difference would an increase of one degree in the last one hundred years matter?"

Russell didn't change his expression at all, but his tone was more somber when he said, "We think it ties into another dark piece of the puzzle. As I've said, there are those who seek immortality, just as men have for centuries. And until they reach the singularity they seek, we believe they are employing other means of life extension. Not only is cloning *far* more advanced than the public has any idea of, but we know there have been scientists who have achieved great success working on what is called the *plasma of the young*. The methods *do* work, and there is nothing unethical about the process unless it's pushed to extremes."

"I'm afraid you've lost me," Graham said.

Thomas leaned forward and took his turn explaining. "There are several methods to extend lifespan and enhance a person's relative quality of life. Some are ethical and some not. One method is plasma transfusions. If a young plasma donor is recruited and is willing and not harmed, the procedure is ethical. But there are those who completely drain donors, just as there are those who harvest organs from unwilling individuals rather than acquire them through normal means or by waiting for a match." He stared unblinking at Graham when he added, "And younger organs last longer."

Graham looked back and forth between them, incredulous. "You can't be serious."

"Tens of thousands of children go missing every year—"

"I had no idea it was so many, and I assumed those were found or went into some sex slave trade."

"Many do. And would that be any less horrific, Graham?" Russell said, raising his voice.

"Of course not! Not what I meant!"

"And those numbers don't take into consideration the organ harvesting in China and other countries." Russell took a calmer posture. "There have been blood sacrifices throughout history for a reason. They aren't myth, they're fact. And they go back to antediluvian times. The modern practitioners have just gotten more sophisticated about it, refined the process, if you will. 'For the life of the flesh is in the blood.'"

"I never thought . . . And you think this is tied to Antarctica somehow?"

"We think so," Thomas said. "But the last member of our group who went to investigate was never heard from again."

"This all seems convoluted . . . Disjointed."

"Convoluted? Really?" Russell shook his head. "My dear Graham, as I've explained before, what we've been showing you goes back centuries and involves *every* power structure, political movement, secret society and major event in history. It may *seem* convoluted on the surface, but I assure you that there are many intersecting and interlocking threads running all through this. We can't boil it down for you in a few meetings. Thomas has been under my tutelage for the better part of three decades, and even *he* hasn't seen everything. We know it's a lot to take in. That's why we chose not to show you all at once. We still aren't going to show you everything. Not that we intend to hide any of the details, but parts of this have been my life's work for almost seventy years. None of it came easily, and much of the knowledge

313

came with *great* cost. And we have a great deal more to show you."

Russell nodded at Thomas.

Thomas handed Graham several sheets of material of various types—some parchment-like and one metal. "This is just a small sampling, mind you."

"What am I looking at?" Graham asked.

Thomas passed him a large magnifying glass. "The metal sheet is similar in material to the scroll you held, so we don't know how old it is. But it was with the sheets of papyrus and vellum that share similar markings. Some of them were in containers that have been dated to be over four thousand years old. The metal could be older, but the readings have been inconclusive."

"Shouldn't these be in scrolls?"

"It would seem they were unrolled and pressed flat and that great care was taken to preserve them," Russell said. "We believe that many of the documents sealed in the crates came from the Library of Alexandria or are copies of documents from that library."

"I thought that was burned?"

"What better way to steal important esoteric information than to burn the building housing it after the theft?" Thomas ran one finger down the metal sheet in Graham's hands. "In addition, there was the Library of Pergamum. And of course there are the vast secret Vatican archives. One of the key components of the Templar treasure was the understanding that knowledge is power. They developed a zealous quest and thirst for information and the advantages it brings. They created a small army of scribes in the early years, followed by their own printing presses and later printers and data banks to utilize what they had accumulated over the centuries. But we'll have to save the full story for future meetings."

Graham used the magnifying glass as he shuffled the sheets. "Well, one of these looks like a representation of a DNA double helix, but that can't be. And this one looks like many thousands of ones and zeros with no spaces, but that can't be either."

Neither Thomas nor Russell replied. Graham peered over the top of the sheets at Russell. "That can't be, right?"

Both men simply stared at Graham with no expression. Then Thomas looked up and away, as if distracted. "You were saying convoluted, I believe," he said blithely. "I think mind-boggling might be a better term. I'm sure you're aware of the possibilities in storing enormous amounts of data on DNA strands."

"Of course. We're researching that storage format ourselves. Not only is the capacity nearly limitless, but it could remain intact for hundreds of years, far longer than any current media—"

"What if the data begins to self-replicate?" Russell asked.

"What if it becomes self-aware?" added Thomas before Graham could answer.

Graham continued to look at the sheets, flipping slowly back and forth between them as he thought about their questions. "Any idea what these say?"

"We've translated random lines and sections," Russell said. "*Decoded* might be a better word. But we've barely scratched the surface. The metal one contains a list of the twenty main archons of the two hundred Watchers talked about in the book of Enoch. The language is an odd blend of Phoenician and ancient Hebrew. Other pages seem to be written in ancient Thracian."

"I have no idea what that means or why it's significant, but it seems hard to believe that something this old hasn't been translated yet."

"We'll leave the significance for later, but that it hasn't been translated really isn't as surprising as you might think. There was a code from the Great Enlightened Society of Oculists that went unbroken for over two hundred and seventy years. You may be interested to know that the code was broken using very powerful computers and artificial intelligence and machine learning. Conventional wisdom says that are over twenty-five other codes from antiquity that remain unbroken. I can assure you from first-hand knowledge that there are substantially more." Russell pointed. "Like what you hold in your hands."

"You say that as if I might have a clue about what I'm holding in my hands."

"It's a lot to grasp, but what we're beginning to share with you isn't far-fetched at all," Thomas explained in his calm and even manner. In this environment he seemed more like a college professor than an ex-Ranger.

"In 1624, in his book *New Atlantis*, Francis Bacon foresaw such inventions as submarines, air conditioning, television, ocean liners, nylon and much more—over three hundred years before they were conceived and created. And that doesn't mean everything presented in the mainstream is amazing unexplained phenomena since much of it is questionable, like the Babylonian Battery and the idea that the Great Pyramid was lit with light bulbs."

"Why have you shown me what you have so far? I don't get it. What do *I* have to do with all of this?" Graham said, popping the back of his hand against the papers he clenched.

Thomas looked at Russell through narrowed eyes. An almost imperceptible wink was Russell's response.

"When I hid the crates for safekeeping," Russell said, "I knew they held secrets that we had no way of understanding. And I knew I needed help. It took me decades to develop a network of people that I could trust. Over time we began to unravel *some* of the mysteries. But only now are many of the details I recall from long ago beginning to make sense. And many of them will still be a total enigma, just like the Oculist code was for over two centuries. World events seem to be moving at an increasingly rapid pace now. We believe it's time to retrieve the crates I hid all over the world and certain items that I've accumulated over the years, and it's certainly time to try to unlock the secrets of what we already have. It may take D-Wave level quantum computing at the qubit level, but we can at least get started with what we have and with what you could bring to the table by collaborating with us."

"Does this include disappearing in Antarctica?"

Thomas laughed. "We *do* have some milk-run tasks that are suitable for navy types if you find these revelations too fearful."

"I can take anything a doggie GI can any d—"

"Thomas is pulling your anchor chain. We need you and we need your expertise. Our resources are far more impressive than you know, but we have limitations. I'm obviously getting long in the tooth, or long in the sabretooth as Thomas would say. We, along with many of our astute associates, believe you could contribute a great deal toward unlocking many mysteries. So we're offering you a red pill, blue pill type of decision."

"To extend the metaphor, how do I know you people aren't part of the dark side?"

Russell barely nodded at Thomas, who was already pulling out a thick file from an unseen briefcase on the left side of his chair.

"That is something you will need to decide for yourself," Thomas said. "You're a bright man, so we're certain you'll determine that our goals are virtuous. In the meantime, that file should help. The first few pages are a detailed executive summary. Substantial documentation follows." Thomas handed Graham the file folder.

Graham began quickly scanning the first few pages. "No way!" He didn't look up from the folder, but it was clear his tone wasn't that of his previous wonder over new revelations. Now his tone had clearly changed to one of anger.

FIFTY-TWO

Graham sat his drink on the table next to him to study more closely the file he was just handed. The color in his face changed slightly, and ire rose as he subtly clenched one fist. "How long have you had this information? If you had it early on, then you're no better than they are." His knee-jerk reaction was to be irate and wonder who he could trust.

Russell's expression was stern, yet it conveyed understanding.

"We had no idea about this until you told us yourself. Since we considered you a friend and potential partner, we took it upon ourselves to dig on your behalf. We're quite good at it and thorough as well. When we originally hacked your system, we did just enough to get your attention and we went no further. In this case, we went very deep, and I think you'll find the information in front of you and the hard drive Thomas will give you to be very useful."

Thomas had already reached for the hard drive, and he set it down beside Graham. "Yes, we were aware of Ambrose, but we hadn't monitored them closely. And fortunately, they don't know about us. We have to pick our battles, and we don't want to risk tipping our hand. That said, when you called and told us that you couldn't make our last meeting and the nature of what happened to your sister, we decided to look at Ambrose much more closely. At the time, you might not have believed us if we'd exposed their plan, but it wouldn't have mattered anyway. You had no choice but to accept the only solution available *at that time*. We've included a new solution for your sister."

"You know of them, but they don't know about you? I would have thought it would have been the other way around. They tout themselves as the be-all-end-all of centuries-old manipulators."

Russell smiled at Graham's take on the hierarchy. "I'm sure they do. And I'm equally sure they're not. Don't get me wrong— they *are* formidable. But in the larger scheme, they aren't considered a major faction. Now, I don't doubt for a moment that they presented such an image to you—and we would have dispelled that at some point down the road. But down the road came more quickly than we'd anticipated. Again, it helps to have some background, so I'll give you the short version." Russell straightened his arms directly forward and then arched his back.

"The Order wisely started with a code declaring that no one would be permitted to intentionally do harm to another within the organization. But over time, some very bad seeds rose to power and the Order splintered into factions. It became increasingly difficult to know who to trust. I had to learn this over a long period of time—and sometimes at great cost and sometimes from near misses."

"Now I'm wondering what to do next. I feel like I'm taking on the Deep State."

"Deeper than you know. Keep your friends close and your enemies closer," Thomas said. "For the time being, I wouldn't let on that you know anything about this. Since they're arrogant, and Dr. Scheer especially so, we were able to get all of their data on the pathogen and the exact cure they used. He loves to brag to his many mistresses on his unsecure server, which made pilfering corporate passwords much easier. We've used our own sources to create an adequate supply of an identical serum. You can test it on your sister with virtually no risk. If we happened to miss something, you'll still have the original serum available. But I think if you have one of your own trusted medical people look at our information, you'll see that it's identical."

"I would rest much easier knowing I had another source. I already had concerns about a sole source, but not for these reasons." He lifted the file and dropped it on the desk. "What do I owe you for all of this?"

"Nothing," Russell said. "Oh, you can reimburse us some nominal amount for the manufacturing cost, but it wasn't that difficult for one of our labs once we had the entire list of ingredients and their exact process. You'll be able to make it at one of your own companies and not ever have to worry about someone using your sister to blackmail you. They'll only *think* they have a trump card."

"I don't know what to say. Thank you doesn't seem like enough. And as appreciative as I am, I still have to consider getting involved in what you've shown me, although I can certainly say I'm fascinated. But now I have to focus on a strategy to protect my companies since I've let the fox get uncomfortably close to the henhouse."

There was another brief pause as Thomas seemed to read Russell's thoughts. Thomas handed Graham another file folder that was very similar to the last—with the same two-hole, top-clasp method of attaching pages for easy perusal. Graham was thinking it was a bit old school as he took the folder from Thomas.

"Of course we could have transmitted all of this to you,"

Thomas said, "but given the gravity of the situation, we thought hard copies and hard drives would be safest at this juncture."

"You're obviously a brilliant man who runs many successful companies," Russell said. "We don't pretend to know the complicated inner workings of any of them. However, we own far more companies and have for many more decades, and we're pretty good at complexities of our own. I have over fifty years on you when it comes to starting and running businesses. And you have to keep in mind that I set up front companies all over the world on behalf of some pretty ruthless and unforgiving people. The second file you hold, along with another hard drive, will provide you with what we know of Ambrose, our ideas on how to protect yourself and what we're willing to do in support. We had this drawn up by some of our most trusted staff in a short time, so I'm sure you'll have your own ideas and ways to modify our suggestions."

Graham was flipping through another executive summary. "This is quite generous of you," he said without looking up. "We did our own typical contingency planning when we agreed to begin a business relationship with Ambrose, and your proposal should strengthen any areas we may have missed."

"I'm sure we'll make money and you won't be torpedoed," Thomas said. "But there is more at stake here than wealth. We believe society is at a tipping point. You could be a part of major paradigm shift to tip the balance in a favorable way. Trust is earned and trust is betrayed. We hope we've earned your trust."

"That you have. I appreciate all of this. That being said, I really have to hit the road. I have a lot to do and I need to get started right away." He waved the folder at Thomas. "I'll keep you posted using the same floating encryption, yes?"

Thomas and Russell both nodded, and Thomas said, "And

we'll let you know if we hear anything further. We still have an open door at Ambrose and several of their facilities. They just don't know it."

After Graham shook Thomas's hand, he walked to Russell's desk and extended his hand again. Russell gripped Graham's hand firmly, his serious eyes staring straight through Graham, and he didn't let go.

"Trust no one. To the best of our knowledge, no one on your senior staff has been compromised, but there are many methods to turn someone. We know your people are loyal and with good reason, but no one can know every detail about another person, and blackmail can be a powerful weapon against loyalty. Just a word of caution from an old soldier."

With that, Thomas showed Graham out and they bid each other a good evening. Thomas scanned the exterior before he returned inside.

Graham sat in his car and stared out into the night sky before turning on the ignition. He had spent years learning to control his emotions, whether it was in combat, martial arts or negotiating a major deal. But if anyone had been watching, it would be plain to see that he wasn't doing the best job of masking his feelings as his face took on a crimson hue and the veins popped out on both of his temples. He had done well to maintain his composure in front of Russell and Thomas, although he doubted his reactions were fully camouflaged. Graham needed to center himself, though he felt the need to scream and to break something. He hoped the trip home would allow him to find that center and regain his mental acuity since everything he'd worked for was riding on him being at the very pinnacle of his game.

As soon as Graham returned to his warehouse to switch

vehicles, and he was certain he hadn't been followed, he reactivated his phone. He touched the message icon and scrolled to his last text exchange with Alex Chen: He typed a new message: *Light the candle*. The response to Graham's coded message was immediate and even more succinct. *On it* was all it said.

FIFTY-THREE

Over The Next Two Weeks

Graham had yet to decide whether Peter was complicit with Ambrose or if they had duped him as well. But for the time being, Peter was being left out of the loop. And as Graham wasn't raising additional capital, there was no need to include him and not doing so would arouse no suspicion.

Graham had long believed in the trust-yet-verify adage, and his relationship with Ambrose was no exception. Since there were many unknowns, he had wanted to make sure that the enthusiasm for expansion capital and enhanced sales hadn't clouded his team's judgment, that they hadn't dropped their collective guards or allowed their financial, legal or technical firewalls to be compromised. In so doing, he, Alex Chen and trusted department heads had looked at many what-if scenarios and had done a great deal of contingency planning. Without being overly paranoid, they were all on the lookout for red flags. Since much of what the company did was classified or patent sensitive, this type of defensive scenario planning wasn't at all foreign to Graham's teams. Now some of the contingencies would swing into effect with fine-tuning directed by Graham.

Ever since he'd left his meeting with Russell and Thomas, the activity at his companies had been racing at breakneck speed, but with a precision that would allow for no wrecks. Graham gave a copy of the information he'd gotten from Russell to Alex and to his CFO, Estella Mendoza, as soon as he arrived at his office complex. Estella was as much a wunderkind in her department as Alex was in his. She had earned a law degree, a Master of International Taxation and both CPA and CFA designations. Estella had full oversight into what became known as the Ambrose project from the very beginning. Graham included his own summary and strategies when he gave them the files. He told them to drop all else they were doing and to meet in his personal conference room in an hour. He now sat across from them and nodded toward the files in front of them.

"I know I haven't given you much time for analysis, but what are your initial thoughts?"

Estella was still adding to what Graham could see were at least a dozen pages of handwritten notes on her legal pad. She looked up and spoke with her typical brevity and candor.

"Bold moves."

"But are they doable?"

She didn't hesitate. "Much of this is included in our prior contingency planning. Given the willingness of the new participants, I don't see any difficulties. It's really just a matter of prioritizing and tweaking." Her cadence was even and methodical.

"Good. Minimum staff on this and maximum effort. Everything else goes on the backburner or you delegate competing critical functions. Alex and I have provided those we think are best suited for this latest iteration of the Ambrose project, but I'll leave any additions to your discretion. Copy me on everything. And don't hesitate to immediately reach out to me if there are any impediments that I can kick out of your way quicker than you can."

Graham stood. "And even though I'm sure I don't need to remind you, I'm reminding you. Absolutely no one outside of the team you assemble is to know anything about this. If anyone gets nosy, I want to know about it."

They both nodded as they gathered up their files and left the conference room. As far as anyone was concerned, they were working on yet another of Graham's dynamic projects that required secrecy—which was completely normal given that they often worked in top secret arenas.

Graham went back to his office where he had another chore to attend to. One that was referenced in the summary he'd given to Alex and Estella. He contacted Vicky via email about her family's interests in his companies, giving her a general sense of what he needed to do and why. He explained that he'd be emailing highly confidential documents for her signature.

He assured her that he would be protecting her family's interests and also their excellent returns. Vicky oversaw her family's investment in Graham's companies. It was very little money for them relative to their vast portfolios, but a significant amount of money from Graham's perspective.

Vicky responded to his email in less than an hour.

"Of course, dear. Just send me the instructions and what I need to sign. You know I find the technical aspects of financial matters tedious and most boring. Besides, you've made the family a great deal of money and it's not like they don't already have more than they can ever spend! Love, V!"

Vicky closed the lid of her laptop and reclined back in the Italian leather seat of her Gulfstream and laughed out loud. "Idiots! It serves them right." She lifted a glass of champagne and toasted Graham. "Well played, my dear."

Graham's ensuing financial moves were as masterful as they were complex. His team was brilliant and resourceful. The escalated financial firewalls they created were ironclad. Graham had purchased the company recommended by von Kleis. And as a result of the obvious synergies heralded by the media's financial analysts, the stock had already seen a major increase in value. Ambrose had intended to slowly acquire more stock so as not to arouse suspicion with Graham, but that plan was now irrelevant. Before Ambrose could act, Graham implemented a stock swap with one of his holding companies. At the same time, several companies controlled by Russell and Thomas quickly bought blocks of stock. Between Graham, Vicky and Russell, they also controlled all of the super voting preferred shares. In addition, and with no protest from the prior owners, Graham, Alex and a few of his corporate officers took control of the board. Whatever von Kleis was planning to do with the company would be far more difficult now and maybe not possible at all.

Graham had been holding on to ready access to low-interest alternative-energy bonds—part of several companies' R&D. He quietly moved to take advantage of the bonds, creating a substantial war chest.

He'd also received offers in the past for some of his peripheral companies. The offers were quite lucrative, but he'd had no reason to sell. The companies weren't integral to the future of his other divisions, and large interests could be sold at a premium, which also provided substantial capital for stock buy-backs. But now, deals concerning two of these were negotiated privately, with the written understanding that there would be no immediate public disclosure of the sale of significant yet not controlling positions in the two companies. Graham had explained that a public announcement would interfere with his expansion and reorganization. Graham informed his board privately as well. They could see that all the moves would benefit the companies, and he set a tentative meeting of the board. Since he didn't require a quorum for the recent financial maneuvers, the Ambrose board member wouldn't hear of them until the next board meeting.

Graham had Alex Chen slow-walk orders that seemed to have originated with Ambrose, giving preference to their existing client base. He was sure the sales would cancel anyway. By manipulating sales fulfillment priorities, it appeared that demand was overrunning their supply when it really wasn't.

He usually turned down invitations to be on the financial shows, but now he reached out to several of the show hosts and apologized for taking so long to get back with them. At that point, invitations were again extended and he *reluctantly* acquiesced. For once he was quite the showman, touting the many new aspects, consolidations and expansions within his company and their greatly increased customer base. However, he talked only about positive news that von Kleis and Ambrose were already aware of. Their stock continued to climb.

One of the key strategies was to completely insulate the most valuable components of his companies. This was done by transferring certain divisions between the various companies and holding companies. The maneuvers were brilliant in that they greatly protected the companies and allowed Graham to essentially hide their most cutting-edge innovations and AI from just about everyone, especially Ambrose. Whatever they were after, it would be nearly impossible to find now.

In the midst of all the maneuverings, Graham tasked Ariel in new and extensive ways, especially along the lines of what he'd been shown by Russell and Thomas. They were good enough to loan him copies of what he'd seen, so Graham could start test queries in an area heretofore unknown to Ariel. He was hopeful of the outcomes on many levels.

He had given a great deal of thought to Russell's request that he go with Thomas to retrieve at least one crate to see how involved he would be willing to become. Russell was clear that the first crate was the most important, but he wouldn't elaborate. They'd helped him immeasurably and had asked for very little in return. Graham thought it might not be a bad idea to be "unavailable" for several days when von Kleis inevitably blew a gasket. Vicky wasn't due back for at least another least ten days, and he had done all he could with his latest barrage of maneuvers, so the timing might be just right.

He owed Russell and Thomas. And frankly, after what he had seen so far, his curiosity was a major factor. He *wanted* to retrieve at least the first crate with Thomas. He hadn't had any real adventure since his military days, and that lack was tugging on him. Graham told Alex he'd be away from the office for a couple days in the near future and that he'd let him know when shortly. He reminded Alex to be sure all messages between them were encrypted with their own system.

Graham had done all he could to protect his companies, family and friends from the threats and contingencies he could plan for or imagine. He wouldn't be able to protect himself as much as he had everyone else because there was little in the way of a viable threat assessment when venturing into the unknown. But it was a risk he was willing to take.

FIFTY-FOUR

As Roth started down the hallway of the hidden passageway, he could hear von Kleis swearing in German. He just laughed. Although what Graham Chastain had done would set back the consortium's plans, it really didn't matter in the larger scope of things. Achieving their plans might take longer, but they had other means at their disposal to get what they wanted. Roth's delight was twofold. First, he relished von Kleis's failure; the pompous egotist was infallible only in his own mind. Second, the Council could give Roth more authority now that von Kleis had been outplayed. They might well infer that von Kleis was slipping and elevate Roth. Von Kleis had too much power to be replaced at this juncture, but Roth was in no hurry, and every movement upward was a movement upward as far as he was concerned.

Roth knew the group was getting more into his own arena—the nastier, darker side of things. Von Kleis was good at strategy and tactics, but Roth doubted he would or even *could* get his hands dirty. Roth relished the many ways he was able to intimidate most people. And since he cared nothing about morality, felt it was both relative and irrelevant, it was no impediment. He was part of the upper class and planned to rule over the sheeple. Roth had always been on the winning side and planned to stay there—no matter what that entailed. And if he enjoyed making his inferiors squirm along the way, so much the better. They were just ants in the sunlight under his magnifying glass.

He didn't have anything against Chastain personally—he was merely an impediment. Roth knew he must be every bit as brilliant as everyone said to see through their machinations so quickly, but that was a good thing. Most of the targets Roth had previously preyed upon melted like so much butter, whining and begging on their way down. But Chastain would be an adversary with a real backbone, and it was a backbone that Roth would enjoy pulverizing. Chastain might keep a stiff upper lip, but Roth smirked to himself that he would most likely feel an involuntary pucker and then have to fight to keep from wetting himself when he got the bad news. Chastain was an all right guy for someone so educated and successful, but he stood in the way of something bigger. And Roth wasn't thinking about von Kleis's grand one-thousand-year master plan either. He was thinking about Chastain being in the way of his own master plan for power and wealth beyond avarice. And for that reason alone, Roth had no regrets and would show no mercy.

Before going into his current tirade, von Kleis had spelled out exactly how, when and where Roth was to roll out their attack on Chastain. He wasn't even giving Roth his normal general directive for a mission or any latitude to use his own judgment. He meticulously detailed the attack in writing and said it was to be carried out to the letter. Roth had never seen von Kleis so incensed. One side of him wanted to buy Chastain drinks and thank him rather than take him down. Von Kleis had been so demeaning in his elementary instructions to Roth that Roth wished he could take him down along with Chastain—but that delightful task would have to wait.

There was one point that Roth did have to have to concede, though; he had thought eliminating the prostitute was risky and a waste. He knew part of his attitude had been his own bias since she'd taken him to places unknown on more than one occasion. At the time he thought her death was overkill and suspected that von Kleis had an ulterior motive in stripping him of one of his favorite indulgences. But now von Kleis's foresight looked like it would be a quick and easy way to bring Chastain into line. Besides, Roth was in the process of stealing Dr. Scheer's women just for spite. That would serve a dual purpose that he would truly relish—enjoying the women and humiliating Scheer. He pulled out his cellphone. As he pushed the button to make the call, he heard the sound of crashing glass back down the hall in von Kleis's office. He laughed and hoped it was something rare and expensive.

Graham found the thick envelope that Suzette had put on his desk. She said it had arrived by special courier from a law office. He read the note from the law office stating that they were instructed to deliver the envelope to him in the event of the death of their client, Harry McGowan. Graham opened the envelope and began scanning the contents. Before he read more than ten pages, he sent a text to Thomas. *I'm in. Let's meet to plan.*

He had already decided to help Russell and Thomas in exchange for all they had done. Even setting aside the huge potential for his own financial benefit, he wanted to be involved. They hadn't asked very much in return, and what he just read confirmed that he was on the right path, a confirmation that also accelerated his decision and timetable. Graham didn't like to admit to himself that he'd been taken in by von Kleis and Ambrose. He reasoned that he'd been duped as a result of love and loyalty for his sister and tried not to beat himself up. But in spite of that, he felt he should have been more careful. He and his staff had been more than thorough in the past, and it was a practice he'd already reinstated. Alex had subtly tried to influence Graham's thinking with regard to Ambrose, and he should have listened. Lesson learned.

And that included investigating James Russell, even though much of his past was shrouded in mystery. But where von Kleis and Ambrose had done everything possible to hide their interests, connections and operations, both past and present, Russell had provided Graham with more information than he would have asked for. Using a sophisticated method of couriers and encryption, Russell and Thomas had delivered a great deal of information to him. The encryption was useless without the sealed hand-delivered keys. Thomas made it clear to him that they were risking far more in what they were exposing to him than was true in the other direction. After much research, analysis and careful reasoning, and after reflecting on the enormity of what he was learning even now, Graham was certain this was true. The more he learned, the more he wanted to be a part of the intrigue and see where it would lead. He envisioned the mysteries of the Templar crates as a massive jigsaw puzzle that required a Rubik's cube solution to attain each puzzle piece. Setting aside the enigma of the golden scroll and what the crates contained, Graham would have been satisfied to investigate potential synergies with Russell's many companies. That alone was something Graham felt he needed to be a part of. Everything else would be icing on a potentially large cake.

He and Thomas had exchanged more encrypted emails regarding when they could next meet and when he could leave for whatever destination Thomas and Russell had in mind. They wouldn't say what the exact location was. Thomas only hinted that Graham should think tropical.

Before he could focus on adventures, Graham took steps to protect his family. He sent one security team posing as a landscape crew to his sister's cottage. Their job was to protect the perimeter and give potential cover for a second security team that Graham sent posing as a home healthcare service. He couldn't risk calling or emailing his sister or Bobby, so one of his security officers would hand-deliver a message from him saying to quickly pack and leave in the healthcare van, which would be a perfectly reasonable cover. He sent a third team to Europe to shadow his wife and her own security from a discreet distance. His remaining security staff would have to take up the slack, but they were trained to go days without sleep if necessary and wouldn't complain about the overtime pay and bonuses he intended to pay them.

Graham had done all he needed to, and Alex and his team had everything under control, so there was no time like the present to accompany Thomas. But before he headed off into an unknown adventure, he needed to send out another encrypted email and ask a favor. It was time to call in a marker.

FIFTY-FIVE

The Guatemalan Jungle

Graham had a great deal running through his mind. No, sprinting was more like it. He was considering the most immensely stupid things he had done in the past and was wondering just where this one ranked. It had to be in the top three. Volunteering to leave the comfort and safety of a perfectly functional navy vessel and putting himself in harm's way to test experimental equipment must be a close second. So close it would require a coin flip. But he couldn't flip a coin now because his hands were occupied with rappelling ropes as he prepared to push off from a cliff.

What had Thomas told him? *Think tropical.* His first thought had been beach, not jungle.

He really didn't want to pass into the afterlife by falling or, more correctly, slamming into the rocks far below. Of course, if he were agile in midair, he might hit the rapids first and drown. Graham was just venting in his own mind, though, since a fall was not at all likely. Even if he hadn't had a good amount of climbing and rappelling experience, the arrester would prevent a free fall.

At the moment, being in the water would be a welcome event since it might thwart the swarms of mosquitoes from draining his blood and replacing it with some form of Southwest Nile virus or neurotoxin. At least the water would wash off the sweat running into his eyes. Land snakes or water snakes? He wondered which were more deadly in this tropical paradise. At least no one was shooting at him. Recognizing his thoughts could be construed as bordering on whining, he decided to keep them to himself.

"Rappelling typically entails some form of downward movement, if you're done daydreaming," said a voice from above and to his right.

"Just taking in the view and wondering if it was you or Uncle James who drugged me and talked me into visiting this humid armpit."

"If you focus on what it would be like climbing up to where we are, it makes the journey down seem easier and more enjoyable."

"I must say, Thomas, that you have an odd view of things. The only upward climb I'll be focusing on is the helicopter ride from the extraction point once we find what we came for." He joked, but he came prepared with Black Diamond ascenders in case their planned exit was blocked. He hoped the contingency devices would stay neatly packed where he had put them.

Even though Graham was in great shape from frequent and intense workouts, his body and muscle groups weren't used to the specific movements—contraction, flexion, tension, twists and bouts of endurance—required of rappelling. And yet he felt little discomfort or fatigue. His mind moved its focus rapidly from a single bead of sweat running down his nose to the water in his barely touched canteen to the cascading mist of the waterfall nearby to the turbulence of the termination of the falls and rapids below. His mind and auditory senses seemed to fluctuate from hearing no sound to hearing all individual sounds nearly simultaneously—all while he adeptly bounced out and dropped effortlessly. He moved quietly and deliberately, stopping on occasion to assess the lower surroundings and to be sure all of his gear was still hanging from carabiners on his harness.

"It's not so bad once you acclimate," Thomas said. "I did my jungle expert training not too far from here. The vegetation and the topography are pretty similar."

"I'm sure if you've seen one jungle, you've seen them all," Graham replied. "Same bugs and snakes. I think I did my snorkeling and sunbathing training on a beach near here. And I don't plan on being here long enough to acclimate." He steadied himself and took off his multicam boonie hat and wiped his brow with the back of his sleeve. "I owe you and your uncle for your help and information, but I'll need more convincing that what we're after could be *that* important."

All joking aside, Graham was quite happy that Thomas had jungle bushcraft skills that far exceeded his own. He had a good deal of training, but his practical land experience was almost entirely confined to desert warfare. The underlying principles were similar, but there was no substitute for specific expertise and tactical awareness. And he was rusty at best. These falls weren't as high as the Salto de Chilascó, but the height was still daunting. Graham was sure that Russell had chosen the area for its seclusion and not for tourist appeal. He wasn't sure exactly where they were going, only knowing that this landmark was their jumping off point.

Getting to the falls hadn't been terribly difficult. The twin-engine plane they used was nondescript, as was their fishing-trip cover. They arrived with the requisite fishing gear that also bore the requisite amount of wear from use. He and Thomas were met by a driver who took them to a well-used but solid Land Rover. The duffels of gear stowed in the back and covered by a dark tarp weren't for fishing—more like hunting. Graham wasn't at all surprised by Russell's planning and contacts. Thomas had explained that his uncle had done business in many countries for many decades, and Guatemala was no exception. Graham turned his reflection to what was immediately at hand.

Thomas scoured his surroundings as he always did. He showed little sweat and no fatigue whatsoever. His head and eyes moved at different speeds, and often his head didn't move at all. His senses were even more finely tuned than Graham's.

"I'm completely certain that you'll be convinced of the importance of our goal over time," Thomas said. "And not just by the mysteries and the intrigue that you'll be exposed to. There are truly dark happenings unfolding unlike anything anyone has ever seen in the past," he added quietly. "You may not want to admit it, but I know you've seen it and felt it."

Graham didn't answer as he pushed off and bounced out to continue his descent, but he knew Thomas was right. And not only had he not spent much time thinking about these events in the past, but before they started educating him, he most likely would have denied such things existed just a few months ago. *Wasn't there always evil in the world*, he would have said, scoffing. Yes, that was true. But not on the scope they faced today. Fifty years ago it was unlikely that a small band of madmen could get their hands on a suitcase nuke or a bioweapon that could be used to wipe out millions just to send a message. It was equally unlikely that unending wars would have served no purpose other than to continue to feed the military industrial complex and create a seemingly endless flow of so-called refugees. Over seventeen years in a backwater prehistoric country like Afghanistan to defeat five thousand Taliban? Millions of missing children that didn't even appear on milk cartons anymore, and it didn't draw a yawn or make the news? Yes, the rich had always gotten richer throughout history, but now wealth was in the hands of fewer and fewer individuals and mega-companies while the truly desperate poor were slaughtered without a thought from those addicted to one electronic device or another. Even in countries as poor and destitute as the one he was in, people who could barely survive were able to find enough money to own a moderately smart phone to stare at constantly.

Graham wasn't sure how much they could do, but he had seen and heard enough to go this far to see if Russell, Thomas and their people had something special or if they were just a bunch of hopeful dreamers tilting at high-tech windmills. They seemed willing to let Graham come to his own conclusions rather than coerce or strong-arm him, but they also continued to send him a steady stream of proof that a number of important attributes of western civilization were going awry and at an increasingly rapid pace.

As they got close to the bottom, Thomas broke into the silence of his deep thoughts by saying, "All that is necessary for evil to prosper is for good men to do nothing."

Graham frowned at Thomas. "You're going to have to teach me that mindreading thing that you and your uncle are so good at."

"Pure logic. You're a good man who has done a great deal to help others. I'm sure you're wondering why you're here and if it's worth it."

"Mind reading. I could have been fantasizing about seeing my smokin' hot wife soon."

"You're a multitasker. *Those* thoughts are constant and a given."

Graham reached the ground first and quickly stripped off his rappelling equipment. He stuffed it into his empty gear bag and gathered the excess Mammut superDRY rope into a neat pile. He attached the gear bag to his pack using a carabiner as Thomas touched down. They weren't taking the equipment with them just because it was top-of-the-line, but because it might come in handy later.

Graham turned his back to Thomas to look at the level ground nearest the river. He wondered if this were some ancient path the Mayans had used long ago. He started to turn back toward Thomas, thinking out loud.

"I recently read that there are over twenty-eight thousand medicinal plants, and I wonder—"

Thomas had pulled his jungle machete out of its scabbard behind his shoulders. He closed the distance between them in less than a blink and swung his blade toward Graham's head in a high, sweeping arc. Graham heard a slight *thunk* above him and watched, mouth agape, when a snake's head dropped in front of him onto the foliage at his feet. Graham had never seen anyone move so quickly or with a more fluid motion than Thomas—and that included some pretty impressive SEALs and high-ranking martial arts masters.

"—wonder just how many poisonous types of plants there are here in comparison to the medicinal ones," he continued, as if nothing happened. He pulled out a KA-BAR Cutlass machete, similar in style to the one Thomas had just used to decapitate the now-dead serpent. He examined the sharp edge of his own knife blade with a slight squint and scowled at Thomas.

"Snakes. Yeah, snakes might be tropical. But my tropical thoughts are more along the lines of Corona, mangos and bikinis. To you, snakes mean dinner."

FIFTY-SIX

Thomas kept his machete in one hand and pulled out his canteen with the other. He took a small drink, replaced the cap and replaced his canteen on his belt. Graham took his cue and decided now was a good time for water. As he took his own drink, Thomas looked in the direction of the flow of the river.

"So I assume, Kemosabe, that you know exactly where we're headed?"

Thomas started walking in the direction he'd been looking. "Not exactly, but this way."

"No map, no GPS, no compass. I hope you can do better than 'not exactly.' I've seen that commercial."

Thomas didn't look back, but spoke over his shoulder. "Uncle James has a very detailed map of exactly where it is. I've studied it. We're headed to a cave near here that's hidden by a smaller waterfall. Even *you* could find it."

Graham laughed and followed behind Thomas, keeping about twenty feet between them. The men fell into a matched rhythm, as if they'd patrolled together for years. Thomas moved as quietly as a cat, and Graham, always a willing student of those with mastery, did his best to emulate his stealthy ways.

They each advanced in a slight crouch and kept their heads

on a swivel, looking back and forth as well as up and down. Occasionally Graham would stop for a few seconds to turn and check behind them.

Ten minutes into their trek, Thomas stopped, lowered his crouch and held up his left fist, his arm bent at the elbow—the military sign to freeze and hold position. Two minutes later, Thomas lowered his arm and fist, but didn't move forward, allowing Graham to creep up beside him.

As the men continued to scan their surroundings, Graham whispered, "I thought this area was uninhabited."

"It was over fifty years ago when James hid the crate, but conditions may have changed since then. He chose the spot because the falls hid the cave and the locals said the place was haunted."

"Haunted by whom?"

"The Ancient Ones," Thomas whispered. "Those who walk without touching the ground. *Keh tah, gah nesh.*"

"That doesn't sound at all Spanish."

"Nor Mayan as far as anyone knows. There are indigenous people in the hills near here who speak of those who came before the Mayans. And there are overgrown Mayan ruins close by, some of which may never have been seen or explored by Europeans. You may not know that early inhabitants from the Incas to the Mayans told legends of white gods prior to the arrival of the Spanish in the 1500s. And here's one you'll really enjoy: one theory is that the white gods were none other than the Templars who arrived around 1307. While you may think that's far-fetched, there's clear evidence that Sir Henry Sinclair, allegedly connected to the Knights Templar, went to the New World in 1398; images of maize and aloe are carved in Rosslyn Chapel, built by Sinclair's grandson, for anyone to see."

"Seems these guys really got around."

"More than you can imagine. And what they collected and amassed from all over the world is nothing short of astonishing."

"Astonishing? Who even talks like that?"

"Those who have been truly astonished."

Not seeing or sensing any threats, Thomas moved forward as he pointed farther down the trail and at a forty-five degree angle away from their present course. "Over that next rise there should be haunted ruins. It would be a great place to come back to and explore someday."

"It must be the heat and humidity, but I'd actually like to do that."

Finally they saw another waterfall ahead and up on the hillside that was a continuation of the general range that they had climbed from. Graham assumed that Russell had chosen the larger waterfall because it was an easy landmark to find. He couldn't imagine finding this completely secluded area without the larger landmark, even if he did possess a detailed map.

Thomas studied their surroundings intently, as if he were taking inventory. Graham was certain he was getting his bearings in relation to what his uncle had told him.

"Wouldn't it have been simpler to have brought the map?"

"Yes, if I wanted to chance it falling into someone else's hands. Or if I didn't think I could remember basic major landmarks like the ones that got us to this point so far. I've already seen where we need to go. I'm just looking for the *easiest* approach for your benefit."

"You don't say much that's positive or helpful. When we get back, we need to work on your people skills. Since you hold me in such low esteem, I don't see why you reached out to me in the first place."

"Mostly because I like your executive assistant."

Graham turned in a rear-facing arc to scan their six. "Not a chance," he whispered. "She has class *and* taste."

Thomas used his machete to clear away some of the vines blocking their ascent. Even if the area hadn't been totally secluded, the vines would have prevented anyone from going in the same direction Thomas took. The approach was totally overgrown.

"Something positive or helpful . . ." Thomas repeated as he hacked away at the vines. "Okay, *we* didn't reach out to you first; you have a mole. That's what put you on our radar."

Graham had moved up to help Thomas, but stopped in his tracks. "I'm going to assume you don't mean a skin blemish."

"Nor small subterranean mammals."

"I find that hard to believe."

Thomas continued to work his way through the overgrowth. "No, I'm pretty sure they're mammals."

"Someone in my organization reached out to you and your uncle."

"Exactly. It wasn't malicious. And at first we thought it was you, and we weren't sure if you were playing some kind of game with us."

"Wasn't me."

"We gathered that."

"Who, then?"

"We honestly have no idea. Somebody pretty bright, though. Main reason we crossed you off the list."

Graham allowed himself a small chuckle. For all of his austerity and toughness, Thomas had a subtle sense of humor. Graham didn't bother to respond, but continued to scan their surroundings. Seeing and sensing nothing threatening, he turned back to following Thomas.

Thomas had quickly hacked a slim path up to a level area right next to the smaller waterfall. Once there, they found it easy to see the opening in the rocks that created a natural archway and path under the falls. A large stone partially blocked what appeared to be a cave. The natural acoustics of the space within the opening served to amplify the sound of the rushing water and turned it into a roar belaying its size.

Thomas sheathed his machete and pulled away some smaller stones on the far side of the large stone blocking the opening. If they hadn't known what to look for, it was doubtful anyone would have been able to budge the huge stone. It was a brilliant locking mechanism that had been in place for many years and one that had become even more camouflaged over time. Thomas began to push the large stone, intending to move it parallel to the opening. Graham put his machete away and helped.

"Why would I make something like that up?" Thomas said, clenching his teeth and using his weight to rock the stone.

Graham stood directly next to Thomas and bent his knees to gain more leverage. "At this point, I might think you're yanking my anchor chain again. Otherwise you might have told me sooner."

"We originally didn't know if the contact had good intentions or bad. Over time we could tell that they—or he or she—were working for your benefit and protection. But if we had told you earlier, you'd have been obsessed with finding out who it was, and this is far more important."

"Not for you to decide."

"We thought it was. I think you'll agree. If not, sue us. Then you can obsess over who it might be. I'm betting you'll give whoever it is a big raise when all of this is over."

Graham stopped to briefly arch his back. He needed to

stretch some of the muscles that were unused to supporting a pack. He had no idea who might reach out to Russell or why. Thomas was right about one thing—he probably would obsess about this until he solved the mystery, but now wasn't the time. And it was equally clear that whoever made the contact had good intentions rather than malicious ones. But why not just approach him? He set those thoughts aside to focus on the task at hand.

With both men dripping sweat, the stone began to roll enough to create an opening to the cave that they could both walk through. Until then, a gap above the stone had been barely visible from their vantage point.

Thomas produced a headlamp from his pack and put it on over his boonie hat. Next he pulled out a powerful LED flashlight; Graham did the same. They both also carried additional lights and neon light sticks. At first Graham had wondered why they carried so many lights, but he soon realized that they had enough protein bars, other rations and water for three days when they intended to be there not more than one day. *And* they were both skilled in foraging for food and water if either ran out. However, ample lighting for a cave search would have been much more difficult since they didn't want smoke or fire. So far, Graham couldn't fault them on their meticulous planning.

Before they fully stepped into the cave, Graham was hit by a unique odor he couldn't place. It was clear that Thomas noticed it as well.

"What *is* that?" Graham asked.

Thomas moved forward and directed the beam of his flashlight in several directions. He stepped forward onto a spongy surface. It sounded like he was walking on popcorn. "Bat guano," he said, pointing in a wide arch with his light. "Very valuable to many cultures."

"The worst thing about bat guano?" Graham said.

"Other than the smell?"

"It means bats. And *just* when I *thought* I was hungry and about to reach for a protein bar!"

They both flipped on their headlamps and slowly entered the cave, hoping not to startle what could be a mass of unhappy bats.

Thomas tested the ground with his boot before taking each of his first few steps. "This is actually old bat guano. Know what that means?"

"Old bats, no fangs?"

"By the looks of things, no bats at all. Something must have caused them to relocate," Thomas said, moving into the cave.

FIFTY-SEVEN

Inside the cave, Graham and Thomas waited to let their eyes adjust. They took in the shadows of the rocks that danced in front of them like specters as the light flashed over the varied surfaces. The roar of the water had diminished somewhat as it was trapped by standing sound waves in the outer archway. They could hear and see evidence of water that had streaked the cave walls and had leaked away through unseen crevices within the many nooks and crannies of the grotto. It was clear that the cave extended several hundred feet, that it split into multiple openings and that the floor rose and fell in many directions.

"My uncle told me a few things about when he hid the crate here. First of all he warned me that what he saw scared him more than a little and he really didn't understand what he was seeing. And he said that he didn't have a lot of time to investigate at that point since he was just beginning to set up safe houses and front businesses for the Company. Then over the years he got busy with his career and finding other places for the other crates, so it's remained here. He said there were times that he wondered if maybe it should remain here permanently."

"As long as *we* aren't here to permanently join it," Graham offered. "I'm guessing Uncle Jim gave you a good idea about the location here inside the cave."

Thomas was already reaching into his pack. He pulled out an irregularly shaped orange pouch. He unsnapped the pouch and pulled out a high-quality folding shovel that when locked at a 90 degree angle also exposed a pick. Without suggestion, Graham retrieved his as well.

"I believe it's right over there," Thomas said, pointing forward. "He said he found a large flat rock that worked well to cover a natural recess between several other large rocks. He put the crate inside, placed the flat rock over the top and then shoveled loose dirt over it. Said it seemed easier than digging a hole just to cover it up and it also looked more natural and seemed elevated enough to remain dry."

"A rock among rocks. We're in the right place. But I do like the not digging part."

Thomas snapped on a couple of neon light sticks and dropped them gently on the ground as they moved forward. They would leave a clear path if their lights failed. He reached the rise he had pointed at and began tapping lightly with the handle of his shovel until he heard a hollow echo. Graham dropped two of his light sticks and set his flashlight nearby to illuminate their intended excavation area. Thomas did likewise. Then, after pulling on their rappelling gloves, they began quietly digging.

Whatever had been loose dirt in the past had long ago become compacted. It wasn't long until they hit the flat rock they were searching for. Graham brushed away enough loose dirt to find the edges of the rock. Then it was a simple matter for them to use the picks on their shovels to pry up the stone and get a grip on it with one hand each.

Once they'd lifted it high enough, they dropped their shovels and were able to get a better grip. They shifted the stone to another relatively flat rock. They didn't need to be gentle, yet they still had no desire to wake any sleeping mammals hanging from the ceiling.

Shining their headlamps inside the enclosure, they could see a square box about two feet by three feet. It was covered in material that looked like several layers of oil cloth that had long ago begun to deteriorate. Underneath that, some metal had become exposed and there was evidence of rust. They lifted the box out of the recess and set it on top of the flat stone.

Graham and Thomas exchanged a look as if to decide who would open the prize.

Before they could decide whether to flip for it or not, the silence was broken by sounds behind them.

"*Hola, amigos. No se muevan.*"

Graham and Thomas turned to face four Guatemalans. The one closest to them pointed a gun in their direction, and the other three carried machetes. They instinctively raised their hands. And shared a look of embarrassment.

"We don't understand Spanish," Graham said. "We're Canadian. I'm a geologist and he's an archeologist."

The man with the gun waved it to signal them to move away and then pointed with the gun toward the box. "*Que es eso?*"

Graham and Thomas were already easing apart to give each other more room.

"*Umleitung,*" Graham said under his breath in German, telling Thomas to look for his diversion. "We don't understand. As I said, we're Canadian, but we don't even like the French."

As Graham spoke, both men continued to adjust their positions for maximum leverage. If they could move to the outside of the slowly approaching line of men, the intruder closest to each of them would act as a shield against the attack of the inner two men. They would take out the outermost men in the line and move inward, effectively making it two against two and then two against two again rather than two against four. Yet regardless of strategies, the gun had to be neutralized first.

The man with the gun became visibly angry. He shook his gun at the box and then pointed it at each of them for emphasis. "Que es eso?" he yelled at them.

As he moved laterally, Graham said, "Oro." Then he paused and repeated, "Mucho oro!" with great enthusiasm. With that, each man's eyes opened wide and they tried to push past each other to see the treasure.

The leader leaned toward the crate—the opening Graham was looking for. He whipped a crescent kick and hit the inside of the forearm of the man's gun hand. The gun dropped to the ground. The leader looked at his throbbing arm first with shock, then with rage. But before he could raise his fist, Graham stepped in with an upward palm strike to the nose, resulting in an instant rag doll. The man wasn't even able to blink as he dropped to his knees and then fell flat on his face. Knowing there was a second assailant with a machete, Graham had already quickly moved back and to his left to keep the leader's fallen body between him and the next attacker.

Thug number two recovered from the shock of watching his friend get taken out of the fight so quickly and easily, and started at Graham, his machete over his head. The body blockade gave Graham more than enough time to reach the folding shovel and use it to fend off the clumsy machete attack. He followed that immediately with a strike to his attacker's throat using the handle. The man dropped his machete and grabbed his fractured larynx with both hands. Graham clubbed his jaw with the flat of the shovel, knocking him out cold. He immediately whirled to see if Thomas needed help, but Thomas was standing over the other two men who were unmoving on the ground.

Thomas held a knife in each hand, handles forward and blades back, both covered in blood. "What took you so long?" he asked.

Before they could congratulate each other, they heard another voice at the cave opening. A man held a gun leveled directly at them.

"Drop your weapons," he barked in heavily accented English.

The new assailant was dressed far better than the four locals they'd taken out—stylishly outfitted for tropical hiking. He was Hispanic like the other men, but taller, and his facial structure was far more European.

Graham began as he had in the earlier encounter. "Why did your men attack us? As I told your friends, we are—"

"You are no archeologist and I am no fool. Drop your weapons!" he hissed. Graham and Thomas looked at each other, and the new man waved his pistol again.

"As I said, *I'm* the geologist and *he's* the archeologist. Don't insult me. We're Canadian, and our feelings are easily hurt."

The new man closed his eyes, leaving only angry slits as his face twisted. "You are neither Canadian nor a geologist, Señor Chastain. You are merely a thief here to enrich yourself by stealing our country's treasure."

"I assure you there is no treasure, and what we find will be shared with the National Museum." Thomas spoke in a controlled, even tone.

"Do you think me a fool?' he snapped.

Graham and Thomas again looked at each other and shrugged slightly.

The man was visibly enraged, his gun hand trembling. He looked as if he'd rather beat them to death than shoot them. "I've been paid a great deal of money to kill you, retrieve the treasure and leave you under a ton of rubble when I blow up this cave." He smiled. "You two thieves will never be seen or heard from again. Say adios."

He raised his gun. A soft pop sounded behind him at the same time the upper right part of his head exploded in a mist of gray and red. He pitched forward and fell on his face, a look of confusion his final expression.

Graham and Thomas instinctively started to move for cover when yet another man appeared from around the same outcropping. He held a suppressed Heckler and Koch MP5 and wore digital camo, with camo paint on his face and a matching baseball cap. He ignored Graham and Thomas and fanned his gun around the room, searching for additional threats.

"Clear!" Graham said. And with that, the man lowered his submachine gun and nodded.

"Friend of yours?" Thomas asked. "He doesn't look Guatemalan." He lowered his hands but didn't drop his knives.

"Irish on my mother's great-aunt's side," said the man in camo.

"Thomas, meet my friend, Master Chief Jason Hart. Our hero," Graham said.

Both men moved forward to thank their backup. But as they extended their hands, Jason's expression went completely cold.

"Not quite," Jason said, raising his weapon again as the two approached.

Thomas tried to raise a knife, but Jason was too quick even for Thomas, and his MP5 coughed two more times.

FIFTY-EIGHT

Both men realized that Jason had fired between them when they heard a body drop to the ground. They didn't even bother to look behind themselves.

Graham thought about Thomas's machete attack on the snake earlier and said, "You both could learn to use the word *duck*," he said. "It's simple. Quick. Easy to pronounce."

"Coming from you, that's pretty funny," Jason said.

Thomas raised a brow at Graham, who simply said, "Long story." Then Graham punched Jason in the chest and said, "Took you long enough to join us."

"Sorry. There are quite a few of his friends littered along the trail leading here. And speaking of that, we probably need to vamoose before quite a few more show up."

Thomas wiped the blood from his knives on one of the dead men and turned to Graham. "When were you going to tell me you brought backup?"

"Had nothing to do with trusting you. Just insurance. When were you going to tell me I had a mole?"

"Just did. And it was before you told me."

"When are you two going to open the box so we can see what's inside and get out of here?"

They both looked at Jason and then at each other and then hurried back to the box. Thomas tossed Graham one of his knives and they cut away the remains of the cloth. The box was well made and tightly sealed. Thomas produced two mini-pry bars from his pack and handed one to Graham while Jason kept a close eye and ear on the cave opening.

With a good deal of work, they were able to pry open the latches and seal. They had newfound enthusiasm when the old hinges creaked to release the decades-old grip. Their enthusiasm was curbed when they found another crate, this one with strange writing on the outside like nothing any of them had ever seen.

Thomas watched Graham stare at the symbols. "We have no idea what any of the inscriptions say. It's as big a mystery as the code we told you about that stayed unbroken for two hundred and seventy years. It's one of the items we thought you might be able to help with."

"I'll put my best gal on it as soon as we get back," Graham said as he focused on the next obstacle. This time he decided to use both his knife and the small pry bar.

Jason was taking another look out the cave entrance when Graham was able to get the lid off and set it aside. Graham and Thomas stared goggle-eyed and silent at the contents of the box.

Jason walked up, leaned between them and looked down. "Huh . . . Sand. You dragged me all the way down here for a wooden box with some sand in it?"

Neither man replied.

"Is it special sand?" Jason asked. "If not, I have *tons* of that where I live. I could have saved you *and* these guys a whole lot of wear and tear."

Graham and Thomas gawked in disbelief.

"You've got to be kidding me," Graham said to Thomas.

"*This* is what struck terror into the heart of your uncle and what we nearly got killed for?"

Ever vigilant, Jason again checked the cave entrance, saying, "You know who's even more disappointed? These dead guys. That last one looks cartel, by the way."

Thomas rubbed his forehead and said, "Surely no one would have stolen the contents and put the box back in such an intact manner—"

"Maybe the sand is a protective covering for something very fragile," Graham said as he put his hand in the box.

When he touched the sand, it began to shimmer. Graham's look of shock returned as the shimmering grew. The sand gave off an energy much like what he'd felt when he held the golden scroll. Or maybe it was his own body's electrochemical energy that was giving power to whatever the sand was. As they watched, the sand began to swirl and vibrate. Graham pulled his hand out, and the men moved back. The swirling stopped, but the sand continued to shimmer. Then, as they watched, the letters *G*, *T* and *J* formed in the sand, as if an invisible finger had written them.

Jason was the first to break the silence. "Okay, I admit it. I don't have any sand that will do that. So what are you guys thinkin' . . . Talk show circuit?"

The sand went flat again and then resumed its previous motion, but it became more like plasma than sand. It began to glow in different shades and hues and to rise up and expand in front of the three of them. They backed up farther, and the sand-plasma continued to expand over and above the box, floating and undulating, forming . . . just what it was forming, they didn't know. Couldn't know. It was like a large hologram, but with no visible projector.

When it finally stopped growing, it looked to Graham like a map of Earth spread out in space. Yet something was out of place. Something . . . Two additional land masses! Before he could mention them, lights began to appear, one by one, across the map.

"Locations," Graham said.

"Locations to what?" Thomas. "James said that it sometimes gave messages, much like the scrolls do. But he said he had no idea what it all means. I do know that whatever was in Colonel Blair's satchel indicated that the contents of one box would be the key to all the others. We speculated that it could be an inventory list of some kind."

As the two men studied the map and pondered the possibilities, Jason spoke from behind them. "What about pyramids and ancient burial mound locations? There's a theory that they sprang up all over the world at approximately the same time. Or they could be plots of ley lines. Or both."

Both men spun to face Jason.

"What? I read," he said, resting the muzzle of his weapon on his collarbone.

Graham shook his head and turned back to the pulsating plasma-hologram. "What if we were supposed to come together for a reason? What if no one person or group could solve the purpose behind all of this?" Graham speculated. "Between our organizations, we have some very unique abilities and horsepower."

"What now?" Jason asked.

"Well, we won't find out here in this cave full of bat guano," Graham said. "Let's get it back to our facilities for thorough analysis before other unwanted guests show up. We have some pretty special capabilities for analysis. If that's okay with Russell."

The other two men nodded.

"I know he'll want to be involved, but I'm sure he has no problem with where the research is done."

"So how do we shut this thing off to pack it up?" Jason asked.

Just as Graham and Thomas turned their heads in Jason's direction, the plasma-hologram flattened into a two-dimensional plane and then a near one-dimensional line that flowed back into the box. The shimmering and vibration diminished and then ceased altogether.

Jason shrugged and moved to cover the cave opening while Graham and Thomas packed up.

Graham began to wonder who he was kidding. With that last spectacular display from the ancient device, he wasn't sure facilities existed anywhere that could unlock its mysteries. What he'd seen was beyond his imagination, the stuff of science fiction, not that of science and computing. What more would they discover? What intelligence was behind the message in the sand? What else . . .

He shook his head. His questions were endless. Maybe fruitless.

No. He didn't believe that.

He was determined to solve the mysteries that had been so long hidden but which were now demanding to be unveiled.

FIFTY-NINE

Graham sat in his Mercedes staring at the photographs in disbelief. After all he had recently been through . . . After finding the amazing sand-plasma holographic map . . . After surviving the attack in the Guatemalan jungle and coming home to secure their crate . . . he's treated to pictures that implicate him in the murder of Caroline Rhea, a woman he'd met briefly. He could barely keep from losing his lunch after seeing what was left of the once beautiful woman. He could think of only one person to ask for help right now.

"Didn't I just get rid of you?" Thomas asked on the other end of the line.

"This is serious. I just found a set of blackmail photos in my car with a note attached. A sick weasel named Roth broke in and put them there while we were in Guatemala. He works with von Kleis at Ambrose. I only met him once, but I remember him well. He leaves an impression and it's not a good one. The note said he'd contact me to arrange a meeting to discuss terms."

"Let me guess—pictures of a beautiful brunette?"

Graham frowned at his phone. "Do you sleep with that golden foil or something? I gave up guessing how you people know things, but now she's a not-beautiful corpse and there are pictures of her entering and leaving my townhome. They're incriminating. I suppose Ambrose planned this if I didn't go along with their eventual plans."

"Circumstantial. Set up the meeting, but not until I send you some files of my own. And don't worry."

"Too late. How can I *not* worry?"

"Trust me. You'll understand when you see the files. Go log in somewhere. Army saves Navy again!" he said, hanging up before Graham could reply.

Graham had no idea what Thomas was up to, but his tone left Graham more hopeful. Even with all of his contingency planning, Graham certainly hadn't seen this coming.

SIXTY

Graham showed up at the park exactly when and where Roth had told him to. He'd had to put up with all Roth's crap about how bad things looked for Caroline and how that was nothing compared to how bad his career and family would look. Roth took joy in telling Graham that he had him by the privates and that he was more than willing to twist if he didn't show up. Not only had Graham never met someone so loathsome and evil, he never fully considered that such evil really existed. He had experienced rage and hatred firsthand in his travels and in combat, but nothing quite like this.

He would enjoy playing along with Roth only to find out what he wanted. Roth had no way of knowing that Thomas had provided him with additional photos proving that Graham was innocent. So for now Graham would have to act out the submissive victim of blackmail and lure Roth into a trap of his own. How Thomas had gotten the exonerating photos of Graham and Caroline was a question that gnawed at him, but which would need to be addressed at a later time.

Graham crossed the commons area slowly, glancing about as he walked. He wore a bulletproof vest under his loose shirt, but he doubted he was being brought here to be shot. There wasn't much point in going into an elaborate blackmail plot just to ambush him. While he walked, he also checked out the area to see if he might recognize anyone from his organization. If there was one mole, there could be a second. But he saw no one familiar.

Then he saw Roth approaching from about fifty yards away. He wore that smiling sneer of his and his usual dreary gray and black attire. Just then, Graham felt and heard the text message alert for his private line. He didn't want to take his eyes off of Roth, but he pulled out his phone for a quick look. He was shocked to see a text from Eric von Kleis.

Emergency! Roth has gone rogue. Acting on his own and trying to frame us and you. Do NOT approach him. He is armed and dangerous! I will provide proof later. vK

Stunned, Graham looked up to see where the sneering Roth was now. He stopped to give Graham a greeting by touching a finger to his eyebrow in a mocking, dismissive salute. His snarky expression said *I can't wait to rub this in.*

At that moment, Graham heard and felt a *fzzzz* go right by his head, and he watched as three puffs seemed to jump off of Roth even as uneven patches of red appeared on his gray shirt and black jacket. Graham had already hit the dirt, looking for cover. He heard no more suppressed rounds but was leery of raising his head to search for the sniper. Based on the hits, he was sure the shooter had to be elevated and behind him. He ducked behind an aggregate stone trash can holder, but could see nothing since he was facing directly into the sun. If the shooter was on one of several of the buildings behind him, he had chosen his spot quite well. Graham wasn't going to go anywhere near Roth, alive or dead.

He ran in a low sprint to a concrete wall and waited. Within seconds both Thomas and Jason weaved toward him through yelling bystanders who were running in all directions. They converged on him a moment later.

"You hit?" Jason asked.

"Not a scratch."

"Can't say the same for the other guy," Thomas said.

Jason continued to search the area like the professional he was. "So I guess the meeting's off then?"

Thomas too was keeping a sharp watch. "It doesn't make much sense to go to the trouble to set you up for blackmail and then kill the blackmailer. I don't get it."

"What I don't get is how you knew to be on my street and to take the pictures of Caroline leaving my townhome very much alive."

"The same mole said you were a good man and you were being set up and that Uncle James and I would understand later. And in exchange the mole would provide assistance in retrieving some of the crates. I can tell you that got James's attention. The rest is history. It would seem that our paths have been more than a little encouraged to cross."

"So I guess this also means you won't be able to test your fancy new voice-activated, Wi-Fi micro-wire with the encoded modulated frequencies, improved battery life and extended range?" Jason asked with a straight face.

"How did you—"

"The bid specs were in your file. Pretty impressive."

SIXTY-ONE

A man with a ski mask crouched under an ingenious low tent made of shade cloth nearly identical to the color of the roof. He had already removed the suppressor and was rapidly breaking down the deadly .306 semi-automatic rifle and scope. Mission accomplished, he thought. So far, anyway.

The sniper quickly rolled up his shooter's blanket and tent and wrapped them around the broken-down sniper rifle and slipped the tight roll into a black duffel. He carried the duffel near the edge of the back of the roof, where a taut black line was attached to an eye-bolt on a wooden post. It was held firmly in place by the snap hook of a carabiner, and he used another carabiner to attach the duffel to the line. He used a remote to pop open the trunk of a car below and gave the bag a shove to start it down the line and into the open trunk. Next he detached the carabiner from the pole, threw the line toward the car and auto-closed the trunk using the remote.

All in less than thirty seconds, he thought smugly. As if he'd rehearsed it a dozen times. Moving deliberately but with haste, he pondered that he'd be 20K richer the next day when he picked up his fee at the locker. He had the fleeting thought that he hoped that his own head would never end up in the crosshairs of a sniper's scope.

He removed the two-by-four he'd wedged under the doorknob of the door leading to the roof. He didn't take off his mask or shooter's gloves until he was inside the stairwell. He removed his shooting glasses and slipped on a pair of nondescript Ray-Bans after he peeled off his mask, turning toward the stairwell wall as he did so. Seeing and hearing no one through the gap between the flights of stairs, he removed his thin rain overshoes and put the mask and shoes in a diaper bag he pulled from the pocket of his windbreaker.

He went down one flight of stairs and opened the door using the diaper bag to prevent prints. Maintaining an expression of disdain, he held the bag away from him like it might explode. He found the elevator and when the door opened, he was relieved to see it empty. Once inside and with the door closed, he took off his jacket and reversed it before pushing the button for the lobby. Seven floors later, he arrived at the lobby, where he maintained his diaper charade and went straight out the back door to where the car was parked. After a quick look around, he again popped the trunk and pitched in the bag and the remaining line he had thrown down from above.

He drove three blocks and parked in a pre-arranged spot. Nothing about or in the vehicle could be tied to him. He got out and started down the street, keeping a steady pace for about three more blocks, listening to the sirens in the distance. He spotted a seedy dive bar and ducked inside. Calling On the Rocks a dive bar was giving dive bars a bad name. It was dark and served alcohol, and that was all he wanted at the moment. He took a seat on what seemed to be a reasonably safe bar stool and pointed toward one of the taps. The bartender nodded, put a glass under the tap and set a full mug in front of him.

He inhaled deeply and exhaled long before he took a large

drink. Only then did he begin to relax and feel he had gotten away clean. He felt the back of a hand give his right elbow a slight smack. The juvenile blow, expected, didn't startle him.

"Took you long enough. I was about to send out the scouts or the cavalry or something. What's the deal?"

"I told you, Sandy. My CI is jumpy and won't meet with anyone but me alone. We go way back."

"Cam, you need to get a better class of CI. This place sucks. No talent and the menu is worse. I know this guy gives you great info, but please," Sandoval complained.

"Okay, your lowness. Let me finish this beer you're buying and we'll go someplace more in line with your highly sophisticated standards and refined palate."

"I'll gladly pay to get out of here. Does this amazing yet low-rent informant of yours have a name?"

"Mr. Smith. And you may very well get to know him someday."

As Camarata drained his beer, Sandoval put some bills on the bar and started for the door. "Fine. Don't tell me, then."

"It's a very common name."

SIXTY-TWO

Graham, Thomas and Jason sat at a round table on the outside patio of Schooner's working on their third bucket of beer and multiple toasts to good friends and absent companions.

"What's next?" Jason asked. "I enjoyed the sandbox op. Hopefully, you have more scenic places to go, though."

"I thought you were still on active duty," Graham said.

"Not anymore. I mustered out to save your butt and keep you out of trouble."

"I'm not going *anywhere* with you two until Thomas tells me who my mole is."

"I already told you that we have no idea. I would tell you if I knew. For the longest time we didn't even know if the mole was male or female."

"But you do now?"

"We aren't one hundred percent certain, but it's a good bet it's a woman."

"What makes you think that?"

Thomas took another drink of beer. "Because we kept asking about an identity. And the only answer we ever got was, 'I'm as elusive as a mermaid.' No dude would ever say that."

"Ariel?" Graham spat out his beer. "Ariel is the mole? That's impossible!"

"Ariel, huh?" Jason said. "Funny. That's the same person who tipped us that the Archangel alert was all a hack and not a real order."

"So no sanction? When were you going to share *that* bit of info?"

"I was going to get to that. And it's the same person at your company who let me know you were making me a great job offer. I was touched by your generosity."

Graham stared out at the water, shaking his head. "Do you have any idea of what this means? The magnitude?"

"I sure do! It means my wife and I can get a bigger house!"

"No, you aren't getting it. This is a major leap in artificial intelligence."

"*My* intelligence led me to believe this shindig was to welcome me on board," Jason said as Thomas roared with laughter. "You *are* still buying, aren't you?"

Graham didn't bother to reply. As he was trying to take in the enormity of the situation that he couldn't fully explain to his two friends, his phone vibrated. When Graham read the message, he could only shake his head again. The number displayed as unknown and the message read: *Who are you who are so wise in the ways of science?*

He took another drink while his two buddies laughed and he listened to the music as it drifted across the deck. "Pretending" by Eric Clapton. How outlandishly appropriate.

Dene is an author, screenplay writer, poet, songwriter and passable musician. He's a recovering business executive who has worked in various industries at the president and vice-president level. Dene is a dog lover, frustrated gardener, non-gourmet cook, innovator and renaissance man who finally figured out that being a writer was what he had wanted his whole life. His friends have wondered why he waited.

Please stay in touch to receive updates about future novels and to be on the lookout for Dene's original screenplay of the same title that is being currently being pitched as a television series:

www.TheQInfinitum.com